PRAISE FOR F. SIONIL JOSÉ

"The foremost Filipino novelist in English, his novels deserve a much wider readership than the Philippines can offer. His major work, the Rosales Saga, can be read as an allegory for the Filipino in search of an identity."
—IAN BURUMA, *The New York Review of Books*

"America has no counterpart . . . no one who is simultaneously a prolific novelist, a social and political organizer, an editor and journalist, and a small-scale entrepreneur. . . . As a writer, José is famous for two bodies of work. One is the Rosales sequence, a set of five novels published over a twenty-year span which has become a kind of national saga. . . . José Rizal's *Noli Me Tangere,* published in Spanish (despite its Latin title) in the late nineteenth century, was an influential *Uncle Tom's Cabin*–style polemic about Spanish rule. The Rosales books are a more literarily satisfying modern equivalent."
—JAMES FALLOWS, *The Atlantic*

"One of the [Philippines'] most distinguished men of letters."
—*Time*

"Marvelous."
—PETER BACHO, *The Christian Science Monitor*

"[José] never flattens his characters in the service of rhetoric. . . . Even more impressive is José's ability to tell important stories in lucid, but never merely simple prose. . . . It's refreshing to see a politically engaged writer who dares to reach for a broader audience."
—LAURA MILLER, *San Francisco Weekly*

"Tolstoy himself, not to mention Italo Svevo, would envy the author of this story. . . . This short . . . scorching work whets our appetite for Sionil José's masterpiece, the five-novel Rosales Saga."
—JOSEPH COATES, *Chicago Tribune*

"The literary work of José is inseparable from the modern politics and history of the Philippines."
—*Le Monde*

"José's writing is simple and direct, appearing deceptively unsophisticated at times. But the stories ring true, and taken together, they provide a compelling picture of the difficulties of modern life and love in this beleaguered island nation."
—STEVE HEILIG, *San Francisco Chronicle*

"[José] is the only writer who has produced a series of novels that constitutes an epic imaginative creation of a century of Philippine life . . . a rich, composite picture."
—LEOPOLDO Y. YABES, *Contemporary Novelists*

"[José is] one of the best and most active writers of contemporary Philippine literature in English. . . . [H]is stories are moving portraits of Philippine society."
—JOSEPH A. GALDON, S.J., *Philippine Studies*

"In Filipino literature in recent years, the creative work of Francisco Sionil José occupies a special place. . . . José is a great artist."
—IGOR PODBEREZSKY, Institute of Oriental Studies, Moscow

"The reader of this slim volume of well-crafted stories will learn more about the Philippines, its people, and its concerns than from any journalistic account or from a holiday trip there. José's book takes us to the heart of the Filipino mind and soul, to the strengths and weaknesses of its men, women, and culture."
—LYNNE BUNDESEN, *Los Angeles Times*

"Sionil José has the ability to write evocatively . . . his descriptions of the rural environment have an intense glow and a lyrical shine . . . truly an emancipated stylist, an interpreter of character and analyst of society."
—ARTHUR LUNDKVIST, The Swedish Academy, Stockholm

"[José is] an outstanding saga writer. If ever a Nobel Prize in literature will be awarded to a Southeast Asian writer, it will be to F. Sionil José."
—*The Mainichi Shimbun* (Tokyo)

"Considered by many to be Asia's most likely candidate for the Nobel Prize for literature."
—*The Singapore Straits Times*

"F. Sionil José could become the first Filipino to win the Nobel Prize for literature . . . he's a fine writer and would be welcome recognition of cultural achievement in his troubled country. [He] is widely known and acclaimed in Asia."
—JOHN GRIFFIN, *The Honolulu Advertiser*

"[José] captures the spirit of his country's sullen and corrupt bureaucracy [and] tells the readers far more about Philippine society than many, far lengthier works of nonfiction."
—STEVE VINES, *South China Morning Post* (Hong Kong)

"The plot [of *Ermita*] is unfolded by concise, vividly picturesque, sometimes humorous, often tender prose. The candor with which Sionil fleshes out his sensuous earthy characters is balanced by his breathtakingly surgical dissection of their minds and souls."
—NINA ESTRADA, *Lifestyle Asia*

"José is one of Asia's most eminent writers and novelists. His passionate, sometimes transcendent writings illuminate contemporary Filipino life in graceful and historically anchored narratives of power brokers and the brokered, of landowners and the indentured."
—SCOTT RUTHERFORD, *Islands* Magazine

"He has achieved a unity in his writings such as that seen in William Faulkner in his stories relating to Yoknapatawpha County in Mississippi or in the Monterey stories of John Steinbeck."
—DOUGLAS LECROY, *St. Louis University Research Journal*

Don Vicente

Don Vicente

TWO NOVELS

✠

F. Sionil José

THE MODERN LIBRARY

NEW YORK

1999 Modern Library Paperback Original

Afterword copyright © 1999 by F. Sionil José
Tree copyright © 1978, 1981, 1988 by F. Sionil José
My Brother, My Executioner copyright © 1988 by F. Sionil José

Modern Library and colophon are registered trademarks of Random House, Inc.

Originally published, in English, as *Tree* and *My Brother, My Executioner* by
Solidaridad Publishing House, in Manila, Philippines.

Don Vicente is a work of fiction. The characters and events are
products of the author's imagination. Where actual historical persons or
incidents are mentioned, their context is entirely fictional.

LIBRARY OF CONGRESS CATALOGING-IN-PUBLICATION DATA
José, F. Sionil (Francisco Sionil).
[Tree]
Don Vicente : two novels / by F. Sionil José.
p. cm.
Contents: Tree—My brother, my executioner.
ISBN 0-375-75243-9
1. Philippines—History—Fiction. I. José, F. Sionil (Francisco Sionil), 1924– My
brother, my executioner. II. Title.
PR9550.9.J67D66   1999
823—dc21   99-10319

Random House website address: www.modernlibrary.com

Printed in the United States of America

For Evelina and Brigida
&
Ephraim and Eugenio

A WORD TO THE READER

These novels contain expressions and words—some Spanish, some specific to the Philippines—that may be unfamiliar to the reader. A glossary has been included at the end of the book.

Tree

CHAPTER

1

THIS IS a journey to the past—a hazardous trek through byways dim and forgotten—forgotten because that is how I choose to regard many things about this past. In moments of great lucidity, I see again people who—though they may no longer be around—are ever present still; I can almost hear their voices and reach out to touch them—my friends, cousins, uncles and aunts, and most of all, Father.

My doctor says it is good that I should remember, for in memory is my salvation. I should say, my curse. This, then, is a recollection as well, of sounds and smells, and if the telling is at times sketchy, it is because there are things I do not want to dwell upon—things that rile and disturb because they lash at me and crucify me in my weakness, in my knowledge of what was. So it was—as Father has said again and again—that the boy became a man.

I am a commuter, not between the city and the village, although I do this quite frequently; I am a commuter between what I am now and what I was and would like to be, and it is this commuting, at lightning speed, at the oddest hours, that has done havoc to me. My

doctor flings at me clichés like "alienation," "guilt feelings," and all
the urban jargon that has cluttered and at the same time compart-
mentalized our genteel, middle-class mores, but what ails me are not
these. I can understand fully my longing to go back, to "return to the
womb"—even the death wish that hounds me when I find it so difficult and enervating to rationalize a middle-aged life that has been
built on a rubble of compromise and procrastination. It is this commuting, the tension and knowledge of its permanence, its rampage
upon my consciousness, that must be borne, suffered, and vanquished, if I am to survive in this arid plateau called living.

At times it can be unbearable, and neither pills nor this writing
can calm my mind; but then, I must go on—that is what the arteries
and the gonads are for—so I hie back to this past wherefrom I can
draw sustenance and the ability to see more clearly how it was and
why it is.

I WAS BORN and I grew up in a small town—any town. I suppose
that from the very beginning, I have always been thus—a stranger to
Rosales, even to the people who knew me—relatives, friends, tenants, and all those fettered beings who had to serve Father as he, too,
had to serve someone bigger than himself. A stranger because that is
how I feel now; the years have really numbed a host of memories—
dew-washed mornings, the tolling of church bells, the precision and
color of my own language.

Sometimes, when I go north to Baguio to recuperate, I stop by
Rosales; it cannot be missed, for Carmen—perhaps the town's
biggest barrio—sits at the crossroad before the long bridge that
spans the Agno; turn right, through Tomana and its makeshift
houses, along what is now an asphalted road, and drive on till a thin
line of decrepit houses forms by the road. They are roofed with nipa
and walled with buri leaves; then the houses multiply—wooden
frames with rusting tin roofs, the marketplace, the main street and its
stores. I sometimes stop here, walk the familiar streets—how narrow,
how weed-choked they are. I pass the creek where I swam, and
its banks are littered with garbage. The old cement schoolhouse
still stands—how shabby it looks, surrounded by scraggly acacia.
I go past broken-down bamboo fences, meet people who sometimes smile and greet me but move on. Many of them I do not rec-

ognize, but I know those faces and the stolid endurance imprinted in them.

My steps lead to the middle of the town, and there, by the side of the road, the balete tree stands—tall, leafy, majestic, and as huge as it has always been. Our house, at one end of the wide yard, is no longer there; it was dismantled long ago, shortly after Father's death, and so was the old brick wall. But the balete tree will perhaps be there for always. There are very few trees of this kind in this part of the province. It has taken decades, perhaps a century, for it to reach this spread and height, taller than the church, than any building in the town—its trunk so huge and veined with vines that six men with their hands joined could not embrace it.

All my life, it has always been to me what Father said it was meant to be—a shade. It was this to countless farmers who came to our yard with their bull carts loaded with grain, or with their problems that only Father could solve—debts that had not been paid and debts that were to be incurred because somebody was dying, somebody was getting married, somebody was born. It was shade from the sun and also from the rain when they who had come to ask Father's favor would get wet under its canopy rather than presume to enter the house.

No one could really say who planted the tree; it seemed ageless like the creek that courses through the town. Father's grandfather had told him he had seen it already crowned with fireflies at night, and though Father did not believe him, he respected the feelings of people, they who believe that this giant tree was endowed with a talisman, that it was more than a tree—it was a guardian over the land and our lives, immemorial like our griefs.

In time, therefore, when the harvest was good, there would be offerings at its base, rice cakes in tin plates, embedded with hard-boiled eggs and hand-rolled cigars between the big roots that cascaded down the trunk and looped into the earth. There were offerings, too, when someone got sick, for the farmers did not consult the town doctor—they relied first on the *herbolario* and sacristan, who recited Latin phrases and plastered the forehead and other afflicted parts of the body with nameless leaves, and then they brought their gifts to the balete tree and, in solemn tones, invoked the spirits—"Come now and accept this humble token of our respect—and please make our dear and loved one well again . . ."

It had provided shade for politicians, for during election time meetings were held beneath it. In the light of kerosene lamps, the politicians would harangue whoever was there to listen, and they would shout their virtues and vilify their enemies. They would butcher a *carabao* or two, and with Father's amen, they would mount wooden planks beneath the tree, spread banana leaves on them, then feed the electorate. Here, too, no less than Quezon had met with the provincial leaders at the behest of Don Vicente, the wealthiest landlord in our part of the country and the man for whom Father worked. And there was the photograph in the living room for all to see—the great man in his *drill de hilo* suit, Don Vicente—plump and smug beside him—and Father at Quezon's right, looking frightened and stiff, and all around them the provincial great. Father had recounted it so often, how the train from Paniqui got in late and how a thousand waiting people had dispersed and Don Vicente would have been put to shame had not Father ridden in great haste out to Carmay and the other barrios, asking the people to return.

During the town fiesta—June 12 and 13—the feast day of San Antonio de Padua, it was shade again for the farmers who rested in the wide yard, unhitched their bull carts, and did their cooking there so that for two days they could watch the freak shows, the garish coronation night in the public market, and the *comedia,* in which brightly clothed farmers and their sons and daughters acted out and danced the ancient drama of the Christian and Moro wars.

Beyond the balete tree and the yard, down the incline of barren ground, is the river, marked on Tio Baldo's maps as the Totonoguen Creek, but because its waters were always swift during the rainy season, I always called it a river. When the rains started in June, continuing all through the early days of the planting season, its waters would be deep and muddy brown. As the rains intensified, within a matter of hours after the first downpour, we could see it rise in a rage of whirlpools, and it would carry the flotsam of the Cordilleras where it had started—the gnarled and twisted roots and branches of trees. Men would line the banks and the wooden bridge, and with wire loops at the end of long poles they would ensnare these gifts of the mountain for firewood. There were times when the river would rise so high it would flood portions of the town and even the *bodega,* which at this time would be quite empty of grain, for almost everything would have been sold by then to Chan Hai. Once it even swept away the wooden bridge, and for weeks the village of Cabugawan was isolated. The floods delighted us, for then we could float our wooden fishes in the ditches.

As the rains subsided and the fields turned green, the mud settled and the river acquired a clear, green hue. It would no longer be swift; it flowed with a rhythm, broken by small ripples in the shallows. It was at this time that we bathed in it and dove to its depths to discover what secrets it held. Now, too, the women took their washing to the banks; they would squat before wide tin basins and whack at clothes with wooden paddles. Where the banks were even and stony or sandy, they laid the clothes to bleach, for now the sun came out not only to help the washerwomen but to ripen the grain. It was also at this time of the year that, once more, Father could go down the riverbank and follow it down, down and beyond to the village of Cabugawan, to a place everyone in town knew; he usually went down at dusk, perhaps because at this time few people would see him, and he did not have to smile at those he met or wave his hand in greeting, for they all knew that at the end of the trail was his secret place.

It was also at this time that Old David, who took care of the horses and the *calesa,* would go to the river with his fine mesh net and kerosene lamp, and before midnight he would be back with a basket of shrimp and silverfish.

By November, the river ceased to move. The smaller streams up in the Cordilleras would have dried, too, and now its sandy bed would be burned, and in between, where there were slivers of earth, thorny weeds and the hardy cogon would thrust out. The depths where we swam would now be shallow pools turned murky with moss that laced the river bottom. It is here where the mudfish and a few silverfish have sought final refuge from Old David's net. Beyond the river that was now dead, the fields would be golden brown and ready for the scythe, and the banks and the narrow delta that could be planted on would be now laced with eggplant, tomato, and watermelon plots that are also ready for harvesting.

I know where the Totonoguen links up with the Andolan creek and how this new river joins the Agno, which never dries even in the years of drought. I have swum in the Agno itself, brought home from its sandy bottom the pieces of pine washed down from the mountains, and these we have splintered to use as kindling wood.

I left Rosales a long time ago; I was grieving then, but they told me I was lucky because I had no quarrel with anyone, that I had everything to look forward to, and that when it would be time for me to return, things would be so changed I would not recognize anything anymore.

Cousin Marcelo was particularly emphatic on that sad, memorable day; I had been away only a year then, and nothing, nothing had changed, and yet he said, "Did you notice that a change has come upon the town? Look at the faces of people—there's hope there, in spite of everything. I tell you, you will forget what happened to your father, and more important, you will forget the past. Even now, people have forgotten that a year has passed and people died, not by ones and twos but by the hundreds. Think of it. You will remember only what is important."

But what is important? I looked around me, at the wide, parched plaza, the shriveled people, the balete tree. All will be the same. I refused to believe that people changed merely because some holocaust had coursed through their lives. They will still know happiness as I had known it, they will still talk of pleasant hours as they have lived them. It is going to be this way with me.

"You will not be coming back until you've finished college then?" Cousin Marcelo asked.

He was past thirty, and he wore his hair unduly long at a time when it was not fashionable to do so. "I don't know," I told him. "I will return, perhaps, on the Day of the Dead, to visit them. And if I cannot come, you will look after them, won't you?"

It was not necessary for me to have told him thus; he held my hand and pressed it. "Yes," he said, trying to smile.

IT DID NOT TAKE ME long to pack, for I was leaving many things behind. Sepa, our cook, had found some of my old books and had brought them in; I picked out one—the Bible—and tucked it in with my clothes. There was still time to look around, to wander around the town, but there was nothing for me to see, no one to visit. I gazed around my room; the hardwood narra floor shone from constant polishing, sometimes with banana leaves, sometimes with coconut meat after the milk had been squeezed. My mementoes were every-where—the air rifle Cousin Marcelo bought for me, the stuffed squirrel Tio Benito brought home from America. The photographs on the wall were starting to brown—me in a white sailor suit when I had my First Communion, my Cousin Pedring and Clarissa when they were married. And there was a big one—dusty yellow with years although all the faces were still very clear as if the picture had been taken only yesterday but it was years ago when we were mourning Grandfather's death. Indeed, here was the entire clan—my relatives, uncles and aunts, the servants, too, and the old, faithful people who had served our household.

I remembered the crowd in the yard, the long table under the balete tree laden with *pancit, dinardaraan,* and *basi* for all the servants and tenants who had come to pay their respects to Grandfather's memory.

In Rosales as in many other Ilokano towns of northern and central Luzon, the ninth day of the burial of the dead is celebrated with dining and drinking, depending on the finances of the bereaved family. We call the feast the *pasiam*—meaning "for the ninth." On this day, those who are not directly related to the deceased may stop wearing the black clothes of mourning, but not the direct descendants—the children and grandchildren.

A host of relatives had descended upon us, cousins to the third degree whom I'd never seen before, aunts and uncles from Manila, and grown-up nephews and nieces who called me Tio with all the respect that the name demands although I still wore short pants. They crowded the house and spilled out into the yard, and some of the menfolk and the entourage of servants had to sleep in the storehouse, where the grain and the corn in jute sacks were piled high. During the last nine days that preceded the *pasiam,* every evening at seven a novena was held in the house. Tomas, the old acolyte, had presided over this, singing in a loud, cracked voice *"Ora pro nobis"* after each of the fifteen mysteries of the rosary. Although the neighbors and the servants prayed with us, we barely filled a corner of the hall. But on the *pasiam,* it was the parish priest himself, Padre Andong, who led the prayers and Tomas—past sixty and a little hard of hearing—bungled as usual his answers as acolyte. The living room could hardly hold all the members of the clan and the servants, and most of the neighbors had to pray in the adjoining room and in the *azotea.*

After Padre Andong had sprinkled holy water on the assemblage, our relatives who were not related directly to Grandfather took off their black mourning clothes, but we who were direct descendants still wore black bands on our sleeves or wore black for another year, after which the period of mourning would end.

At around ten in the morning, the prayers concluded, someone in the yard ignited a rocket, which swished up and exploded—the signal for the festivities to begin, for the gin and the *basi* to flow; it would need another minor calamity for the clan to gather, and for this occasion the town photographer was on hand. His camera, a bulky contraption, staggered him when he carried it up the stairs and posed us all at one end of the hall. "It is not bright," he complained after he had peeped out of his red velvet shroud, so he poured some powder on a rack, told us to stand still, and at the appropriate signal sent an orange flame spurting up. For some time the smoke and the acrid odor filled the hall. It was then that Father said he would like a bigger picture, which would show part of the house, so we broke up, the cameraman bundling his huge camera again, and filed after him in one burbling procession down the stairs into the yard. There was much laughter and joking as he lined us up on one of the benches before the eating table, the morning sun blazing on our faces.

Looking about him, a bit uncomfortable perhaps in his close-necked alpaca suit, Tio Doro said aloud above the sonorous talk: "We are such a big family, why don't we have a coat of arms like the great families during the Spanish times?"

Cousin Andring, the perennial jester, shouted: "That's an excellent idea, Tio. I suggest that our coat of arms shows a demijohn of *basi,* which shall symbolize our hardiness and, of course, our pleasant disposition."

In spite of his mother's angry glare, Cousin Andring was unruffled, and his remark was greeted with prolonged laughter. "And we will have Tio Marcelo do the design, too," he continued.

My relatives must have considered his second joke in bad taste, for now most of them scowled. It was not difficult to understand their reaction; Cousin Marcelo, though he was pleasant and reliable to some extent, had long been regarded as "the problem" in the family because they considered him unstable. He was the only one who greeted the reference to him with laughter.

Tio Doro was alive with ideas. "We should have someone chronicle our lives, our successes and failures."

"Mostly the failures—particularly when there is too much gin," Cousin Andring remarked, happy again.

Tio Doro turned around to look at his relatives, almost all of us still in identical black. Then his eyes rested on me.

"Espiridion," he called to Father, who sat on the bench behind me. "That's the job for your boy—he may grow up to be a writer and give us some permanence."

The blood rushed to my head, and I glowed all over. Behind me, Father said happily, "You can depend on him to do that."

The photographer shouted that he was ready, and everyone preened. Almost everyone. I saw them then in the shade of the balete tree—the servants, Old David, Sepa, Angel, Tio Baldo—all of them watching us and seeming left out. I turned to Father, who was straightening the creases of his white alpaca suit. "Father, couldn't we have Sepa and all the others with us in the picture?"

He frowned at me.

"Just one," I pleaded.

"All right," he said, still frowning, then he called out to them to stand on the low benches in our rear. They hastened to their places, smiling.

Now the picture is before me. Where are they now, these familiar faces? Tio Baldo, Ludovico, and, perhaps, Angel were already dead. Others have left for places unknown—perhaps to Mindanao and the promise of new lands, perhaps to the labyrinths of Tondo and Santa Cruz, where they would work as drivers and house servants, in places where there will be little light and they, too, will be among strangers just as I am now in this blighted town. I knew this from the very beginning—that oil and water could not mix, just as Teresita had told me once.

I am also my father's son.

CHAPTER

ALL WHO SERVED US used to tell me that I was born under a dark cloud not so much because my mother died giving birth to me, but because I never saw her. She was, they said with candor and reverence, the most beautiful woman they ever saw, and whenever they would start talking about her who nourished me in her womb, I listened attentively. I would be vastly proud and at the same time feel this sense of loss and futility, and foolishly I would wish to see her even though she be but a pallid ghost.

But I never did, although she lingered in every nook of the house, among the old iron pedestals and the tarnished mirrors, in the garden she once tended, and most of all in the big and troubled room that she had shared with Father. Her portrait there, by Cousin Marcelo, the servants told me, was lifelike. I often stood before it and marveled, for in the light that came in a flood when the sash shutters were open, I could almost feel her long hair, her benign smile upon me, her oval face, her dark eyes. Her expression exuded tenderness, patience, and that virtue of compassion, of forgiveness for even the deepest hurt such as that which Father could inflict.

The painting hung before Father's writing desk—an old narra masterpiece with a cover that slid down. Cousin Marcelo knew how to capture every nuance in a person's face, but more than this, he had also rendered in paint my mother's luminous skin, the very flutter of her eyelashes.

Seeing me there gazing at the picture once, Sepa said: "Don't you ever think she was that homely; she was much prettier than that—and her hair, her beautiful hair!" Then she called me to the kitchen, and among her shining pots and pans, she told of those times when she helped my mother wash her hair with lye from straw ash, treat it with coconut oil when it was dry, and comb it slowly as if she were combing fragile threads of gold.

Sepa was past fifty and stout like a pampered sow. Like Old David, who looked after the horses, she could not read or write. She used those black, thick slippers called *cochos*, and she always wore the traditional Ilokano handwoven skirt and rough cotton blouse. She had served the family all her life, and she spoke to Father and me with an intimacy none of the other help ventured to imitate. "If your mother were here now—if she were only here now."

I remember my first visit to my mother's grave on a windy October afternoon a few days before All Saints' Day. I was five or six years old. I was chasing dragonflies in the yard under the watchful eyes of one of the maids when Old David scooped me up in his arms and took me to the house, where Sepa gave me a good scrubbing. She dressed me in my sailor suit, and when I was ready, Father emerged from his room in a white drill suit looking as if he was going to an important feast, for his hair was neatly combed and his robust cheeks shone.

Near the family altar in the *sala* he picked up a bouquet of roses wrapped in palm leaves. They came from my mother's rose garden, which Father now tended. Then, taking my hand, he led me down to the yard, where Old David was waiting for us in the *calesa*. The drive to the cemetery was pleasant; the afternoon was mild, and the smell of grass, the good earth, and the fields yellow with grain filled the air. The wind whistled in the bamboo groves by the side of the road, and Old David sang snatches of his favorite Ilokano song, "If You Still Doubt."

Father was silent all the way, his eyes at the distance. The road narrowed and was now devoid of gravel; rutted in the rainy season, it was now drying up, the deep lines drawn by bull carts and sleds hardening into neat furrows. We reached the cemetery, its low stone wall shrouded by vagabond *cadena de amor.* The earth was carpeted in amorseco weeds, and in the empty spaces stood leafless sinegue-las trees. The cemetery was busy with people painting the crosses and the slabs with white lime. At the dead end Old David stopped, jumped down, and helped us off.

We walked down a gravel path bordered with rosal, bloomless now till next June, when it would sprout white, scented flowers, to the small chapel at the center of the cemetery. It was already quite late in the afternoon, and the sun was soft on the skin. The vestiges of work were everywhere—the freshly cut grass and the splashes of whitewash on the picket fences and on the figures of plump baby angels that adorned the tombs.

Father held my hand and guided me through the narrow passageways between the tombs. We reached a lot fenced off from the rest by a low iron grill, and in its center was a narrow slab of black marble, bordered with freshly trimmed San Francisco. Father let go of my hand. He removed the palm wrap of the bouquet and placed it at the foot of the slab, then, as if his legs were suddenly knocked away from under him, he fell on his knees on the grass and I, too, compelled by some magic force, knelt beside him. When he spoke, his voice was hollow and sounded far away. "Nena, I've brought your son to you now that he is old enough . . ."

I glanced at Father in the thickening dusk; his hair was tousled by the wind, his white unbuttoned coat flapped about him, and tears streamed down his cheeks.

It was the first time I saw him cry, and I realized how much he must have loved—and still loved—her who was no more.

OURS WAS AN OLD HOUSE with a steep, galvanized-iron roof grown rusty red over the years. It had unpainted wooden siding and sash windows with balustrades that could be flung open to let the breeze in when the days were hot. The ground floor was red tile, and its walls were red brick, scarred in places but whitewashed. The flooring was solid mahogany—long planks two inches thick and a foot wide—laid side by side without a single nail piercing them.

When the servants scrubbed the floor, the fine grain of the wood shone.

The furniture was just as old; though some pieces were lost during the Japanese occupation, most of the bigger ones were still with us: the mirrored lockers, the steel pedestals, the marble-topped tables.

A few paintings hung in the living room—just pretty pictures done by my Cousin Marcelo. One that should not have been there was the picture of Don Vicente. The modern frame, a *media cuerpo*, shows Don Vicente, massive and impregnable, wearing a Panama hat, his corpulent chest almost breaking out from his tight-fitting, collarless suit. The picture hung on the wall by the big clock as a symbol, I think, of the vast authority the rich man wielded over us, particularly Father.

I could not understand then why Father worked for Don Vicente. We had enough to get by, and Father had his own lands to look after. Maybe, as Cousin Marcelo said, he did not have enough courage to leave Don Vicente, or maybe Father knew that if he ceased being close to the Great Man, there would be a hundred fawning and greedy men who would be only too glad to take on his job. This could be the reason, but I don't think it was; Father took the job because Don Vicente trusted him and, more than that, it gave Father a sense of power such as he would never have known if he tended no more than the land and properties under his name. Once I heard him say to a tenant, "Don't you know that I can drive you all away from your homes today, right now, if I wanted to? Where will you live? Don Vicente's word is law, and I am that law!"

But knowing Father, his bluster seldom meant anything, for he was, I always like to believe, just and fair.

The living room, through a door at the right, led to the dining room and the kitchen, which were in a separate structure roofed with clay tile upon which weeds sprouted. At the left of the kitchen, which was Sepa's domain, was a stone *azotea* that stretched to the wing of the house including the living room. On warm evenings, when the moon bloomed over the town, it was Father's haunt and mine.

The wide yard—all the way up to the storehouse roofed and walled with galvanized-iron sheets, too—was not grassy like the plaza. The earth was bare and packed tight and clean with *carabao* dung but for the green patch of garden planted with roses, azucenas, and other flowering plants. Guava trees—their slender branches seldom laden with fruit—stood in the yard, and to their trunks the *carabaos* of the tenants were often tethered when they came during the harvest season with their bull carts. A woodshed and a stable stood near the storehouse. In all three buildings, big rodents lived, burrowing under the piles of chopped acacia boughs or in the sacks of grain.

ONE OF THE PLEASANT PASTIMES I used to enjoy as a child was to discover the alien things in the crannies of our home. I used to climb to the attic, endure the sun as it lashed on the iron roof. There, among the dust of years, I poked at old boxes that stored strange shapes and wanton objects. The place I enjoyed best, however, was Father's room. It adjoined mine, but I seldom had freedom in it except when he was in the field during the planting and harvesting seasons looking after the *hacendero*'s tenants under his care as *encargado* and also after our own. Then I would sneak into the room, open his drawers and trunks. There was one beside his dresser that fascinated me most, because it was made of handsome and polished Chinese rosewood embedded with ivory carved into birds and bamboo. It was always locked, and though I had seen him open the other trunks, I never saw him touch this one. I heard him riding down from the stable to the street one Sunday morning, and after he had galloped toward the creek, I was in his room before the rosewood trunk. I lifted the lid, and this time, to my surprise, it was open. The biting scent of naphthalene balls assailed my nostrils. There before me, filled to the brim, were women's things. I knew at once I had opened my mother's wardrobe.

I picked up a garment and held it in the light—a bright silk shawl embroidered with red roses and edged with lace. I placed it back, then lifted a thick wad of clothes, and underneath, close to the bottom of the trunk, was a small wooden box with two small ivory angels on its lacquered cover. I opened it and found a heap of letters and dried petals of what looked like a big red rose. The box smelled of perfume, and in a moment the heavy and wonderful scent pervaded the room. It was then that Martina, one of the new maids, drifted by the open door and for a moment stood there, watching me. I opened one of the letters. It was in fine, feminine script, and addressed to Father. I could not read all of it; at the end, "Always— Nena." I felt as if I was trespassing into a secret realm, where I belonged but was not, at the moment, allowed in. Trembling, I put the letters back and gently placed the box under the pile of clothes.

Her pert brown face screwed up, Martina asked, "What is that?" She did not dare venture into Father's room.

"Letters," I said. "My mother's letters to my father."

"Those are her clothes?"

I nodded.

"They look beautiful," she said, still standing at the door. "Why don't you try one?"

"I am a man," I said, frowning at her.

"Go on," she said. "I just want to see how women's clothes looked years ago. I won't tell anyone."

In another moment, I was flailing my arms and thrashing as I put on a blue silk dress.

It did not fit, of course; it hung loose, well below my feet, and seeing me attired thus, Martina let go a delighted squeal. I laughed with her and was, in fact, enjoying myself so much I did not realize that Father had returned, was at the door in his riding breeches, the whip in his hand. Martina must have seen him approach, for she had disappeared.

Although his countenance was severe, Father did not whip me; in fact, there was more sadness in his eyes than anger. "Never again," he said softly but sternly. "Never again shall I see you open this trunk."

And never again did I do it. After Father died I kept the trunk, and it has always been closed as he had willed it; with the years its locks rusted, and there came a time when the key no longer worked and it would take a crowbar and a sturdy hand to open it—but that hand would not be mine.

NEXT TO DECEMBER AND its holidays, June was the most welcome month in our town. The floodgates of heaven were finally opened, the rains started, and the rice planting began. The fields that were brown began to stir with the emerald of new grass. Grasshoppers were on the wing, and the frogs came alive. But more than these, June was the time when we celebrated our town fiesta. A full month before the festivities, they had already started coming, the *feria* people who erected tin sheds near the church, in which they sold cheap dolls with plump cheeks and bright eyes, and ran shooting galleries and stalls for other forms of gambling.

It was during this time, too, that the *comedia* players—the farmers and their children—from Carmay came and stayed in the *bodega*, where they practiced their prancing and their lines before they acted them out on the stage in the plaza. As fiesta patron, Father provided for their meals, their mirror-spangled clothes, the papier-mâché helmets and wooden swords, as well as the five-piece band that accompanied their acting.

The year I was twelve, two weeks before the fiesta, a circus came.

Three big trucks immediately transformed the plaza into a mud puddle as they manueuvered into position. I did not know anyone from
the circus except a girl about my age; she walked the tightrope—so
well, up there in the heights, she could have been walking on even
ground. Her name was Hilda.

She and I did not have much in common, but during the two
weeks that she was in Rosales, we became friends. I lived in a big
house with old people. The young sons of Father's tenants acted ill
at ease in my presence, but Hilda did not. She lived in a tent—that
was the home she knew—with old people, too, who did not care
about what went on inside young minds, what made them want to
go swimming even in dirty creeks the whole day, or what drove them,
naked, splashing and singing in the rain.

I should not have told Hilda about my going to Grandfather's
house, but we got to talking about where we would like to be most;
she had come that morning as usual to draw water from our artesian
well, and I was waiting for her there. She had a ready answer for me:
"I would like to be up there, feeling the height, knowing that people
are looking at you—tensely, waiting for you to fall."

She said she started walking the tightrope when she was five
years old along with her parents, who were trapeze artists. She did
not sound boastful at all. At six, when she should have been in
school, she was already earning, starring in the circus act.

I described to her what Carmay was, and I did not exaggerate. I
told her about the buri palms, how in the dry season they were
tapped and the sap was boiled in huge iron vats into sugar or drunk
sweet and cool and soothing in the sweaty afternoons. Cornfields
laced Carmay, and water lilies decked its irrigation ditches in flaming
violet. Beyond the village was the Agno, swift and murky during the
wet season, and in its wide delta, corn and watermelons grew. In
Grandfather's yard were fruit trees—santol, duhat, and orange—all
of which I climbed. I also often went with the men to the river to
watch them fish till their bamboo baskets were full. And now that the
rains had come, the banabas lining the paths were flowering. It is a
heavenly place, Carmay!

"I must go with you," Hilda said.

During the first week of June, the vacant lot beyond the house,
which was often regarded as an extension of the plaza—which it was
not—was transformed into a field of green amorseco weeds that had

started to flower. Before Father built the storehouse behind the house, his tenants used to fill the place with their loaded bull carts while waiting for Chan Hai, the Chinese merchant who came for the grain with his battered truck and a huge weighing machine. But every time there was an athletic competition of the grade schools in the district, the town mayor always asked Father's permission to use the place in addition to the plaza. Father did not ask for any rent, and perhaps in recognition of his charity, his name was always prominently included in the programs.

The balloting for the fiesta queen was not yet over—it was usually held two weeks before the fiesta—when the circus came. The trucks—their radiators spewing steam, their tops brimming with poles, trunks, and people—rumbled past the house, drawing the servants from their chores to the windows. They proceeded to the plaza and to Father's vacant lot and started to unload.

Father saw the crates spilled on the grass, the wooden stakes piled high, the lot now churned by heavy tires. Shaking his head, he went on with his figures. In a while, three policemen from the nearby *municipio* approached the visitors, who had already started driving stakes on Father's land. They went into a huddle and finally broke up, the policemen leading the way to our house.

Ever correct and polite, Father met them in the hall where they piled in with their muddy shoes and flopped on the rattan sofas with their brash city ways. From their ranks, a well-built man with a balding top came forward; his tone was apologetic, and he was saying how sorry he was that they had used Father's land without realizing it was not part of the town plaza. A girl tugged at his hand continually, and when he could not ignore her anymore, he said, "This is my daughter. She walks the tightwire." Another tug. "And she is the star of the show."

She was not even ten, I think; she certainly was no taller than I. She preened her faded overalls and grinned exuberantly, her big eyes shining, then she stepped back a little and executed a neat curtsy. Everyone broke into laughter, even Father, then she walked away from the assembly. I followed her to the middle of the hall near the picture of Father's grandfather; from it her gaze turned to the chandelier in the rose-colored ceiling as it tinkled to a slight breeze, then she walked to the grandfather clock by the foot of the stairs, and finally, catching a glimpse of me watching her, she came to me and asked if I lived in the house.

I nodded.

"It looks so big," she said, scowling. She was on the verge of another question, but the circus people seemed to have obtained Father's permission, for they started for the stairs, her father still profuse with thanks. Hilda joined them.

"Please come when we start," her father said at the top of the stairs. "We have a good program, and it is known through all of the province. There will be people from as far as Lingayen, Dagupan, and, of course, from Urdaneta."

Father nodded, then went back to his seat in the *sala*.

"It is not much of a circus," he told me afterward. It was dusk, and I had lingered by the window watching the men work, listening to the rhythmic pounding of their sledgehammers on the wooden stakes. A stage took shape, and a wire fence, and within the enclosure they rolled out a mound of canvas that occupied one whole truck. Amid shouts and creaking pulleys, they hoisted the giant tent.

"When you go to the city," Father continued, "you will see a real circus at the carnival. This is just a big sideshow, although it is quite famous. A circus has wild animals, maybe five elephants, lions, and tigers. And look at them—they have only two elephants."

"Father said yours is not a real circus," I told Hilda the next morning. She had come to the backyard where the artesian well was, as did the other members of the troupe before her. They had also parked some of the trailers near our *bodega,* and in the wide threshold of the building they had set up some of their cots. "A real circus," I went on reciting what Father had said, "has lions and tigers."

"It is a real circus," Hilda retorted. She put down her battered pail, braced herself before the pump, and glared at me. I did not move from the bottom rung of the stone stairs that led to the *azotea.* For a while, it seemed that she would shout at me or do something rash, but she lowered her pail and started to pump.

"There was a time," she said, throwing angry glances at me, "we had two lions and two tigers. Three elephants, tall and strong as trucks."

"They are not here now," I said.

"No," she said, pumping furiously. "The trainer was killed by the tigers. They were all sold to the zoo—but not the elephants because they are easy to take care of. And they work—but even without them ours is still a real circus. Come with me." Her pail was full. I turned apprehensively to the house to see if anyone was watching. Sensing my reluctance, she taunted, "Don't be a sissy."

I helped her with the bucket, spilling the water on our legs as we hurried behind the house and out to the plaza until we were behind the tent. The previous night, rain had fallen, and now the morning was polished to a sheen. The tent was a dull white hump fringed by acacias. In its cool shadow, on planks that were laid side by side, the menfolk rested. The women were washing and cooking, and when they saw me, they smiled in recognition. Hilda was holding my hand, and as we entered the wide awning, her grip tightened. "Wait here," she said, and darted out. It was warm inside the tent. Tufts of grass rose above the narrow slits between the boards that were laid in the middle for a stage. Around it, on the sides, were boards fastened together, tier upon tier. From the top of the tent, which now looked patched up from within, bits of sun stole in and lay in bright silver puddles on the ground. The two poles crowned by a blue halo of the June sky soared up, and near the halos were swings and ropes that stretched from one pole to the other.

Hilda returned wearing red tights. Her feet were encased in thin-soled leather shoes, and she trotted to one of the poles where the end of a rope ladder dangled. She bade me follow her as she started the climb, nimbly scaling each swaying rung. It was warmer up on the precarious perch near the top, but Hilda did not seem to care. She smiled when she turned and saw me holding tightly to the pole, not venturing as high as she had climbed. She put one foot forward on the high wire that extended out into space—and there was no net beneath her. I called at her to stop, but she answered with a resonant laugh. As she lifted each foot in her slow progress, the wire swayed. Balancing on her right foot, she raised her hands. The wire ominously zagged, and by then, I thought that even the poles were swaying. I turned away, unable to look.

When I looked again at her urging, the swaying had ceased. Hilda was not on the wire anymore; she was perched safe and smiling on the small platform near the other pole.

I was weak and trembling when I got down. Hilda waited for me at the entrance and walked cheerfully with me to the outside, where the sunlight was waiting.

HILDA'S FATHER dropped by the house again the next afternoon, reiterating his invitation. But Father, always enigmatic and aloof, merely nodded and said he would try.

The plaza was in a gala mood that night; the small town band whose services the circus had secured started tooting around the town, even before dusk, carrying placards about Hilda's death-defying act and the world's strongest man pitting his strength against an elephant. After a hurried supper, I asked Father if I could go. He called Tio Baldo—I don't know why I called him Tio when he was really just one of the help; perhaps it was because Father had con-sidered him bright enough to be patron to him; perhaps because of all those who helped in the house, it was only he who attended to my school problems. He was to accompany me with no less than the circus manager, so that I would be given the best seat that night.

The plaza was illuminated by carbide lamps of dice tables and other enticements. Before the makeshift stage that was actually part of a truck with the sides removed, a big electric bulb blazed, drawing many moths, showing the painted faces, the baggy pants of the cir-cus clown, and the barker, urging the crowd to hurry, hurry—the seats were being filled. Some members of the troupe were seated at one end of the stage, and I recognized Hilda at once in the same red tights she had worn that morning, but her face was now thick with paint. She did not recognize me in the crowd as she sat there in the center, basking in her glory while the barker pointed to her and shouted her virtues, her mockery of death. The band stopped playing and went inside the tent, followed by the troupe; the show was about to begin.

Tio Baldo and I had the best seats, beside the mayor and his wife, at the rim of the circular stage. Although outside it was cool, within the tent it was warm, and the smells of perspiration and to-bacco smoke were all around us. I did not mind this so much, for soon the clown came out, Hilda's father recognizable even in his baggy pants and with a pillow tied to his girth; he and the other clowns went through their paces while the kids up on the tiers squealed at their pratfalls. A magician enthralled us as he made balls vanish, drew doves out of a black hat, put a woman to sleep, then proceeded to saw her in two. Next, the strongest man in the world—a hefty six-footer with bulging biceps—bent a steel rod, let a truck run him over slowly, and, as a finale, pushed an elephant toward the other end of the stage. Then the trapeze artists, and finally, Hilda.

Now the lights blinked out except for one spotlight atop a tall tripod. In the middle of the stage, in that circle of white, she seemed so tiny and fragile. While the barker described what she would do, she did somersaults, splits, and back bends; it was as if she were made of rubber. She could put her head down between her feet and contort into every imaginable shape. She did several curtsies, turning around to face the audience, then she trotted to the pole and went up, up to her perch, the spotlight never leaving her. The band ceased playing, only the snare drum rumbled, and now an apprehensive murmur coursed through the audience. The beat of the snare drum quickened as she rose from the narrow platform; she stepped onto the high taut wire on her dainty feet, tested it like a frightened child learning how to walk. One shaky step forward, then a short, ominous pause. Balancing herself, she repeated the same staggering process until—or almost until—she got to the center, for now the wire had started to sway, and from the audience exploded one despairing cry as she slipped and then toppled.

But Hilda did not fall. Below the first wire was another; she had jumped into a dance, each step sure and steady this time, below her no net at all. When she had finished, the applause was deafening.

HILDA WAS IN THE YARD again the following morning and, of course, in the succeeding mornings with the same battered pail. She worked like the others and did not seem to mind. She did not have much to say when I asked about the different towns she had visited, but her face always brightened as she recounted each.

"I will go to the city someday," I told her a week later when she said she liked performing best in Manila, for she did not have to work so hard helping in the kitchen. Her chores for the day were over, and we were idling in the *bodega*, which was now, save for a few sacks of seed rice, almost empty.

"I will study there," I said, and she told me, too, how she had taken snatches of schooling during the rainy season; Rosales, as a matter of fact, was their last performance for the season, for the circus closed when the rains came, and they started on the road again in November.

Within the week, more sideshows came to town and decked the main street with their gaudy fronts and raucous shooting galleries. The people flocked to them—children wide-eyed and amazed at the freaks, the wild man from Borneo who ate live animals, the cobra woman, half snake, half human—but it was really the circus that attracted people, for this was the first time it traveled to our part of the country. The two elephants alone, feeding on sugarcane and mountains of grass—drew crowds from other towns and the distant villages. Two weeks before the actual fiesta, the streets were rigged up with varicolored bulbs and from all the houses stretched bunting of brightly colored Japanese paper. Above every street corner soared a bamboo arch, festooned with woven palm flowers, proclaiming Her Majesty, the Queen, for whom the town market was decorated, and on one end a stage with a throne and across the white canvas, Her Majesty's name and that of her two princesses—the annual handiwork of Cousin Marcelo.

The day before the feast of San Antonio de Padua, Hilda came as usual to the artesian well. I was in the yard, waiting for Old David to hitch the *calesa;* beside me was my air rifle and my canvas bag. Father had expected a few guests to arrive in the afternoon for the fiesta; as a matter of fact, some of the tenants had already appropriated places under the balete tree and others were camped inside the *bodega.* We needed some chicken and fresh vegetables, perhaps fruits from the farm. We fell to talking again about Carmay, and when the *calesa* was ready, Hilda cast her pail aside and said firmly, "Take me with you."

"But your folks might look for you," I tried to dissuade her.

"They won't," she replied. "They do that only if they don't see me on the high wire. I haven't been to any farm, really. You know, I have ridden two elephants in the parade, but I have not ridden any *carabao* yet."

All argument was useless. She clambered up the *calesa* after me, and we drove out. From the asphalted main street we veered to the left, to the graveled provincial road and Carmay three kilometers away. The *calesa* jerked over the ruts, but Hilda did not mind. Beyond the town, Father's fields lay green and vast, extending to the banks of the Agno. Some of these he had bought from Don Vicente, whose lands were in the opposite end of the town; some were cleared by his grandfather, who had come with the first settlers from the Ilocos; some he had taken bit by bit from farmers who owed him money and could not pay. The sun punctuated every tree, the buri palms, the mounds that dotted the fields and on whose crests tall grass waved with each breath of wind.

We reached Carmay, a neat huddle of farmhouses beside a creek. She crinkled her nose and said it was not much—just like all the other villages in this part of the country. We dipped down the provincial road into a narrow path and got off before the biggest house in the village, the only one roofed with tin. We found Grandfather knitting fishnets by the stairs. In his old age, he should not have been living alone, but he preferred the Carmay, where he was born and where he grew, where he worked and saved enough not only to buy out his other neighbors' farms but also to send all his children to college, so that they would not be farmers like him.

I kissed his gnarled and wrinkled hand, then embraced him, smelling once again his tobacco. Old David told him what we had come for, and while our servant tended to his chores, Hilda and I went to the irrigation ditches, which had begun to fill. We romped in the newly stirring fields and chased grasshoppers. For lunch, Old David had brought hard-boiled eggs and broiled catfish; he then broiled a slice of dried *carabao* meat, tough as rubber, all of which we ate with our hands in Grandfather's cluttered kitchen. After this, we went back to the cornfields and gathered a few ears, which we roasted over coals that Grandfather had kept alive for us in the shade of one of his mango trees. Under the tree, with the scent of June and the living world around us, we were shielded from the sun, which was shining on the rich brown earth, freshly plowed and shining still where the plowshares had ripped into it. I went to the furrow and picked up a clod. It was warm and moist.

Hilda was lying on the sled. I sat beside her and told her to raise the hem of her dress up to the navel. She turned to me, half-rising, and said angrily, "I will not do such a thing."

I told her then, "I want you to belong to Carmay, to be free from the sickness of other earths. I will rub this on your stomach"—I held the clod before her eyes—"and just as Grandfather said, you will never get sick, not while you are here."

She seemed apprehensive, but she smiled. Though she did not seem fully convinced about the efficacy of my magic, she finally raised her dress. "You are like an old man," she said, shaking her head. "You believe in spirits."

I did not speak. Her legs were white and clean, and her skin was smooth. I crushed the clod and let particles trickle on her skin. The grains fell on her navel and rolled down her sides. With my palm, I spread the clod on her belly, slowly, softly, and when this was done, she snapped her dress down and pinched my hand. "Foolish!" she said, laughing.

IT WAS LATE AFTERNOON when we headed for home. Shortly before dusk, rain fell in torrents and flooded the newly dug canals along the streets. When she saw the clouds darken, Hilda had hoped it would not rain so hard so that the tent entrance would not be muddy. She had asked me to go see her again, but I was tired, and besides, the program would not be changed till the morrow—on the first night of the fiesta—when there would be some variations.

I went to bed after a supper that we shared with Father's talkative guests from Manila. The rain stopped, but soon there was a slight insistent patter on the roof again. Occasionally a streak of lightning knifed across the sky. I closed the sash shutters and went to sleep. The patter was still on the roof when I woke up and discerned weighted voices in the hall. They persisted, anxious and harried, not the soft sounds of a dream. I rose and walked to the door. The hall was ablaze, and even the big chandelier, which was used only on special occasions, was lighted. Beyond the balcony, however, the plaza was dark and quiet and the lights of the many vendors and dice tables were out.

I recognized at once the members of the troupe. Hilda's father paced the floor, still wearing his baggy pants and multicolored coat, but the paint was erased from his face. Hilda's mother was a forlorn figure near the sofa where most of them were gathered.

Catching a glimpse of Father, I went to him and asked what it was all about. He told me to go back to sleep, but I could see that he was greatly disturbed. "Who is it, Father?" I asked. He said it simply: "Hilda, the girl from the circus, the tightwire artist. She slipped."

"Isn't the doctor coming?" one of the women asked. She did not get any reply. The others slouched on the sofas, their faces tense with waiting, and soon they started mumbling. Hilda's father told them to be quiet. He approached Father and said softly, "I hope you don't mind the inconvenience we are causing you, but the plaza, with all those people, and the rain . . ."

Father dismissed him with a nod. Then I saw her. I went to the sofa where the older women were gathered about. Hilda lay there, pale and motionless, and in the corners of her mouth were little streams of red that had dried. As she opened her eyes, her mother bent over her, whispering, "My poor, poor darling . . ."

She was not listening; she closed her eyes again, and as she stirred, she moaned. "Don't crowd around her," Father said when they started hurrying to the sofa again. With the exception of her mother, they went back to their seats.

"Our star is no more," Hilda's mother wept bitterly, casting a beseeching look at Father, who turned away. "She always did it right— she could do it even with a blindfold on."

Hilda opened her eyes again, and briefly our eyes locked. She opened her mouth as if to speak, and I bent low only to hear her say, "I hate you," almost in a whisper. But her mother heard, and she cried, "You naughty girl!"

I wheeled and ran to my room. Father followed me there. I did not know what to do, what to say. "She came to Carmay with me this morning," I said. "I did not want to bring her along, but she insisted—"

"I know," Father said, sitting on my bed. "David told me."

"I did not do anything," I said.

Father nodded, then bade me go to sleep. Outside, the rain and the wind grew stronger. The leaves of the balete tree rustled, and there were sounds of people scurrying below the house seeking shelter in the wide sweep of the *media agua*. They would be drenched if they went under the balete tree; its cover would not be enough. Above the monotonous patter on the roof, the merry music of a brass band somewhere beyond the plaza drifted into the house, and the dusky magic of June clung like a wanton spell to my troubled mind.

CHAPTER

I N ANOTHER TWO DAYS the fiesta was over, but the circus did not wait for the last rocket to be fired. The morning after the accident, it packed up, leaving the plaza looking sullen and desolate. The bamboo arches in the street corners and the paper buntings that were soaked and frayed were not dismantled till after a week, but when the circus left I was miserable. Not even the strong afternoon rains, which brought my friends out—racing in the streets and shrieking and splashing in the solid jets of water from the roofs— could lure me away from the sad, sad thought that bedeviled my mind.

My depression would have lasted much longer, but by the end of the month, another celebration came. After more than ten years in America, Tio Benito finally returned home.

Among our many relatives, only he could claim the distinction of having been to America. He went there in the 1920s at the age of eighteen when many Ilokanos were lured by the promise of high wages on the sugar plantations in Hawaii and in the orange orchards of California. There was also the dubious expectation of being able to go to bed with an *Americana*. It was the question often asked of Tio Benito when he settled down to talk with old friends and neighbors.

Grandfather had objected to his leaving, for it meant Tio Benito's denying himself a college education, which his brothers and sisters had. But Tio Benito was bent on his adventure; he pilfered *cavans* of grain from the *bodega* over which he kept watch, sold them to the Chinese *comprador,* then scampered off to Manila and across the Pacific.

Grandfather was very angry, not so much at the minor thievery as at the fact that Tio Benito had gone without bidding him goodbye. But the old man was quick to forgive, particularly after Tio Benito's letters started coming and with them an occasional dollar bill or a shipment of clothes that, alas, may have been all right for Alaska and Northern California but certainly not for Carmay.

But in his letters Tio Benito asked for money more often than he sent it. He got, of course, what he wanted, plus pleadings from all in the family that he hurry back to the land of his birth because Grandfather was becoming old, and there was need for him to look after his inheritance, for his brothers and sisters were too involved with their own.

Everything about Tio Benito was wonderful and done with style. But Tia Antonia, on the occasions that she visited us, always derided him for having gone wrong; she said he had become a "pagan." She had an ally in Sepa, our cook, who believed in religion as convert Protestants devoutly do. Almost all of my relatives were a religious lot, though they were very democratic about their beliefs; they went to any church of their liking. It was almost a rule that hardly anyone stayed home Sunday mornings—all must go to church. I found this not too disturbing, for I was serving then as sacristan to Padre Andong, the Catholic priest—a chore I appreciated, as I always managed to swipe a few coins when I passed the collection plate on Sundays.

Tio Benito's explanation for his "paganism" was pragmatic. "Look," he would say. "What is the need for one to go to church or pray to God? He is everywhere. God knows that when something miserable has happened to you, you need help. Why go to church and make the preacher or the priest grow rich? God knows you are thankful for the things He has done for you. Besides, He isn't like a young girl whom you must flatter every day with words so that His love for you won't diminish. He isn't like that because He is God. He is good. He knows that you like Him, and there is no need to be repetitive—mumbling prayers over and over, prayers said yesterday or a thousand years previous. He gets tired of that."

Still Tia Antonia insisted that he did not even know how to make the sign of the cross. It was hard to believe that a man as old as he did not know that.

Father, however, recalled that Tio Benito was quite religious before he left for the United States; consequently, he explained his brother's sanctimonious behavior as a result of American influence.

To this, Tio Benito retorted, "Don't you dare say that the Americans have no religion, that they don't know how to worship. Yes, they do worship—and it is the buck, the dollar, they revere. It is the end and the beginning—an American without money has nothing, not even God. And that is why America is strong—because it worships money. And look at all of you, worshipping something that cannot help you. Is God responsible for the droughts, the typhoons that destroy the crops?"

Tia Antonia looked at his recalcitrance in a slightly different manner: "America is rich and, therefore, licentious and without God. Look at the absence of modesty of its women." And then she would go into a tirade against the magazines showing American girls in the briefest of bathing suits.

"And that is precisely what I like," Tio Benito admitted to me one day when he was regaling me again with his stories about the United States.

"But surely, Tio," I said, "there must be something in America that you did not like." He was silent for a while, then, in quiet tones, he told me of days of hunger, how difficult it was to get a job because he was brown, how he was treated no different from the Chinese, and how he pitied the Negroes most. "They are not regarded as people," he told me.

"But America is the land of equality, of the free—"

"Bullshit," Tio Benito said, raising his voice.

I quoted at length from Lincoln's Gettysburg Address, which I had already memorized.

"It is the land of opportunity—that is right," Tio Benito said. "If you are white, if you are Protestant, and you are Anglo-Saxon."

"Meaning you cannot play the saxophone?"

He laughed and tousled my hair. "You are too young to be discussing religion with me," he said. Then off again he went, this time to Carmay to be with Grandfather. But after being there for a month, the farm must have bored him, for he moved into the house again, this time sharing Cousin Marcelo's room on the ground floor. He did not seem to have a care in the world. He had obviously saved some money to fool around with, and he continued his meanderings, holding court in the marketplace and at the town barbershop, and ready with the bottle even for the slightest acquaintance. Spending as he did, his savings soon petered out but not the heckling, particularly from Tia Antonia and from Sepa. His impending bankruptcy and the unrelenting nagging about his profligate ways must have done something, for one Sunday morning he decided to give God a chance.

To please Sepa, he went with her to the Protestant chapel. He played no favorite, for on the following Sundays he tried them all—the Catholic church, the Seventh-Day Adventists, even the Aglipayans. Not one of the denominations, however, appealed to him. After he had tried them all, he did not hide his loathing for "the stuffy crowdedness in the churches—even God would have been uncomfortable there. With all those many converts, they have no need for me. The priests talk in a language I cannot understand," he said. He complained, too, of people with bad voices singing.

"What did you do in California on Sundays, Tio?" I asked.

"I had a good time," he said, a grin breaking across his rotund, oily face.

"Did you play games? Cockfights?"

His eyes twinkled. He looked at me expansively. "Cockfights—yes, although the Americans never liked them; they always tried to haul us to jail for it. And games . . . yes." He turned to Father and to Sepa, who was hovering by, ready with another helping of his favorite *dinardaraan*. "I will tell you later . . . later . . ."

That afternoon, I cornered him in the *bodega,* where he was making an inventory of the sacks of grain gnawed by rats. "We followed the crops in California," he explained. "We would be picking beans, tomatoes, lettuce. Then strawberries and grapes. And apples, yes, apples. I would smell of apples even on Sundays."

I could picture him munching an apple, although he said apples made him sick. On Sundays, he went on, he had plenty of money. He brushed his teeth, wore his flashiest suit and his black Stetson, then boarded the silver bus that was fast and smooth, and soon he was in town. He went around a corner, and when he came out, he was holding the waist of a tall blonde, who was, all the while, laughing and immensely enjoying herself.

I did not like her laughter. I did not like her looks, even if she was as white as a newly washed radish. She destroyed the picture of baskets and baskets of golden apples that Tio Benito had picked.

A year after Tio Benito had returned, I noticed that the talk about his ways and the questions that were posed to him diminished, then almost disappeared. Everyone began to accept him for what he was—even his profanities, his showing off, and his attachment to his black Stetson when a lighter, airier hat would have sufficed. On Tio Benito's part, he seemed to have become more morose each day, for he had finally spent all his money and had started to sell some of his things; he even tried to sell his woolens, which no one would buy. Now he often asked for money from Father, but knowing his ways, Father would only give him pin money; after all, Tio Benito was assured a roof over his head and meals every time he was hungry. More than that, he had his share of the harvest, which, alas, was months away. He wandered less and less to the marketplace and to the barbershop on the main street and kept more to the house, talking with Sepa, Tio Baldo, and Old David, for they listened dutifully to his jokes and his stateside stories. Sometimes he also ventured to Carmay to be with Grandfather on weekends.

Then one day he announced pompously at the breakfast table that he would go to the neighboring town to look after a business deal involving the buying and selling of the mongo harvest, and would Father be gracious enough to advance him a small loan of fifty pesos, which he would repay within the month? Father was a bit puzzled but was pleased nonetheless; at last—American commercialism had made its mark in a time of need.

Tio Benito was away for a week, but on the next Sunday he returned at about lunchtime. He looked pleased. His shirt was wet with perspiration, for the sun was bright and the streets were baking in the heat. He did not seem to mind, although I knew him to curse even at the slightest rise in temperature. Now his eyes danced with a light I had never seen before, except when he described his Sundays in America.

Tio Benito had a companion—a woman. She looked at least twenty years older than he. Tio Benito was middle-aged, but he did not have any of the wrinkles that lined the woman's face. I told myself, of course, that she must be just a business associate and not someone toward whom he had amorous intentions; after all those blondes in America, such a thought was unthinkable.

Not that she was ugly; she was brown—very—and she had classic Ilokano features: a broad forehead, a small nose, and lips that were quite thick. What struck me were her upper teeth, which were all set in gold so that when she smiled it seemed as if her mouth was on fire. From snatches of conversation while they were talking with Father in the *sala*, I learned that the woman lived three towns away, that she had come to pay my very surprised and very amused father the fifty pesos that Tio Benito owed him plus whatever interest there was. But more than this, she also wanted to talk to all of us about a very urgent matter "concerning salvation and the soul."

"Yes," Father said. "This is very good to hear. But let us eat first."

We stood up and went to the dining room, and when Sepa saw Tio Benito, she told him he was lucky, for she had prepared *dinardaraan,* his favorite dish. It consisted of pork and the innards of the pig stewed in its own blood and in vinegar. The day before, a neighbor had butchered his pig, and Father gave a *cavan* of palay for five kilos and the innards.

At the mention of *dinardaraan,* Tio Benito scowled at the cook, but he did not say anything. We sat before the long narra table, in the middle of which was the glass fruit tray topped with oranges and apples. Like Tio Benito, I also relished *dinardaraan,* but I could have been knocked down with the paper wand Sepa waved to drive the flies away. There he was, straight as a bamboo, his head bowed, his eyes closed; with his woman companion, he was praying! Father was all smiles; it seemed that we no longer had a pagan in our midst. After this surprise, I pushed toward him the bowl of *dinardaraan,* reminding him it was my favorite, too.

It happened then; with disdain clouding his greasy face, he pushed the bowl away as if it were poison.

"I prepared it," Sepa said, surprised and defensive.

But Tio Benito ignored her; he stood up abruptly, and in sudden inspiration, he began the best speech—or sermon—I ever heard on the importance of eating the right food so as not to pollute the body or offend God. He spoke with power and conviction, and we stopped eating; even the maids paused in their chores and crowded in to listen to the words of wisdom that now poured from his lips. He spoke of the growing evil in the world, of the need for brotherhood, community, kindred spirit that would not only allow us to enter the kingdom of God but also banish the usurpers of His word in this land. He railed against the friars who established a church subservient to Rome: look at the money collected in the Catholic churches—it is sent to a foreign land to fatten foreign priests. The Americans were no better; they also sent their own missionaries to perpetuate the subservience of Filipinos to them. The Catholic priests, the Protestant pastors—they talk in a foreign language, they are ashamed of their own, of Ilokano or of Tagalog, which are the languages of the people. And then he spoke of the reasons why he could not eat *dinardaraan* or anything with blood, for such food was not fit for anyone who believed in the true God, for anyone who could read the Bible and regard it as sacred, for it is right there—and he proceeded to quote from memory the particular chapter and verse. It was my first experience with a convert of the *Iglesia Ni Kristo.* Sepa was very pleased, although her particular sect was Protestant; what was important was that Tio Benito finally believed.

"I will convert you," he enthused. Turning to Father and me, and of course to Tia Antonia, then to all the maids and house help gathered around us, he added, "All of you, all of you."

The woman was silent, but on her face was the most beatific smile I had ever seen—her mouth was aglow. So my Tio Benito became a Christian—of that much I was sure. Although I doubted if his hortatory rhetoric could move as much as an inch any of the people who listened to him, I was sure that the woman with him had some uncanny power of conversion, for it was she who did it and no one else. She married Tio Benito, and though I am not very positive about what Tio Benito said about not eating *dinardaraan* because it is cooked in blood, of this I am certain: In our town, it used to be fashionable for the very rich to have as many gold teeth as they could afford. Tio Benito's wife had all her upper teeth in gold, and that, in itself, was enough proof to Christians and pagans alike that she was, indeed, a very wealthy woman.

NOTHING PLEASED GRANDFATHER more than Tio
Benito's wedding; he once said that only a woman could tie my
uncle down to Rosales and banish once and for all the itch that had
sent him drifting to alien lands. Now that Tio Benito had settled
down, the old man was at peace because all his children were where
he wanted them: within his reach should the time come for him to die.

The wedding was celebrated in Carmay; in the mud-packed yard
of Grandfather's house, the tenants built a long shed roofed with coconut leaves and fenced with old bamboo fish traps. Here the entire
village gathered to feast on three *carabaos,* two cows, and half a
dozen pigs. The wedding ceremony itself, in the absence of a chapel
of the new sect in Rosales, was performed in Grandfather's living
room, which was decorated by Cousin Marcelo with sprays of pa-
paya blossoms and palmetto fronds. Many members of the sect arrived in a fleet of *caretelas,* and while their minister ranted and flung
his hands to the roof, the women sang and cried. Grandfather made
it clear, however, that he was not now going to stop enjoying *dinar-*

daraan or tolerate any attempt of the newlyweds to interfere with his bucolic peace and the future of his soul.

Even before the china used at the feast was dry, Grandfather told Tio Benito to pack his overcoat and his thick, dark suits and, like a good husband, follow his wife to her home three towns away. It would have been ideal if Tio Benito and his wife lived with the old man, but Grandfather valued his independence and isolation. "Since your grandmother died," he once said, "I have lived alone and I like it that way." Nevertheless, he followed Father's advice and kept a handyman, not to serve him but to see to it that in his twilight he did no unnecessary work that could cut his days still shorter.

Two days before Christmas, Grandfather came to the house; the helper who kept watch over him had crossed the Agno to spend the holiday with his family, and knowing this, we tried to dissuade Grandfather from returning to Carmay and spending Christmas there alone.

He was too stubborn and set in his ways to accede. He arrived hobbling up the graveled path with his long, ivory-handled cane, a relic of his younger days when he was *gobernadorcillo,* his feet encased in leather sandals firmly tied to his ankles by thongs. On his head was a crumpled *buntal* hat. Although he tried to walk as if his bones were those of a frisky youth still, he could not refrain from stooping. It was only when he paused at the foot of the stairs that his fatigue became apparent, though he had walked but a short distance from the bus station. He was panting, and as I tried to help him up, he looked at me, at the young hand that held his arm, and a flash of scorn crossed his face. The expression changed quickly into a wry smile. "I am all right, boy," he said.

But he did not go up to the house alone, for quickly Father came rushing down, saying he should have sent us word so that Old David could have fetched him in the *calesa.*

It was one of the old man's rare visits, usually made three or four times a year. He had chosen to stay on the farm, which he had helped clear out of the wilderness that had once stretched from the Andolan creek to the banks of the Agno. He had also imparted to the farmers around him his knowledge of farming amassed through years of frugal Ilokano existence, which were interrupted only when he held office and participated in the revolution or when he visited town.

If Father did not tell me, I would never have known, for instance, what he did during the revolution, that among other things, he knew Apolinario Mabini and took care of the Sublime Paralytic when he fled to Rosales, that Mabini stayed in our house, where he wrote a lot before he went to Cuyapo, where later on he was captured by the Americans.

The only time I heard Grandfather really raise his voice was when I was perhaps nine or ten years old. I had gotten ill, and he had come to see me on the third day that I had this high fever and hardly noticed the people fleeting about my sickroom. He had made inquiries about what had happened, and Sepa told him I had played at the foot of the balete tree together with some classmates and that we had constructed a playhouse on the veined trunk of the tree.

I remember him roaring at Father, why knowing this, he had not sent an offering so that I would get well, and how Sepa immediately went to the kitchen at Father's harried command to do what Grandfather wanted although I knew that Father did not really believe in all that superstition.

Father used to threaten me when I misbehaved, saying that he would banish me to Carmay. Though I had always regarded Grandfather with awe, he never terrified me. After all, I loved listening to his stories of the supernatural and the mysterious. He was particularly fond of telling stories about the balete tree, for he believed that the tree was blessed and that it was bound to protect us from the curses and onslaught of evil. When Father realized that packing me off to Carmay would cause me no suffering, he resorted to the whip instead.

For a man over eighty, Grandfather seemed in good health. As far as I could recall, he had been sick only once, and I distinctly remember how, on a stormy September night, Father and the doctor had to rush in the *calesa* to Carmay and slosh through rice fields to attend to him; he lay in his old rattan bed saying that if death were to strike, no one would be able to thwart the blow, and for that reason he refused absolutely to take any medication.

Grandfather was more than prepared. It was no secret that he had ordered a coffin made of the finest narra when he was just a few years over seventy. Somehow, Father had disposed of the relic when the old man ceased asking about it. Many marveled over his ability to maintain an agile mind, and his memory for faces was superb; he could identify his grandchildren, his great-grandchildren, and the host of farmers and their families who lived around him.

What was the secret of his longevity? His tenant neighbors, especially the more superstitious, had an explanation. It could be, they said, that once upon a time, he had heard the bells on Christmas Eve. On that very hour of midnight when Christ was born, a heavenly chime would peal; only the chosen would hear it, and they who are so blessed would live to a ripe old age, their fondest wishes all come true.

I recounted this to Grandfather, but he ignored it; he was not really all that keen about things said of him, for his religiosity pertained mostly to the land, whose yield was greatly influenced by God and the elements. He had not stepped within the portals of the church for ages, though he was not one to deride those who did. During the dark days of the revolution against Spain, he had developed an apathy about the Spanish friars and, eventually, the church.

That December evening as he sat down with us at the head of the table, he seemed exuberant. He relished the mudfish and sipped his chicken broth, as if he thoroughly enjoyed every drop. We waited for him to finish and had expected him to talk, but he was adamant. "I came here for no other reason than to take my grandson with me," he said. "He can return when Basilio returns from his family."

It was a time I did not particularly care for Carmay, because on Christmas I would rather be at home. The provincial road sliced through the far end of the barrio, which was really nothing but a few thatched houses huddled together with Grandfather's—the biggest of them all and the only one with a tin roof—standing closest to the narrow bull-cart path that leads down from the road. There was peace and quiet in Carmay on Christmas Day, and perhaps its only attraction during the holidays was its excellent rice cakes, better than those available in town. It was livelier in Rosales—the early-morning mass, the chill permeating our bones, the jaunty band music rousing all of us. We would then stagger from our warm beds to go to church, where first we would drink scalding ginger tea from the convent kitchen. Afterward there would be the happy sight of flickering candles on the altar, the smell of incense swirling about, and above everything our voices swelling in the choir loft. Later the sun would rise from behind the heavily wooded hills of Balungao, and suddenly it was morning.

The evenings were just as memorable. Tio Baldo, come Christmastime, always fashioned a bamboo cannon for me, and as soon as it was dark we filled one end with heated kerosene, stuck empty milk cans in the mouth, and fired away at the youngsters across the street, who also had the same noisy toy. Or with Angel, Ludovico, and the other boys, we would play from house to house as a bamboo orchestra, all the rest tooting and puffing at a weird assortment of bamboo flutes, clappers, and jingles, while I played the harmonica—the only instrument that somehow managed to give a running tune to the noise that we emitted. The money we made was not much, but for the boys it meant a merrier Christmas. Shortly before midnight, when we returned to the house, we also had something for the help—maybe a cigar for Sepa and a bottle of gin for Old David.

But Grandfather had spoken, and what was Carmay at Christmastime but a wide, dreary field ripe with grain? There was nothing there to dispel the quiet but the booming voice of some farmer calling his children from their river bathing or the martins cawing in the lofty buri palms.

"We are not going to sleep in the house," Grandfather said. "We are going to sleep in the field to watch the new harvest."

It was only then that I perked up, for the prospect of sleeping in the open—something I had never done before—was vastly appealing.

"Why should we sleep in the field, Grandfather?" I asked. "Aren't you afraid you might get a cough?"

He tousled my hair, then went on to explain that times had changed. "Years ago," he said, "during harvest time, the newly cut stalks of palay were piled in the fields, where they were not removed, or brought to the granaries till they were to be husked. Now, with hunger slowly stalking the land, one has to keep watch over the harvest, lest it be stolen."

I AM SURE we made a fine sight that afternoon as we walked down the main street to the bus station. Grandfather walked stiffly in his sandals, ivory cane in his hand and his crumpled hat propped straight on his head. I felt proud walking behind the old man who had helped build the town and who was, perhaps, the oldest man for miles and miles around.

When we passed the church I said, "If I were not coming along, Grandfather, I would sing in the choir tonight during the Christmas mass."

A scowl swept across his face, and knowing I had displeased him with my remark, I did not speak again.

The trip to Carmay was uneventful. We reached it in a few minutes. The sun lay bright on the countryside, and the golden fields were alive with reapers in brightly colored clothes. The boundaries of our land, which Grandfather had cleared, blended with the tall dikes running parallel to the banks of the Agno.

We went up to his house. Ears of corn and fishnets were piled near the door. In the kitchen, chickens were pecking at grains scattered on the floor. The nippy December wind stole in, and Grandfather told me to bundle the blankets and a couple of pillows. We hitched a bull cart, then headed for the open fields where the harvest was stacked high. Soon it had become dark, and stars began to sparkle in the black bowl of sky.

After we had fixed our beds in the bull cart and in the sled with a thin canopy of hay over us, Grandfather sat on the sled quietly. Distant wisps of singing and the ring of laughter from the farmhouses reached us. Rosales was far away—a halo of light on the horizon. No sound from it could reach us, not even the boom of the bamboo cannons or the sharp crackle of firecrackers.

It was peaceful and quiet. After a while, with his head resting on the rump of the sled, Grandfather began to tell stories of the days when this field was a jungle of cogon grass and mounds, and snakes lurked in every hole. He spoke of the Bagos, who trekked down the Cordillera ranges and traded venison for cloth and matches. It was a time when the Agno River was not so wild and the Andolan creek had plenty of fish and, in his own backyard, he hunted the wild pig. He spoke, too, of past Christmases, though he was not keen about them, of the nights he slept in the open during the hunt and harvest evenings, when he kept watch over the grain that could not be carted off to his granary.

"Boy," Grandfather said, "the silence of a field can give a man beautiful thoughts. Here, more than anyplace, you are nearer God."

I did not understand then what he meant, for I was Padre Andong's acolyte in the Catholic church and had quite a different idea about worship. But I listened just the same to his stories of the revolution till the singing and the hoarse shouting of the tenants from across the fields waned and a heaviness stole over my eyes.

Perhaps I dozed, for when I looked up from my seat of hay, Grandfather was no longer near me. Over the land, a moon shone, a cool, silver lamp. The Balungao mountain in the east slumped like a sleeping beast, and all around us was the night, the endless river of night insects and crickets, and the rich, heady smell of new hay. It was cold, and I wrapped the blanket tighter around my quivering body. I looked around apprehensively to where the camachile tree stood, and where the *carabao,* tied to a saluyot shrub, was chewing its cud. I saw Grandfather then standing in the open behind the cart, his head raised to the sheen of the starlit heavens and his right hand clutching his old ivory cane.

He stood there erect as a spear, for how long I can't remember. I went to him, but he did not seem to feel my presence. Staring closer at his upturned face, I saw tears trickling down his coarse, wrinkle-furrowed face, to his lips, which were parted in an exultant smile.

I remembered then that he was a little deaf, but he must have known I was near, for he spoke without looking at me: "Listen, boy."

I held his hand.

"Listen, boy, listen," he repeated in a soft, tremulous voice.

"What is it, Grandfather?" I asked, hearing nothing.

"Listen," he repeated severely.

Across the silent fields where the farmers' homes were huddled a dog howled. The evening wind whimpered in the camachile saplings, a *carabao* snorted. Somewhere in the shaggy grass that covered the dikes, cicadas were chirping, and farther down, the river gurgled as it meandered in its course.

"I hear only the river, a dog, the wind, and insects," I said.

It seemed as if his thoughts were far, far away.

"The bells, boy," he said, a glow on his face bright as happiness, clear as morning. "The bells are ringing."

I remembered again the legend of the bells, how men like Grandfather had defied time and circumstance, lived through the years crowned with bliss and fortune, because, once on a Christmas night, they heard the bells. And here was this old man, who had always said this was not so, straining his old deaf ears listening, crying.

I looked at his face again, at the drooping eyelids, at the thin lips mumbling a prayer, perhaps, and it occurred to me that he no longer belonged to my time. He had taken on a countenance that struck me with awe. In the next instant, I drew away from him and slowly turned and ran across the new hay, over the irrigation ditches, down the incline, beyond the towering palms standing like hooded sentinels of darkness, all the way to Carmay in the Christmas night. I went breathlessly up to the old man's house, my heart thundering in my chest, and cuddled among the pillows in his damp room, not wanting to return, cursing myself for not hearing anything and, most of all, for not believing what the old man said he heard.

When Christmas morning broke over Carmay, a neighbor and I went where Grandfather and I camped in the night. I had expected the old man to be angry with me for having left him.

I told no one about what Grandfather said he heard, not even the doctor who declared that Grandfather, whom we found lying serenely on the sled with an angelic smile on his face, had finally died of old age.

CHAPTER

AFTER GRANDFATHER'S DEATH, Father asked Tio Benito if he wanted to live in Carmay, but my uncle was too comfortable in his new residence to care for the virtues of the village. Before the elements could claim Grandfather's house, Father had it torn apart, and all its good planks of wood were brought to Rosales. The other materials—the galvanized-iron sheets, sash windows, and wooden sidings, even the kitchen utensils—were given by Father to his tenants.

The wooden shed, which was full, he gave to a tenant family that had suffered a disaster that year; while the woman of the house was preparing charcoal, some sparks flew and their house burned down. They were so poor that they would have slept on the ground and without a roof had not Father taken pity on them and given them the woodshed.

I remember this family very well, particularly Ludovico, the son. Among the many farmer boys whom I knew, Ludovico alone dared show me his true feelings and speak to me in anger, as if I were no more than a worthless younger brother.

But then, Ludovico's anger was not the long, smouldering kind. The moment he had given vent to his feelings, he was again his old likeable self. He was a tall, gangling youth with eyes that gave the impression he was sleepy all the time, but those eyes became instantly alive the moment he spoke. He seldom talked, though, and when he did, he seemed always to be groping for the proper words to say.

He was dark like most of the other barrio boys who had no education except the practical kind that one absorbed after knowing hunger quite as well as the endless drudgery that went with being a tenant. He had only a pair of pants—blue denims, well worn, faded at the knees and the buttocks—which he washed himself and ironed with such consuming care, as if it were a *de hilo* suit.

Ludovico came to the house on a Sunday after the first mass was said. He accompanied his mother, Feliza—a thin little woman who always spoke in a whisper, whose face was as pale as a banana stalk. Her wide bamboo basket was usually filled with vegetables—sweet-potato tops, bamboo shoots, eggplants, greens that she could not have sold for much, because in Rosales vegetables are cheap and could be had for the asking. She would give some of the vegetables to Sepa, for these were raised on Father's farm, and by some unwritten law, a part of such harvest belonged to us.

Feliza was very industrious—this much could be seen in the way she swept the storehouse or the yard so thoroughly whenever Father asked her.

Ludovico always carried the firewood—dried acacia or dalipawen branches on a pliant pole balanced across his shoulder. One bundle was for us, and the other was for sale in the public market.

They always came barefoot, and their feet were thick and black with mud or dust depending on the season. Like most of the tenants in Carmay, Ludovico would have probably grown to a venerable old age without having known how it was to wear shoes. I would ask them to come up to the house for a while, but like the other tenants, they would refuse with plenty of head-shaking. They would look bashfully at their dirty feet and still decline to come up to the house even after they had gone to the artesian well below the kitchen to wash.

After Ludovico had stacked the firewood in the woodshed and carried the other bundle to market, he would return to the house and wait in the yard while his mother sold the greens and the extra firewood.

Feliza would return at about eleven, her face damp with sweat. With the little money she had made from the vegetables, she would have bought a bottle of kerosene, salted fish wrapped in dried banana leaves, sometimes a bundle of rice cakes, laundry soap, and cheap little items from the Chinese stores that occupied Father's building along the main street.

They would not depart until Father had acknowledged their presence, not by talking with them as they stood motionless at the bottom of the stairs but by simply waving his hand in their direction and occasionally inquiring how things were in Carmay.

It was while waiting for his mother that Ludovico and I became friends. I would often join him on the stone bench in the shade of the balete tree. He was never voluble; he would shift his position when cramped, or sometimes he would venture into the graveled street and loiter there.

I asked him once if he had gone to school.

He had reached the third grade, he said, his face aglow as if reaching the third grade and being able to write one's name were an achievement.

During the harvest season, I would get permission to go to Carmay regularly with Old David. The old servant would leave me in Ludovico's care, and Ludovico would lift me and carry me around on his shoulders while I held on to his short, dry hair.

One day, we went to gather camachile fruits along the provincial road. That was the day Ludovico was scared, for I had messed with some poisonous vine, and the whole day my arms swelled and ached. Father gave him three lashes with the horse whip, and after that Ludovico waited on me as if I were a sultan's son.

I remember the time we were standing by the half-dried irrigation ditch and my straw hat was blown into the ditch by a strong gust of wind. He crouched low on the embankment to retrieve my hat. On a sudden impulse, I gave him a little shove and into the muddy ditch he fell. He got splashed all over with black mud. He cussed, but I laughed and laughed till I found out that he was really angry. I thought he would give me a thrashing, but when he noticed I was scared, he began laughing, too. He laughed so madly I thought he would never stop.

After the harvest season, the open spaces no longer fascinated me. In a few months the rains came, in driblets at first and then in torrents. Just the same, Ludovico walked three kilometers to our house from the barrio with his two bundles of firewood balanced on a pole.

Once, sitting on the top rung of the kitchen stairs, I watched him drink from the artesian well. I was in a mood for pranks. I went down, splashed water on him and, while at it, I slipped and fell at his feet. We laughed together till Sepa told him to go away, which he did immediately, as if he were a whipped dog.

I cannot now forget the last time Feliza, his mother, came to our house. Balanced on her head was the same old load of greens to sell at the market, but she didn't put it down. After Ludovico finished drinking, she suddenly started to cough.

Ludovico took the basket off his mother's head and placed it on the ground, then patted his mother gently on the back.

"I told you not to come," he said. "Now look—it has started again."

Feliza stooped and beat her flat chest with her knotted fists. She shook convulsively, then spat out something red, very red.

"What is that?" I asked.

She sat down and gurgled. Seeing that she had nothing to use, I got a glass from the kitchen shelf and handed it to her. She thanked me when her coughing ceased.

Father came out then. He asked what the matter was, and reluctantly, I told him.

Father said, "Don't carry so heavy a load, Feliza. After all, Ludovico is a big man now and he can do that for you. Or is Ludovico lazy?"

Ludovico reddened. "No, Apo," he said softly, "I am not lazy."

After they had gone, Father asked me if it was I who had given the glass to Feliza. He instructed Sepa to immerse the glass in boiling water, then he turned to me: "Don't give Feliza any of the things we use."

Once, perched on Ludovico's shoulders, I asked him: "What would you want to be when you grow up?"

He replied he was already "almost a man" like his father, but I insisted there must be something, someone he would still want to be.

"All right," he said, laughing. Behind us was Rosales, and in front of us were sprawled the hills of Balungao.

He jabbed a finger at them. "I want to own one of those. You have never been there. You don't know how it is to own a few trees. Giant trees that can mean a lot of firewood. Sagat and parunapin. These make good house posts, too."

He went on talking about the trees, how they were felled and later tediously dragged down the slopes. And how he caught the slippery mudfish in the creeks, how his father had a row with an uncle over the irrigation ditches, how his cousin was hurt in a drinking spree. Then, unconsciously, his mother was sucked into the whirlpool of his thoughts, and he told of the work she did at home, which might as well pass for that of a *carabao*'s—washing clothes, pounding rice, helping in the tilling of the soil.

The harvest season passed. The tenants littered the yard again with their bull carts filled with grain. They tucked the jute sacks in neat piles in Father's storehouse. And one morning, Chan Hai drove into the yard with his trucks, joked with Father, weighed the palay, then took most of it away. Father counted over and over the money the Chinese had handed him and placed it in the steel safe in his room.

Father always bought a lot of things when he made a sale. Even the servants were provided with new clothes, and a new set of furniture found its way into the house. I wondered what Ludovico's father did with his share of the crop, for when Ludovico came to town on Sundays, he still wore those faded denims.

Then the rains came. Now the mornings were cool and refreshing, and the world had a sharp, clean aroma that made one glad to have a nose.

Ludovico's father and the other tenants came to Father's *bodega*, talked of the planting season and the harvest. It would be something to be reckoned with, they said. That was immaculately clear in the stars, in the aura of the full moon, in the red-blood sun as it sank beyond the coconut groves of Tomana. When they left, they carted a few sacks for seed.

It was in the first week of October that Ludovico stopped coming to our house and headed for the hills to gather more firewood to make charcoal with. His mother was very sick, and she needed all the money he could earn. His father suffered in his stead with the firewood—small branches of madre de cacao and twigs that were damp and did not kindle so easily.

He apologized when Sepa fumed because the firewood he brought did not give off charcoal for broiling.

He does not know much about firewood, I mused.

He came one Thursday in the hush of twilight with the same two bundles. Since his usual day to come was Sunday, from the dimly lighted kitchen Sepa inquired why he was rather early. He said he was going to the hills the following day.

"I'll be back as soon as I can. Sunday, probably," he said complacently. "I am just going to take Ludovico home. He caught something bad over there. Typhoid, I think."

That Sunday, as he said he would, Ludovico's father did return. He came to the house with a black piece of cloth tied around his head. He had freshly ironed, well-starched pants folded at the ankles.

His peasant feet, big and spread, were washed and clean.

Father, whom he sought, emerged from the front door. Father did not ask why he had the black piece of cloth tied around his head. Instead, the first question Father prodded him with was: "Has the rice started to flower already, and has the dike in the west end of the farm been fixed?"

"Everything is all right, Apo." Ludovico's father smiled broadly, but almost as precipitately as it came, his grin vanished as he now spoke in low, even tones. He had come to borrow money for a funeral. Ludovico had died.

Father went to the house, shaking his balding head. When he returned, he handed some bills to Ludovico's father, who in his relief pocketed them at once.

"There will be the usual interest to that," Father reminded him.

Ludovico's father nodded and was all smiles. Then his voice faltered. "But Apo, I cannot return this after the harvest this year. Feliza, my wife . . . Next harvest time, maybe . . ."

"And why not, may I know?" Father demanded.

Ludovico's father explained hurriedly. At first, Father was unmoved. Then he said. "All right, next harvest time. But don't forget, the interest will then be twice."

I did not quite understand what it was all about, so I tugged at Father's hand. He did not mind me—he went his way. I did not attend Ludovico's funeral, but Sepa, who was fond of him, did, and she described how Ludovico was brought to church without the pealing of bells, wrapped in an old buri mat and slung on a pole carried by his father and a farmer neighbor.

And only afterward did I understand why there was not even a wooden coffin for Ludovico, why the next harvest, which might be bountiful, would be meaningless. I remembered Ludovico's mother—so tiny and thin and overworked, her wracking cough, her pale, tired face, and the ripening grain that she would neither harvest nor see.

CHAPTER

7

ALL THE LURES of Carmay and its feeling of space seemed dulled after Grandfather and Ludovico were gone. Even when the irrigation ditches were finally shallow and the fishing there with bamboo traps was good, even when the melons in the delta were ripe and beckoning, I did not go there. The dry season was upon us—a glaze of sun and honeyed air; it touched the green mangoes and made them golden yellow, took the roar and the brownish tint from the Agno and made it placid and green. The dry season and school vacation also brought to Rosales my Cousin Pedring (on Father's side) and my Cousin Clarissa (on my mother's side). Pedring had just finished law school in Manila and had come to Rosales ostensibly for some quiet and to review for the coming bar examinations. He was about twenty-four. He must have been miserable, cooped up in the city for so long, and on his first day in Rosales he got me to go with him to Carmay "to fill his lungs with clean air."

He was handsome and fair, and he recalled how once he had vacationed in Rosales when I was still a baby; he had bathed in the irrigation ditch in Carmay then, and now he wanted to relive that experience. But in the dry season all the irrigation ditches had dried up except in spots where the water was stagnant and green. This did not deter him; he would have immersed himself the whole morning there like a *carabao* if I did not tell him that we had to return to town before noon. Gathering his clothes, his hair still streaked with bits of moss, his pale skin shiny with a patina of mud, he dressed hurriedly. We boarded the next *caretela* that passed.

It had been one of my chores to proceed shortly after noon to the post office in the *municipio* to pick up Father's mail and newspapers that were brought in by the train connection from Paniqui. It was a chore I enjoyed because it afforded me the first look at the comics section of the papers, and even in the midday sun on the way back I would be reading *Tarzan* and *Mutt & Jeff.*

It was lunchtime when Cousin Pedring and I reached the town, and the sun was warm. On the street, dust rose at the gentlest stirring of the breeze. With mud now caked on his hair, he rushed to the artesian well for another bath with Old David working the pump.

When both of us were through, Father called us up. "You go to the station," he said.

"But the mail, Father."

"It is all right," Father said. "For once the mail carrier will do his job."

"Who is arriving?" Pedring asked.

"Clarissa," Father said, and dismissed us with a wave of his hand.

Old David was readying the *calesa* when we got to him at the stable. It was a short ride, and, from the elevated station platform we could see the train rounding the bend at Calanutan, blowing its whistle shrilly. Pedring helped me down the *calesa* and said, "Tell me about Clarissa."

"A cousin like you, but on Mother's side," I said.

"I know," he said, passing his hand over his hair, which had dried. Without pomade, it was unruly. "How old is she?"

I made a hasty mental calculation. "About eighteen, I think."

He stomped his feet on the stone platform to shake off the dust from his shoes. "I have not seen her yet," he said. "What does she look like?"

I remembered Clarissa very well. Father and I once went to Cebu for a two-week vacation, and she and her parents met us at the pier; I was barely nine then, but everything about that visit was etched clearly in my mind—the pungent smell of copra at the pier, the sloping, narrow streets, their beautiful stone house, its sash windows festooned with butterfly orchids. There was a party in her honor, for she was sixteen and it was her first time to dance in public. She wore a white lace dress, and her hair was knotted with a red ribbon. I remember how flushed and anxious she looked as she kept in step with her father, and when it was over and the small band changed tune, she sought me, literally pulled me to the floor and, amidst much laughter and coaxing, tried to dance with me. I remember her moist, warm hand, her sweet breath upon my face, and my stepping on her feet many times.

"Is she pretty?" Cousin Pedring was insistent. I hardly heard him above the clangor as the train pulled into the station and shot blasts of white steam into the noonday glare.

"Yes," I said, "very pretty."

"Will she stay long in Rosales?"

"I don't know," I said.

I could not miss her when she alighted. One could not but pause and cast a lingering look at her, even if she was in a crowd; she really had bloomed—a regal head, full lips, and eyes filled with laughter. When she saw me, she waved at once, and moved away from the women with their baskets of vegetables.

"You have become so tall," she said, bussing me on the cheek. I introduced Pedring, and they shook hands, then we walked down the cement platform to the palisaded yard, where Old David waited. We helped her with her rattan suitcase, then boarded.

"How is Tio?" she asked as we cantered off to town. After I replied, she did not speak again all through the drive. Pedring attempted some conversation: "It is good to have you here." But to his attempts, she merely nodded or smiled, and her smile—if it was one—was as dry as the dust that Old David's horse raised.

"WHAT ARE YOU THINKING OF, Clarissa?" I asked later as we ate lunch.

She shook her head and looked pensive. I would have pressed

for a clearer answer, but I caught Father's eye; he sat at the other end of the table, and though he did not speak, I knew he did not want me to press the query further.

The following day, though Father did not explain it clearly, I learned why Clarissa was with us. It seemed that a young man in Cebu had taken an interest in her—he was the son of a clerk, had no chance of going to college, and Clarissa's parents did not approve—after all, they were well-to-do and all their children had studied in convent schools. She was therefore exiled to Rosales, so that in time she would forget.

Before we went to bed that night, I invited Pedring and Clarissa to play dominoes in the *azotea;* I knew that she did not relish being in Rosales, in this small dusty town away from the delights of home. "We can go to Carmay tomorrow," I said. "The camachile trees are now bearing fruit, and we can gather them. We can bring a lunch basket, and we can go to the Agno, swim, or stay there and gather pine splinters. There are so many wonderful things one can do in Carmay." She shook her head and said something listless, that she did not like hiking.

We did not go, and Cousin Pedring, who had wanted very much to stay in Carmay, seemed pleased that Clarissa had elected to be in the old dreary house instead. And there came a time afterward that he lost all interest in Carmay and would rather be cooped up in the house with her.

The following day, before I was to leave for the post office to get the mail, Father called me to his room and said that all the letters addressed to Clarissa should not be given to her. I should give them all to him.

Clarissa must have expected them, for on the day she arrived, she asked what time the postman usually came to deliver the mail, and I told her it was I who was the mail carrier. She met me at the yard when I returned and breathlessly inquired if there was any letter for her.

"Nothing," I said, and it was true.

But the following day three did arrive. I followed Father's instruction and gave them all to him. He opened them and read them briefly, then instructed me to burn them in the kitchen. It was a job I did not relish. As I proceeded to burn them, I got curious and started reading one. It was a love letter—mushy words strung together—and having memorized the penmanship, I never bothered reading any of the many that came afterward. Every day Clarissa would ask and I would lie; she had me mail letters, and like the letters she was supposed to receive, they never reached their destination.

"Are you sure I don't have any mail today?" she asked one particularly trying day when the heat seemed to scorch everything, even my patience. She had been in Rosales for more than three weeks.

"Yes," I said sourly. "Why should I hide it from you?"

"Well then," she said with determination. "Tomorrow, I will be at the post office ahead of you so Tio will not know."

But on that day she did not come because Pedring managed—by some miracle—to take her to Carmay instead; they left shortly after breakfast with a basket that was amply prepared by Sepa. And in the afternoon when they returned, the wind and the sun in her hair, the basket was filled with camachile fruits. She forgot to ask about her letters.

On the days that followed, she no longer seemed to care whether she received a letter or not, and soon the letters from the boy in Cebu stopped coming altogether, and I was glad and relieved, for then I no longer had to lie. I began to see less of Pedring, too. He was not reviewing, nor did he like to go swimming in the Agno. He had time only for Clarissa.

May came quickly, and once more the land turned green; somehow, the life and vivacity came back to Clarissa, too, and she seemed to enjoy my cousin's company, for many a time I would catch them laughing on the bench in the yard.

When we played dominoes in the *azotea,* they would often get to talking and it would be difficult for me to catch the thread of what it was all about. More and more, they would clam up when I asked what it was that they were so secretive about.

At the end of the month, before the town fiesta and the opening of the school year, the parents of both Clarissa and Pedring came to Rosales. With Father joining them, they talked far into the night, while on the moon-drenched balcony Pedring, Clarissa, and I played a listless game of dominoes. I won most of the time, for they did not have their minds on the game; they did not speak much, for they seemed all ears, instead, to the talk and the occasional laughter that went on in the living room.

The following day the tenants came, and with isis leaves and wax they cleaned every nook of the house; they also polished the silver that had started to tarnish. All through the week the preparation went on, and, when it finally came, it was the grandest wedding Rosales had seen in years. There was a battery of photographers, and two days after the wedding, I saw our picture in the papers, Pedring looking bewildered, Clarissa radiant and pretty as always, and I in my white suit looking dandy—too dandy and too old to be a ring bearer.

Pedring took his bride to Hong Kong, and from there he wrote to Father and to me saying they would return to Manila, where they would make their home, then visit us before Christmas. He also took the bar examinations and passed.

I did not see them again until I went to Manila to continue my studies, and then and only then did I realize what I had done, what fate I had helped to shape.

CHAPTER

LACK OF HOUSEHOLD HELP was one problem we never had to face. In fact, Father used to have some difficulty turning away many youngsters who wanted to serve in the house, the sons and daughters of tenants who wanted their children to be with us, so that they would be assured of three meals a day, particularly during the lean months of the planting season—June to August—when many a rice bin was empty. Some of those who came to work, of course, knew that their servitude was payment for debts incurred, debts that their fathers had accumulated through the years. They all came to Rosales without much education, barefoot, their brown, emaciated bodies slowly putting on flesh after the first few weeks of eating regularly, their blemished skin becoming clear, their deportment less awkward as in the first few days when, awed by Father's presence and the proportions of the house, they would walk or go about their chores in reverential silence.

Not Martina; of all the maids who came to serve us it was she I remembered best, for there was a brashness in her ways that was self-confidence rather than arrogance; it was not that she did not respect

Father or that she looked with condescension at the timidity of the other help. She was, from the very beginning, herself, untrammeled by convention and uncaring toward those who thought she was without the refinements that any growing girl—barrio-born or from the heart of town—should have. They said that no good would ever come to her—that she would end up in the streets; I cannot believe this conclusion, and though I never saw her again after she left us, I am sure that wherever she is, she can cope with most of the problems life would shower on her.

She was fifteen when she came to the house. She had had some schooling, for she knew how to write her name and many a time, too, did I see her go over the old papers Sepa used to kindle the firewood. She was well on the way to becoming a woman, and I remember the ogling of the boys in the barbershop when they watched her go to market and the guarded language they used when they spoke with her. She never bothered with them. She would flop on the bench in the yard in a most unwomanly manner, exposing her thin thighs. Sometimes, too, I would catch the other boys in the house stealing glances at her low neckline and her small firm breasts, as she bent doing her chores, sweeping the yard or pumping water from the artesian well.

At first she came to the house only on weekends to do odd jobs, and she would do them as fast as she could, sweeping the wide yard cluttered with acacia and guava leaves and the dung of work animals when the tenants brought their bull carts in. She also helped clean the *bodega,* which was always in disarray, and once her chores were done, she would disappear. She did not seem to bother with her looks, her hair hanging in damp, uncombed locks, her face stained with dirt, although I was sure with some care and with a little bit more to eat, she would be good-looking.

Once, as Old David told me, her father operated Father's rice mill, but by some accident, his feet got caught in the gears. It was a miracle that he survived, but he was maimed for life. Earning a living with both legs gone was impossible, so Father gave him an annual pension of twenty *cavans* of palay, more as a result of a court order, I think, than of sympathy.

Martina always took the shortcut from her house, which was a distance, and hurdled the tall barbed-wire fence in the rear of the *bodega.* Seeing her scrambling over the fence one afternoon, Father shook his head and said, "Knowing that girl's future is like being sure that tomorrow the sun will rise from behind the Balungao mountain."

One afternoon I saw her up a guava tree in the yard; I had refrained from climbing it for one week so that by the end of that time the fruits would be ripe. She had tied a piece of string around her waist, then filled her dress with the hard green fruits so that her tummy bulged out front.

"Get down there!" I shouted. "Or I'll call Father and he will flog you." She did not mind me, and angered by her insolence, I started to whimper and cry. As she scurried down, the string around her middle snapped; the fruits all came tumbling out.

"Cry—cry all you can," she said, jumping to the ground. I stopped crying and scrambled after the fruits, grabbing with both hands all that I could and stuffing them into my pockets until they were full. And while I was at it, she never made an attempt to take anything; she just stood there watching me. When I could no longer gather more fruit, I looked up to meet her gaze, contempt, pity, perhaps, in her sullen eyes. She turned and walked to the house.

There seemed to be a gulf between us after that incident, but somehow, in another week we were friends again. She told me little about herself, but she did talk a lot about her father, who was not feeling well, so that she had to go home for about an hour every day to see him. She was not hindered from doing so; after all, she was not needed much in the house, and I think that Father tolerated her presence only because he felt some obligation toward his former employee.

I went with Martina to the river, too, and we bathed there, her clothes sticking to her thin body, her hair wet and dripping. We dove into the cold depths and tried to stay there as long as our breath could hold, and in the murky greenness, I would open my eyes to see her flapping and holding her nose. After the swim, we crossed the fields glinting brown in the sun and took the path that went by the rice mill, climbed the barbed-wire fence, and then we were home, dry and ruddy from the swim.

I HAD NOT SEEN Martina's father, and once or twice I asked her to take me so that I could see how a man without legs moved about, but she always said, "Some other time." Her mother died when she was a baby, and she did not remember her; she was more like a shadow in the past, without any importance.

Martina was very clumsy but could be very gentle, particularly with animals. She was cleaning my room one morning when she tipped the china vase—my bank—from my *aparador* top, and it fell with a resounding crash on the hardwood floor. She had said earlier that her mother brought bad luck to her father, that her father said so, and now that Martina was growing up, she, too, was bringing bad luck to him.

"See?" she said as I looked aghast at what remained of my vase. "I am bad luck, too."

She was etched against the bright frame of window where the morning sun came in. "I was simply cleaning this . . ." she said as she picked up the fragments and placed them in the dustpan.

I faced her squarely, my suspicions aroused. "Where is the money?" I asked. "There were two one-peso bills there."

She glared at me, her hands fingering the frayed hem of her soiled cotton dress. She had raised it so that her dirty bones stuck out. "Am I to know?" she retorted.

I was angry and could not hold back. I took one step forward. "You are a thief!" I hissed at her.

She did not budge; she lowered the hem of her dress, then pointed a finger straight, almost into my face. "Don't you ever repeat that word to me," she said coldly, evenly. "The thieves in this town are not us; if I ever hear you call me a thief again . . ."

I was helpless facing her, knowing how capable she was of doing whatever she threatened to do.

"I will tell Father," I said finally.

"Go tell him," she said in the same even voice.

BUT I DID NOT TELL Father, and it was not that I was afraid to do so; rather, I was bothered by what she had said, that the thieves in Rosales were not people like her. Yet, I had heard Father say so often that the tenants could not be trusted, that during the harvest season they should be watched carefully for they were always hiding part of the grain or harvesting the fields in spots where it could not readily be discovered. They never gave our rightful share of the vegetable harvest, the fruits of the orchards—the bananas, the pomelos—and in time of need, they went to no one but him.

I could not ask Martina about these, so we never talked about the money in the vase again. I could have easily forgotten about it, but the next day, after she had gone to visit her father, I found that the coconut-shell bank that I had filled with coins had grown very light, and there had not been a day that I had not put something in it. But who would I blame? There were other servants in the house who went to my room—Old David, Sepa—I had no proof and will never have one, but nonetheless, Martina was always on my mind.

SHE CAME TO ME once while I was in the *bodega* chasing the rats, which were eating the palay and the corn stored in huge piles. She asked if I wanted to go with her to her father's. It was an invitation I had waited for, more out of curiosity than anything else. Now I would see a legless man who did nothing but weave fishnets every day.

Again, we went by the backyard, hurdled the barbed-wire fence, and headed for the open fields. It was a long walk to the other end of town. We paused in the shade of a mango tree, which had started to bloom, then followed the path that led to the big ash mound behind the rice mill.

"You have never been on top of that," she said. "When you are there, on top of that black mound, you stand so high, you can see almost all of the town and the river, too."

"Let's climb," I said.

She took my hand to lead me, and we followed the black path up the huge mound—the ashes spewed by the rice mill for more than two decades. Her palms were rough and her grip was strong. The rice mill came into view, and we heard the faint *chug-chug* of its engine, saw its smoke, like a careless lock of Martina's dark, uncombed hair, trailing off from the tall chimney that stabbed black and straight into the afternoon sky.

When we reached the top of the mound, I was breathless and my hands and brow were moist; there was not much to see—the mound was not high enough the way Balungao mountain and its foothills were. Just a stretch of the river, farms baked in the sun, and the shapeless forms of farmer houses. But for Martina this was the pinnacle, the top of the world, and on her face was happiness and triumph. "This—all this," she said, "my father put this here. How many years did he work to put this here? And now, I am on top of it—and look at what both of us can see."

I did not want to spoil her pleasure. "Yes," I said softly. "You can see farther and more from up here." A sharp wind rose and the ash swirled around us. For some time the view was marred. A speck got into my eye and blinded me, hurt me, and I went down with her, half seeing what was ahead of the soft and powdery path that led to the fields.

We reached the tobacco rows, the green plants taller than we were, their green speckled leaves, their white flowers like plumes glinting in the sun.

It was a stupid question I asked on impulse: "What did he do before?"

She paused and looked sternly at me: "You know that," she said. "He built that mound where we were. A mountain of ashes—a mountain! How long do you think it took to collect all that ash? Certainly, it was not a week."

I regretted having asked again when it was so unnecessary. Now we were silent, unusually so. We walked across the tobacco plots, the leaves brushing against our faces, the air around us strong and compounded with the aroma of tobacco and the brilliant sun.

"I am his bad luck," she finally said. "He says he had plenty of good luck before. Then he married my mother . . . then I came. Bad luck . . . bad luck, that is all he says . . ."

"Why was your mother bad luck?"

"Mother?" she turned quickly to me, anger flashing in her eyes. But the anger quickly fled, and in its place, this ineffable sadness, and she shook her head as we walked on. We had reached the end of the tobacco farm, and before us was a narrow strip of fallow land given to dried brown shrubs and the amorseco weeds. "Wait here," she commanded.

Across the weed-choked strip was her father's shack. Its windows of battered buri palm were closed, and it stood alone and desolate, no life pulsating from it. But I wanted to look within, and I objected shrilly. "You asked me to come, to see your father. You asked me!"

Her tone was final. "You stay here and wait."

I watched her gallop away; her lithe, catlike figure disappeared behind a curtain of grass, then emerged again only to go up the bamboo ladder and into the hut.

Its windows did not open, and no sound seeped from it.

We got home at dusk, and Father was already eating. I was breathless, and when he asked where I had been, I said simply, "I climbed the ash mountain, Father. Martina and I. We went to her house, too."

"So. Did you see her father?" I turned briefly to Martina and could see the look of displeasure on her face, the anxiety.

"No," I said.

Father continued with his chicken *adobo,* and, when Martina returned from the kitchen with the water pitcher, he said, "Don't go with Martina to that place again." And to Martina, who was filling the glasses, he said icily, "Don't take him there again, understand?"

"Yes, Apo," she said, looking straight at Father, and then she turned to me, the ancient sadness in her eyes.

Martina and I did not talk anymore about that afternoon, though I wished we had. And when I saw her leave, I wanted each time to go with her, but she merely smiled and said there would be a time when the sun would not rise from the east.

She continued to do her work with frenzy, so that Sepa and all the others could not complain when, having nothing more to do, she would be out in the yard, playing marbles with me, or out in the fields chasing the grasshoppers that had come with the rains.

Then on that week before school opened, she asked me if I wanted to go with her. She had a bottle of medicine that she had bought with her savings; it was for her father, who, I now learned, had not been feeling well for weeks but, in spite of this, had sent his daughter to work for us, and this was what Martina had done, knowing that her place was at home. What was it that made him do this? And for her to accept it? I did not know, Father did not know, but it had to be done if that black mound of ash was anything.

I did not want to disobey Father, though, and the thought held me back, but only briefly. He had gone to Carmay that day, and it would be late in the night when he would return. "It will be I who will tell him. Only I will know that you had come along," Martina assured me.

It was almost dusk; the farmer boys were bringing home their *carabaos* from the creek where they had been bathed, and the pigs were being called in for their meal.

"We may be late coming back," I said.

"Are you afraid?"

"Of course not," I said.

We hastened to the backyard and climbed over the barbed-wire fence, and as we dropped on the other side, she turned apprehensively toward the house, almost hidden from view by a screen of guava trees, to see if Sepa or any of the help had seen us. We were secure; there was no one in the kitchen or in the *azotea*.

We walked quickly toward the river, passed the clump of thorny camachile trees, and found the path that led to the gully, which the *carabaos* had widened when they were herded down for their daily bath. We skirted the bank, then went up the path that crossed the tobacco patches. I had begun to tire, for she walked at a fast pace; she did not want the darkness to catch up with us, and now my breath came in heavy gusts. We went over a bamboo bridge that spanned a dry irrigation ditch, and I sat down to rest. She jeered at me. "You are not tired. I sometimes run all the way from your house to ours!" And I recalled those mornings when she came to sweep the yard and she was pale and breathless, sweat trickling down her forehead.

"No, I am not tired," I said, and rose.

We rounded the curve where the grass was tall, and in the deepening hush of afternoon, the sound of insects was sharper, the smell of the earth stronger. Then we were at the foot of the black mound, and Martina was saying softly, "How long did it take to build? How long did it take the balete tree to grow? Only those who have memories can tell, and I would like nothing better than not to remember . . . to forget . . ."

The small hut was ahead of us, somber and alone against the purpling sky. She held my hand, and I could feel the sudden sprint of life coursing through her with the tightening of her grip.

"Do you know what to say if he asks you who you are?"

"Do I have to say anything?" I was disturbed by what her question implied.

"Only if he asks," was her hurried reply. "Just tell him anything—anything—that you live across the street. Anything. But don't tell him you live in the big house—that you are your father's son!"

I nodded dumbly, and her grip on my wrist relaxed. She continued quietly: "We may be little people . . . but you must understand, we are not beggars."

"Whoever said you are a beggar?" I objected vehemently.

"Everyone does," she said. "Why should you be different?"

We were in the yard and had hurdled the low bamboo gate. Martina headed for the short flight of bamboo stairs, and at the top, she beckoned me to follow her. I did. She slowly opened the door of the *sipi*—the small room where farmers kept their precious things, their rice, their fishnets, their clothes—and stepped in.

"Father?" tentatively, then, "Father, Father!"

Silence.

In a while, she came out slowly, and in that instant, I should have known from the dumb despair on her face. I should have stayed with her and learned to understand her ways, why she came to the house swiftly and disappeared just as fast when she had done her work, how hurriedly she ate her meals—like a hog—especially during those first days she was with us, the hunger in her belly that could not be easily appeased. Most of all, I should have understood how steadfastly, how proudly she took care of that cripple inside, how he, too, had sought to live his way by sending his only child to work for us, making believe that what was given to him by Father was not charity, when all of us—but not the two of them—knew it was theirs by right. Who built the ash mound?

But I did not know. I was only twelve.

Martina did not fumble for words. "Father is dead," she said quietly.

I remember having peeped briefly into that darkened room at the legless figure there lying still and stiff, its eyes staring blankly in the gathering dusk, the buzz of mosquitoes around us. And this feeling came to me, freeing me of other feelings, all other thoughts, this feeling of dread that I had intruded into a misshapen world that I had somehow helped to shape, and that, if I did not flee it, it would entrap and destroy me. I do not recall what else Martina said, for I had quickly turned, rushed down the stairs and across the barren ground, away from this house and the ash mound beyond it. I ran and ran—away from the macabre shadows that trailed me, away from Martina and her dead father, into the comforting brightness of our home. I remember, too, her voice, her face determined and calm, and that last look of hurt and abandonment, as I ran out of a beautiful friendship into the certitude of ease that awaited me. And much later, I wished that I could see Martina again, that I could reclaim her friendship, but she left Rosales that very night and did not even attend her father's funeral, which Father had grudgingly arranged.

CHAPTER

ONE OF THE CRUDE insinuations I often heard from class-mates and neighbors when I was young was that I should be tol-erated and my tantrums ignored for the simple reason that insanity ran in our family. It was no joke considering that almost everyone is related—no matter how tenuously and distantly—to a person who may not be exactly insane, but whose behavior is often delightfully unbalanced. We had one such individual in our midst, and thinking about him now, I envy Cousin Marcelo for his being able to do what he wanted and not be disturbed by eccentric labels that our relatives and even some of the townspeople had attached to him.

There were, of course, past evidences of why he had gotten his reputation—that night he returned from Carmay drunk from *basi* and singing all the way in the loudest possible voice. "The bird sings when it is happy. Why shouldn't a man do the same?" And what about that time he exploded a box of firecrackers during the Rizal Day program in the plaza? "I hate verbose speeches—they never can explain the Noli and the Fili the way firecrackers can."

I am, of course, on my Cousin Marcelo's side, and if he was insane, so was I. He was the happiest man I knew, although much, much later he was just as burdened with the prosaic chores of looking after properties that enabled him to indulge in the kind of independence I wanted for myself.

Cousin Marcelo was not really a cousin; he was Father's youngest brother, the youngest in the family, and I should have called him Tio and in the most deferential tones, but he did not relish that. "Can you see a single white hair on my head?" he had asked. There was none, of course, in the jet-black mane that reached to his nape, and in time, his asking me to search for one became a ritual. "Call me cousin, then," he concluded.

He had finished with the highest honors in a Jesuit school in Manila—a fact that, perhaps, explained his rambunctious good humor particularly when it came to his schooling and the church. "Be careful when you go with priests," he said when I became a sacristan. "He who walks with Jesuits never walks with Jesus."

He knew a bit of Latin, a bit of Greek, and lots of Spanish, which he spoke with Father and Grandfather, liberally spiced with sexual epithets; if you heard him and did not see him, you would conclude he was some Spaniard. In actual fact, Cousin Marcelo looked very much like a peasant and also dressed like one; he was always going around in denim shorts, which were comfortable—but they also showed how atrociously bowlegged he was, and he was also partial to wooden shoes in spite of the racket they caused. But he had a warm, friendly face, a little squint, and long hair when no one wore his hair long. He was past thirty, but his disposition must have done some physiological magic to his face; he looked no older than twenty. When Grandmother died, he lived for a while with Grandfather but had to go to the city to study and had to live alone—"not in a garret because there are no garrets in the Philippines."   .

He had majored in philosophy and was easily the most learned man in town, and his favorite high-sounding expression always had "aesthetics" to it—Don Vicente had no "moral aesthetics," Father had "no aesthetics" in his life, and he worried about my becoming "an aesthete."

He chose to return home to paint shop signs, *calesas* and *caretelas,* and, for the town fiesta, arches to the auditorium and, of course, his annual masterpiece, the stage and throne of the fiesta queen and her princesses. He could not make a living in Manila doing portraits or the still lifes and landscapes he wanted to do, so he lavished some of his talents on the mundane things in our town, and it was our *calesa,* its tin inlay aside, that was the most colorful, for he had covered it with cloud and floral designs, as he did with jeepneys in a much later period.

He went to Manila perhaps once a month, sometimes twice, to "unburden" himself, and I always looked forward to his return after three or four days, for he always had something for me—books, chocolates. Indeed, he was my favorite relative, and his big room on the ground floor was almost mine. It was airy, with frosted windows that were open most of the time. One side opened to the garden, and in the morning when the sun flooded the green, his room would be ablaze with light, which never seemed enough. He had Aladdin lamps without their shades, and they were almost always on so that, as he said, he should be able to see everything, even the sins that were hiding under every speck of dirt.

This was his domain, and its main difference, I think, from rooms or the *sala* of most houses I have been to was not its brightness. He had this diploma—a fine document from his college in a gilt frame, with silver lettering in Latin and a pompous seal. All the diplomas I had seen in our town were in living rooms, prominently displayed for everyone to see.

"Diplomas are turds," he said, and his hung right in front of the toilet bowl in his closet.

His room, as I have said, was always open, and I often wandered in and out, poked among his things, his paints and brushes, his sketches of nudes, and heaps and heaps of old magazines, pieces of string, bits of glass, old bottles, all of which he said he would shape into living and breathing objects.

Of all his paintings, it was his portrait of Don Vicente that intrigued me most, for he had, more than with any other, enjoyed doing it. As the youngest, he always spoke to Father and all those older than him with some diffidence, but he cast aside the familial hierarchy when he spoke about Don Vicente. "It is time you end your servitude to him," he had said. "What do you want a hacienda as big as his for? You will be getting many problems, and in the end you will not even be able to enjoy the simplest food that the farmers have."

Father chose to ignore tirades such as these, reminding Cousin

Marcelo that he did not know much about the mundane ways of the world, because as an artist he was confined to the ozone regions of the mind. It was, of course, a rebuttal that Cousin Marcelo did not accept, for he felt he was closer than most to reality, to people, and to the tune of living.

"That is what an artist is," he said, defining himself.

One warm April afternoon, a delegation of the town's civic leaders had come to the house seeking Father's approval for a project that would endear them all to Don Vicente. A case of sarsaparilla, a bottle of gin, and cracked ice had enlivened the discussion, which centered on the forthcoming celebration of the town fiesta. It was Mr. Alafriz, the councilor from the market district, who suggested that, aside from crowning the fiesta queen, Don Vicente should also be honored with a statue, so that "he would look toward the town with kindlier eyes."

In the haze of Alhambra smoke and the torpor of Fundador, Cousin Marcelo barged in and bellowed, "You will do no such thing."

All eyes turned to him. His face visibly red with embarrassment, Father said, "Explain, Celo."

"And who would do the statue of Don Vicente? Would you be able to get someone bright enough to chisel out all the secret recesses of his personality? Show all the different layers and folds of his fat and his character? And where will you get the mountain of marble, not just for the shape of his corpulent body but for the immensity of his greed? You will insult the memory of Rizal by building this man a monument. Images of stone can only be for beings like Mabini, Bonifacio, Rizal. For someone like Don Vicente, you need something different, something that is equal to his rapacity."

"What are you thinking of?" Father asked.

"You don't have to spend. And he can take it with him if he wants to."

"Please tell us what it is," Councilor Alafriz said.

"I will paint his portrait," Cousin Marcelo said.

The politicians could not afford to insult Cousin Marcelo; he was Father's brother, he was far more educated than all of them put together. There were hesitant murmurs, but in the end they agreed, convinced by the most practical of reasons—that the portrait would not cost them one centavo.

For one whole week, Cousin Marcelo labored in his room, which, for once, was locked. When Mr. Alafriz checked on him afterward, he always assured the councillor that the portrait would be finished on time. The great day came, but Don Vicente was not able to come to the fiesta; his piles had gotten worse, and he had to go through surgery. The first time I saw the portrait, I wondered why it was done the way it was—the blobs of black, the smouldering face—and to my question, Cousin Marcelo had grinned: "Just picture Don Vicente in your mind, what you feel about him, what you think he is, and there you have it."

His second chance to be of use to the town as an artist came when Padre Andong rebuilt the church. Cousin Marcelo said he would do murals for it, to depict God as he saw Him—not a just God but a vengeful one. I suppose that if Padre Andong had lived longer, he would have acceded to Cousin Marcelo's services.

There is something about a new church that attracts people and bids them welcome. They wander in, their eyes go over the newly painted walls, the shiny altar still flavored with the smell of mortar. Then they pray a little and make the wish, which is supposed to come true sooner or later because it was made during their first visit to the church.

I am sure that, since then, many strangers have entered the new church more in the spirit of adventure than to commune with their faith. Built of hollow blocks with a new tin roof, it adjoins a convent with hardwood panels and a brick porch.

We never had an old venerable church such as those moss-covered edifices farther north, because our church—like our town—is new. The old church had been a ramshackle building that, somehow, was not refurbished even at the time when Rosales was at the height of its prosperity as the rice-trading center of eastern Pangasinan. But it had a quiet and simple atmosphere, and any man who wanted peace could enter and never bother asking if it was Protestant, Aglipayan, or Seventh-Day Adventist.

The façade was a triangle mounted by a white cross. The churchyard was plain *carabao* grass, with a gravel path lined with rosal. The floor of the church was plain cement, rough and uneven in parts. A skeleton of a belfry was attached to one side of the church, and it shook every time we climbed it to toll the Angelus, the elevation of the host, or the arrival of the dead. A mango tree squatted by the belfry, and on the days that we had nothing to do, we often climbed it, roosted on its branches, and told fool stories.

Everything is changed now; the mango tree has been cut. On the days that it was laden with fruit, Padre Andong used to count them like some miser and would rail at us when he saw us eating the sour green mangoes. "Why can you not wait till they ripen?" he lamented.

"Some people cannot wait for heaven," Cousin Marcelo would have retorted.

Padre Andong came to the house one Sunday afternoon. He was a short, bulky man in his seventies. For the past three decades or so, he had been our parish priest. He used to be quite slim—that was what the old people say—but the town must have agreed with him, for he had put on weight. His bulk was covered by tight, ill-fitting soutanes, which were always frayed in the cuffs and collars and patched in the buttocks. He had a slight squint, which was not noticeable when he wore glasses. Somehow, that strong smell of tobacco and of public places never eluded him.

He could not have chosen a more propitious time to visit Father, although the visit was not necessary, for even if Father no longer went to church, he sometimes went to the convent to play chess with the old priest or with Chan Hai, another chess player, waiting in the wings for his turn. But Padre Andong wanted to be correct; he had come to ask Father a favor.

The harvest that year had been very good, and the wide yard was filled with bull carts laden with grain. Upon seeing the priest approach, Father gave the ledger to Tio Baldo and went to the gate to meet him.

Up in the *azotea* where they had gone to sit in the shade, Sepa was preparing the *merienda* table. It was like this during harvest time, this ritual visit, and Father was in a boasting mood: "Is there any man in town, Padre," he was saying, "who will give you thirty sacks of palay this year? Thirty fat sacks—you cannot eat that in a year!"

"No, Espiridion," Padre Andong was saying, "but there is a man who will give me forty sacks next year."

"I don't believe it!" Father said.

"You will," Padre Andong said. "Because it is you who will do it. But I did not come here for the palay, Espiridion. I know that you will give it to me, even if I did not come. As you told me, it's time that you send your boy over to be an acolyte."

His words jolted me; serving him was not easy, for he had flogged his erring sacristans and worked them hard and long. It did not seem to me an equable arrangement for Father, who did not go to church, to send me there, but it was his wish and I walked to the church that afternoon with Padre Andong, who was silent most of the way except for his quiet assurance that I would be a good acolyte. Old Tomas, the sacristan, immediately took me under his care, and we proceeded to the sacristy, where he showed me the vestments; he could have said mass himself, for he had served there so long, he knew the Latin liturgy backward.

I served in the church for many months without pay, though money did come in, not just in the Sunday collection but from services: the baptisms, for which there were special rates, if celebrated at the main altar or in his residence; for burials, depending on how long the bells were tolled, on whether we met the funeral procession outside the church, halfway from the residence of the deceased, or when we went to the residence itself. The most expensive, of course, was if Padre Andong went with us to the house and accompanied the hearse to the cemetery. Even weddings had to be priced accordingly, and it was Old Tomas who recited the rates as well as the "specials" that went with them.

The larder was never full; Padre Andong's breakfast often consisted of just plain rice and dried fish, and as if to save on food, he often made the rounds of his parishioners, as we were having lunch or supper, which was good, for he became known to everyone and was involved not just as confessor but as counselor in many of the problems of small-town families.

I was talking once to Sepa about there being no food in the convent, and she said, "That priest—he would boil a stone, add salt to it, and then call it excellent soup!"

And it was not just with his food that he was niggardly; his clothes, as I have said, were a pauper's. I had to consider, however, the fact that Sepa was not a Catholic and, therefore, had a biased view.

About Padre Andong's sternness—there was enough evidence of it to go around. I could start with Father, although I was not there when it happened. Father persistently kept away from the mass but not from the chess games that he, Chan Hai, and Padre Andong played in the convent patio. Father ceased attending church in the month of July, I think, when the rains were particularly strong and even the sturdy blooms of the rosal in the churchyard were frayed. That Sunday the rains had lifted briefly, and as usual, Father had gone to hear mass. Padre Andong was a disciplinarian when it came to how the faithful should act during the elevation of the Host. There were instances when he would interrupt this portion of the mass to shout at an erring parishioner and tell him to kneel.

The old roof had long been leaking, and many portions of the church were wet. Father's special pew near the altar was drenched, and even if Padre Andong knew it, I suppose he did not really feel it enough reason why now Father should stand up during the elevation.

He spotted Father standing thus, and Padre Andong shouted, "*Hoy*, there, kneel down. Kneel down!"

Father continued standing, straight as a spear, so the story went, and next Padre Andong shouted: "Espiridion, kneel down not for me but for God!" And Father, in his white alpaca suit, head drooping, crumpled to his knees in the puddle before him.

Unlike God, said Cousin Marcelo, Father was not a vengeful man, and came harvest time, he sent the usual sacks of palay to Padre Andong. And Padre Andong came to the house on the occasions that warranted his being there—the thank-you call, Father's birthday—as if nothing had transpired.

He was more Ilokano than most of us, though he was Tagalog; when he first delivered his sermon in Ilokano, so the story goes, he had the whole congregation buckling in laughter, for some Ilokano words that he mispronounced easily became obscene. But what really labeled him as a native was his practicality around the church; he had planted fruit trees like the mango later, guava, pomelo, and avocado. He kept poultry, too, and even coaxed us to work with him several plots of pechay, eggplant, and tomatoes so that his larder was literally independent of the marketplace.

But while his hens were always fenced in and properly kept away, the garden was not free from the chickens of the neighbors, which often flew over the fence and pecked on our plants. On one such occasion, Padre Andong was so incensed that he chased a white leghorn and felled it with a stick.

He did not know where the chicken came from, and we certainly did not want to bring it home. The problem was solved by him, and that afternoon, in the convent, we sat down to a wonderful meal of *arroz caldo con gallina*. When given the opportunity, Padre Andong was also a good cook.

Even in his seventies, Padre Andong saw to it that we were strong of build. He built a chinning bar behind the sacristy, which he often tried himself, and during the Eucharistic Congress in Manila he also bought for us a pair of boxing gloves.

He was an indefatigable hiker, and when he was to say mass in the barrios, he was the first to wake up in the deep quiet of dawn. If it was my turn to go with him, he would rouse me in the convent where I slept for the night, and still drowsy, I would go down to the kitchen where Old Tomas would have a cup of chocolate and *pan de sal* ready; then we would be on our way, his soutane tucked in his waist, so that he would be able to walk faster, and I would keep pace with him with the small canvas bag that held the chalice, the candles, and the bottle of holy water.

It happened on one such trip to the barrio of Calanutan. On the way back that afternoon, instead of taking a *calesa*, he decided that we would walk the shortcut, via the railroad tracks. We were halfway when we were caught by a pelting shower, and we got back to the convent drenched to the bone. The following morning Padre Andong was flushed with fever and had difficulty saying mass. The doctor came, and only then did we know that the old priest had never been too well—he had heart murmurs and as a matter of fact, we should never have hiked to Calanutan at all.

We cooked liver broth and gave it to him at lunchtime together with his medicine that the doctor had prescribed. He was grateful for the broth, but he did not take the medicine. In his rasping breath, he said, "Prayer is good medicine, particularly if you are as old as I am."

That evening I offered him a prayer.

The fever left him, but he never regained his strength. He was pale and listless. One afternoon a nun came to the convent, and I learned afterward that she was Padre Andong's youngest sister. They talked in Tagalog, some of which I understood. The nun was saying that it was time for him to go to the hospital, or to retire in the *hospicio* in Manila, where he would be taken care of in his old age. He could no longer say mass regularly, listen to confessions, or visit the villages where there were no churches; Rosales needed a younger priest. This was the way not only of the world but of the church itself.

That afternoon, after Padre Andong had made his decision, he told me to go fetch Father.

"He is leaving Rosales for good, Father," I said, not quite sure that Father would come. "He is a sick man."

Father tousled my hair. "I am going to see him," he assured me.

The old priest's room was airy and light, but it was bare except for his ancient rattan bed and his shabby clothes in the open *aparador*. He asked Old Tomas to draw from under the bed an old wooden trunk, to which he had a shiny iron key always in his pocket. Bending over, he opened it and removed from the top the same old black soutane that he wore frayed at the cuffs and the hem but pressed and clean.

And beneath this was a heap of coins and paper bills—many of the coins already greenish with mold. I had never seen so much silver in my life, and I looked at it in sheer wonder. Then, Padre Andong's cracked voice: "All of it I have saved these many years—the new church will not leak . . . you don't have to kneel in a puddle anymore, Espiridion. And you will come back . . . The new church I will leave . . . and it is what the people shall have built."

So they came that week, the carpenters and the masons, and they dumped their lumber and their cement in the churchyard. They tore the façade off the old church first, then the tottering belfry, and through the hellish sound of building, Padre Andong seemed pleased with the world. He rose early, staggered to the churchyard, and looked at what was taking shape, and until the last day of his stay in Rosales, he seemed to want to linger a moment longer.

The day Padre Andong finally took the train to Manila and his resting place, I asked Father during the evening meal, "What happens when old priests can no longer say mass? Who will take care of them, since they have no children?"

Father was in a quiet mood. "Then it is time, I suppose," he said with a wry smile, "that they sprout wings and go up there."

I am sure Padre Andong would have preferred it down here, in the new church, if he only could have stayed.

CHAPTER
10

A WEEK BEFORE Padre Andong left, the new priest arrived in Rosales. He was a young Pangasinense with short-cropped hair and a bounce in his walk. He had just graduated from the seminary near the provincial capital, and Rosales was his first assignment. During his first week in town, he was always up and about, visiting his wealthy parishioners and supervising the completion of the church.

He came to the house, too, and after losing two successive games of chess with Father, he practically got Father to promise that henceforth he would hear mass again.

He must have made some impression not only on Father but with the townspeople as well, for on his first Sunday mass, the church was filled to overflowing and the crowd spilled all over the sacristy and beyond the open doors onto the lawn.

Shortly after his arrival, however, I stopped serving in the church. I no longer relished working for him; for one, he turned down Cousin Marcelo's plan to paint murals. He wanted the wall plain. But what really angered me was his refusal to give Tio Baldo a

Christian burial. I know that the laws of the church are steadfast, but still, I believe that Tio Baldo—because of his goodness—should have been given a church burial, and that he should not have been buried as if he were a swine.

It is easy to forgive a person his faults when he is dead because in death he atones for his sins somewhat before the eyes of people who are still living and who have yet to add more on the parchment where their sins are listed. But even if Tio Baldo had lived to this day, I would not nurse within me the slightest displeasure toward him for his having taunted Father. I would, instead, honor him as I do honor him now, although in the end his courage seemed futile.

It happened that year when the harvest was so good, Old David had to remove the sacks of rice bran from the *bodega* so that every available space there could be used for storing grain. I thought that Father's tenants—and also those of Don Vicente—could buy new clothes at last, but they did not; all they saved they gave to Tio Baldo, who, I'm sure, spent it wisely and well.

Tio Baldo was not really an uncle. In fact, he was no relation at all. He had lived in a battered nipa shack near our house with his mother, who had been, like him, in Father's employ. She took in washing and did odd jobs for as far back as I could remember.

Tio Baldo helped Father with the books. He had gone through grade school and high school with Father's money and insistence, and when Father was in a gracious mood, he spoke of him in terms that always brought color to Tio Baldo's dark, oily face.

He would be a teacher someday if he continued enjoying Father's beneficence. Indeed, Tio Baldo was made for teaching. He used to solve my arithmetic and my spelling problems in such a lucid manner that he never had to do the same trick twice. He also taught me how to fashion a well-balanced kite out of bamboo sticks, so that once it was airborne, it would not swoop down—too heavy in the nose. He taught me how to make the best guava handle for a slingshot, how to ride curves on a bicycle without holding the handlebar, and most important, how to swim.

One hot, raw afternoon he came to the garden and saw Angel, one of the houseboys, squirting the garden hose at me. He asked if I wanted to go with him to the creek. No invitation would have been more welcome.

We stripped at the riverbank. From a rise of ground on the bank, he stood straight and still, his muscles spare and relaxed, then he fell forward in a dive that hardly stirred the cool, green water as he slid into it.

When he bobbed up for air, he looked up at me and shouted: "Come!"

And seeing him there, so strong and ever ready to protect me, it did not matter that I did not know how to swim, that the water was deep. I jumped after him without a second thought.

One June morning, Tio Baldo came to the house with his mother—an aging woman with a crumpled face, whose hair was knotted into a tight ball at her nape. They talked briefly with Father in the hall; then the old woman suddenly scooped up Father's hand and, with tears in her eyes, covered it with kisses.

The following day Old David hitched his *calesa,* and we picked up Tio Baldo at his house, loaded his bamboo valise, and took him to the railroad station. He was to stay in Tia Antonia's house in the city, and while he served her family, he would go to college to be an *agrimensor*—a surveyor.

For the next two years that he was in the city, Tio Baldo never took a vacation. He returned one April afternoon; he went straight to the house from the station, carrying a wooden trunk on his shoulders all the way. He had grown lighter in complexion. His clothes were old and shabby, but he wore them with a confidence that was not there before.

Father stood up from his chocolate and *galletas* to meet him. Tio Baldo took Father's hand, and though Father tried clumsily to shake off his hold, Tio Baldo brought the hand to his lips.

The following day he resumed his old chores, but Father had other ideas. Father took the broom and ledger from him. "I did not send you to college so you can count sacks," he said in mock anger. "Go train a surveying party. You've work to do."

Tio Baldo was delighted, particularly so when Father bought him a second-hand transit and a complete line of surveyor's instruments. With these and some of the farm hands trained as linemen and transit men, he straightened out the boundaries of Father's farms, apart from Don Vicente's hacienda.

For half a year he worked very hard; he would start for the fields early in the morning with his huge canvas umbrella, chain, and stakes, and he would return to Rosales late in the evening. He did not work for Father alone; he worked, too, for the tenants.

Then, one evening, Father came home in an extremely bad humor. He struck my dog with his cane when it came yelping down the gravel path to meet him.

"See if Baldo is in," he told me at the top of the stairs in a manner that was enough to send me scampering down from the house to the nipa hut.

Tio Baldo rushed to the house at once, to the dining room where Father had sat down to supper and was slurping a bowl of cold chicken soup. The moment he saw Tio Baldo, Father pushed the soup aside.

"Sit down!" he shouted, pointing to the vacant chair at his side. "I want to talk to you, you ungrateful dog."

Tio Baldo, his face surprisingly unruffled, took the seat beside Father.

Father did not waste words. "I've always considered a little knowledge dangerous. Baldo, the truth. Is it true you are starting trouble against Don Vicente?"

I admired Tio Baldo's courage. "Forgive me, Manong," he said softly. "I am grieved, but I've already given them—the old people in Carmay—my word. I only want to get their lands back. Don Vicente can still live in luxury even without those lands, Manong. It's common knowledge he grabbed these lands because the farmers didn't know anything about cadastral surveys and Torrens titles. You said so yourself."

The steady glow of the Aladdin lamp above him lighted up Father's face. It was very red. "You accuse Don Vicente of being a thief? You might as well shout to the world that I'm a robber, too, because I'm his overseer."

"You are his employee," Tio Baldo said.

"And that I'm only doing my job?" Father screamed. He flung his spoon to the wall, and Sepa picked it up quietly.

Tio Baldo nodded.

"What are you doing, Baldo?" Father asked, his face distorted with rage. "What has gone into your head?"

"You knew my father," Tio Baldo said simply. "You said he was not impoverished until Don Vicente took his land. I'm locating the old Spanish markers. The old men are very helpful, Manong. Please don't be angry with them."

As if by an unknown alchemy, Father's anger slowly diminished, and when he spoke again after a long silence, his voice was calm. "Well, then, so that is how it will be. I'll tell Don Vicente about this, of course. You will have lots to answer for, Baldo. I only hope you know what you are doing."

Tio Baldo nodded.

Father looked at him with resignation. "I don't know what to do with you, Baldo," he said finally. "You have so much to learn. I'm sorry for you."

That night I could not sleep for a long time. Father stayed up late in his room, writing, pacing. Occasionally, he would curse aloud and slap his writing desk. When morning came, he roused me from sleep and handed me a fat envelope to mail. It was addressed to Don Vicente.

Four days later, a woman came.

It was early November then. The first harvest was being brought in by the tenants, and their bull carts were scattered in the wide, balete-shaded yard.

She arrived in Don Vicente's black Packard, and from the balcony, I saw her step out with the lightness of a cat. She must have been Father's old acquaintance, for she shouted his name in greeting when she saw him padding down the stairs to greet her.

They embraced effusively. "Ah, Nimia!" Father sighed. "I didn't expect you. This is a surprise."

She grinned and tried to press away the wrinkles on her elegant blue dress. She went up to the house, sat daintily on Father's rocking chair in the *sala,* and shucking off her high heels, curled her toes. Her toenails were as brightly painted as her lips. She must have been near forty and used to having her way, to getting what she wanted, and the very way she talked with Father, the coyness of her gestures, the instances when she touched his arm or smiled at him, suggested not just how well she knew how to use her femininity but how well prepared she was to go all the way if that, too, was the ultimate necessity. That she was brought to Rosales in Don Vicente's own car from Manila indicated just as well the extent to which the rich man would go to protect his interests; he knew the people in the country who mattered, men who made the laws, who rendered justice, but, more than all of these, he knew, too, the primordial weakness of all men, and I suppose that included Father.

Nimia, as Father called her, fascinated me—how she swung her hips when she walked, how she crossed her legs when she sat down, revealing just a bit of thigh, how everything in the world seemed pleasant and beyond cavil, for there was this smile plastered on her face and it never seemed to leave her.

She came to me when she finally saw me, her perfume swirling around her, and kissed me on the cheek—a wet, motherly kiss—then looked at me with those black witch eyes kindling with delight. "How you have grown!" Then to Father, "He was just a baby when I saw him," and I thought she would talk more with me, but she wheeled around and relegated me to limbo, while she asked Father about the town, about the problems of Don Vicente and his tenants, and finally about this Baldo.

Father lingered around her with his light talk, ignoring her question. He asked what she would have for refreshments—a glass of sarsaparilla or *halo-halo*? "Nothing," she said, then in all earnestness she asked, "Tell me, what does Baldo look like?"

"You have handled worse people." Father patted her arm. "He is not handsome, of course. A little bit on the lean side, with an average peasant's face, but I'm sure you'll have a hard time with him."

"Vicente always says that in the beginning," she said, waving Father away with a deft motion of her hand.

"I know Baldo better than you," Father said.

"After I'm through, I'll know him better. When do I start?" she asked.

"Right now, if you want," Father said.

But she did not start at once. Like a bat, she waited for the dark. After supper, she peered out the window; light burned in the *sala* of the small house, and before a big table there, Tio Baldo was poring over maps.

She smiled confidently at Father, then she went down to the house.

I did not notice her return, but after breakfast the following morning, she started packing her things. Her face was sour when she bade Father good-bye at the gate.

"Don Vicente must try something new," Father said.

"I'll tell him you can do just that, but you aren't lifting a finger," she said angrily.

Father waved as she boarded the Packard that would take her back to Manila. "I have limitations, my dear," he said lightly.

She did not wave back.

After the woman left, things moved quickly. November tapered off into December, and the harvest came in a steady stream. Shortly after lunch one afternoon, the black Packard with a uniformed chauffeur drove into the yard, its horn blaring.

Father dressed hurriedly. Our visitor was Don Vicente himself. It was the first time I had seen him, although almost every day his name was mentioned in the house. Father tried to talk him into getting up into the house, but he firmly refused. He sat inside his car, gesticulating, his fat white face tightly drawn. Occasionally, he would shake a stubby finger at Father, and though I could not understand much of their conversation, which was in Spanish, I knew that the rich man was very angry.

Don Vicente concluded his tirade by thrusting a cardboard box in Father's hand, and then, at a wave of his hand, his chauffeur started the car. Father stood stiffly and said good-bye, and the car sped away.

After we had supped, Father bade me follow him to his room. He handed me the box, then we went to Tio Baldo's house.

I had not been in it for some time, and now I noticed how really small it was. The *sala* was bare except for the big table and a sorry-looking bookcase made of packing crates. The only costly fixture in the house was the Coleman lamp hanging from a rafter, and below it Tio Baldo was drafting. When he saw us, he stopped and came forward to meet us.

"You know why I'm here?" Father asked.

"Does it matter, Manong?" Tio Baldo said. "It is always good to have you visit."

Father took the cardboard box from me, and ripping its cover away, he spilled its contents on the large blue map on which Tio Baldo was working.

"It's all yours. There's five thousand pesos there. Count it. Not a centavo less."

"If you say it's a million, Manong," Tio Baldo said, "it's a million."

"Don Vicente brought it this afternoon."

"I heard he was here," Tio Baldo said. "But I didn't expect this."

"All the money you got from the old men—you can return it now, and there would still be enough left to tide you through five lifetimes. Is the price all right?"

"Don Vicente hasn't enough to buy us out," Tio Baldo said. "We have all the proofs we need now. We will charge him for damages, too, when we get the land back."

"You are not taking this money, then?" Father asked, moving toward him.

Tio Baldo did not speak.

"What's wrong with you?" Father asked sternly. "Don't you know an opportunity when you see it? You'll never earn this in a thousand years. Think of it!"

Baldo gathered the bills and returned them carefully to the box. "If you were in my place," he asked, facing Father, "would you take it?"

Father blanched and his lips quivered.

"Tell me," Tio Baldo pressed. "Would you take it?"

Father picked up the box and, muttering, he stomped to the door.

The next morning, Father left for the city. When he returned the following day, the first thing he did was tell me to call Tio Baldo to the house.

He came obediently. I followed him to Father's room and stood guard at the door to see to it that no one ventured near.

"Well, Baldo," Father said, a hint of sadness in his voice, "I've done everything I could. That money . . . if you want it, it's still available."

"I have all the maps and papers ready," Tio Baldo told Father quietly instead. "I'll leave for the city tomorrow. The old people who have opened their bamboo banks—all of them—they are expecting so much. I think we have enough to present to the officials. They'll give us justice, I'm sure."

Father spoke calmly. "So you think you can win. You are at the end of your road, Baldo."

"I'm not afraid," he said with conviction. "There are people on our side."

Father controlled himself; the veins in his temples were bloated, and his fists were balled. "Do you think you'll matter?"

"You are wrong to think otherwise," Tio Baldo said.

"You think I am?" Father brought his fist down on the small table beside him and sent paper clips and pencils flying around the room.

Tio Baldo simply looked at him.

"You think I'm afraid, too?"

Tio Baldo turned away from Father and walked to the window. The yard below was littered with bull carts. A cool wind sprang and wafted up to the house the heady scent of harvest.

"Am I afraid?" Father held him by the shoulder.

"I never said that," Tio Baldo said, without making the slightest move to shake off Father's hold. "I think you are only acting your age."

"Now I'm old!" Father said. "Now I'm a fool. But let me tell you this. Need I remind you it's not only me you are destroying but yourself, and, perhaps, all those dear to you?"

Tio Baldo, still gripped by Father's hands, smiled wanly. "I owe you for many things," he said. "An education, but above all, a sense of right. Please don't take the last away."

Father's hands dropped from Tio Baldo's shoulders.

"Baldo," he said softly after a bit of silence, "I'm not taking anything back. Education and righteousness, they are good." He slapped his thigh in languid resignation. "But we have to live. All of us. All right, I have a few hectares to my name, a rice mill, some houses. But still, I'm nothing. And you know that. Don Vicente—he has everything. He can ruin not only you or me but all of us—not because he wants to, but he may be forced to."

"We have nothing to lose," Tio Baldo said. Tears began to well in his eyes.

Father took him to the door. "There's nothing more I can say," he said.

Tio Baldo's gait quickened as he crossed the hall. He hurried down the stairs and stepped into the afternoon.

We did not hear from him the whole month that he was in the city. Christmas passed, and we would not have known that he was finally home had not Old David seen him hurry from the railroad station to his house without speaking to anyone.

The news must have reached Carmay, for at dusk Don Vicente's tenants started coming, some riding their work animals to town straight from the fields and bearing still the strong odor of earth and sun. The young ones came, too, but there were more old men, farmers who had known nothing but the cycle of plowing and planting. They gathered in the yard, talked quietly among themselves, and wondered perhaps why Tio Baldo did not come out at once to speak to them.

At about eight, he finally came down from the hut and walked among his people. From underneath his house, he rolled out a wooden mortar into their midst and perched himself on top of it. His mother took a kerosene lamp from their kitchen and strung it up on a low branch of the balete tree.

It took him some time before he finally spoke, louder now than the mere whispers with which he half acknowledged those who welcomed him. No sound rippled from the crowd; they hung on to each word, and each was like a huge, dull knife plunged into their breasts.

Then, when he paused, someone spoke, loud enough for all to hear: "And our money, have you cheated us?"

Tio Baldo exclaimed, "All my life, I've lived in virtue, but now, with you condemning me, I'll crawl in the dust to beg your forgiveness." Lifting his palms to a darkened sky, his voice shaking with his grief, he turned around into the silent crowd that flowed beyond the yard of the little house to the street.

"Tell me," he said. "Tell me, you who are older than I, upon whose brows wisdom sits. I've tried, but we cannot fight money with money, nor force with force because we haven't enough of these. Where have I failed? Have I not been true to all of you? Tell me, my fathers who are old and wise, tell me what to do. I have no money to pay you back. Even the house where I live is not mine. But my blood—take it. Tell me, my elders, if it's enough."

But they did not tell him; they stood like many stolid posts, unable to speak.

"What has happened to the world?" Tio Baldo cried. "Since when could justice be bought, and men have become strangers to honor? And we who have been marked for this kind of life, shall we be slaves forever? I am your son and will always be; why do you fling me now to the dogs? Tell me, oh my elders, who are wise!"

Still they did not speak.

Then, from their ranks a cry broke out—very soft and plaintive—and in the light of the storm lamp, as I stood there in their midst, I could see tears in many eyes. Numbly I looked at the ancient, care-worn faces. Someone started to sob aloud, and he was quickly joined by three or four, and I could feel each sob being torn out of chests, for they were only old men, enfeebled and ready for the grave, crying now that their last dream had gone to waste. And as I looked at them, at Tio Baldo alone atop the mortar, as I listened to their grief, I felt a vise tighten in my throat; I knew I did not belong here, that I had to join Father in our comfortable house.

It was to it that I returned. And there, from the balcony, I watched the farmers slowly scatter and head back for their homes. In a while the night was quiet again and the light in the small house was snuffed out. The crickets in the balete tree started whirring, and from the asphalted provincial road came the muffled clatter of bull-cart wheels and *carabao* hooves carrying the harvest to the storehouse of Chan Hai.

"How did Baldo take it?" Father asked as I passed him on the *azotea* on my way to my room.

"Bravely, Father," I said.

I knew how right I was, even when, the following morning, we woke up to shrill cries from outside, in the wide yard, where people had gathered to see Tio Baldo hanging by the neck from one of the lofty branches of the balete tree.

CHAPTER

11

A MAN'S SUICIDE is the ultimate violence he can fling against the granite circumstance he could not vanquish. It is a lonely and desperate act of supreme courage, not weakness. But it is also an admission of total failure; the destruction of the self is the end of one person's struggle, an end wherefrom there will be no rebirth or resurrection—nothing but the blackness, the impenetrable muck that hides everything, sometimes even the reason for death itself.

Tio Baldo never left a note, and I can only surmise the depths of that despair that had claimed him. It was not, I think, that Don Vicente had defeated him; that would not have dented his courage so much, for someone like Don Vicente—all-powerful and all-devouring—could have done that and that would be explainable. It was, I think, Tio Baldo's complete destruction at the hands of his own people that not only humiliated him; their mistrust—though not so widely voiced—simply destroyed his last shred of dignity.

But when a person commits suicide, he does not do violence only to himself; he inflicts his death upon those whom he least considered would be so afflicted. I have thought of Tio Baldo a lot, admired him, the simplicity of his final response; he has taunted me and haunted me in a way no wraith ever will, for I saw in him not just a way out of my own dilemmas but the capacity of man to have in his hands—and in no other—his own destiny. But in thinking this way, I also realized how finite everything is, how vulnerable a human being is as I now know—victim that I am, not just of memory but of that accursed attachment that I have felt for all those who have been good to me.

As for Father, he, too, was not inured to the turmoil of conscience and self-blame. In the days that followed, he became more morose and withdrawn. At the dinner table, he would stare blankly, his face drawn and haggard. He seldom spoke, and when he did, even when he was not really angry at anyone, his words had a cutting edge.

There were nights, too, when sleep eluded him, and once I heard him curse: "Ungrateful wretches! I gave you everything and you give me hell!" He moved about in his room, his slippers scraping the floor, and I slept through, then woke again to listen to him still awake and moving about.

He did not have breakfast with me that morning, and when I saw him again late in the day after school, his eyes were deep-set and glazed, and for the first time I realized that he was drunk; his breath stank.

He had called me to the *azotea*, where he reclined on his armchair, the ash from his cigar scattered on the front of his white coat.

"Son," he said, "when you grow up, don't think of other people. Think only of yourself. Others don't matter, because they don't think of you anyway."

It was comments like these that, more than anything, showed how Tio Baldo's death had now warped Father's thinking. There may have been occasions when his spirits were buoyed up, but they were far between. I thought, for instance, that the coming of Miss Santillan to our house would brighten our lives, and it surely did, but only for a while.

Miss Santillan was brought to the house by the high school principal. She was a young, handsome woman, a teacher. They talked with Father for some time in the *sala*, then the principal left and Miss Santillan stayed to board with us. Father told her to make herself really at home. I'm sure the gesture was but a nicety; Father could not have meant what he said, because he loathed intrusions into his privacy. The only reason, I presume, why he took Miss Santillan as a boarder was that she was the only teacher in the high school who was not a native of our town. The principal had suggested to her that nothing but the best boardinghouse would do for her.

And the "best," actually, was our house.

Miss Santillan was around twenty-four. Her complexion was clear brown like a baby's, and she wore her hair short like a movie actress. Her shoes had high heels, and her toenails, like her fingernails, were painted red. She did not, however, wear the slightest smudge of rouge or lipstick. In spite of this, her lips and her cheeks shone with the pale pink of *macopa*.

During the holidays, when the wooden schoolhouse beyond the plaza looked haunted, she stayed in her room. And if the weather was balmy, she would read, comfortably seated on the bench shaded by the balete tree. She came up only when the sun finally toppled over the foothills and the leaves of the acacias that lined the provincial road had closed.

On this particular evening, a few days before the celebration of our high school concert, we were idling in the *sala*, having finished supper. Miss Santillan was feeling exuberant the whole day, and though it was Saturday, she did not shut herself up in her room or read in the yard. She had puttered around the house instead, joking with the maids in the kitchen and with the boys in the storehouse. The echo of the Angelus had waned; I had kissed Father's hand, and he had taken his silver-handled cane and gone down for the stroll that would lead to Chan Hai's. Sepa had lighted the bronze Aladdin lamp in the *sala*. The cool blue haze steadied, and Sepa dropped on the sofa and leafed through the *Bannawag*, which she could not read but whose pictures and Kulafu comics attracted her.

Miss Santillan, who was looking out into the town slowly succumbing to the dark, turned and beckoned me.

"You want to know something?" she asked. She held my hand and pressed her forefinger to her lips as if to warn me to share with no one her beautiful secret. "It is supposed to be a surprise," she said.

I nodded.

"You won't believe it, but Mr. Sanchez and I—"

"You are getting married?"

Her face reddened; she drew back and laughed. "No, of course not." She stopped laughing, but her voice was still rich with happiness. "For the high school program, the principal has asked us to sing. A duet."

Now it was evident why she felt lighthearted the whole day, and suddenly it struck me as wonderful—her singing on a stage. From bits of talk in the school, I gleaned that she had studied voice once, but never during the past few weeks that she had stayed with us had she raised her voice in a full-bodied song.

As for Mr. Sanchez, our mathematics teacher, he made not the slightest effort to hide his rich baritone as big as himself, and he could best any male teacher in the school, I am sure, not only in hog-calling but in wrestling.

Miss Santillan turned around and looked at the piano in the hall—a relic that had belonged to my mother. It was more of a prop whose presence was a status necessity in all big houses. Its dark mahogany shone dully through the red shawllike cover that ran down the keyboard and almost hid the rectangular stool. It sulked in the west corner, flanked by two wrought-iron pedestals that supported palmetto fronds. Its stage was elevated a step high, and surrounding it, lining the curving wall, were square glass plates that reflected bits of light. Though constantly cleaned by Sepa, its thin casing had started to crack and peel. I could knock out a tune with one finger, but I never heard it played properly; its only complaint against the obscurity to which it had been flung was a disconcerting jangle of the chords when Sepa ran a rag over the keyboard to wipe off the dust.

"I think I will yet play a tune on that," Miss Santillan suddenly said, moving toward it.

Sepa dropped the magazine.

"Why doesn't someone play it, anyway?" Miss Santillan asked me. "It's easy to learn, you know. Was it never intended to be played?"

"It is, ma'am," I said.

A cryptic smile crossed her face, then she strode toward it. Before she could lift the cover, Sepa ran to her side and clamped a firm hand on the piano cover.

"No, *maestra,*" the aghast housekeeper said.

"Don't be foolish," Miss Santillan reproached her.

"But Apo—he might know. No one has touched it in a long, long time."

"It's all right," Miss Santillan assured her. "I'll play softly. Besides," she turned to me, "your father won't be back till midnight."

Sepa backed helplessly away. "I'll explain it to him," the teacher said. She eased herself onto the stool and cracked her knuckles. "I haven't touched a piano in ages."

She played a folk song and occasionally struck a broken string. She did not step on the pedals because they did not respond, and with the piano lid closed, the music was muffled, distant. She did not complete a piece; she just rippled through snatches of melody.

She turned to me afterward to ask what song I wanted to hear. She would play a complete piece. Her question lost urgency, and her face quickly darkened.

"Play a mazurka. Any mazurka," Father answered for me; he had returned much earlier than we had expected and had perhaps stood by the door, for how long we did not know.

"Sepa told me not to touch it," Miss Santillan explained. "I thought I might still be able to play . . . it was such a long time . . ."

Father did not listen to her blurted explanation. "I should have known that you play well—with fire, with emotion." He was euphoric. He brushed aside the housekeeper, who had gone to him with a mouthful of excuses.

"We didn't expect you to come home so soon," Miss Santillan said, stepping down from the platform.

Father was still grinning. "Chan Hai has had too much *cerveza,* and his moves weren't wise. But go on. Play."

Miss Santillan reluctantly returned to the piano. Her long housedress swished against her legs. "Some of the keys are out of tune," she said, and struck one to emphasize her point. "And a few strings are broken." She struck a few keys again.

"I know," Father said, "but go on. Play."

He turned and went to his rocking chair in the *azotea,* wheeled the chair around so he would face us, and digging a pouch from his shirt pocket, filled his pipe and lighted it. In the cool light of the Aladdin lamp Miss Santillan looked very pretty. Her hair was brushed up and tied with a blue ribbon at her nape. Her forehead, her cheeks were smooth. As she played, her lips were half open as if in a smile. Father's eyes were on her hands.

MR. SANCHEZ VISITED US the following afternoon. It was the first time he or any other teacher came to the house. Only the principal visited us; even Miss Santillan's female coteachers waited at the gate when they wanted something from her. We walked from the schoolhouse with Miss Santillan. Mr. Sanchez was short and dark, with a fleshy face and wavy hair. He wore a white shirt loudly printed with red and green birds. Though he was seldom jovial in school, all the way to the house he teased Miss Santillan on the prospects of their forthcoming stage appearance. What they did not know was that the entire school already shared their secret. He did not want to come up to the house, but when I told him that Father was not home and would not be in until evening, he went up with us. It was not long before he was at ease and Miss Santillan had him sitting beside her on the piano stool as they played "Chopsticks." It seemed to be the only tune the mathematics teacher could play.

"I haven't done that in years," Mr. Sanchez gushed, and Miss Santillan's eyes shone. They sang a little, Miss Santillan softly, while most of the time Mr. Sanchez's baritone boomed. After the Angelus had pealed, he said he was going home. Since our supper was not ready yet, would Miss Santillan care for *halo-halo* in the refreshment parlor by the bus station, and would I please come along as Miss Santillan's chaperon?

Father returned early, and we met him at the gate. He rattled the iron bars of the fence with his cane. The two teachers greeted him. Father did not ask where we were headed, but Mr. Sanchez felt he had to explain, his baritone changing into a squeaky stammer.

ON OUR WAY BACK, the night was black and the balete tree was crowned with fireflies. Mr. Sanchez walked close to Miss Santillan, and sometimes they talked in whispers punctuated by Miss Santillan's soft laughter.

Roosters perched on the acacia trees along the street crowed. At our gate, I saw Father smoking in the *azotea*. He rose when we approached. "Your supper is cold," Father said as he opened the door for us. Without listening to Miss Santillan's greeting, he hied back to his seat.

After supper, Miss Santillan took her lesson plan and went to the table in the *sala* where I also did my homework. There Father joined us, his unlighted pipe in his hand. "Aren't you going to play tonight?" he asked.

"I am tired," she said politely, "and, really, I don't know any other piece except those that you've already heard."

Father struck a match.

"Besides, the piano is . . ."

Father snuffed the light out without kindling his pipe. "I know." He sounded sorry. "The piano is no good."

Before Miss Santillan could speak again, he went back to his rocking chair. When we left the table after some time, he was still there, neither smoking nor rocking, the quiet night all around him.

I was not asleep when the familiar scrape of his slippers came down the hall. He paused before my door, then came in, his pipe still unlighted in his hand.

"You went very far this afternoon," he said.

"No, Father," I said, trying to make out his face in the dark. "We just had *halo-halo* at the bus station."

"With that teacher?"

"Yes."

He nodded and left.

The following week, Father spent little time in the fields. He came home early; at five he was already in the house, and he always asked Miss Santillan to play after supper. In spite of the repeated invitations of Chan Hai and the new priest, Father paid little attention to chess. One afternoon, four days before the high school concert, a man from Dagupan arrived. He brought the piano to the *azotea,* where he dismantled it, and it lay, a heap of strings and pieces of anonymous wood, its many felt-covered hammers scattered on the stone floor.

"The mice gnawed some parts," he explained, pointing to a mess of shredded paper where pink baby mice, their eyes still shut, were cuddled together and making soft squeaking noises. For the next two days he stayed in our house, working far into the night. When he was through, the piano was returned to its old niche. It had a new coat of varnish, the lid was propped up and polished to a sheen, and the white ivory keys were no longer yellow.

After supper, upon Father's prodding, Miss Santillan walked over to the piano. We watched her settle primly on the stool, then tentatively run her fingers over the keys. The music that bloomed later was full, magical, and Father rocked quietly in his chair.

Then it was their last rehearsal, and Mr. Sanchez came to the house again. The block-glass window in the corner was flung open, and the last vestiges of sun that came in made the piano shine like burnished gold. Miss Santillan played "One Kiss" several times. On Father's rocking chair, which had not been returned to the *azotea* yet, Mr. Sanchez sat and listened. After a while he went to Miss Santillan's side. He rested his arm on the piano ledge, looked at Miss Santillan's face, then sang. His voice was tremulous and without much timbre at first, but as the melody held him, it soon filled the house.

After "Oh Promise Me," a Spanish song, he sang another, whose words I could not understand. They were not able to finish the last, because there was a brisk clapping behind me. I turned and saw Father standing at the top of the stairs. He did not return the greeting of Mr. Sanchez. To Miss Santillan, he said gravely: "I didn't know you could sing, too," then he walked briskly to his room and his ledgers.

Miss Santillan played softly after Father had gone, and in a while Mr. Sanchez begged to be excused. He said he had something important to do at home.

"But won't we sing just once more?" She tried to hold him back. "We might not be able to practice again."

"Oh, yes, we will," Mr. Sanchez stammered, then he stepped back to the door, mumbling unintelligibly about his work.

Father appeared at the supper table. He was very quiet, and it was only after the dessert that he spoke. Without looking at Miss Santillan, he dug his spoon into the bits of *nanca* sweet and said: "I see you sing, too."

Miss Santillan could not face Father. "I had no formal training," she said.

"And the other teacher, too?" His voice dripped with sarcasm. "You made a nice duet, indeed!"

"We will sing in the high school program tomorrow."

"Really?" Father said. "Well, that's good! I think you'll make a good show. It's really all right for you to like singing very much, to like a man even . . ."

Miss Santillan gripped the table's edge; a flush of red had crept to her face. "Isn't this becoming too personal, sir?" she asked.

Father glared at her. "Personal or not, I cannot let any lovemaking take place in this house."

"Lovemaking!" Miss Santillan slumped, shocked, on her seat. "We were only singing a . . . a duet!"

Father had not raised his voice, but it was stern. "I don't care which men you want to meet. But as long as you are staying here, under my care, I want you to know that I am like—like your father here."

He stopped and, in all dignity, stood up, walked to the *sala*, and pushed his rocking chair back to the *azotea*. Miss Santillan, speechless for a long while, finally rose and made for her room.

The next morning she was back in her perch under the balete tree. The day of the high school show had come, and though she was needed at school, she did not go. Father arrived late for supper, and when it was over he got his cane from the rack and went down the darkening streets. A boy came from the high school where the program was about to begin and asked for Miss Santillan, but she told me to tell the messenger that she was not feeling well. After the Angelus, Sepa lighted the bronze Aladdin lamp, and Miss Santillan brought out her sewing box. The quiet in the house was awful.

"Aren't you going to play tonight?" I asked.

She shook her head and did not even turn to me.

"I am going to the school to watch the program," I said. "Aren't you coming along?"

Another vehement shaking of the head.

It was sheer waste, and I loathed it. I went to the piano at the far corner. I wanted to run my fingers over its keys, so I tried to lift the lid, but to my surprise, it would not budge. The man who repaired and tuned it had installed a shiny, silver-plated lock—and it was on.

THREE DAYS AFTER our high school day, Miss Santillan packed her things and told Father she was moving to another house with one of her female colleagues because she "needed help and guidance on some of her class projects."

Father objected a little, but I did try very hard to dissuade her.

Later in the afternoon, Father went down, his white coat crumpled and dirtied, and he stayed out the whole night. He did the same thing many times afterward, and though I suspected where he went, I did not ask.

I was having a snack in the kitchen one late afternoon when Sepa, who was serving me, said: "I hope you don't think ill of your father when he leaves in the late afternoons."

"You are speaking in riddles," I said. "He plays chess in the convent or in Chan Hai's shop."

The old woman sighed, and her small, bleary eyes were slits as her cheeks puffed up in a smile. "Maybe he does . . ."

"You old fool." I waved her away with my spoon. "You know nothing but make stories."

She called me to the window, and I reached it in time to see Father hurrying out of the yard, past the screen of bananas in the direction of the rice mill.

"Do you know where he's going?" she asked. She wiped her fat, oily face with her apron and went back to the stove.

"He is taking a shortcut to the rice mill," I said. "If you have something to say, say it."

"You'll find out yourself," she said. "You'll find out."

"You are a witch!"

"Follow him, then," she said. She shook the ladle at me and laughed again.

"You old witch," I said, flinging the spoon at her.

For a woman of her build, she dodged nimbly. As I left, her roiling laughter trailed me.

It was not easy to forget what Sepa had said, but in time I did forget, for there was Carmay and boys like Angel with whom I played. Father started leaving the house more often. He would be out the whole night and return only in the morning. I never bothered asking him, for he worked hard, managing his farm and Don Vicente's, and if he did play chess even for a whole week, it was his business and I would not interfere.

Angel and I were out in the fields near the rice mill one gusty April afternoon. We were flying a kite I fashioned out of Father's extra Christmas wrapping papers the year past. Angel let me launch it alone; it was a perfect kite, for I had just run a short distance when a puff of wind picked it up and sent it soaring to the sky. It wavered sideways, then hovered motionless in the air, its string uncoiled to the very handle, taut and tugging at my hand.

With my kite safely up, I sat down in the shade of a banaba and dismissed Angel, for I no longer needed his help. He had barely disappeared beyond the turn of the path when a strong wind swept the sky; the string snapped, and the kite started its slow, swaying descent.

I raced across the field and followed the kite as it was blown farther away. In a while I found myself near the river, beyond the rice mill. I ran up the mountain of black ash, and as I reached the top I looked down and saw Father walking swiftly along the bend of the river to the new nipa house on the lot where Martina and her father had once lived.

For an instant, I wanted to call out to him and tell him of the kite that was now drifting down the river, but it became apparent that he was in a hurry. What Sepa had said rankled in my mind, and I hurried down the ash mound and trailed him.

Father walked quickly, as if he was afraid someone was following him. As he neared the nipa house, a woman I had never seen before came out. She hurried past the bamboo gate to the path, and as Father drew near, her arm went around his waist, and arm in arm they went up to the house.

I crouched behind a sapling, numb in spirit, and forgot all about the kite. I remembered Mother's whitewashed grave and Father's angry voice when he saw me wearing her dress. When I finally went home, the sun had sunk and Rosales was empty and dark.

ALL THROUGH THE NIGHT, I could not sleep. When Father arrived at dawn amidst the howling of the dogs, for the first time I loathed him.

He appeared at the breakfast table in excellent spirits, his face radiating happiness. He must have noticed my glumness, for he asked me what the matter was. I shook my head and did not answer.

The whole day I stayed in the *bodega* with my air gun idle in my hands. Many rats were out in the open, scampering in the eaves and on the sacks of grain, clear targets all, but somehow they no longer interested me.

And at the supper table after all had left, Sepa came and tried to humor me.

Unable to contain myself anymore, I went to Father, who was smoking in the *azotea*.

"I was near the rice mill yesterday afternoon," I said, hedging close to him. The rocking of his chair stopped; he knocked his pipe on the sill and turned to me.

"What were you doing there?"

"I was flying a kite," I said, looking down at my rubber shoes, unable to meet his gaze. "Its string snapped and I chased it. I went near the new house by the river."

I looked quickly at him and saw in the cool light of the Aladdin lamp his tired, aging face.

"What else did you do?" he asked, his voice barely rising above a whisper.

"Nothing," I said. "I saw you."

He looked away and said quietly, "I don't have to explain anything." And with a wave of his hand, he ordered me away.

I WAITED until I was sure the house was quiet, then I stole into the kitchen and with the meat cleaver, I busted my bamboo bank and filled my pockets with the silver coins. The back door was open, and without a sound I stepped out into the moonlight.

Sepa was at the gate. She sat beneath the pergola, smoking a hand-rolled cigar whose light burned clear like sapphire in the soft dark.

"Where are you going?" she asked.

"Do not interfere," I said. "You are a cook and nothing else."

She held my arm, but I brushed her away. Undaunted, she stood up and followed me to the street. In the moonlight, she peered at me. "Young one," she said, "it's a nice night for taking a walk, isn't it?"

I did not speak.

She said lightly, "It's a lot better sleeping out in the open than in a room stuffy with curtains and mosquito nets." Her hand alighted on my shoulder. "But then sometimes it rains, and then there's the heat of the highway, and the awful dust that spreads and itches and soon pocks your body with sores."

"Leave me alone," I said.

"I should, but listen. It is a man who understands, who knows that life isn't always cozy," she said with a wisp of sadness in her voice. "We would like to see things as we want them to be. Unfortunately, that can't always be."

We reached the town plaza, which was now deserted of promenaders and the children skating in the kiosk. The plaza was lined with rows of banaba trees glistening in the moonlight.

"Take these trees," she said, "how wonderful it would be if all through the year they were blooming. But the seasons change just like people. There is nothing really that lasts. Even the mountains don't stand forever. But people, I am sure, can be steadfast if they have faith."

Her hand on my shoulder was light, and as I walked slowly she kept pace with me. With her wooden shoe, she kicked at a tin can and sent it clattering down the asphalt.

"Who is she, Sepa?" I asked after a while.

"Who?"

"You know whom I mean."

"She is good-looking. She came from a village in the next town . . . was a barrio fiesta queen."

"Did Father build the new house for her?"

"That's all I know," she said. After a while, from out of the quiet, she spoke again: "You know how it is with the *hilot*—the midwives who deliver babies. I'm one, too. Remember? Sometimes they have to use force to hasten birth and lessen the mother's suffering. It's always better for the mother and the baby, but it doesn't always look good with the *hilot*. She is misunderstood."

"I understand you perfectly," I said flatly.

Sepa sighed: "I still believe your mother was the most beautiful woman I've ever seen, and more than that I believe, too, that she bequeathed much of her graciousness to her only child. And your father—he is a wonderful man."

T HEN IT WAS November again, and the rains no longer came in gusts; the sun shone and the grain ripened, and all over the land the rich smell of harvest hung heavy and sweet. There would be smoke in the early evenings and the delicious odor of roasting, half-ripe, gelatinous rice, and there would be pots of bubbling sweets— camotes, bananas, langka. The mornings would be washed with dew, and I would lie longer in bed till the sun roasted my brain.

It was on one such morning that I was roused from sleep. Father had swept into my room, his leather boots creaking; he tapped the iron bedpost with the steel butt of his riding stick, and in the bronze glimmer of day, he stood before me, big and impressive. "A hunter must rise ahead of the sun," he said.

I stirred, but when Father had gone I slowly sank back into this bog of blissful sleep. It was brief, though, for the dogs started howling in the grounds, and Old David was shouting at the boys not to tarry with the saddles. Above the clangor of everything, I could distinguish the neighing of the black pony that Father had given me. The world was alive; we were going to hunt together for the first time, for I was already old enough to handle a gun. It was a time I had waited for, and looking back, all through those trying times, Father really needed not just the woman I had yet to meet but a diversion from the cares that had begun to nag and depress him.

At this time of the year, Old David said, the delta was dry again; the waters had receded from their pockets, and in the mornings shrouded with mist the quail would gather at the water holes. It was time for Father to mount his chestnut horse, gallop past the iron gate through the still-sleeping town. On mornings like this when I was not yet allowed to go with him, I would rise early, too, and wrapped in bedsheets, I would linger at the balcony and watch Old David help him mount. The face of the old man would always turn up to me in a smile as he and Father passed below. I loved his work, his closeness to the horses to whom he often spoke, and I often idled in the stables, all around me the pungent smell of urine and sawdust, while he tinkered with the leather. And in the stable, he dismantled father's *escopetas*—the twelve-gauge double-barreled shotguns—and cleaned them till their bores shone and their hand-carved stocks glistened. With his permission and watchful eye, I had touched them, listening to the double click of the trigger. By the time I was ten, I could handle the guns, though I could barely lift them, and I had learned not just how to shoot but how to treat them with respect and caution.

"Do you think he would take me hunting now?" I had asked so often, it had become a ritual for us. But Old David, chewing his leaf tobacco, merely shrugged: "Next year, perhaps. Your father knows best." At the end of the day, as the sun toppled over the foothills, I returned to the balcony, knowing they would soon come, and by dusk Father would ride in slowly, Old David cantering behind him. But many a time, however, the saddle pack did not hold even one skinny bird, and many a time, too, Father tramped to the house with thunder in his boots, banged at the doors and did not even look at me when I rushed down the stairs to kiss his hand.

There were times in the years long past, Old David said, when they did not know where to put the quail and the heron that they had shot, but now the birds hid in the fastness, driven there by men who no longer had enough rice to eat. More babies were born, they grew up, and there being no more land to farm in the plain, they moved to the foothills and razed them of their cogon grass. They tried planting in the delta, too, when the rains stopped, but the course of the river had always been erratic, and what could be a fertile field this year could be a sandy bar next year.

I prodded Old David again to go ask Father if I could go with him to hunt; he had said that my voice was changing and, yes, perhaps this time it would be all right. We went up to Father's room, but only he entered; I tarried at the door, which was ajar, and heard Father say, "But why must he come? There is nothing there but wasteland. Here he has everything, has he not? An air rifle, a bicycle, companions . . ."

"He wants to hunt, Apo."

"And if he gets lost? Or if he drowns? No one will replace him . . ."

"I have forgotten, Apo."

"Can he take care of himself?"

"Yes, Apo. He knows how to handle a gun now."

A long pause, then Old David came out, his craggy face bright with a smile. And later that day, from the open window of Father's room, I aimed at a brown kapok pod buffeted high in the wind. This was the moment I had waited for, to load and aim a gun, and when I fired, my bones rattled, my teeth jarred, and in my ears the roar was deafening. When the acrid smoke cleared, the pod no longer swung in the tall and slender tree across the street.

Father was grinning when I turned to him. "All right, eh, David?" then to me, "But if you come, you must carry something, like the lunch bag. And you keep track behind me so you won't get lost."

But doubts persisted. "Tell me, am I not ready yet?" I asked. Old David shook his head. He had often watched me aim a slingshot at Father's empty beer bottles lined up in the yard, and each brown exploding glass was like the shattered body of a bird. Then, with an air rifle and at a greater distance. Now with the gun.

"You'll do," Old David said simply.

So on this November morning when smoke from the kitchen stoves and yard fires of the neighbors curled up to a sky polished with sun, I finally was to see the delta. I had new rubber boots and denim overalls. I went to the dining room, where Sepa and Old David were serving Father coffee and fried rice, and sat at the other end of the long mahogany table. The chocolate the old man placed before me steamed fragrantly, but it was not enough. I motioned to

Old David to pass the fried eggs, but Father warned: "A hunter must always eat light before the hunt."

I waited till Father rose. At the door, without his seeing it, Old David slipped into my hand a white lump of native cheese wrapped in banana leaf.

Down at the stable, the boys ringed me and wished me luck, then they dispersed hurriedly when Father came. After he had mounted, Old David helped me up onto my pony. For the past few days I had studied the animal's temper, raced it to the meadow beyond the barbed-wire fence, anticipating the time I would ride it to the delta. Now the frisky animal reared, then pawed the ground. I held its reins steadily.

Old David mounted his low-chinned mare. With Father on his *castaño* before us, we rode down the driveway. Through the town the dogs followed us in howling packs. The early risers, who sat haunched before yard fires warming their hands, stood up and watched us and our horses, whose breath spouted from their nostrils like blasts of steam in the morning chill. We clattered over the new wooden bridge across the creek, then turned to a weedy bull-cart road, and down to the fields where farmers were already harvesting. They paused in their work to watch.

"We will be there soon," Father said. We were halfway, so Old David said, when Father told us not to follow him, and jabbing his stirrups into the hinds of his mount, he galloped ahead.

I turned to the old man as Father disappeared at the bend of the road. "Tell me, Old David, can I really get lost in the delta?"

Old David maneuvered his mount away from the mud pits and the deep wheel ruts that sliced the road and moved away from me. He did not answer.

"Are there many birds there?"

"You know what the delta is. There isn't anything about it that I haven't told you," he said.

I brought my horse beside the old man's mare so that as we jogged on, our legs brushed.

"*Ay,*" the old man sighed. "Long before your father ever went there, when your grandfather and I were still boys, we hunted there. One night we kept vigil at the edge of a brook. With a powerful gun you track just one bird. One skinny bird! We let the pagaw and the heron alone, but you can't do that now. You know what were there once? Wild pigs and deer that cavorted in the light of the moon and stood unafraid at the edge of the clearings!"

Once, before I knew what a deer was like, in Father's study I gazed at the mounted heads of boars that adorned the wall, their tusks sticking out of their petrified snouts like Moro daggers. Beside Father's folding desk I touched the smooth tapering antlers that served as cane-and-hat rack. On Father's high, carved chair, I perched myself to reach the blades of the spears, the forked arrows, and the double-barreled shotguns on the wall.

"People didn't crowd the delta then, nor was it planted with crops. Deer and wild pigs roamed it freely, scared not by the sight of men. They nibbled at the corn; like disciplined soldiers they drank at the riverbank without muddying it. The river was very clear then, like a spring, and the land wasn't dead. But more people came, sapped it dry of its milk. The animals fled to the deeper hills. Then there was no more place to flee to but here. Everything was cleared. The hills. The mountains." Old David's ancient face looked wistful.

"You must love going to the delta," I said. "Year after year, you go there."

"So does your father," the old man said. He smiled enigmatically, then whacked the rump of his mare with his rattan whip. The animal doubled into an awkward trot, and sensing the prospects of a race, I whipped my pony, too, and in a burst of speed I passed him.

The wind whipped my face; the road exploded in a blaze of orange and green. Then the dike loomed, a high mound that followed every turn of the river's bank. At the base of the dike, I stopped and waited.

Old David rode up to me, and we went together, without speaking, our horses straining up the path. Now, atop its narrow crest, I could see the whirling waters of the river and, beyond the tufts of grass and camachile brambles, the vast green spread—the delta sprawled toward the sun.

"Your hunting ground." Old David nudged me. Then down the patch of land below the dike we saw Father signaling us to hurry.

"The river is not deep," Old David said as we trotted to where Father waited.

"And what if it be a hundred bamboos deep?" Father glared at the old man. "You said he can take care of himself. Hurry with the pack, and no more talk."

The old man alighted slowly and helped me down. He unstrapped the pack from the saddle, unholstered the gun, and laid it on the grass. I held the barrel up and asked Father if I could carry it.

Father shook his head. He pointed to the saddle pack that contained our lunch and the water bottle. Leaving the horses tied to knots of grass near the dike, we walked to the riverbank and down a narrow gully; at its bottom, a bamboo raft swayed with the current. A tenant setting fish traps in the shallows told Father that the first cucumber and watermelon seeds in the small clearings were planted the other day.

"So it's like last year, eh, David?" Father said happily. "Pray that the birds haven't been frightened away yet. We should have come earlier."

Old David strained at the raft line that stretched across the river. The raft moved closer and hugged the muddy river edge. Father leaped into the raft, and I followed him with the lunch bag and the water bottle. The raft swayed giddily.

"You come back for us at sunset with the horses, David," Father told the old man. "This time, since you aren't coming, we may have better luck."

Old David pulled the line, and the raft slithered with the current. We balanced ourselves on the dry bamboo floats, safe from the waters that lapped and swished at our perch. With Old David's every heave at the line, the steel wire above us sang. The land and the mossy reeds jutting up the waterline drew near, and in a while the braced prow of the raft smashed into the delta. The tamarind tree, on whose trunk the steel line gnawed deep, quivered with the impact.

I leaped into the sandy landing, the bag and the bottle narrowly missing the tree. Father followed; he wasn't much of a jumper. He splashed into the river's edge, and I turned just in time to grasp the gun, which had slipped from his hand.

"I'll hold it, Father," I suggested. I raised the bottle and the lunch bag. "These aren't heavy."

Father grabbed the gun from me and did not answer. He started out immediately on one of the paths that forked from the landing, Swinging the lunch bag and the bottle over my shoulders, I followed the measured drift of his steps. He did not speak. We plodded on until the trail we followed vanished into a high, blank wall of grass that fringed a small brook.

"Shall we stay here, Father, and wait?" I asked, wiping the sweat on my forehead. I had begun to tire, and I had not seen a single bird. "Old David said the delta birds usually roost near the mudholes."

"We rest here," Father said. He parted the grass and the undergrowth with the muzzle of the gun.

"But won't we go deeper?" I asked. "Old David said we have more chances of finding something to shoot at . . . if we go deeper."

Father scowled at me. My other questions remained unasked. "We stay here," he said firmly. "Maybe the herons weren't driven away by the tenants yesterday."

I sank on the dank black earth. My legs started to numb, and my throat was parched. I opened the bottle and took a hasty gulp.

Father saw me. "And what will happen if you are lost with no drinking water?"

I hastily screwed the bottle cap. This was no hunt at all; we were sitting on the edge of a stagnant brook, just waiting. After a long while, when nothing stirred in the grass, Father stood up and threw the gun over his shoulder. "Let us move," he said without turning to me.

"Where do they really stay, Father?" I asked, following him.

"Anywhere."

Were they in the high grass that rustled with every stirring of the wind? Or in the shade of the low camachile trees?

We came upon untidy clearings that were already planted and lingered in the empty watch houses at their fringes. The sun scorched the sky, and on and on we probed into the grass. Once, I listened to a faint, undefined tremolo—perhaps a birdcall—but nothing came out of it, no quarry taunted the sight of Father's gun. Only tiny rice birds and still smaller mayas twittered and shrieked in the green.

Our shadows became black patches at our feet, and I felt the first twinges of hunger. I did not open the lunch box. As we walked on, I nibbled at the cheese Old David had given me, and its salty tang heightened my thirst. We reached the fire tree at noon. It would be some time before it bloomed. Old David said it was a landmark we could not miss. It rose above the monotony of rushes and thorny saplings.

"You never notice a fire tree that's young," Old David had said. "Not until it's in bloom. You never see it as sapling or seed. You see it just like the way God had planted it and meant it to be, a blazing marker on the land."

"I know this tree well," Father said, pointing to his rudely carved initials on its trunk. "I did that years ago."

I unslung the lunch bag and the water bottle. "Old David and Grandfather spared this tree when it was still small," I said.

Father did not listen to me. He ripped the lunch bag open and handed me two cheese sandwiches. He ate hastily, and when he drank, small streams trickled down his chin. He smacked his lips contentedly as the water ran down his neck and drenched his shirt front. After eating, Father slumped on the big roots that crawled up the trunk and lowered his wide-brimmed cap over his face to shield off a piece of sun that filtered through.

"I'll steal a wink," he said. "Try it, too."

Father took his hat off and fanned his face. He looked at me quizzically, then laid his head back against the trunk.

I laid the empty bag on a gnarled root beside him and perched my head on it. Above, hemmed in by branches and the grass, in the blue sky, swallows circled slowly. When I turned on my side, I saw that Father's jaw had dropped. He was snoring, and a small line of saliva ran down the corner of his mouth. Later, when the sun shone through the branches on his face, he stood up. His eyes crinkled. Tightening the cartridge belt around his wide waist, he bade me follow him.

He said, "You will find hunting is luck. Mostly luck." He straightened the wrinkles on his breeches, then walked again. I kept pace behind him and flayed the grass with a stick, sometimes with my feet. But no matter how vigorously I worked at it, not one heron or quail soared up from the grass. We were finally stopped by a brook, wide and still, and its quiet and opaque blue meant it was also deep.

"Shall we cross it, Father?"

Father contemplated the glazed waters and shook his head. "We can have as much luck here as across it."

We hiked back to where we came from, where the ledda grass was burned by Father's tenants the other day and many charred tufts still smoked.

"Are we going home?"

"You ask too many questions," Father said.

The sun dipped. From the green before us, a pagaw suddenly whirred up and disappeared in the grass. Father raised the rifle too late. He did not fire. "Not even your grandfather or David could hit that," he said, lowering the gun. "We are heading home."

But where was the way? I followed him, and then we were once more near the tree in whose shade we had rested.

Was our aimless meandering now one of the cursed tricks of the delta? It is so easy to get lost in it, Old David had warned, especially at this time of the year when the grass was still high and the water holes were deep. And the thought that we were drifting in its fastness without finding our way soon frightened me.

"Aren't we lost, Father?"

"Lost?" Father laughed. "Lost?" he repeated but did not look at me. He paused, whipped out a handkerchief from his pocket, and wiped his face. He studied the thin trace of a trail—if it was a trail—that led to the west, then peered at the sun. We followed the trail hurriedly, and when we heard the river finally gurgling in the shallows, Father's steps quickened. When we reached the bank, however, the raft was not in sight, nor the tamarind tree to which it was moored. We scanned the other bank, but there was no familiar gully there—only the long hump of earth, the dike.

"Can't we swim, Father?" I asked. "Old David said the river is not deep."

Father shook his head vehemently. "We are still hunting."

"I wish Old David were here," I said. "He knows this place so well."

"Don't say that!" Father's voice was stern. "No one really knows this land. I've come to it year after year long before you were born. Each time, the landmarks are lost except for the fire tree. Even the brooks change their course. The river washes everything away. Nothing remains constant here."

Father closed his eyes and leaned on the gun barrel, his feet wide apart.

"Let me find the way, Father," I suggested.

When he did not speak, I parted the high grass and walked ahead. After a few paces, I heard the swoosh of his boots and the crackling of dry camachile twigs behind me.

I walked briskly; to the left from the tree, straight to the left, I remembered Old David's advice. Pushing through the tall grass, I felt my knees start to wobble. But soon the dunes that sloped before me looked familiar, and finally the clear prints of Father's boots, the water holes where some water buffalo had wallowed—all the places we had passed that morning.

"Old David said no one can really get lost here," I said. There was a rustle behind me but no answer.

I was heading straight to the right bank, and I broke into a run. I found the big path used by *carabaos,* and as I rounded the last scraggly growth of low camachile trees, at last—the river, the tamarind tree, the raft.

The rope that held the raft bit my hand as I untied it hastily. After drawing the raft nearer the landing, I turned around: Father was still not behind me. I called aloud but no answer; I called again, and after a while the grass before me rustled. Father emerged from the green, clutching his gun. He looked tired.

I wanted to brag about what I knew of the delta, all that Old David taught me, but then I heard the distinct flapping of wings.

Wings, bird wings—not the lapping of the water on the reeds or the moaning of the afternoon wind against the brambles. I glanced abruptly at the water's edge by the raft, and there, only a few paces before the unruly growth, a big, white, long-limbed bird alighted. For an instant it seemed as if it was an illusion, but the bird tilted its head and calmly stood on one leg like one of the porcelain figurines in the house. I turned to Father going out of the grass to the landing.

"Look," I called softly, afraid lest the thing be disturbed.

Father did not heed me. "There," I repeated, pointing a trembling finger to where the bird stood. He paused, saw the bird at last, and slid a shell into the gun.

The roar thundered across marsh and river, but the bird did not fall; it hopped slowly to the nearest bush before Father could fire again.

I ran to where it vanished and was still cursing as I jumped upon the brambles that scratched my hands and legs, when I felt Father hold my shoulders and shake me. He looked at the scratches on my arms that had begun to redden.

"You couldn't have missed," I flung at him. "Old David said the buckshot spreads." I was shouting. "And it was so close, so close!"

He did not speak. I walked to the raft and jumped into it first. Neither Old David nor any of the tenants were by the gully to pull us to the other bank, and we both strained at the line.

In midstream Father paused and asked, "What did David tell you about the delta?"

I did not answer.

Father sat on the low bamboo platform, and the eddy that breasted the floats slapped at his muddy boots. "I won't get angry if you tell me."

"Stories," I said, "just stories."

"I never saw you speaking to the old crow."

"We talk a lot," I said uncomfortably. "Under the balete tree, in the stable. Usually when you are away."

Father bit his lower lip and turned away.

"I wanted to know about the delta," I said.

"Well," Father said gruffly, "you know it now." He rose and gave the line a violent tug. The raft lurched forward, and I almost fell into the water. It smashed into the landing, and I jumped off and raced the incline up the river's bank.

The sun was buried in a fluff of clouds, and the hilly rim of the world burned with the fires of sunset. Beyond the blurred turn of the dike Old David came leading the horses.

I turned and saw Father swaying up the gully, clutching at each strand of grass that sprouted on its sides. He loosened the earth with each step and brought down a small avalanche of pebbles and loam. When he neared the top, he placed his right leg over the rim and extended the gun muzzle to me. I pulled, and with a grunt, he heaved himself on level ground. He sank on the grass, panting, and did not get the gun back.

"I'll go ahead, Father," I said. "I'll tell Old David to hurry with your horse."

I hooked the water bottle on the gun barrel and swung it on my shoulder. After a few paces, Father followed. His arms were not swinging.

Old David came with the horses, whistling an old Ilokano ballad, and in the hush of afternoon the tune was clear and sad. "A fine hunt?" The old man grinned as he handed me the reins of my horse. He took the gun and gently placed it in its holster in his saddle. "I heard the shot, and I said, this time, the last bird in the delta is done for."

I stared at him, wordless, then mounted my horse and jabbed my heels into its flanks. The spirited animal reared, and sprang. I brought the horse down with a jerk of the reins, and Old David grabbed the mouth bit, held it firmly, murmured unintelligible words, and patted the animal's glossy coat. The horse became still.

"There will be other years. Next year, perhaps," Old David told me gravely, then he led his mare and Father's mount away.

I was still gazing at the delta darkening swiftly when I heard Father cursing behind me. Turning around, I saw him walk up to Old David; his hand rose, then descended on the old man's face, but Old David, holding on to the reins of the big chestnut horse and his own bony mare, stood motionless, unappalled before the hand—the bludgeon—that shot up, then cut into his withered face once more.

CHAPTER

13

THE DAY I was to go hunting again never came that year or the next, for that December the war came and Father surrendered his shotguns to the Japanese. They also got all of the riding horses, save one—the old skinny nag that was Old David's. The delta where our prey was safe became the sanctuary of brave and angry men.

The war changed the delta and Rosales but hardly altered us. Father and our relatives, we retained our leisurely manners, our luxuries, and the primeval quirks of our nature. Only Tio Doro, I am now sure, was profoundly affected by the war, and I am glad he had survived it. Of all my uncles, it was only he who devoted the best years of his life to politics. There has always been some distaste in our family for any activity that was political, but Tio Doro was simply made of a different fiber. He took to its swagger and blather not for personal honor, but because he found in politics an outlet for his nationalistic passions.

He had no delusions or misgivings, however, in his last days when the ideas that once propelled him to great wrath seemed finally jaded. Maybe he was consoled somewhat by the thought that in his time he had lived fully and well.

After the war, when the Philippines was granted independence, I was sure he would be the main speaker in his town during the program that marked that momentous hour. The honor would have been his by right, because he was Balungao's first citizen and all his life independence was his one consuming obsession.

I had expected him to say so many things, and those who knew how fiery he had been would have been surprised at the change. Not that he had forsaken his old beliefs for new, pragmatic ones; he simply had outgrown them, I suppose, just as I had outgrown my short pants.

If it were not for his daughter, Cousin Emma, I would not have gone often to Tio Doro's place. Not that his big, blue house was far from Rosales—it was only five kilometers away. He was awesome, and moreover, he seldom talked with me, maybe because he felt I was not ready for his ideas. I had heard Tio Doro deliver speeches in public, and I recall vividly his Rizal Day speech many years ago. At that time I had enough of a grasp of English. Tio Doro had always occupied a prominent niche in his town, and he was the program's principal speaker.

It was highly fashionable then to speak in English, although only a few understood it, and Tio Doro spoke in that language for the benefit of the high school students and town officials who occupied the first rows of rattan chairs. A platform had been set up on empty gasoline drums, bordered with split coconut fronds and draped with the national tricolor. Everywhere around the stage, people were sprawled on the grass, on the amorseco weeds, on *caretelas* and bull carts, and on the floats decked with tobacco sheaves and girls in native costumes.

He wore one of those ill-fitting, collarless drill suits that was the uniform of bureaucrats. His stiffly starched pants almost shackled the ankles, but they heightened his patriarchal dignity. When he strode to the stage, there was a discernible clapping from the front seats. After clearing his throat, Tio Doro cast a solemn glance at the newly painted Rizal monument, whose base was covered with amarillo wreaths, and then he broke into a resonant voice that became more vigorous as he progressed.

He spoke of death, declared that dying could not be more glorious than when one gives up his life for the native land. He said this with such intensity that it made me wonder if he remembered it on his deathbed. He relived the days when, at the age of thirteen, he was already with the revolutionary forces. And on he meandered, no longer elaborating on dying but attacking Occidentals, the despicable manner in which they had exploited Filipinos for centuries. He dissected the Monroe Doctrine and its distorted implications, the hypocrisy of the Americans in exercising it, their much touted entry into World War I to make the world safe for their democracy. His voice rose as he lambasted whites for their rapacity and deliberate blindness to the Filipinos' right to self-government. He gesticulated and swore to high heaven and evoked the wrath of the gods, because on earth nobody would act as Tio Doro wanted.

He finally concluded: "God forbid that I will ever have ties with foreigners who ravaged this beautiful Philippines!"

As if precipitately timed with the end of his speech, the brass band played the hymn "My Country," and the notes hammered at the already excited audience. The ensuing ovation was ringing and long.

As I said, Tio Doro seldom spoke to me, and when he did, he was aloof and dull. On one visit, however, we finally had a chat. I was browsing in his library, and Cousin Emma was banging on the piano. I had picked out the *Noli* from his Rizaliana and was giving it a cursory look when he emerged from his room, propped himself comfortably on a sofa, and asked what I would want to be when I grew up.

There was a note of concern in his throaty voice. For a moment I did not know what to say. I was but a sophomore in high school. I finally blurted out that I had not yet given the matter much thought, but Father had insisted on my becoming a doctor. Tio Doro remarked that I might be a writer someday, because I was always reading. But being a doctor, I told him, impressed me more. Whereupon, he tried to dissuade me from becoming one, arguing that there were too many doctors who had M.D.'s only as honorary suffixes to their names. And that was when, for the first time, Tio Doro talked with me as though I were grown-up.

"It is just too bad," he mused, gazing at the unlighted Aladdin lamp above us. "We don't have a language that is known throughout the world. Even if we could have a national language someday, it would still be better if our writers wrote in English. Then they will have a wider following. However, if you will ever write, use a pen name. If you use your own, you might be mistaken for a Latin or even an Italian. Now, if you wrote under such a name like Lawag or Way-waya, no one would doubt your being Malayan."

Though I did not quite know his motives then except for what I gleaned from his impassioned speeches and from textbooks about Bonifacio and Del Pilar, I said I understood.

Tio Doro was an elementary school principal and was among the first batch of graduates of the Philippine Normal School. After his wife passed away, he gave up teaching and focused more attention on his estate, which, after all, was the main source of his income. He plunged into active politics immediately after he quit his teaching job, and that was even before I was born. Several times he ran for the presidency of his town, but every time he lost. His political enemies had a tough time dislodging him from the political platform, though. He was that kind of a man—he could be stopped but not knocked out. And when he finally retired from the political arena because of physical disability, never again were elections in his town thrillingly anticipated. Under the tattered banner of the Democrata-Nacional he waged his fight, and when this party irrevocably split over the Hare-Hawes-Cutting Law, he sided eventually with the Democratas.

He should not have suffered defeat as often as he did. It was not because he squandered on campaigns, filling the insatiable stomachs of voters, for his wife's and his own resources were quite formidable. There was nothing questionable, either, in the way the ballots were counted, for the time when birds and bees could vote was yet to come. It was just that he had a horde of implacable enemies.

In his town the Chinese up to this day carry considerable influence. Tio Doro did not have a single Chinese friend then, and he derided Father for being on affable terms with Chan Hai. He attacked Mon Luk, the rice merchant in his town, whenever he could and at his political meetings accused him of controlling the retail trade. Tio Doro never failed to point out how many people owed money to the Chinese middlemen.

Tio Doro would not have won in the 1934 elections if the Nacionalistas had not split and backed two other candidates for the presidency. As town executive at last, he effected no radical changes during his term. Many had thought he would forcibly padlock all the Chinese stores or do something equally drastic, but he did not. On the routinary side of his term, he sliced a narrow graveled road behind the cockpit and named it after himself, as was the practice of almost all town presidents. He built a new wing for the elementary school building, planted rows of ornamental bougainvillea in the town plaza, erected a water tank, and dug drainage ditches on the sides of the streets.

Anyone would have asserted that Tio Doro truly loved himself, but no one could deny him his charity when in 1934 he gave half of his rice harvest to the poor, as the great storm of that year ravaged the crops. At the close of his term, the Commonwealth was inaugurated. He expressed his usual skepticism about the new arrangement, but he did not run for reelection. Not that he was tired of politics. I used to see him limp often. Now his legs were paralyzed, and that ultimately meant he could not campaign anymore. This did not mean, however, that he left politics completely. His heavy hand was still felt as he welded the Democratas in his district as the last phalanx of the opposition. Though none of his weakling protégés got elevated past the municipal council, he scrupulously supported them to such an extent that he became a local power broker.

Being a true Democrata, Tio Doro would not support President Manuel Quezon, but when Quezon made his now oft-quoted "Better a government run like hell by the Filipinos than a government run like heaven by the Americans," Tio Doro tersely commented: *Tama!*

After high school, Cousin Emma continued her piano studies at the state university conservatory. Tio Doro might have at times been smothered with loneliness in his big house, and the wheelchair to which he was tied might have depressed him no end. Emma was not around to play his nostalgic *kundimans,* the nonpopularity of which he lamented. "These songs," he said, "express the soul of our people."

I seldom went to see him, but on those occasions that I did, he spoke to me of the conflict between Japan and China as if I were now grown-up. But clearly the flare-ups loomed nearer, darker. Mussolini had attached Ethiopia to his empire. In Spain the civil war raged. Then Germany invaded the Balkans. Developments came quickly: Japan joined the Axis, and he predicted that, with Japan now on one side and America on the other, Filipinos would soon be involved more precariously than ever in the whirlpool of the White Man's destiny.

Hitler must have slightly piqued Tio Doro's interest, for he bought a copy of *Mein Kampf*. He never trusted foreigners, and now he justified the racism of the totalitarians as long as national progress was their goal. When the Atlantic Charter was promulgated, Tio Doro was inclined to be sarcastic about it. It is a very interesting scrap of paper, he averred, but the Americans and the British have common imperialistic designs, as history had proved in Cuba and India. Do you think they will come to the succor of the colonials without considering their private interests first?

War engulfed the Philippines shortly afterward. The Japanese landed on the beaches of my province, and Tio Doro's town, like ours, was one of the first to be occupied. Father saw no reason for us to leave the province. We were not molested, and we had enough to eat. But the transportation was slow and difficult, and I rarely visited Tio Doro and Emma, although Father did see him frequently.

Cousin Emma wrote to me occasionally. In her letters she could not say much because the mails were censored. For Tio Doro, however, his writing days were over; the dread paralysis had crept to his hands.

Then Emma's letters ceased. The country was liberated, and we weathered a few scary nights. When the fighting was over, Emma wrote in one long letter everything of importance that had happened. She told of how her father had been humiliated by the Japanese. His frailty had proved to be no shield. He had been asked to serve as town mayor, a figurehead, but he had flatly refused. Yet, before the war, he had appreciated the Japanese love of country and emperor that amounted to fanaticism, and he believed in the validity of the Japanese catchword: Asia for the Asiatics, the Philippines for the Filipinos. Then, inconsistently, he secretly gave most of his harvest to the guerrillas rather than sell it to the Japanese rice agency, the BIBA. Cousin Emma recounted some gory episodes, among which was how the only son of Mon Luk in their town was executed for underground activities, and how the rice mill of the Chinese had been razed to the ground, transforming the Chinese merchant into a pauper. To all these incidents Tio Doro had been an eyewitness. At one time he was a prisoner, too.

But for all that happened, Tio Doro's absorption in politics had not waned. Although the war had added to his worries, he still managed to dabble in politics. His health was deteriorating, and his resistance was petering away. He was sick most of the time from complications of his paralysis so that the doctor's visits became more frequent. He was never really physically strong; even when his legs had not yet succumbed, his frame was meager and he was susceptible to colds, so that when he made his nighttime speeches he was always wrapped up. Emma asked if I would like to see the old invalid before he passed away.

I arrived on an Army truck transformed into a bus. The Balungao municipal building was a gaunt remnant of a once imposing edifice, and beyond it, Tio Doro's blue house still stood above the rubble of the other residences, which had not been as fortunate. At my right loomed the chimney of Mon Luk's rice mill, a monolith pointing to a sodden sky as a reminder of a once-flourishing business, over which Tio Doro would have pleasantly chuckled years ago if by some occult and terrible power it suddenly collapsed.

I passed through the stirring May streets, felt the cool whiff of the rainy season through the thick afternoon heat, recalled how every house once stood, how edges of gumamela had not yet sprung up in the yard of the demolished schoolhouse, which was now alive with American GI's. The acacia trees that lined the main road were bigger—they had been but puny saplings once. The asphalted road, which they lined, was rutted and scarred by the tracks of tanks and bulldozers. A couple of makeshift bars were filled with soldiers in olive uniforms, laughing boisterously and singing "You'll Never Know."

As I neared the blue house—its paint peeling off, its fence shabby and crooked—jazz welled up from within. I pushed the heavy iron gate that squeaked open with a metallic tinkle from the bronze bell above it. Up the graveled path I hurried, and from the direction of the back-door stairs, Cousin Emma came beaming.

I hurried up the polished stairs, on each side of which stood little statues of discus throwers. Cousin Emma took me to the spacious drawing room and told me that the old man's days were numbered.

We went to the room where Tio Doro was confined. He was propped up in a wheelchair near the wide-open window. The afternoon sun streamed in. His cheeks were sallow, the crop of distinguished white hair sparse. He was apparently resigned, as would be the earth to the whims of the elements. But now in the room were two middle-aged American officers and Tio Doro's former archenemy, Mon Luk, who, I later learned, had just borrowed a little capital from him to start business anew.

I held his soft, nerveless hand and kissed it, and almost forgot to answer when he inquired how Father was.

At that time when no explanations were possible, I was hurtling back to those blurred yesteryears, to that conspicuous Rizal Day program long ago, when as the main speaker he discoursed despicably on all foreigners, when on his election platform he damned all Chinese. And now, in the privacy of his home—in his own room—were these strangers laughing with him as if they were his long-lost brothers.

CHAPTER

14

WHAT HAPPENED to Tio Doro was one of those profound transformations that the Occupation wrought. Rosales itself underwent irreparable changes—the great fire that burned down the business area and Father's commercial buildings, the guerrilla war that brought death to more Filipinos, I think, than to Japanese. For me, neither death nor suffering was trivialized. I had seen both and was touched, but not by lesser forms of travail. Father had seen to it that his family and those under his wing were well provided for. He had also played superb politician by keeping away from entanglements either with the guerrillas or with the Japanese puppets. As I heard him say all too often, "The bamboo survives by bending to the storm."

As for the balete tree, it weathered the war handsomely. The belief of the people in its sacredness, in its being the embodiment of spirits that watched over us, was even reinforced. At one time, the Japanese needed some poles or timber for additional construction in the schoolhouse they had taken over, and they ordered some civilian laborers to cut down a few branches. The laborers—as was to be expected—ran away for fear that they would displease the spirits. Faced with having to do the job themselves, a couple of bald-shaved Japanese proceeded to the tree with their handsaws. No one really saw what happened, but the two soldiers were killed by a grenade that exploded while they were up in the tree. How the grenade got there is one of those riddles that will never be unraveled. Then, when the Americans came, they pitched their tents in the plaza and had a bulldozer level or cover up the bomb shelters with which the Japanese had pocked the plaza. The bulldozer had grazed the balete trunk—much to the shock of the people who were watching the machine work, for they had warned the American sergeant driving it not to go near the tree. He had, perhaps, never heeded the warning. As he turned around, an explosion rent the air, and after the smoke had cleared, the bulldozer was in shambles and the American was seriously injured. He had hit a land mine that had lain there all the time, undisturbed, planted by whom, nobody knew. The American detachment in Rosales left soon after the accident, and the bulldozer lay by the tree in a crumpled heap. It was there for some time, rusting in a pile of scrap, till someone dismantled it, testimony again to the sorcery of the balete tree.

The war was over—we thought there would be no more killing. But we were wrong, for now, all around us in the plain, the men who had fought the Japanese so well as Huk guerrillas now fought their landlords and the Army, which they perceived as instruments of the landlords to perpetuate their ancient, miserable lot.

But even if this was so, Father's tenants did not seem affected by the dissidence that had broken out in their midst; they went about their duties promptly, and for all the memories of Tio Baldo, they seemed as docile as always. Yet I knew that it was not so—the surface calm was deceptive.

It had been growing—I am conscious of that now—like the yellow, poisonous yam; and though there were mere tendrils above the earth, crawling and withered, underneath was this root, massive and deformed, with appendages of the most grotesque shape, burrowed deep. To bring out the whole would require careful prodding and digging, so that all of the root would be lanced from its mooring, for any remaining shred could well be nurtured again by the rich and loving earth, not just into life, but into something bigger than the original root wherefrom it had sprung.

"It is so clear," Cousin Marcelo said. "The war showed the farmers, the poor, how they could survive and how the rich and the powerful could not. Look around you—the tenants are no longer the cowed starvelings they used to be. They know that if they are united and if they have guns, they can do almost anything. Anything! We have to be aware of these changes and adjust to them. We cannot live in the past forever."

Indeed, the war altered many things but again not us, not us. We knew no hunger as did our neighbors, who lived on buri-palm flour; no lack of clothes as did many of our tenants, who learned the feel of sackcloth on their backs.

"We are fortunate," Cousin Marcelo continued. "But look at the thousands of young people with no future. They either become soldiers or bandits in the hills whom the soldiers seek without pity. Look at Angel, and you'll know what I'm talking about."

I knew what Cousin Marcelo meant. I also know now that the changes that came upon the country were very profound and much more all-embracing than we had the courage to perceive. The farmers, the tenants—we did not realize then how they saw and understood that the power of the rich, of Don Vicente and Father himself, had been eroded, that in those four abject years it was really each man for himself. The old loyalties held insofar as we were concerned, but they were rendered fragile, as only time would soon show. For what the Japanese did was not to destroy the landlords; they were not interested in social change, in the restructuring of classes; they were interested only in the produce of the land, and they got the rice and whatever bounties the land gave and in the process leveled everyone.

But with the Japanese gone, the old arrangements were quickly resumed—or so we thought—little realizing that what had been broken could never be brought together again. And all these now come sharply to mind as I think of Angel and that morning during the dry season, when Father woke me up with his swearing in the garden. I rose and went to the window.

Below, Angel struck the stone bench by the balete tree with his straw hat and stirred the dust and dry leaves that covered it. As if he were a participant in a primal ritual, without looking at Father poised before him, Angel lay flat on his stomach.

I hurried down the flight in time to see Father lash the horse whip across Angel's buttocks for the last time. The servant's lips were drawn, his eyes were shut, and he did not rise. Panting and cursing still, Father flung the whip to the caked earth and with his forefinger scraped off the beads of sweat that glistened on his forehead.

Father was a tired shadow of his former self; he forgave the servants their manners, their barging into the *sala* before the guests, tongue-tied and fumbling for words, when he asked what brought them there; he did not mind their forgetting to polish his boots when he galloped off on his *castaño* to the fields. But it seemed that the mistake Angel had committed was beyond reprieve.

"And you say you will soon buy a *cédula,* ha?" Though Father's wrath was spent, his voice was threatening still. "Not in ten years will a stupid one like you need one!"

Angel finally stood up. He passed a hand over his buttocks and mumbled, "It won't happen again, Apo."

Father did not hear him, as he turned away and stomped back to the house.

Since he came to serve us, Angel was to tend Mother's garden—the roses, dahlias, and sparse rows of azucena that had survived the rainy season. He had failed to water the unpotted roses to which Father was particularly devoted because the rose plots were what Mother had lavished her care on. Father himself padded them with horse dung from the stable, but now the rose plots were whitish patches of dry soil.

Father had found Angel behind the *bodega,* sitting on a sled and gazing at the faraway hills, unable to explain why he was there on a morning when he should be working and—most of all—why he neglected the rose garden.

AFTER HIS WHIPPING, Angel returned to the garden and sprinkled water on the wilted plants, shielding each with his palm.

"It won't do any good," I said.

He turned to me and smiled sadly. "I shouldn't have forgotten." He dropped the tin can back to the water pail. "I just couldn't forget what happened to Father and Mother. It seemed so impossible . . ." He drew the can from the pail again and, his palm over the withered plants, sprinkled them. "These are difficult times," he murmured.

Angel was eighteen, but he looked shriveled and lines of premature age furrowed his brow. He stood up when his pail was empty and returned to the artesian well by the kitchen stairs, where three soldiers stationed in the town plaza were filling canvas buckets. They belonged to a company supposed to patrol the nearby foothills, which were now alive with Huks. Angel was soon conversing with them.

He was back in the garden in the late afternoon.

"Will you teach me now?" he called. I was at my window watching him. I went down to the back of the storehouse where Father had seen him loafing. We sat on a ledge; against the back of an old chair, he balanced the dog-eared primer I gave him and turned to its last pages.

He tackled a few sentences, and after one page he paused and leaned on the warm stone wall. His eyes wandered to the tamarind tan of May that covered the land. From his shirt pocket, he dug out the last frayed letter from Mindanao, which, as one would a Bible, I had read to him many times before. Exasperated at the thought of reading it again, I said, "No, not this time."

He seemed hurt, and he thrust the letter back into his pocket without unfolding it.

"What can you do now?" I said, feeling badgered. "You should burn it. All the other letters, too."

He came close to me, smelling of the stable and the dry earth. His voice trailed off: "About this morning, when your father saw me here, I was thinking . . ." Again his eyes were on the barren land beyond the barbed-wire fence and farther, the mountain half-hidden by coconut trees. He spoke brokenly. "I just cannot believe it. How they both died . . ."

I looked at the dust where with his finger he had spelled his name wrong. I did not want to remember the stooped, pallid woman, his mother, and the slight balding man, his father. "You never learn!" I said, and stood up to leave.

ANGEL WAS TO SERVE US for ten years without pay. In the ledger in Father's room, on the list of debtors, was the name of his father. As with all the other tenants, Angel's father had often been in great need.

"Why do you butcher your *carabao* and feed a throng because your son is getting a wife?" Father always blustered to them who came asking for loans. But always, in the end, the tenants got the money—what they needed for a "decent" funeral, a baptism, a wedding. And as their debts piled up, they promised, "Next harvest will be good . . ." Sometimes, when their forecast was right, they did pay, but during the planting season—in the lean days of June, July, and August—they would again be before Father with the same old plea.

When Angel came to the house, his flesh was mottled with a skin disease caused by long hours of work in the waterlogged fields. Father bade him sleep in the *bodega,* by the wall near the west window. It was a shelf, actually, which was used to hold jars of fermenting sugarcane wine, and when the harvests came he was hemmed in by sacks, and there was only enough space for him to crawl onto his board and snuggle there. When the grain was sold and the storehouse was emptied, the cavern was all his again.

In time the coarse board was polished by his back. The seasons changed, the balete tree lost its leaves, then sprouted them again. The fiesta filled the house with loquacious cousins from the city, and before long, Christmas. The boys and Old David received new clothes, they sang carols in the yard. New Year—the boys from across the street dueled Angel and me with bamboo cannons loaded with empty milk cans—and, finally, harvest time, and Chan Hai cluttered the yard again with his trucks.

"THIS IS A HARSH YEAR," Angel said, when his parents came to stay in the *bodega* with him. May rain fell at its appointed time, and Old David hoped the harvest would really be good, for he had observed the sun sink blood-red behind the foothills and seen the full moon and its indigo halo. Weren't those the signs that augured beneficence?

But shortly after the seedlings sprouted from the beds, the worms crawled out and devoured them. What the worms spared was transplanted into the irrigated fields, but barely grown, the sprouts were parched by a long August drought. Only those near the waterways survived to be lashed later on by an October storm. For a week the winds whipped the crops and the farmers scurried in the fields. But no matter how fast they cut the ripened grain, they could not pick each seed from the mud where the wind had embedded it. Father's share did not even reach up to Angel's pallet, and Chan Hai made but a few trips to the *bodega*. By February all that was left were a few sacks of seed rice, over which Angel kept watch, because every day some hungry tenant came to town and peeped into the *bodega* before going up to Father to ask for a loan.

Hunger precipitated despair. But more than despair was the nagging belief that the land they had patiently and lovingly groomed never really belonged to them but to Father or Don Vicente. This rankled in their hearts—Tio Baldo had long been dead, but they remembered. They knew that in the unrecorded past their forebears cleared the land but were cheated when influential men made the Torrens titles. This belief alone united them and gave them strength.

One late February afternoon, Angel's father rushed to the storeroom and told his son to leave immediately. Angel refused; instead, he convinced his father to go see Father, who was in the *azotea*, watching a ball game in the plaza.

"They are coming tonight," Angel's father said. "They will force the storehouse open. The grain will be divided among them."

Father listened without stirring, and when Angel's father was through, he walked briskly to his room. When Father came out, the new Garand that the soldiers had given him was slung on his arm.

He looked at Angel's father coldly. "By God, I'll use this if I have to! I'll call the constabulary. The bastards will not get a single grain."

They came at dusk, their bolos tied to their waists, their talk a drone of many bees that rose ominously to the house where, from the half-closed windows, the maids tried to make out their brothers and fathers. They spread out in the yard restlessly, then one of them strode to the door and rattled the iron latch and called, "Apo, we want to talk with you!"

Father was waiting for them at the top of the stairs. He went down, brushing aside Old David, who tried to hold him back by saying, "Blood must not be spilled," for Father was unarmed. I rushed down after him, walked among the strangers whose brown faces were indistinct in the shadows cast by the storm lamp Old David held high in front of Father.

His tenants followed him like steel filings drawn by a magnet. Walking behind him, I expected anytime the shining arc of a *bolo* to descend on him. He walked on, silent and sure, and when he reached the bench under the balete tree, he mounted it. Old David hung the storm lamp on an overhanging branch, and in its yellow glow Father's face was livid with rage. He looked at all of them gathered before him, the men whose first names he knew, and when he spoke, his voice trembled.

"I knew you were coming," Father said. "I know you want to tear down the gate of the storeroom, so you can get what is in there."

The men shuffled and murmured among themselves.

"And I know, too," Father went on, his voice now pitched and stern, "that you are saying, 'Why must we pay a yearly rent when the land we farm is ours?'

"I'll tell you. I was not born a hundred years ago, but I know that when my father came down from the north, he cleared this land. I bought the rest. You know that. Maybe Don Vicente did steal from you, but not I! I can drive you from your farms, use machines. It is cheaper, easier, less trouble. Maybe I'll even harvest more."

Father paused. His hands shook. "You came here to tear down doors. Well, go ahead. You'll get a few sacks of grain. You'll have full stomachs for a week. But after that, what? When the planting season comes, where will you get seed rice?"

No answer. Then, slowly, some of them drifted away from where Father harangued at them and sat under the awning of the storeroom, mumbling a babble of solutions.

"But can't you give us something to eat, Apo?" someone finally asked.

Father stepped down from the bench and went to the *bodega*. At the door Father called Angel. The massive doors swung open, and in the light of the storm lamp, which Old David raised, Angel stepped forward, the shotgun in his hands. The tenants glared at him, and from their curses I knew that they had disowned him.

"I am not the government, nor is Don Vicente," Father said. "If I give one, I must give all. Go home, all of you, or I'll run you out of this yard!"

"Hunger can't wait, Apo," one was brave enough to shout.

"You'll die of starvation tomorrow if you eat your seed rice!" Father shouted back. "Go home, all of you. I'm not the government—nor a philanthropist!"

THEN THE DRY SEASON—the land beyond the fence browned. Heavy clouds formed overhead, but rain did not fall and light passed on to darkness. The boys gathered edible moss from the creeks, the women returned empty-handed from the withered vegetable patches, and the men scanned the blue, burning sky.

Angel's father, who came to the house every Sunday to give his share of firewood as did Ludovico's father, stopped coming, and one April morning Angel and I rode a bull cart to Carmay to trim the madre de cacao and acacia trees that lined the barrio road.

On our return, the cart loaded with green twigs, Angel said, "It is hardest this year." Angel's parents came with us with all their things, and upon reaching the house, they sought Father.

He was smoking in the *azotea*.

"We have nothing left to eat in Carmay, Apo," Angel's father said. "The sweet potato has been shorn of its green leaves."

Angel's mother said, "We have tried everything. Even banana roots."

Father listened placidly, rocking his chair, his arms limp on his lap. The smoke from his pipe curled above his head. "I have many mouths to feed," he said finally, "and your debts—you haven't paid them yet."

"We won't stay here long, Apo," Angel's father pleaded. "Before the planting season comes we will leave Carmay."

"For where?" Father asked.

"We are selling our house and our *carabao*, Apo, for our fare to Mindanao."

"Like the others, ha?"

Angel's father did not answer. There being no alternative for Father but to let them stay, they carried their things to the storehouse and swept away from a corner the cobwebs, bat droppings, and bran. They did not mean to be idle. Angel's father fixed the fence, and his mother helped in the kitchen, until one May morning Father chanced upon her coughing hoarsely there. He told her never to work in the house again.

Father did not send them away as the town sanitary inspector had recommended. It was June at last, and the first showers of the rainy season blanketed Rosales. All the things Angel's parents owned were packed in two bundles, and Angel drove them in Father's *calesa* to the train station. All through the narrow, shrub-lined dirt road, they did not speak. They loaded their bundles into a boxcar.

As the train chugged to start, Angel reminded his father, "Don't forget to write. Tell me what is happening. And someday"—he stared at his big toe digging into the sodden, coal-sprinkled bed of the ties—"I'll come, too."

Angel's father nudged his wife. "Hear that, woman? Don't forget what your son said."

A slight drizzle started as they climbed into the boxcar, and Angel and I ran back to the rig. They lifted their hands in awkward farewell, but Angel did not look back. We drove back slowly, and he held the reins in check so that we reached home in a walk.

A full month passed and the land finally stirred. The rains became fuller and stronger, and the fresh green of June darkened to a dirty hue. The banabas bloomed and amorseco weeds wove violet patterns around the mud holes that pocked the plaza. One afternoon, as was my daily chore, I returned from the post office with a bundle of letters. At the foot of the stairs, I called Angel, who was in the garden weeding the gladiolus bulbs, and threw him the bundle.

"From Mindanao," I said.

In the storehouse that night, in the light of the storm lamp, I pored over the letters. They told of how his folks barely had enough seed rice to start the planting season in that distant land. They were isolated, and in the evening only the flickering of a faraway neighbor's lamp in the trackless dark impinged upon them the consoling thought that they were not alone at the edge of the forest.

The succeeding letters arrived regularly, and I answered some for Angel, who now mastered the alphabet but could not yet write legibly. The boys envied him for his parent's luck. He told them of the wonderful Cotabato fields, how his father caught a wild pig under their house, how one evening his father killed a python in the chicken coop. As to what was in store for them, Angel had no foreboding. In another year Angel's mother told of how they were plagued by moneylenders who wanted to get all they harvested for the little that they owed.

"Tell me why it is like this," Angel asked.

I could not explain the tragedy that stalked his folks before the next harvest was in. When he received the fateful letter, he managed to have one of the boys read it. In the afternoon, when I came upon him filling the horse trough with water, his eyes were swollen from crying.

"Father is dead," he said simply.

"Let me see the letter," I said.

He washed the bran and black molasses dripping off his hands and gave me a folded sheet from the ruled pad on which his mother always wrote. "Read it, please," he said.

I started cautiously, feeling out the words: "My dear son:" (The letters always started that way.) "This old and aching heart will overflow with joy if, when this letter reaches you, you are in the best of health.

"There is not much for me to do now [there was an erasure that blotted out two lines] . . . now that your father is no more.

"Sometimes I think we should have never come here, but in this land the rice grows tall. We thought we would never know hunger again, but hunger will always be with us. Your father could not even fight when they got him . . ."

Somewhere in the stable, a neighing horse drowned out my words. Angel leaned on the wooden rail that separated the trough from the stall of Father's *castaño*.

"Why did they do it?" he asked.

"We came here," I went on with the letter, "because they said that for us who cannot wait for the three-month rice to bear grain, there is plenty here. The trees—they are in the forests. The cogon grass and bamboo, too. We can build strong houses here, but we shall always be cowering before the big men around us, doomed to die, paying . . .

"We will always fall prey, chick to the hawk. They said this land is ours and we can own all we plant. But here there is hunger, too, as elsewhere in the world. We fear not only God's wrath, but the field rats that devour our grain, the animals that trample our fields. We fear men because they have made the world too small for us. There is not enough of it for us to plant, we who have never known what lay beyond the waters we crossed or the high mountains that now surround us . . ."

"What about Mother?" Angel bent forward, his eyes burning. "What does she say of herself?"

I turned the letter over. "There is nothing more," I said.

IN THE DAYS that followed, Angel would rush to meet me every time I appeared at the bend of the road with the mail from the municipal building. He would trail me up the stairs, and without bothering to look at him, I always shook my head. There were no more letters.

I chanced upon him in the *bodega* one afternoon while hunting house lizards and mice. He was hidden by piles of firewood and corn, poking a rod into the piles to flush out the mice. He did not speak until I saw him. His eyes were hollow, his voice was heavy. "Mother is dead, too," he finally said.

"You are not sure," I said, cocking my air rifle as a mouse raced across the eaves.

"She is dead," he said.

I fired, and the lead pellet whammed into the tin roof with a sharp metallic twang. I lowered the air gun with a curse.

"Two months," Angel said, breathing hard, "and not a letter. Can't you see? How was she buried, who dug the grave, was there a cross?"

Silence.

"And if someday I'll go there, how will I look for them?"

There was nothing I could say. I stood up and left him, his words ringing in my ears. The next day Father found him behind the *bodega,* seated in the wide drop of the driveway. He did not water the rose plots for a week, and in the heat, the young plants that Father loved were dead.

Hard times, Angel said, for during the last harvest Father did not go to the fields anymore as was his wont. But for a company of soldiers who had their camp—an untidy blotch of olive-colored tents— in the town plaza, who drew their water from the artesian well behind the house, Father and I would have gone to the city to return to Rosales only when he could safely canter on his horse to his fields again.

A few weeks back, the Huks swooped down on the next town and all through the long night the sad boding chatter of machine guns and the scream of speeding trucks on the provincial road kept us awake. Since then it was prohibited to walk in town at night without a light, and Father slept with his shotgun and his new revolver within easy reach.

SHORTLY AFTER the Angelus, Sepa came to the *sala,* where, beneath the new Coleman lamp, I was reading. "Angel has something for you," the old woman said, and gestured that he was waiting for me in the *bodega*. I went down to the silent yard. Inside the big building I flashed a light on the broad wooden board where Angel sat leaning against the wall.

"Do you want ointment for blisters?" I bantered, playing the light on his face.

He did not answer. I turned the light off, and in the pale haze from the barred window above him, his gaunt, tired face became softer.

He stretched his hand to me. "Here," he said in a tone that was supplicating. I took from him the battered cardboard box where he kept his mother's letters. "Keep it for me."

I climbed to his side and sat on the pallet. I flashed a light on the stone floor, saw that his trunk fashioned out of packing boards was tied. He wore shoes, too, the worn-out pair Father thought he had thrown away.

"Are you leaving because Father whipped you? Why, he whips everyone. Even me!"

Angel shook his head.

"Where are you going, then?" I asked, gripping the box.

"Don't tell Apo," he said. "I am leaving tonight. With the soldiers."

"But where?"

The alien sounds of evening filled the storehouse. In its blackness rats moved. Outside, in the balete tree, cicadas were alive.

"I don't know where they will send us," Angel said carelessly. "I am not going to Mindanao, though. Maybe, someday, I'll go to the United States, like your Tio Benito. But for the next few years . . ." He turned reflectively to the barred window and pointed to the starlit west where the mountains loomed. "We will go there. Fight there."

In my mind flashed the vivid sight of the uncovered bodies of soldiers brought to the town plaza after the all-night fighting in the nearby hills—the stiff, half-naked dead, some barefoot, all their faces anonymously stolid in death—dumped by the camp roadside to be identified.

"You are stupid, just as Father said."

"I am eighteen," he retorted.

"You don't know what is waiting there for you. You'll die."

His rough hand slid into mine. "It doesn't make a difference." His voice quavered. "But what can I do? Will I stay here forever like

David, tending the garden, feeding the horses? I would have joined the Huks if they came and asked me. I am sure that with them I'd be in a place other than here. Can't you see? I have to go. Where I am going I'll have my own life. The soldiers have that much to offer. And they are here."

"You are going to die."

He let go of my hand. In the dark, his teeth gleamed in a quick smile. "That should worry your father," he said with a trace of sarcasm, "but don't think I'm running away from my father's debt. My salary, most of it, will go to Apo. Until we are free."

"You are going to die."

His head drooped. He eased himself down the pallet and paced the stone floor. "Yes, but I'll die decently," he said, pausing. He leaned on his elbows and faced me. "Isn't that what we should live for?" His questions had a quality of coldness, of challenge.

I swung down the pallet and beamed a ray across the black void to the open door. His letters were in my hand. I walked away without answering him, Angel, my servant, my friend.

CHAPTER

15

IN THE MORNING the household was agog over Angel's sudden departure, the servants speculating on where and when he would die.

"I can't understand it," Father said at the lunch table. He was angry and perplexed. "So I did whip him, but was that enough to make him leave?"

"Maybe he wanted to be free," said Sepa, who was serving us.

"Free?" Father asked incredulously. "Wasn't he free here to do his foolishness?" He turned to me. "You were the last one he saw. What did he tell you? Why didn't you stop him?"

"He said he would send you the money, Father, to pay the debt of his parents."

"And I'll believe that? Why didn't you stop him?"

I could not speak.

"So Angel is gone," he said aloud for all the servants to hear. "Ingrate! I gave him a roof and three meals a day, and he could at least have come to me and said, 'Oy, I'm leaving now because my belly is full and my limbs are strong.' See what I get for my kindness to people. Nothing but insults that claw the mind!"

Father's anger, however, did not persist, nor did the talk of the servants about Angel. In a week, all attention centered on the forthcoming celebration of Father's birthday. It was not really for him alone; more than anything, it was an occasion for all of his tenants to come to town to partake of his food, and at the same time bring their children and grandchildren, so that Father would get to know them. It was a time for them to render us service, to fix the fences, clean the yard, and whitewash the walls.

For Father's close friends, too, it was a time to gather in the house and share his liquor. For our relatives who lived in other parts of the province or in the city, this was a time for remembering old ties.

Among our Manila relatives, it was Tia Antonia and her children who came most often "to have a better whiff of air." I suspect, however, that she came to Rosales almost every month not only for the country air but to save on groceries, for Tia Antonia was the prototype of the Ilokano housewife—a tightwad as only Ilokanos could be. For the big feast she was the first to arrive.

Old David and I met her at the railroad station. I was peeved at Father's sending me there, for it interrupted my mouse hunting in the storehouse. Tia Antonia and her children needed no welcoming committee—Rosales was practically their home. As we came within sight of the red brick station, Old David's horse paused and its bony head dropped. He prodded its skinny rump with his big toe and whacked the reins on its back.

"Thank heavens, this *calesa* is not for hire," he sighed as the horse finally lifted its head and plodded on.

The old man turned to me and grinned. His breath stank with nipa wine, but he talked soberly: "If it were, no one would use it. You can't expect much from horses now. But you should have seen the horses I tended then in your grandfather's stable. Colts, roans, all spirited, from the provinces of Abra and Batangas. They could race the wind and come out winners by how far the east is to the west!"

The train from Paniqui had long come in and was now leaving the station, the steel bumpers of its three dilapidated coaches whanging as they lurched forward. *Calesas* filled with passengers were pulling out of the parking lot under the acacias, and the platform was almost empty of people. We could have reached the station earlier, but through the main street, along the shrub-lined road that skirted the creek to the station, though Old David always clacked his tongue, never once did his horse perk up.

"There they are," I said, nudging the old man as we reached the shade of the acacias where now not a single *calesa* was parked. Even from a distance it was easy to recognize Cousin Andring, with his paunch and round balding head, and Tia Antonia, who always wore a severe chocolate-colored *terno,* her gray hair tightly knotted.

Old David tied the reins to one of the posts that palisaded the station yard. I jumped down and ran to Tia Antonia, who was standing by the ticket window, and kissed her bony hand. She was past fifty and looked ascetic but still used perfume liberally, a brand that had a particular scent similar to that of crushed bedbugs. Andring tousled my hair.

"If I didn't know you were coming," Tia Antonia said drily, peering down at me through her steel-rimmed eyeglasses, "we would have taken one of the *caretelas.*"

Cousin Andring beckoned to the old man. "David," he called pointedly, "don't tell me you were drunk again and forgot."

The old man mumbled something about the horse being slow, but Cousin Andring went on: "Hurry with the bags." Three pieces of baggage lay at his feet. David picked up one—a leather valise, the biggest of the three, and sagged under its weight.

"Careful!" Tia Antonia hissed. "My thermos bottle and medicines are in there."

Old David smiled as he picked up the bag and walked away. Cousin Andring called him back and told him to take one more bag, but the old man walked on.

"The old lazy drunk!" Cousin Andring swore. "I cannot understand why Tio tolerates him. He is late, and now he is also insolent."

He picked up the two bags and, overtaking the old man, dumped one on his shoulder. Old David momentarily staggered, but he balanced the bag and carried it to the back of the *calesa.*

"It is about time Tio bought a car," Cousin Andring said as we joggled up the dirt road to town. "I don't see why he doesn't. He has the money."

"Whip the horse, David," Tia Antonia said irritably. "I'm hungry."

Old David whacked the reins on the back of the animal, but its pace did not change. Cousin Andring grabbed the rattan whip slung on the brace beside the old man. He moved to the front and sat beside me on the front seat, then leaning forward, he lashed at the horse. Our speed did not pick up, so he gave up after a while. "The servants and the horses Tio keeps," Cousin Andring said in disgust, "they are all impossible."

Father met us at the gate. After they had alighted, Old David took the *calesa* to the stable. He carried the bags upstairs and let me take the heavy leather harness off the horse.

I led the animal to its watering trough and watched it take long draughts. Old David came to my side and, breathing heavily, told me to go up to the house, where they were waiting for me at lunch.

"I'm not hungry," I said.

Old David shook his head, then scrubbed the moist, steaming hide of the animal. "All morning you have been bringing rice and vegetables from Carmay," he spoke softly to the horse's ear. "Then you are whipped and cursed." He laughed mirthlessly. "*Ay!* It's the life of a horse for you."

From the kitchen window Sepa called me; Father would be angry if I did not eat my lunch on time. I turned and left Old David.

THE KITCHEN HUMMED that night; the stove fires burned bright, and the servants moved briskly about. In the wide yard, under the balete tree, Father's tenants butchered a *carabao*, several pigs, and a goat. The activity in the house, the boisterous laughter of Cousin Andring in the *sala*, where he told stories to Father and the other arrivals, made sleep difficult.

A light flickered in the stable—an old squat building with a rusty tin roof at one end of the yard. It was strange that a light should still be on there, so I went down to look. The door was bolted from the inside. I peeped through a crack and saw the horse prostrate on the sawdust, and Old David sitting on an empty can beside it. He let me in.

"He is very sick," he explained. He watched the beast's dilated nostrils, its dull, rasping breath. He had covered the animal with jute sacks soaked in warm water.

"Will it die?"

He lifted the storm lamp on the ground and looked at me. "There is a limit even to the strength of a horse," he said.

I stayed with him for some time and helped drive away the flies that crawled on the horse's head. He carried pails of boiling water from where the tenants were heating water in big iron vats, and when the water was no longer very warm, he poured it on the jute sacks that covered the animal.

Soon the roosters perched on the guava trees crowed. It was past eleven. "Go to sleep now," Old David told me. "Tomorrow is a big day, and don't let a sick horse worry you." He thanked me and walked with me to the stairs.

Sleep was long in coming. The laughter in the hall, the incessant hammering in the yard, the scurrying feet of servants persisted all through the night. Between brief lapses of sleep I thought I heard the insistent neighing of the horse.

IN THE MORNING more of Father's tenants and their wives and children trooped to town. Under the balete tree a long table made of loose planks and bamboo stands was set. Big chunks of *carabao* meat and pork with green papayas steamed in cauldrons for them. I passed the drinks—gin and *basi*—and played no favorites. To each I gave only a cup.

The tenants never went up to the house where Father's relatives and friends gathered in the *sala* around a big round table laden with our food, fat rolls of *morcon, caldereta, dinardaraan, lechon,* and, from La Granja, *tinto dulce,* sherry, *anisado.*

Before the food was served to the tenants Old David came to me with a big bottle.

"Fill it up," he pleaded.

"You'll get drunk again," I said, knowing I already had given him three cups of gin.

"It's for the horse," he said. "A little alcohol might help it."

I could not refuse the old man.

Before noon, when the food was about to be served to the tenants, the five demijohns under my care were empty. I went to the stable to see how the horse was. It will be better in the morning, Old David had told me the night before. He was still in the stable. His withered face was red, and the bottle of gin I had given him was on the ground, half empty.

"Old David, you drank the wine," I said, angered by his lie.

He nodded and grinned foolishly, his black teeth showing. "It's no use," he said, pointing to the horse that now lay still on the sawdust, its eyes wide open. Several flies were feasting on its eyes, on the streams of saliva that had dried on its mouth. The jute sacks that had covered its brown hide were scattered around.

"Only a while ago," Old David explained, shaking his head.

"Father must know," I said.

"No, not on a day like this. All these people. What will he say?"

"It is his horse," I said. "Tell him."

"It's an old horse, and it was more mine than his," Old David whined. "He never liked it. He had no need for it."

"If I tell him myself, it will not be good for you," I told him.

He stood up and, with wobbly steps, followed me to the house. In the *sala* Father and his guests were already eating. I went to him and told him Old David had something important to say. He beckoned to the old man, who remained standing at the top of the stairs where I had left him. He walked to the table and whispered the news in Father's ear.

"No!" Father exclaimed. He turned to the startled assemblage. "Of all things to happen on my birthday!"

Cousin Andring, who sat near him, bent over and asked, "Not bad news, is it?"

"It is," Father said, but there was no trace of grief in his voice. "My old horse is dead. All the rest the Japanese took. But this. Now it's dead." He turned to the old man. "What did it die of?"

"I don't really know, Apo. Maybe exhaustion."

"I always knew that horse couldn't endure it," Cousin Andring said. "You should have hitched another yesterday, David."

"There is none other," Old David said. He turned to Father. "What shall we do now, Apo?"

Father stroked his chin, exaggerating the gesture. "Well, inasmuch as no one wants to eat the meat of a dead horse, there is only one alternative left. David, you bury the horse."

Father's guests roared.

"Tell us," Father went on when the laughter subsided, "when did it die?"

"Just now, Apo."

"How long have you been tending horses, David?" Cousin Andring asked. "You were not able to cure this one, even with your experience."

"The Apo knows I've been in this household since I was a child. Ever since, I have tended not only horses but also children. One can cure sickness, but death . . ."

"Tell us, then," Cousin Andring leaned forward, his eyes bulging with inspiration, "about your experiences tending horses. God, let us saddle up David and have some fun," he said, turning to our other relatives, all of whom smiled approval.

The old servant moved to the middle of the hall near the table stacked with wine and food. He looked anxiously at Father, but Father was now occupied with the leg of a fried chicken. When he caught Father's eye, Father merely nodded and said, "Go ahead, David. Speak up."

Old David blinked, wiped his bloodshot eyes with his shirtsleeve.

"Here," Cousin Andring said, rising and offering the old man his unfinished glass of Scotch. "You may have had too much, but this is different. It may even refresh your memory."

"Thank you," Old David said. He took the proffered glass and emptied it into the brass flower vase on the table. Again, the bumptious howling.

Cousin Andring relished it. "If you can't tell us about horses, David," he went on, "tell us the story of your life. Anyone who has lived as long as you, and has drunk as much, must have an interesting life."

Old David turned briefly to me, but I could not look at him; I felt dismal and responsible for his predicament. He turned to Father, but again Father nodded.

"My life," he said finally, softly, without the slightest trace of emotion, his red eyes steady on my Cousin Andring, "is like an insect's. So small it can be crushed with the fingers like this." He paused, and with his thumb and forefinger lifted, he made the motions of crushing an imaginary insect.

"Ah, but for an insect—a flea, for instance—you are very durable," Cousin Andring said. The guests smiled.

"Now tell us," Cousin Andring said, "your life as a man, not as a butterfly." More laughter. Cousin Andring beamed. He was apparently enjoying himself.

Old David held the table edge. His voice was calm. "Yes, I'll tell you all." His eyes swept the hall. "I was born here. I knew this place when it was a wilderness, when the creek . . . you'd be surprised—it wasn't wide then. Why, there were some parts of it that one could cross merely by jumping. And the fish . . .

"I have watched young people grow so quickly like the shoots of bamboo. Most of you here, Benito, Antonia, Marcelo—all of you. And I said, someday, maybe, among these fine children, there would be one like their father. You must all revere his name, you whose lips still smell of milk . . ."

"And Carlos Primero!" Cousin Andring roared. Laughter swelled in the hall again.

"There was kindness in the hearts of men," Old David said, undistracted. "I recall similar parties like this, which your grandfather used to give. His servants—us—we did not eat in the yard. We ate with him at his table, and we drank wine from the same cup he used!"

"More wine!" Cousin Andring howled again.

"There was less greed, less faithlessness. Men were brothers—the rich and the poor. It was a day for living, but now the past is forgotten and it can never be relived again even by those who used to belong to it. It was a good time, a time for loving one another, for forgiving one's faults and understanding one's weaknesses. Now the people don't even know what kindness means to a horse . . ."

"Let's drink to the health of the horse," Cousin Andring said. "By God, we'll give that horse a decent funeral, eh, Tio?" Cousin Andring winked at Father.

More laughter. The guests raised their glasses of wine and beer and smacked their lips. Then they fell to eating again, nibbling at drumsticks, reaching for the mountains of prawn and crab on the table.

Old David turned to Father and said in a quavering voice, "I have said enough, Apo."

Father laid the spoon on his plate. "All right, David. We lost all the horses. No, I am not blaming you and your drinking. After all, even horses die. Now, maybe, I'll buy a pickup truck, a jeep, or a car. You can't drive—and even if you can, I won't let you be the driver. What good would you be in the household then?"

"There is still the garden, Apo," Old David said. He bent forward, his arms twitching. "And I can clean the car, wash it every day, till it shines like the bronze studs of the harness. And I can help in the housekeeping. I'll sweep the yard twice a day, Apo. Even the streetfront of the house . . ."

"You are too old for that, David," Father said, smiling wryly.

"And too slow," Tia Antonia chimed in, "and too drunk."

Cousin Andring stood up and faced the old man. "Well," he said, gesturing with his fat hands. "Since you seem to have no more use for David here, we can bring him with us to the city." He turned to Father. "What do you say, Tio? You don't know the trouble with the servants we are having there. You cannot trust anyone except those whom you have known long and well. Tell Tio, Mother, about our last maid who ran off with the houseboy across the street, bringing with her your pearl earrings and some of the silver. David drinks too much, more than he can hold, but . . ."

Tia Antonia nudged Father. "It is true," she said gravely.

"I'd rather stay here, Apo," Old David said, his eyes pleading. "I was born here. I'll die here."

Father grumbled. "Don't worry about dying, David. You'll live to be a hundred. You'll still be around long after we are turned to dust." Father turned to his sister: "I have no objection." Then to the old man, "You'll go, David. Maybe just for half a year—"

"My days are numbered, Apo. I feel it in my bones, in the lungs that are dried in my chest," Old David said.

"Who wants to live forever?" Cousin Andring asked. "Drink, David." He extended another glass of Scotch. "There's more of this where you are going. None of the cheap nipa wine and gin you have here."

But the old man did not even look at my cousin; he turned and shuffled out of the hall.

THE NEXT MORNING the house was quiet again. Several women from Carmay stayed behind, and, after the guests had gone, they swept the yard, then scrubbed the narra floors. The stable was being torn down by the boys. Earlier, the horse had been dragged to the nearby field and buried there.

I lingered in the stable, waiting for Old David to go. He was dressed in his best denim—a little faded on the knees and on the buttocks but still quite new because, unlike his other pair of pants, it was not patched. He watched the planks being torn down. The dirty harnesses cluttered up a corner together with those that he had cleaned, their bronze plates polished to a sheen. His battered bamboo suitcase, lashed tight with abaca twine, was beside him.

"When will you return?" I asked.

His eyes were smoky red as they always were. He gazed at the ground, at the black streaks of molasses, which the boys had carelessly spilled in their hurry to dismantle the stable. Upstairs in the house, Cousin Andring traded parting pleasantries with Father. Then they came noisily down the stairs.

"Must you really go?" I asked the old man again.

Old David's voice was hollow and distant. "So it must be. This is the time for leaving. Just as there was a time for beginning, planting, growing. I watched them all grow—your uncles, your father—all of them. Your grandfather—he was a spirited young man. I remember how he dared his father's wrath, how he would flee to the forest with me in search of game. We swam the swollen creek together, even when logs hurtled down with the current. Ay, he was not born to the wilderness, but he defeated me in almost every contest except running. We would race to the edge of the river, but my legs—they were young and agile then, and they always carried me there first. He could shoot straight with the bow or with a gun. But he died, too." A long pause. "Then your father—I would carry him perched on my shoulders, just like you. I used to drive him around, just the two of us, in the *calesa* to Calanutan and Carmay. I remember we spilled out once when the wheel fell into a deep rut and broke. I carried him to town on my shoulders, and never once did I put him down. Balungao it was, and that's five kilometers away."

"You are drunk again," I said.

He dug his big toe into the sawdust and shook his head. "Ay—I knew them all. I watched them grow into big men, learned men. But no one lives forever—that's what your cousin said. I can die here, where I saw them all grow. There is nothing like the land you belong to claiming you back. But everywhere the earth is the same."

Father, his hands on the shoulders of Tia Antonia and Cousin Andring, walked idly to the gate where the jeep was parked. The servants were loading it with vegetables, two sacks of rice, chicken, and bunches of green bananas.

Cousin Andring turned to us. "And why isn't David moving yet?" he shouted. "Is he drunk again?"

The old man stood up and tried lifting his valise, but it was cumbersome. I grasped its lashing at one end, and we carried it to the jeep.

"Does he have to bring all that junk to the city?" Cousin Andring asked, looking apprehensively at the jeep that was now overloaded. "I'll bet anything it's all bottles of nipa wine. A year's ration, that's what."

Father smiled. "Let him," he said.

"Hurry, David," Cousin Andring urged the old man, "we'll miss the train."

We raised the suitcase, but the old man's hold was not firm enough and the trunk fell. I stepped aside lithely just in time to avoid being hit by it. Its lashing broke, and out spilled his things—an old prayer book, his clothes, a leather case in which he kept his betel nuts, and a bottle of nipa wine. The bottle broke when it hit the ground, and its contents were spilled.

Tia Antonia buckled over laughing, but Cousin Andring was angry. "God," he cursed, "can't you be more careful, David?"

Pushing the old man aside, he picked up his things and dumped them into the open suitcase, then heaved everything into the jeep.

Old David's face was pale and expressionless. He was the last to board the vehicle, and as it started, he turned briefly to me. I could not tell whether what glistened on his cheeks was beads of sweat or tears.

CHAPTER

16

SHORTLY AFTER Old David left to serve in Tia Antonia's house in the city, I, too, had to pack my bags. I always knew that someday, after I finished high school, I would proceed to Manila and to college. In my younger days I had looked ahead to the event, but when the moment finally came, leaving Rosales filled me with a nameless dread and a great, numbing unhappiness. Maybe it was friendship—huge and granitelike—or just plain sympathy. I could not be too sure anymore. Maybe I fell in love for the first time when I was fifteen.

Her name was Teresita. She was a stubborn girl with many fixed ideas, and she admonished me once: "Just because you have so much to give does not mean it will all be accepted. Just like that. There's more to giving than just giving."

She was sixteen then, and looking at her made me think of moments bright and beautiful, of the banaba in bloom.

I did not expect her to be vexed when I brought her a dress, for it was not really expensive. Besides, as the daughter of one of Father's tenants, she knew me well enough, better perhaps than any of the people who lived in Carmay, the young folks who always greeted me politely, doffed their straw hats, then closed-mouthed went their way.

I always had coins in my pockets, but that March afternoon, after counting all of them and the stray pieces that I had tucked away in my dresser, I knew I needed more.

I approached Father. He was at his working table, writing on a ledger, while behind him one of the new servants stood erect swinging a palm-leaf fan over his head. I stood beside him, watching him scrawl the figures on the ledger, his wide brow and his shirt damp with sweat. When he finally noticed me, I could not tell him what I wanted. He unbuttoned his shirt down to his paunch. "Well, what is it?"

"I'm going to take my classmates this afternoon to the restaurant, Father," I said.

He turned to the sheaf of papers before him. "Yes," he said. "You can tell Chan Hai to take off from his rent this month what you and your friends can eat."

I lingered uneasily, avoiding the servant's eyes.

"Well, won't that do?" Father asked.

It was March, and the high school graduation was but a matter of days away. "I also need some money, Father," I said. "I have to buy something."

Father nodded. He groped for his keys in his drawer, then he opened the iron money box beside him, drew out a ten-peso bill, and laid it on the table.

"I'm going to buy—" I tried to explain, but with a wave of his hand he dismissed me and went back to his figures.

It was getting late. After feeding the hogs, Sepa was getting the chickens to the coops. I hurried down the stairs to the main road, which was quiet and deserted now except in the vicinity of the round cement embankment in front of the *municipio,* where the town loafers were taking in the stale afternoon sun.

The Chinese storekeepers who occupied Father's building had lighted their lamps. From the ancient artesian well at the rim of the town plaza, the water carriers and servant girls babbled while they waited for their turn at the pump. Nearby, traveling merchants had unhitched their bull carts after a whole day of slow travel from town to town and were cooking their supper on broad blackened stones that littered the place. At Chan Hai's store there was a boy with a stick of candy in his mouth, a couple of men drinking beer and smacking their lips portentously, and a woman haggling over a can of sardines.

I went to the huge bales of cloth that slumped in one corner and picked out the white silk cloth with glossy printed flowers. I asked Chan Hai, who was perched on a stool smoking his long pipe, how much he would ask for the material I had picked for a gown.

Chan Hai peered at me in surprise. "Ten pesos," he said.

With the package, I hurried to Carmay. Dusk was falling very fast, the leaves of the acacias had folded, and the solemn, mellow chime of the Angelus echoed to the flat stretches of the town. The women who had been sweeping their yards paused. Children reluctantly hurried to their homes, for now the town was draped with a dreamy stillness.

Teresita and her father lived by the creek in Carmay. Their house sat on a sandy lot that belonged to Father, set apart from the cluster of huts of the village. Its roof, as it was with the other farmhouses, was thatched and disheveled, its walls were battered buri leaves. It stood alone near the gully that had been widened to let the bull carts and *calesas* through when the bridge was washed away. Madre de cacao trees abounded in the vicinity but offered scanty shade. Piles of burnt rubbish rose in little mounds in the yard, and a disrupted line of ornamental San Francisco ringed the house.

Teresita was in the kitchen, sampling the broth of what she was cooking. There was a dampness on her brow and a redness in her eyes.

"What are you doing here at this hour?" she confronted me. In the glow of the crackling stove fire, she looked genuinely surprised.

I could not tell her at once or show her what I brought.

"I wanted to see you," I said, which was true.

"But it's already late, and you have to walk quite a long way back." She laid down the ladle on the table and looked puzzled. She must have noticed then that I was hiding something behind me.

"What do you have there?" she asked, moving toward me.

I laid my package on the wooden table cluttered with battered tin plates and vegetables.

"It's for you," I said. My face burned like kindling wood. "I hope you'll like it."

Her eyes still on me, she opened the package. When she saw what it was, she gave a tiny, muffled cry. She shook her head, wrapped the package again, then gave it to me. "I can't," she said softly. "It does not seem right at all."

"But you need it, and I'm giving it to you," I said firmly. The burning in my face had subsided. "Is there anything wrong with giving one a gift?"

And that was when she said, "There are things you just can't give like what you are doing now . . ."

I THINK it all started that evening when we were in the third year and Teresita recited a poem. It was during the graduation exercises, and she was the only junior in the program. I cannot remember distinctly what the piece was about, except that she spoke of faith and love, and how suffering and loss could be borne with fortitude, and as she did, a clamminess gripped me, smothered me with a feeling I'd never felt before. I recall her resonant voice cleaving the hushed evening, and I was silently one with her.

I did not go home immediately after the program, for a dance in honor of the graduates followed. Miss Santillan, who was in charge of the refreshments, had asked me to help Teresita in serving them. I sat on one of the school benches after I got tired, watching the dancers file in and out, giggling. When most of them had eaten, Teresita asked Miss Santillan for permission to leave.

"My father, ma'am," she said. "He doesn't want me to stay out very late, because of my cough. Besides, I have work to do early tomorrow."

"Going home alone?" Miss Santillan asked.

"I'm not afraid," she said resolutely.

I stood up, strode past the table laden with an assortment of trays and glasses. Beyond the window, a moon dangled over the sprawling school buildings like a huge sieve, and the world was pulsating and young.

"I'll walk with you," I said.

She protested at first, but Miss Santillan said it would be best if I went along. After Miss Santillan had wrapped up some cakes for her, we went down the stone steps. The evening was clean and cool like a newly washed sheet, and it engulfed us with an intimacy that seemed unreal and elusive. We did not speak for some time.

"I live very far," she reminded me, drawing a shabby shawl over her thin shoulders.

"I know," I told her. "I've been there."

"You'll be very tired."

"I've walked longer distances. I can take Carmay in a run," I said, trying to impress her.

"I'm sure of that," she said. "You are strong. Once I was washing in the river, and you were swimming with Angel, and you outraced him."

"I did not see you," I said.

"Of course," she said, "you never notice the children of your tenants, except those who serve in your house."

I was so upset that I could not speak at once. "That is not true," I objected. "I go to Carmay often."

She must have realized that she had hurt me, for when she spoke again she sounded genuinely sorry. "That was not what I meant, and I didn't say that to spite you."

Again, silence.

The moon drifted out of the clouds in a sudden smudge of silver, lighting up the dusty road. It glimmered on the parched fields and on the giant buri palms that stood like hooded sentinels. Most of the houses we passed had long extinguished their kerosene lamps. Once in a while a dog stirred in its bed of dust and growled at us.

"You won't be afraid going home alone?" she asked after a while.

"There is a giant *capre* in the balete tree that comes out when the moon is full," I said. "I'd like to see it. I've never seen a ghost."

"When I die," she laughed, "I'll appear before you."

"You'll be a good ghost, and I won't be afraid," I said.

We walked on. We talked about ourselves, the friends that we ought to have had but did not. We reached the edge of the village where the row of homes receded and finally her house, near the river that murmured as it cut a course through reeds and shallows.

When we went up to the house, her father was already asleep. In fact he was snoring heavily. At the door she bade me good night and thanked me. Then, slowly, she closed the door behind her.

So the eventful year passed, and the rains came on time. The fields became green, and the banabas in the streets blossomed. The land became soggy, and the winds lashed at Rosales severely, bowling over a score of flimsy huts that stood on bamboo stilts. Our house did not tremble in the mightiest typhoon. With us, nothing changed. The harvest with its usual bustle passed, the tenants—among them Teresita's father—filled our spacious *bodega* with their crops. The drab, dry season with its choking dust settled oppressively, and then it was March—time for Teresita and me to graduate.

Throughout the hot afternoon, we rehearsed our parts for the graduation program. We would march to the platform to receive our high school diplomas, then return solemnly to our seats. When the sham was over, Teresita and I rested on the crude benches lined before the stage.

She said softly, "I will not attend the graduation exercises. I can feign illness. I can say I had a fever or my cough got worse, which is the truth, anyway."

"Why?"

"No one would miss me in the march if I don't come."

"You are foolish," I said.

"I can't have my picture, too, I'm sure."

"I don't believe you."

"I can't come. I just can't," she repeated with finality.

She did not have to say anything more. I understood, and that afternoon I asked for money from Father to buy a graduation dress for Teresita.

And that same week Father ordered Teresita's father, who farmed a lot in the delta in Carmay, to vacate the place, as Father had sold it. Teresita's father had to settle in the hills of Balungao, where there were small vacant parcels, arable patches on the otherwise rocky mountainside. There he might literally scratch the earth to eke out a living.

April, and a hot glaring sun filtered through the dusty glass shutters and formed dazzling puddles on the floor. The dogs that lolled in the shade of the balete tree stuck out their tongues and panted. The smudges of grass in the plaza were a stubbly brown. The sky was cloudless and azure. Sepa told me to see Father, who had something important to tell me.

He was in the *azotea* reading the papers and fanning himself vigorously. The question he asked stunned me. "When do you want to leave for the city?"

For some time I could not say a word. The school vacation had just started, and the school opening was still two months away. "It's only April, Father," I finally said.

"I know," he said. "But I want you to get well acquainted with your cousins there."

Heat waves rose, shimmering in the street, swallowed up by the dust that fluffed high when a jeepney passed. Father's voice: "You will grow older." He hammered this notion into me. "You will grow older and realize how important—this thing that I'm doing. You will leave many faces here. You will outgrow boyish whims. In the city you'll meet new friends."

I did not speak.

"The time will come when you will return to me—a man."

"Yes, Father," I said as he, having spoken, went on with his reading.

THE DARK came quickly. The sun sank behind the coconut groves of Tomana and disappeared below the jagged horizon. Before darkness fell, I left the house and journeyed to where the houses were decrepit, where children were clad most of the time in unkempt rags and, when a stranger would stumble into their midst, they would gape at him with awe. Beyond the cluster of homes came the barking of dogs stirring in the dust.

I went up the ladder that squeaked, and when Teresita's father recognized me in the light of the flickering kerosene lamp hanging from a rafter, a shadow of a scowl crept into his leathery face. Even when I said, "Good evening," his sullen countenance remained. He returned my greeting coldly, then went down and left us alone.

"I'm leaving," I began. Teresita was washing the dishes and now she wiped the soap suds from her hands. "I'll go to the city tomorrow to study. Father is sending me there."

She said nothing—she just looked at me. She turned and walked to the window that opened to the banks of the river and the fields.

"We'll soon leave, too," she murmured, her hands on the windowsill. "Your father sold this place, you know," she said without emotion.

"I'm very sad."

"There is nothing to be sad about."

"Yes, there is," I said. "Many things."

She remained by the window. Outside, the night was alive with crickets.

"Won't you go to school anymore?" I asked after a while. She did not reply, and I did not prod her for an answer.

"What course are you going to take?" she asked.

"I'm not very sure," I said. "Maybe I'll follow your advice."

"Please do," she said. "Please be a doctor." With conviction, "You can do so much if you are one."

I did not know what else to say.

"Don't write to me when you are there," she said.

"But I will."

"Nothing will happen," she insisted. "Besides, it will not be necessary. Thank you very much for coming to see me."

"I have to," I said.

She followed me to the door. The bamboo floor creaked under me. She called my name as I stepped down the first rung, and I turned momentarily to catch one last glimpse of her young, fragile face, and on it a smile, half-born, half-free.

"Please don't write," she reiterated, raising her hand. "It's useless, you know."

"But I will," I said, and in my heart I cried, "I will, I will!"

"I'd be happier, and so would Father, if you didn't," she said. "And besides, I wouldn't be able to answer your letters. Stamps cost—"

"I'll send you some," I said.

The smile fled from her face. "You cannot buy everything," she said.

I headed for the gate. The children who played nearby stopped and looked at us. And in the other houses, though it was very dark, I knew the farmers and their wives watched me leave, knowing how it was going to be with us, how I would leave Teresita and thus make Father happy, how I would forget everything—the orchids I gave her that now adorned her window and that, I am sure, would someday wither, the books I lent her, which she rapaciously read, the eager laughter that welled from the depths of her. I would forget, too, how we hummed to the music of the town's brass band and walked one sultry night from the high school to Carmay.

The night was vast and the stars were hidden by clouds. In the blackness I could not see banabas along the path, but I could imagine the purple of their blooms.

CHAPTER

17

O N T H E M O R N I N G that I left, Sepa came and thrust into my hand pieces of *pan de sal* with coconut syrup. The syrup had oozed, and the paper bag with which she had wrapped the bread was soiled.

"For the trip," she said, attempting a smile.

I went down to the yard, where one of the boys had the jeep waiting. The air was heady, compounded with the clean tang of morning. The sun was mild, and one could drink it and never feel that the body was full. It touched the fading grass and gave it a tinge of jade. It glinted, too, in the leaves of the coconut palms and transformed them into a thousand blades gleaming and unsheathed. It was a beautiful day, but not for me.

Father was at the gate. When I kissed his hand, he held my chin up and said: "You'll be all right in the city. But that's not important. It's the learning that counts, and the growing up."

He dug out his gold watch from his waist pocket. "You have plenty of time," he said. "Now listen. You are young and you don't know many things, but do remember this: you are alone on this earth. Alone. You must act for yourself and no other. Kindness is not appreciated anymore, nor friendship. Think of yourself before you think of others. It's a cruel world, and you have to be hard and cruel, too. They will strangle you if you don't strangle them first. Trust no one but your judgment—and even then don't trust too much."

He laid a hand on my shoulder and smiled wanly. "Son," he whispered. He had not spoken the word in a long, long time. "Be good."

I wanted to fling my arms around his neck, tell him that I loved him, but my throat was dry. I only said, "I'll remember, Father."

I boarded the jeep, and we drove out into the street. I did not look back.

It was early evening when I reached Tutuban Station. The jostling crowd in the giant, gloomy building baffled me, but I had no difficulty because Cousin Andring was on the platform to greet me. When we emerged into the lobby, Old David came forward from the nameless phalanx of people. He had aged so much. I did not want him to carry my suitcase, but his grip was strong and determined.

We hurried to Cousin Andring's jeep, which was parked outside the station, then we drove off to the suburbs. The long trip did not tire me, but in the jeep, watching the brilliant neon lights and the depressing huddle of tall buildings, I felt lost and tired.

My first days in the city were restless and uneventful. In the mornings, I'd wander around the shops or see a movie. I'd return to their house in Santa Mesa shortly before lunchtime. Tia Antonia seldom talked with me, and Old David did not have the time, either, for he was always busy in the garage or in the garden. I imagine that he purposely avoided me and busied himself whenever I went near.

Tia Antonia's children—since most of them were already grown-up—were correct but not friendly, and, if they talked with me at all, they asked the most asinine questions.

I was very glad when, one morning, Cousin Pedring telephoned and said he would come in the afternoon to pick me up, so that I could stay in his house in Cubao until classes started. It had been ages since I saw him last, when he and Clarissa got married, and I was very glad he had not forgotten.

He had changed a lot. His girth was wider and so was his forehead. Clarissa, too, looked different from the young girl I used to know. Her cheeks were plump, and she moved about with a matriarchal dignity rather than the gay sprightliness that was her. She had three children now, the youngest a darling girl about two years old. Clarissa hummed incessantly as she prepared the supper table.

In the early evening Cousin Pedring and I got to talking about the old times, and we would have talked far into the night if he did not have a poker session with friends. He kissed Clarissa at the door, as if he were going on a long journey.

I was alone with her, and as she served me a second helping of ice cream we talked about Rosales and how it was. "That was the most beautiful wedding I have ever seen," I said, recalling theirs.

"In a short time yours, too, will come," she said. "And then you'll be raising your own family. But you men never know the trouble women go through."

I remembered the secret I had kept and decided that now was the time to get it off my chest.

"It was good you came to Rosales that vacation," I said. "I don't know what would have happened if you hadn't come."

"What do you think would have happened?" Her eyes lighted up.

I remember the letters postmarked Cebu, which I showed Father first, then burned. "Well," I said, "you might have ended up marrying that fellow from Cebu and not Pedring."

"Why do you say that?" she asked, the laughter drained from her.

"After all, he wrote to you so many times when you were in Rosales. He was very insistent, you know."

"He did write to me?" She was incredulous.

"Yes," I said. "But you never knew it, did you? Father told me never to tell you. As a matter of fact, I burned the letters myself."

Her face became blank. "And I thought all along he had decided to forget. I was all wrong," she mumbled, a faraway look in her eyes. And then her head drooped, and her body shook with silent sobs.

"Clarissa." I went to her. "Is there anything wrong?"

She kept sobbing for some time, and I stood before her, not knowing what to do. She looked up at me and hurriedly wiped her tears.

"Tell me," I said. "Does Pedring beat you?"

A smile bloomed again. "Foolish!" she said, rising from her chair. She tweaked my ear. "Of course, he treats me well. He doesn't beat me at all. Whoever gave you that idea?"

"Why are you crying, then?"

"You don't understand," she said. "You are too young."

"Tell me," I urged her. "I won't tell your secret."

She turned away. A trace of sadness lined her voice. "I was thinking of all those letters . . . and it seems as if it was only yesterday . . ."

"You've not grown up," I said, but she did not hear, for the baby had started crying and she rushed to the crib, baby talk gushing from her lips.

THEN JUNE, and I was in college at last, engrossed with botany, zoology, chemistry, and a host of other subjects for preparatory medicine. College was an exhilarating experience, and for a time the old nagging aches were soothed and I was immersed in new interests.

Until one October afternoon: I was in the college cafeteria drinking Coke, when one of my classmates rushed to me white-faced and asked if I had seen the evening paper.

I shook my head. He thrust the front page in front of me and asked if the photograph before me was that of Father.

I could not believe what I read, how he was brought out of our house the evening before by men who were armed. The soldiers had gone after his kidnappers, so the paper reported, but they had returned empty-handed.

I rushed to the dormitory, and at the lobby I met the father dean. He must have read the story, too, and had come to tell me about it. He held my shoulders, and his cool blue eyes gazed into mine.

"You have to be brave," he said.

I went to my room and shut the door. No tears came; a tightness gripped my chest, and I could not breathe. I lay on my cot and could not think.

At dusk Cousin Marcelo and Tia Antonia came mouthing platitudes. "Maybe," they said, "the men did not harm him." Cousin Pedring came, too, with Clarissa. He said he would leave for Rosales the following morning.

I did not go down for supper. My roommate came in shortly before lights-out and brought me a glass of warm milk and crackers.

AFTER THREE DAYS, Cousin Pedring came, the grime of travel still on his face. There was no news at all about Father. Then, after a week, a tenant stumbled upon Father in the delta. He had died terribly, said Cousin Marcelo, who came with the news. The body bore more than a dozen bolo wounds. The day they found Father, they buried him beside Mother's grave.

"You do not have to go home," Cousin Marcelo said. "There's nothing you can do now."

"But I'm going home," I told him, suddenly aware that it was now my duty to look after his ledgers, the farm. "I'd like to look at the papers."

"Yes, of course," Cousin Marcelo said. "Now you have to study a lot of things and make decisions." He looked ruefully at me. "And you . . . so young and not even through with school."

But it would not do for me to stay in Rosales anymore; everywhere I would turn, there would always be something familiar, yet alien.

"You'll be free now," Cousin Marcelo said. "You must not be like your father. He was a slave to what he owned. You must begin again—that is most important."

Words meant not to be heard, a few drops of rain on parched ground.

WE ARRIVED at the station at dusk. No one met us but the baggage boys, who recognized me at once. They gathered around, and one got hold of my canvas bag, while another hurried down the platform to hail a *calesa*. They did not speak much.

Even the *calesa* driver did not speak until we were close to home. Cousin Marcelo placed a *salapi* in his palm, and as we got down, he turned to me and said he was sorry about what had happened. Sepa could not contain herself when she saw me coming up the stairs. She waddled down and exclaimed: "You are so tall!" Then she broke down and cried. Cousin Marcelo held her shoulder, then freed me from her. I did not cry; for a long time now I have not tasted the salt of tears. Darkness fell quickly, and since it was too late to go to the cemetery, I hastened to my old room and unpacked.

The supper that Sepa prepared was excellent—roasted eggplant, crab and meat stew—but I had no appetite. I went to the *azotea.* Sepa followed me; she had lighted her hand-rolled cigar.

"Tell me," I asked after some silence. "What has become of the people in Carmay? Who did it? Surely you have an idea."

"I do not know," she said feebly. She leaned on the *azotea* ledge and turned away. "I'm just an old, worthless woman imprisoned in the kitchen. All I know is this: death hides now, not only in the delta but in Carmay as well."

"Will they kill me, too?"

"Drive the thought away," the old woman said. "You are young and good, and you have no enemies."

"And Father was old and bad and he had a hundred?"

Sepa flung her cigar away. In the soft dark I could make out her face. Her voice was sharp, "Your father was good. He was not seen clearly, that's all. Now don't let such thoughts grow lush in your mind. Drive them away quickly."

Silence again.

"Tell me, what has happened to the people in Carmay?"

"There are a hundred people there," she said, "and all of them are still alive." Then she must have guessed what I wanted to know. "You are asking about Teresita?"

"I wrote to her many times," I said. "She never answered. Not even once."

"She died last month," Sepa said softly. She shifted her weight on the ledge. "The old sickness in her family . . ."

I could not speak for some time. The old woman prattled on: "It wasn't much of a funeral. I wanted someone to write a letter to you, but I couldn't find anyone I could trust."

"Maybe," I said after another uneasy silence, "it's better this way. She won't suffer anymore."

Sepa grunted: "Yes, death is a blessing. People who grow old should remember that. How is David?"

"I didn't see him when I left," I said. "Tia Antonia must be taking good care of him. He's well, I suppose. I visited Tia Antonia often. But Old David, he always seemed busy. He avoided me. At first, it was difficult; I couldn't understand. I do now."

She grunted again.

"You have no news about Angel? Where is he now?"

"He's lost," Sepa said without emotion. "He is a soldier. But he is no problem, really, the way she is."

"Who?" I asked, leaning over to hear her every word.

"Your father's woman. It must be very sad, being cooped up in that house by the river, unable to show her face . . ."

"How did you know?" I asked. Sepa did not answer; she stood up shaking her head and left me to the night.

Morning came to Rosales in a flood of sunlight. I woke up, a stranger to my old room but not to the happy sounds of morning, the barking of dogs in the street and the cackling of hens in the yard. Cousin Marcelo was in the *sala*, waiting.

"I know my way to the cemetery," I said.

He pressed my arm. "All right then, if you want to go alone. But be sure to be back as soon as you can. We have many things to talk about. You are an heir, remember."

Breakfast was waiting. I took a small cup of chocolate, then went down to the street. Day was clear, and the sky was swept clean and blue with but wisps of clouds pressed flat against its rim. The banabas along the road seemed greener maybe because my eyes had so long been dulled by the dirty browns and grays of the city. Housewives were hanging their wash in their yards, and their half-naked children played in the street, their runny noses outlined in dirt. The day smelled good with the witchery of October, the tingling sun. Tomorrow, it would probably rain.

It was a long walk to the cemetery. The morning etched clearly all the white crosses and the gumamela shrubs that the grave watchers tended. I walked through narrow paths between the tombs, past the small chapel in the center of the cemetery, beyond which was Mother's tomb, and now Father's, too.

A woman was bent before the white slab of stone, and, as she turned I caught a view of her face. I was not mistaken—it was Father's woman. When she saw me, she stood up and walked swiftly away. I followed her with my eyes, until she disappeared behind a sprout of cogon that hid the road.

I went to the tomb and picked up the bouquet she had left—a simple bundle of sampaguitas—then placed it back on the slab. It was not yet completely dry, and the gray cement that the masons had left unleavened still cluttered the base.

I remembered my first visit, Father's quavering voice again: Nena, I've brought your son to you now that he is old enough.

I MUST SEE HER, tell her it's useless harboring ill will. I hurried from the warren of white crosses and headed for the river, down a gully, and along the riverbed until I came to another gully beyond where she lived.

The footpath was widened by *carabaos* that went down to the river to bathe, and beyond the bank was her house. It looked shabby from the outside, with its grass roof and buri walls already bleached and battered. A bamboo gate was at the end of the narrow path. I pushed it open.

Within the yard, I called: "Man. There's a man. Good morning."

No answer. I went up the bamboo stairs. From the half-open door I could see the narrow living room furnished with three rattan chairs, a coffee table with crocheted doilies, and some magazines. A Coleman lamp dangled from the beam above the room. In a corner was a table clock and a sewing machine. A vase with wilted gumamelas was on a mahogany dresser near the open window.

"Man. There's a man," I repeated. Still no answer.

In the room that adjoined the *sala*, someone stirred.

"Please," I said, rapping on the bamboo post by the door, "I have to see you. I wanted to talk with you at the cemetery, but you left so quickly."

A shuffle of feet, then she flung the door open and I saw her—not she who was gay and laughing but a tired and unhappy woman, her eyes swollen from crying. Her hair, which would have looked elegant if it were combed, cascaded down her shoulders. She was dressed in a dark shapeless blouse. From her neck dangled a red bead necklace whose medallion of polished gold rested in the valley of her bosom.

"What do you want?" she asked, glaring at me. Then recognition came, and the annoyance in her face vanished.

"You are his son," she said simply.

"I want to talk with you," I said.

She came to me. "Why did you come? You don't have to. It is not necessary."

"I have to," I said. "Maybe, because we both lost someone. Maybe . . ."

"But you didn't love him," she said, looking straight at me.

I was too surprised to answer.

"I suspected it all along," she said sadly. "Many did not like him, and I wouldn't blame his only son for feeling the same way. Sometimes blood isn't really enough."

"You are wrong," I said. Coherent speech was mine again. "I respected him."

"Respected him! What a difference!"

I did not know how to argue with her; she did not give me a chance.

"Let me tell you," she said hastily. "He was not good and he was not kind, and that is why they killed him. But he had virtues, and he was really good in his own way. Not many understood, but I did, and that's why—" She brought the handkerchief to her eyes and started sobbing. She slumped on one of the chairs, her body shaking with her sobs.

"Please don't cry," I said.

She dropped the handkerchief on her lap and turned to me. "He loved you," she said. "He used to talk so much about you."

"That's not true," I said, unable to hold it back any longer. "That's not true at all!"

"*Ay!*" She sighed. She rose and walked to the window. "If only we know the things that are hidden in the hearts of others, the world wouldn't be such a sad place." Outside, the sunshine was a silver flood. The birds on the grass roof twittered.

"He never cared for me," I said plainly. "He tried to but—"

"But he did! And you call him Father! You didn't even understand him!" she exclaimed. "You were very close to him, and you didn't even know how he felt! And here I was, seeing him only once or twice a week, and I knew so many things. But maybe it's because I'm a woman. I do know! You have to believe it now that he's dead. We could have gotten married, lived together. He loved you, and he said he failed you because of me and many other things that he had to do, although he didn't want to. The death of this Baldo, his help-lessness before your Don Vicente. All these he told me and blamed himself. How will you ever understand? You have to be a man . . ."

There was nothing for me to say.

"How old are you?" she asked.

"Seventeen."

"So young," she said, "so very young!"

I gazed out of the window, at the caved banks of the river. "I'll be leaving, maybe tomorrow," I said.

She came to me again and held my arm lightly. We walked to the door. A breeze stirred the tall cogon grass that surrounded the house.

"What will you do now?" I asked.

She bit her lower lip, and when she looked at me, resignation was on her face. "What can I do?"

"You'll stay here?"

Her voice was dry: "Yes. Where will I go? To the city, like you? I've been there. You are thinking perhaps that if I leave I can start anew? I ask you: what for?"

She left me at the door and walked to her dresser. Before the oval mirror she examined her face, her swollen eyes. She was beautiful, even though grief had distorted her face.

"If there is anything you need, you can go to the house, to my Cousin Marcelo. I'll tell him to give you everything you need."

She turned quickly to me. "No," she said sharply. "No, thank you. I don't think I'll ever go there. I've some pride, you know."

"I want to help."

"You can't," she said, trying to smile. "Thank you for the thought. I am ashamed, that's all. But not with him. Only in the beginning. Then I wasn't ashamed anymore, even when I felt a hundred eyes stab me in the market, in church; one gets used to it. The skin thick-ens with the years." Fresh tears welled in her eyes. "But believe me, with him I was not ashamed. Never. Maybe I loved him deeply, al-though that didn't seem possible."

"Please, don't cry," I said.

She daubed her eyes. "Well, you see me crying now, but I will stop. I'll powder my face and comb my hair, then go out. And should another man come up that path, do you expect me to shut the door?"

I did not answer. I turned and stepped down the stairs into the blinding sunlight.

SO IT MUST BE; I left Rosales, relegating that town to a sweet oblivion in the mind. I left behind people who should not intrude into the peace that, I thought, I could build and reinforce with a wealth of means that is mine by inheritance.

I have lived in pleasant solitude, breathed God's pure air, and wallowed in sybaritic comfort, although, occasionally, I do think about those who were around me, and do feel deeply about the travail of my youth. But I see their anguish as something caused by human cussedness itself, that this is man's certitude and destiny— irrevocable, final—that one cannot make anything different from it any more than I can stir ashes back to life.

Yet, much as I am sure of these, I also know that the present, this now, is yesterday, and anything and everything that I find detestable are outgrowths of something equally detestable in this not-so-distant past.

I wish I could be honest and true, but truth as I see it is not something abstract, a pious generality—it is justice at work, righteous, demanding, disciplined, sincere, and unswerving; otherwise, it is not, it cannot be truth at all.

But the past was not permanent, nor is the present—who was it who said you cannot cross the river twice? Motion, change, birth, and death—these are the imperatives (what a horrible, heavy word!) of life.

I SOMETIMES pass by Rosales and see that so little has changed. The people are the same, victims of their own circumstance as Old David, Angel, Ludovico, and even Father had all been. God, should I think and feel, or should I just plod on and forget? I know in the depths of me that I'll always remember, and I am not as tough as they were. Nor do I have the humor and the zest to cope as Tio Marcelo did, looking at what I see not as an apocalypse but as revelation; as he said once, paraphrasing a Spanish poet, he was born on a day that God was roaring drunk.

I think that I was born on a day God was fast asleep. And whatever happened after my birth was nothing but dreamless ignorance. But there was a waking that traumatized, a waking that also trivialized, because in it, the insolence and the nastiness of human nature became commonplace and I grew up taking all these as inevitable. In the end, the satisfaction that all of us seek, it seems, can come only from our discovering that we really have molded our lives into whatever we want them to be. In my failure to do this, I could have taken the easy way out, but I have always been too much of a coward to covet my illusions rather than dispel them.

I continue, for instance, to hope that there is reward in virtue, that those who pursue it should do so because it pleases them. This then becomes a very personal form of ethics, or belief, premised on pleasure. It would require no high-sounding motivation, no philosophical explanation for the self, and its desires are animal, basic— the desire for food, for fornication. If this be the case, then we could very well do away with the church, with all those institutions that pretend to hammer into the human being attributes that would make him inherit God's vestments, if not His kingdom.

But what kind of man is he who will suffer for truth, for justice, when all the world knows that it is the evil and the grasping who succeed, who flourish, whose tables are laden, whose houses are palaces? Surely he who sacrifices for what is just is not of the common breed or of an earthly shape. Surely there must be something in him that should make us beware, for since he is dogged and stubborn as compared with the submissive many, he will question not just the pronouncements of leaders but the leaders themselves. He may even opt for the more demanding decision, the more difficult courses of action. In the end, we may see him not just as selfless but as the epitome of that very man whom autocrats would like to have on their side, for this man has no fear of heights, of gross temptations, and of death itself.

Alas, I cannot be this man, although sometimes I aspire to be like him. I am too much a creature of comfort, a victim of my past. Around me the largesse of corruption rises as titles of vaunted power, and I am often in the ranks of princes, smelling the perfume of their office. I glide in the dank, nocturnal caverns that are their mansions and gorge on their sumptuous food, and I love it all, envy them even for the ease with which they live without remorse, without regret even though they know (I suspect they do) that to get to this lofty status, they had to butcher—perhaps not with their own hands—their own hapless countrymen.

Today I see young men packed off to a war that's neither their making nor their choice, and I recall Angel, who is perhaps long dead, joining the Army not because he was a patriot but because there was no other way. So it has not changed really, how in another war in another time, young men have died believing that it was their duty to defend these blighted islands. It may well be, but the politicians and the generals—they live as weeds always will—accumulating wealth and enjoying the land the young have died to defend. This is how it was, and this is how it will be.

Who was Don Vicente, after all? I should not be angered then, when men in the highest places, sworn to serve this country as public servants, end up as millionaires in Pobres Park, while using the people's money in the name of beauty, the public good, and all those shallow shibboleths about discipline and nationalism that we have come to hear incessantly. I should not shudder anymore in disgust or contempt when the most powerful people in the land use the public coffers for their foreign shopping trips or build ghastly fascist monuments in the name of culture or of the Filipino spirit. I see artists—even those who cannot draw a hand or a face—pass themselves off as modernists and demand thousands of pesos for their work, which, of course, equally phony art patrons willingly give. And I remember Tio Marcelo—how he did not hesitate to paint *calesas* and, in his later years, even jeepneys, so that his work would be seen and used, and not be a miser's gain in some living room to be viewed by people who may not know what art is. I hear politicians belching the same old clichés, and I remember Tio Doro and how he spent his own money for his candidacy and how he had bowed to the demands of change. When I see justice sold to the highest bidder I remember Tio Baldo and how he lost. So honesty, then, and service are rewarded by banishment, and people sell themselves without so much ado because they have no beliefs—only a price.

I would like to see all this as a big joke that is being played upon us, but I have seen what was wrought in the past—the men who were destroyed without being lifted from the dung heap of poverty, without recourse to justice.

But like my father, I have not done anything. I could not, because I am me, because I died long ago.

Who, then, lives? Who, then, triumphs when all others have succumbed? The balete tree—it is there for always, tall and leafy and majestic. In the beginning, it sprang from the earth as vines coiled around a sapling. The vines strangled the young tree they had embraced. They multiplied, fattened, and grew, became the sturdy trunk, the branches spread out to catch the sun. And beneath this tree, nothing grows!

Baguio
October 26, 1977

My Brother,
My Executioner

CALVARIA

Luis Asperri

I

This is the beginning—
We started here and followed them,
They who had their backs to us,
They who began here, too,
Who cut the trees and uprooted weeds.

We prepared the fallow earth
And planted the seed
And all that had to be done is done.

They will also begin here—
They whose faces are young still,
Whose deeds we cannot know.
Will they also end here
Like all of us, without meaning?

II

Land without change, claim me now—
Grasshopper and dragonfly
Beyond duhat tree, over the river,
The greenest hill and plain.

III

The road is long, dusty and crooked,
And at the end, a decrepit fence
Around a straw house.

What can it hold? A sun grown cold,
Fruit of the field that is husk.
I walked away from it,
Morning dew that washed my feet.
My eyes are clear and what do I see?
A stone wilderness that wearies me.

IV

On my knees in Quiapo till my knees ache
Lisping a prayer in Quiapo till my tongue numbs
I shall lacerate myself till I bleed
Because it is Friday—
On my knees in Quiapo, in the poisoned air,
Listening to hope that is not there.

V

Dark beneath this white—
Thoughts curdle the mind;
I was lost, searching among ghosts.
Where have you been, my brother,
What springs have you tasted,
What mountains have you scaled?

We are one in a pod
But one will wither.
Now we sow in anger
And the thunder of words deafens us.

Truth burns the mind, but how—
Yes, how to utter it!

VI

I should hasten back to the cave
Where there is no light, no presence,
And perhaps no end.

The mirror is not cracked
Nor the mind with which I see.

VII

The shadow I cast is long;
My forehead is moist, my hand is cold.
I have gone to a field to glean
And now, my pillow is a rock
And night without stars
Surrounds me.

Even the trees are still
Shriveled in the air . . .
There is no dream.

VIII

I do not think there will be meaning
To an end as trite as death
Nothing really dies,
Not this blue of the sea; nor will this breath
Sour as long as loving
And the brilliance you bring
Tarry as you pass by.

The wave we watched, the dunes we shaped,
The grains of sand that slipped
Through our fingers—
What could I give?
As long as we shun regret, and time remember,
Then my life is blessed.

There is no meaning now to death.
I am secure in this treasure we share—
We really dared, we dare.

IX

The eclipse passes
And leaves no trace;
We can deceive the eagle eye
And draw rings around the sun.

Filler of my need,
Quencher of my thirst,
We have scanned the twisted sky
And dug a land that is scabbed.
Where did we bury them—the hopes
We could not hold?

X

God, when I was weak-kneed
And frightened; when my voice was hoarse
And my breath was short,
You did not come.

If I was your son, blood of your blood,
If you are true as blood is true
Then, listen, God—
Your feet are rooted on this earth
On which I also stand.
I hurl to you this gall
To deafen you, to blind you.

Leave now
For you have long feasted on my rice
And the bin has long been empty.

These hands—gnarled and nerveless now
Can serve no more,
Nor this heart beat for you.

You cannot feed me in my hunger
Or comfort me in my cell;
Dusk chokes my breath.

XI

We slept late last night
Soaked in the heat.
We marched on blistered feet
And burnt-out lungs
And our stomachs were cold and wrought.
We knew where we were going
As hungry dogs know the scent of home.
The sky was black and ghosts wreathed our way
And because we could not see,
We plodded on to where we started
As the others before us, and yet before us . . .
When will we know how to pause?
When will we know the quiet shade?

Even in our deepest dreams we are awake
Listening to the dreaded footfall of those who hate us.
Even in our quietest peace we are awake,
Tortured by the touch of conscience,
Listless, because . . .

We all slept late last night
And now it is morning, but, God—
Where is the sun?

XII

My Brother, the season is here;
The earth is seared, the grass is browned,
And dust covers everything.
The *carabaos* call for their young;
The dogs howl in the wind.
The frogs are buried in the clod
And the creek where we swam is dry.

We whose wounds are tattooed on our breasts,
Whose throats are aching and parched—
When can we heal? How can we ever speak?

All the laughter that rings
Comes in the wake—
The music that beguiles us
Accompanies the parade to the north.

My Brother, the season is here,
The sun that is kind now ripens no grain
And rain that falls, falls on barren clay.

My Brother, I am alone.

CHAPTER
18

Luis Asperri could have gone home to Rosales every weekend if he had wanted to. There was a host of legitimate reasons
for going home: his father's birthday, the town fiesta in June, Christmas, the Holy Week. After all, Rosales was a mere two hundred kilometers away from Manila. But after he had left the town and gone
through college, he had always found it inconvenient to go home,
and though he knew the real reason for staying away, there were always excuses that were credible, so that in time he came to believe
them. Seeming to understand, his father did not press him all
through the four years. After all, it was easy for the old man to go to
Manila, at least five times a year, to visit his favorite gambling den in
San Juan, have a *lengua* dinner in the casino, of which he was one of
the oldest members, and after that, polish off the evening with a visit
to his whorehouse in Pasay.

The old man, however, had not come to Manila for the last six
months. As Trining had said, Don Vicente was ill. He had always
been robust and even obese, so it must have been the Carlos
Primero, the pork *asado,* and the *sin vergüenzas* that had finally

taken their toll. The thought that his father might finally die lingered in Luis's mind with a touch of melancholy, although it did not strike him with apprehension. It was, after all, something that would happen someday to his father as well as to everybody else. Besides, the old man had gotten what he had wished for: a son who bore his name, though his complexion was not as fair nor his nose as aquiline.

Luis had picked up his cousin Trining from her convent school the previous evening to sleep in his house so that they could start early. Indeed, they had had a six o'clock breakfast, but the traffic in Balintawak, at the northern exit from the city, was overwhelming, and when they finally managed to reach the open highway the sun was already blazing down, its rage over the land white and consuming. It was March, and the fields were *chico* brown. The emerald green that burnished everything during the rainy season had long become faded except in patches of irrigated plots where grew watermelons and mongo.

He seldom went outside the city. There had been excursions to the south, to Negros, where some of his sugar-planter friends often asked him to spend the weekend, and a couple of shopping trips to Hong Kong, but no lengthy car rides like this one. Looking fretfully at the land around him, he realized that in all the years he had been in Manila nothing in the countryside had changed, not the thatched houses, not the ragged vegetation, not the stolid people.

Changeless land, burning sun—the words turned in his mind and he decided that they would someday make the opening line for a poem.

Changeless land?

He could see the blight sweeping over this land like a thunderstorm creeping over the near horizon. Quickly the sky above the line of trees darkens and the clouds start to boil. The muggy heat disappears, and the air is quiet and still. Then the wind stirs and the dust in the street rises in billows, as if some giant fan has been turned on. A blackness starts to descend and cover everything, the browned fields of May, the old cracked earth. A flash ignites the sky, and the crack of lightning hurtles across, reverberating into a long, roiling boom—and then silence, coolness, and blackness again. Now a rattle from the distance, like a thousand pebbles cast on tin roofs, on the steaming asphalt, on everything that has waited and waited. The rain has come, the season for green things.

It was not rain that was coming; it was another season, and he could see it as darkness, could feel its electric tension as he had felt the touch of life itself. But this was not life, not even the promise of it, and the fact that he was no longer part of this land, this changeless miasma from which he sprang, filled him with sadness and guilt.

His kind of life was not what he had sought; it had been thrust upon him. His consciousness hounded him, and it made all the difference, the nagging qualm, for though he had fled Rosales, there was no escaping this blight, and he saw it clearly as the Chrysler sped through the monotonous drabness of the plain.

This is the changeless land, scorched by sun and lashed by typhoon, and on it the peasant—as much a part of the land as the barren trees and the meager grain that grow on it—is changeless, too. Barefoot, ill-clothed, a fighting cock under his arm, here is the peasant, working with scythe and plow, plodding along, as slow and as patient as his water buffalo.

How to be completely free from this land—this was what he had sought, and yet he was going back now, not just to Rosales but to the beginning.

His cousin who was beside him would never understand what it was that cankered him. She had not bothered to understand; she welcomed his company—that seemed enough. She was eighteen, and the life in Manila was waiting to be lived. To her, going to Rosales was but the savoring of another life—and perhaps she could make the experience more sweet than it promised to be.

The two other men in the car, the driver and the *encargado,* were incidental, servants to be ordered around, to warrant a safe, comfortable passage, and they did their best, making small noises, running to the restaurant in Angeles to get cold drinks for them. Both these men, however, could have been his relatives, for they came from the village where he was born.

Santos, the caretaker, could have been an uncle. In his own self-deprecating way he hid a sharp mind and a capacity for observation that was both peasant and sophisticated. He had been his father's caretaker for years and had maintained the position by sheer talent. Simeon, who was Santos's cousin, was stolid like a buffalo but not dim-witted. He lived with his childless wife, Marta, in the garage be-hind Luis's house on the boulevard. He was also part-time gardener, handyman, bodyguard, and messenger for the young mestizo. The two could be mistaken for brothers because they were both short and dark and their Ilokano faces were broad and solemn, as if they had never learned to laugh.

The big black car slowed to a stop, and the warm, gummy spell of the dry season rushed in. Luis stopped reading the manuscript and put it back into the brown pigskin portfolio beside him. Five soldiers in battle green were seated on a wooden bench in the thatched shed by the road. A tall, lean one with a steel helmet, his carbine dipping from the crook of his arm, approached the car.

"It will be night when we reach home," Trining said edgily. "It's more than two hours lost, these stupid checkpoints."

Luis pressed her hand, then turned to the window. The soldier peered briefly into the car. He doesn't even look eighteen, Luis thought as their eyes met.

The soldier moved toward the front and asked Simeon where they were going. Santos, the caretaker, answered, "To Rosales," and turning to Luis and Trining, "we are taking our master's children home for a vacation."

"I didn't ask you," the soldier said gruffly. "You," he said, thrust-ing a chin at Simeon.

"We are going to Rosales," Simeon said.

The soldier looked at Luis again and then at Trining; on her, his eyes lingered. He waved his hand: "Roll!" The gears clashed and the car surged forward.

"Son of a whore," Luis said softly under his breath.

"Don't curse," Trining admonished him. She was a sophomore in an exclusive girls' college run by German nuns, and her obsession with clean speech bothered him.

"Whore," he repeated. "That's the truth, isn't it?"

"You have been in the city too long," Santos said. "There are many things in the province that have changed, Luis."

The car picked up speed, and it was cool again. Luis returned to the manuscript he was reading.

"Do you really have to work?" Trining asked. "We are almost there." Turning to her, Luis saw her pout; he had not been too attentive to her, so he placed the manuscript back and zippered the portfolio. She smiled and pressed his hand.

They were nearing Rosales—one more village and they would be there. To his right, beyond the clumps of bamboo on the horizon, the thin finger of the town's yellow water tank towered above the trees, the coconut groves and the buri palms. The car slowed down as Simeon let a herd of *carabaos* cross. Then the car turned right to a dirt road, leaving the main cement highway.

Santos turned to Luis. "I might just as well tell you," he said evenly. "Do not be alarmed when you see him and find him changed. We all grow old . . ."

Luis nodded.

"But in his case," Santos continued, "he seems to have grown old suddenly—and tired. I am not saying he is different from what he has been in the last few months. But all day now he does nothing but stay in the house. He doesn't go out anymore. Does not even read like he used to. He is just there, propped up on his bed with an ice bag on his head. The doctors say his heart is not getting any better, but he doesn't believe them. He says it is the times, the mood. And at his age there is everything to make his heart worse. The troubles we are having in Lagasit, for instance. That's why we now have civilian guards—twenty of them. You can never tell how useful they will be—in the north, particularly in Sipnget."

"Sipnget? What is there?" Luis bent forward, anxious to know more.

Santos turned to him again, an assuring grin on his face. He seemed to know just what made Luis apprehensive. "Do not worry," he said lightly. "Your grandfather and your mother, they are well. And your brother, Victor—I think he has found work."

Luis leaned back, relieved.

"It's another kind of trouble," Santos elaborated. "You know about it, I am sure. You are working for a newspaper, and this is no secret anymore."

"What is no secret?"

"Times are changing, Luis. People, too. The tenants are getting organized, and they cannot be frightened anymore—nor impressed by what is being done for them. The last time I was in Sipnget to supervise the division of the mongo harvest they were dissatisfied. All of them. One even said, 'Well, the law says you only get a third of the harvest and we keep the rest. But you still get half. Remember, it isn't far off when you won't be able to get anything. In fact, it is you who will have to pay.' "

"You told Father this?"

"No, but I think he knows. And now, with all this bothering him, he is touchier every day."

"You don't have to tell me that," Trining said, turning balefully to Luis. "Twice a month I go home. But you!"

"Please, it's different with you," Luis said.

"He reads your letters," Simeon interrupted their private war, "and he gets your magazine and reads what you write. Sometimes he asks me to read for him. His eyes were never strong, and they are weaker now. But my knowledge of English is poor, and his eye-glasses—he breaks one almost every month." Santos laughed nervously. "They are handy to throw when you are angry, you know."

The ride was no longer comfortable, for the roadbed of pebble and stone, unleveled throughout the wet season, was laced with ridges, and where the pebbles had been scattered, the ruts were deep and the bigger boulders that were road foundations thrust up like mounds. The land had not changed—this vast brown land his father's great-grandfather from that small pine-clad town in the Basque had claimed long ago in the name of the Spanish sovereign and the Asperris yet to come. On both sides of the road the fields, long shorn of their harvest, had become scraggly with growths of grass. Everything was tinted with brown and the dazzling sunlight, but beyond the fields, the foothills of Balungao, where his great-grandfather had once stood to gaze upon this plain—as his father never tired of retelling—were purplish and scabbed with black where the cogon grass had been burned. It was there that his father had gone in the past to hunt. It was to these foothills, gold-streaked and blue and bathed with translucent haze, that the farmers who could no longer farm in the plain eventually went to eke out a living from rock and thin soil.

The forest had long been shaved off, and where the deer and the wild boar used to roam, there remained only cogon wastes splintered into tenant farms for the hundreds of patient and land-hungry Ilokanos who had come down from their narrow and inhospitable homeland in the north. After three generations the footpaths had become roads leading to Acop, to Carmay, to Cabugawan, and to Sipnget and the small village called Rosales had become the center of the rice trade from the Cagayan Valley and had grown, as had the fortunes of the Asperris. They built *bodegas,* which they rented out to Chinese rice merchants and moneylenders. They also built a rice mill for the cheap grain their tenants produced and what they cornered in the harvest months, when the price of grain was very low. But difficult times soon came to the eastern portion of the province and to Rosales: a railroad to San Jose farther north cut down the importance of the town as a trading center. Left on its own, Rosales did not progress or produce more; there was no effort to build a dam across the two rain-fed creeks that hemmed the town and converged to drain the precious water into the Agno River. The Asperri clan did not manage the land well, and there finally came a time when only two were left—Don Vicente, who preferred the sybaritic pleasures of Manila and Europe, and Don Alfredo, his brother, who lived in the old brick house their grandfather had built. It was spared by revolutionary ire in 1898, but not by the *colorums* in the thirties.

Because Rosales is not astride the main Luzon highway, it is, like all small towns, condemned to anonymity and to that disquietude that has pervaded the rural areas for decades. The Ilokanos who inhabit it are hardy and given to *carabao*-like drudgery, but they are also in constant debt, not only to the Asperris but to the leaseholders, the *encargados,* and the Chinese shopkeepers or the lesser landlords, men like Santos who are Ilokanos, too.

Luis had not missed all this. The comforts of his Manila home had bothered him. It was in this Ermita house where his father had lived as an absentee landlord. It was here, too, where Luis had grown to manhood, away from the cares of Rosales and of Sipnget, away from his grandfather and his brother and his mother. Thinking of Sipnget now, Luis felt a dull ache pass through him, but it was nothing, nothing but a wisp in the wind; he was here in this place called Rosales—and how small, how nondescript and immemorial the town appeared.

It seemed as if in Rosales nothing had stirred from its ancient lethargy, as if no breath of life had blown through. Even the people in the streets, in front of nondescript stores, seemed to move about with the imprint of lassitude and surrender on their tired brown faces. Here was the herd, inured to everything; here was stone-hard patience not as virtue but as deadly vice—not only in the faces of people but in the physiognomy of the town itself, in the pathetic row of low, squat buildings with horrid soft-drink signs. The dirt road now had been asphalted as the center of the town has drawn near, with its main street and the town plaza—an expanse of withered grass, a cement basketball court with its cracked floor, and at one edge of the plaza this giant, gnarled balete tree, which, as small-town legends go, was supposed to be the home of spirits and all those anonymous wraiths that bode evil if they are not flattered with offerings. At the other end of the plaza was the *municipio*. It stood on the same spot where several years back, before the war, it was burned down. Fronting the *municipio* was the white monument of Rizal, stolid in the brilliant sunshine, and to its left was the Catholic church. The houses thinned out, and beyond was a line of small cogon-roofed houses on bamboo stilts and a few big houses of the merchants and lesser landlords.

A shallow curve, then the Asperri house comes into view, fortresslike, surrounded by a brick wall covered with dying strands of *cadena de amor,* which would turn lush and green with the first rains of May. As a little boy, he had seen another house, of brick, paned with colored glass as this house was now paned, overlooking the whole town, higher than the church steeple, taller than the coconut palm but not as high as the balete tree. Before the war, as with the *municipio,* this house was burned by a small band of men—fanatics who professed an implacable hatred for the Asperris, members of some native religion that enshrined Bonifacio and Rizal and the whole phalanx of heroes who had fought the Spaniards. He had read about them, heard about them from his grandfather and his mother, and secretly he had shared the sentiments that had propelled them to violence. There were even times when Luis had mused how it would have turned out if they had chanced upon his father in the old house and killed him, too, as they had killed his uncle and his aunt. Then he would not have been born—a wish that came to him in those moments of anguished self-doubt that were far more frequent now that he was secure and never in want than in the days when he was sunburned, barefoot, and perpetually hungry in that godforsaken corner called Sipnget.

A new house had been built—a replica of what had been destroyed in one night of fury, but sturdier of foundation and with the latest accoutrements, for his father loved comfort, ease, and of course, the power that his lands and other forms of wealth had brought him. He had lived in Europe and in Manila indulging in his pleasures; he had not intended to go back to Rosales to manage a hacienda and those simple Ilokanos and live like a hermit as his brother had done; he had gone through that experience already, had loathed Rosales and would have found the small town unlivable— but there was duty, not just to what his forebears had carved, but to his young niece, who had survived that indescribable night.

This was home, this was the repository of the past, and every boy in town regarded it with awe. It was as secret as the sacristy, for very few had been inside it and hardly anybody knew what moved within its caverns.

In its yard were the ancient trees that had been spared by the fire. From a distance they looked like green mounds from which the battlements rose, dull red and white, their glass windows reflecting bits of sun. Wooden caryatids of buxom women naked from the waist up adorned the corners that faced the street. Although the house was not old, the original red paint had not been renewed and the cracked red walls gave the house an ancient, medieval look.

It was just as well, for Luis had once likened the house to a storybook castle, sinister with dungeons—but dungeons in which the prisoners had a beautiful time, served as they were with bread and water. In Sipnget, where Luis had grown up, he had tasted bread only on Sundays, when his mother went to town to sell a few greens and came back with her rattan basket half-filled with soap, matches, salt, sugar, and a couple of *pan de sal* for her two boys.

He had lived part of his boyhood in this house, but he had never regarded it as home, not as he did that poor hut in Sipnget. This huge house was nothing but slabs of stone, solid pieces of wood, and polished floors, and servants who flitted about at his slightest whim, barefoot and nameless, although he knew where they came from. They were his people once upon a time, but he was an Asperri now and that made all the difference.

"I did not really expect you to come," Santos said quietly.

"And why not?" Luis felt badgered again, for Santos was right. Luis had been transparent to persons other than himself and his cousin. "It's vacation time, isn't it?" He did not care to hear Santos's reply, and he did not hear him mumble it. They were nearing home, and they slowed down as they passed the Chinese *accesorias* his father owned, the bootblacks, and the travelers at the bus station. They paused once as Simeon let a *caromata* pass, then he swerved to the right, to the wide-open driveway lines with well-tended azucena plots and potted roses. The car stopped on the broad tile landing of the marble stairway.

A young man he had never seen before, in faded khaki, a pistol tucked on his hip, appeared from behind the stairway, opened the door, and saluted. At first Luis took him for one of the soldiers who manned the outpost they had passed and who must somehow have strayed into the house. Beyond the driveway, at the door of the storehouse, were more men in khaki, armed with Garands and carbines.

"Who are they?" Luis pointed to the armed men.

Simeon turned to him. "Our civilian guards," he said matter-of-factly. It suddenly became clear that Rosales was like the rest of the country—in turmoil—and it was here, right in this very house, that the turmoil was perhaps keenest and deepest.

"Shall I go tell him now that you are here?" Santos asked, turning to Luis and Trining as he stepped out of the car.

"No," Trining said, "you may go."

Luis got out. He had not driven such a distance in a long time, and a sense of relief filled him. He greeted the servants who had emerged from the shadows and were now around them, vying with one another for the leather luggage in the trunk. Luis went up with his cousin. The stuffiness converged upon them—the mustiness, the meticulous polish of the woodwork, the stifling opulence, the magnificent pink chandelier from Venice in the center of the hall, which his father had brought back from one of his trips to the Continent before Luis was born, and the bronze statue of the farmer with the plow at the end of the hall, fashioned by a nameless sculptor from Manila.

Trining led Luis to his father's bedroom. On the carved narra door he rapped twice. The voice from within—hollow and expectant—told them to enter. All the blinds of the room were down and it was almost dark, but Luis saw Don Vicente Asperri at once on the high-canopied bed. The old man was propped up by a stack of pillows. He was in pajamas, and his huge body seemed to melt into the thick slab of mattress. His eyes were squinting now, and his thick lips were half open, as if in a smile.

Luis went to him and held his father's big hand to his forehead. As he and Trining withdrew to sit on two wrought-iron chairs near the window, Don Vicente beckoned to them, his voice soft but firm. "Come nearer, I can't see you well."

"Luis, so you have finished college," he said after they had drawn their chairs close to the bed. Luis turned to Trining briefly, but her expression was noncommittal. "In a way, Papa. But I have no diploma yet."

Luis watched his father's face. Don Vicente grunted, but whether his reaction meant displeasure or plain indifference Luis was not able to fathom. The old man turned to the girl: "And how's college?"

Trining sighed. "Fine, Tio, but don't ask me about my grades. Those nuns, they are never satisfied with my term papers." Don Vicente shook his head, and the loose folds of fat on his chin trembled. His countenance was happy. "What do you intend to do now, Luis?" he asked, blinking.

"I hope you won't object, Father," Luis said hesitantly. He had grown familiar with the dimness, and looking at his father's face, at his red misty eyes for any sign of disapproval, he continued, "I have found a job."

"You are working?" Don Vicente asked in disbelief.

Trining nodded. "At least it will keep him out of mischief. He will no longer go around fighting priests."

"Luis—fighting priests?" Don Vicente asked in alarm. He stretched himself upon his pile of pillows and stared at his son.

"But you know, Tio," Trining said. "That is why he wasn't able to get his diploma." She was apparently enjoying herself, and she started laughing.

"A fighter like his father, then," Don Vicente said, his lips quivering. "Tell me about it sometime, *hijo.* I don't remember the story very well. It must be in the files Santos keeps."

Luis felt relieved that the old man had not shown any desire to muddy the niceties of welcome, but his uneasiness was not easily dispelled. For four years he had not returned to Rosales, and here he was again before this man he called Papa, this man whose face his mother said she could spit at without blinking. He had loathed coming back to this town, this house, five kilometers away from a village where his mother, his brother, and his grandfather still lived in great need, while here he was, secure and never wanting.

Don Vicente rubbed his chest. "And what about affairs of the heart?" he asked, a smile flickering across his face.

Trining turned to Luis and said gaily, "Tio, his score is zero. He rarely comes to see me in school, where I have so many pretty friends all waiting to see my handsome, intelligent cousin. And when I introduce him to them he becomes an ice cube."

Don Vicente grunted again, but from the light in his eyes Luis knew his father was pleased. "It's about time you started getting more interests, *hijo*," he said.

"I don't have to look for more," Luis said, feeling miserable and piqued with his cousin. He crossed his legs and studied the interlocking hand-embroidered design on the bedsheet. "My work, it's so demanding and really keeps me busy."

"Don't let your work do that," his father said. "Visit Trining every week next school year, even every day if you can. I think you should live together, so that you can meet her friends."

"It's once a month he comes," Trining complained, "and he doesn't even want to take me out unless I beg him. It's so embarrassing. I would like to do some shopping and see some movies—but he won't let me."

Don Vicente laughed, and as peals of his laughter burst out, Luis imagined that they gathered in his belly and belched out of his mouth with the sharp crack of splitting bamboo.

"*Hijo*," he said, "try to understand how difficult it is for a girl to be cooped up in that convent school. And you don't have to work all that hard."

"I have no specific working hours, but we do have to exert extra effort all the time."

"But your health—look at yourself, frail as a toothpick." Don Vicente sounded alarmed.

"I sleep well, eat well."

"But is your allowance enough? I can give you another opening in the bank," Don Vicente offered.

"It's more than enough, Father," Luis said firmly. "You know that."

"And the house, nothing needs repair? New furniture?" Don Vicente pressed on.

Luis shook his head. "I live like a sultan, Father," he said. "I cannot ask for more. Besides, I am earning a little now."

"Starvation wage!" Don Vicente roared, and then fell into a fit of deep coughing. After a pause, "All right—remember this—no one asked you to work. It is my remotest desire. But if you want to die slowly . . ." His coughing stopped, and leaning forward, he said softly, "You know I am always interested in your welfare, and I've told Simeon and Santos to look after your needs even if you don't want to tell me . . ."

A gap of uneasy silence.

Then, turning to the girl, Don Vicente said, "Run along to the kitchen and see that we have a good supper." Trining stood up, and as the door closed after her, Don Vicente beckoned to his son to come closer. "Listen, I do not want you to go astray. But you should have women—that is natural. Only, do not let your sexual urges confuse you about the real purpose of marriage, which is the formation of a home. Marriage is a social contract, not just for children but for your future."

"You seem to have forgotten the most important element, Father," Luis said. "There has to be love."

Don Vicente smiled patronizingly, his nicotine-tinted teeth showing. "Young romantic love! Yes—you must know the feeling, the experience. But don't forget what marriage is for. You can have mistresses, Luis. But marriage must be for more than love. Politics, economics, stability. Now, look around you, at your own publisher. Dantes—he married his cousin, or did you not know that? The politicians that I knew—the powerful men in government—they married not for love. So, keep your romantic notions and do the right thing just the same."

Don Vicente looked at the ceiling, shaking his head. "Young people," he continued, "they waste not only time. But then, I was young once, too. And I enjoyed life—my wine, my gambling. Do you gamble, son?" He turned briefly to Luis.

The young man shook his head.

"What are you so sensitive about?" the old man asked. "I am a man, I understand. Nothing like gambling or risks to temper the soul. But even here, you must keep your head. And you must know how to lose. I did lose a bit—on the tables, but I gained a lot away from them. Do you know what I am talking about?"

Luis would have to hear it again, how the old man had played poker with Quezon and all those who gravitated around Malacañan, the big men, the mestizos who blabbered in Spanish and bludgeoned the *Indios* just as their forebears had done. "I almost had a street named after me in Quezon City," Don Vicente was saying, "but Quezon forgot—and I was too proud to remind him about it. And as I was saying, you must also choose your gambling partners—not just any riffraff, and don't patronize just any gambling den. Politics is total, son. Total. And even women should be tools in it. If you ever go to a whorehouse, don't forget to look after your health; use condoms. Be protected always, by insurance, by connections. This is what I really want to tell you. Have you considered taking up law, Luis?"

Luis shook his head again.

"You are still very young," the old man continued. "You can take up law in the evenings. You don't have to become a lawyer, or if you pass the bar, you don't have to practice law. Four years—and the knowledge of the law is a good form of preparation. With it, you can be a surer, more skillful politician. Then run for public office, for Congress. This is how I see it. Times are changing, Luis. I did not have to go into politics because I knew the best politicians in the country. Wealth—you cannot keep it, nor will it grow if you have no political power: I am not too sure that you know the men who are in power now, or those who are coming up. Be a congressman, then, from this district. Not mayor, that is much too low for you. I have supported so many of them, and they—Nacionalistas and Liberals— they owe me favors. So you will have not just a name or wealth but real power. You understand, don't you?"

Luis nodded. There came quickly to mind the parade of politicians in the Ermita house, the gregarious talk and the handshakes, the government clerks meekly seeking audience with his father, the carefully coined phrases of corruption, the undertones and the exultant "*areglados.*" So, he would be a politician, too, but the prospect did not attract him. "We have such a surplus of lawyers, Father, and noisy politicians who do nothing but cheat." He had not intended to argue or displease the old man.

"But am I asking you to cheat?" Don Vicente raised his voice. "When did millionaires cheat? I am asking you simply to understand what power is, more than I can give you, with my name, my properties. I am thinking of the future—and just between us, *hijo,* you have made a very good start. The people know now that there is an Asperri who is intelligent. And with your pen, you have influence—which is also power."

"I understand, Father," Luis said. He had wanted to ask, of what use is power when it is coveted just by one man, or one group, without the consent of those who are ruled? How long can it last? But the question did not need to be asked, for he knew, too, what the old man would say—that there are those who are destined to rule, to hold power, not because it is their blood but because they are created to rule, to manipulate, in the same way that there are men who are destined to work, to be slaves, to be patronized, to be cared for like children. History is like that, and the Philippines and the Filipinos are no exceptions.

His father was being redundant again. "It is obvious, of course, particularly to those of us who know. The Dantes family—you know Dantes is not in politics, but his brothers and relatives are. They have the whole of the Visayas—perhaps I exaggerate—but Negros and Panay are in their hands. They have intermarried with one another. Not all of Dantes's papers are making money, but they are forms of investment. Look how scared the politicians are of him. I read in the columns that even the president does not dare cross his path. And why? He has political power, and he can also manipulate public opinion. Do not forget, I may be shut off here, but I read—and think—and remember. I knew the Dantes family when they had nothing but a couple of *bancas*. Now look at their shipping, their transport system, their bank, their publishing—and the politicians they control. Do you know that they could be hurt if the Philippine Bank, which they think they own, were to foreclose their loans? The bank, of course, will not do such a thing . . ."

Luis knew of the vast political and economic power that the Danteses, as the country's leading sugar family, wielded. He also knew that to work for Dantes meant giving him not only one's loyalty, sweat, and blood, et cetera, but also, as the boys in the Press Club often said, "giving him your balls."

But Dantes was an ideal employer. When he traveled, which was twice a year, he always brought six or more of the staffers—first class, of course. For his particular pets he bought cars, homes, vacations—and when they became too old or too unwieldy in his publications he kicked them upstairs as vice presidents or consultants in his other enterprises.

It was common knowledge on newspaper row that his editorial writers and columnists, like Abelardo Cruz and Etang Papel, were reduced to lackeys and wrote according to rote, but Luis did not have to go through such an ordeal.

In his one and only job interview, the publisher had told him, "I will give you complete freedom, not only in the way you run your magazine but in picking your staff. I know of your quarrel with your father rector. I admire your independence; just remember that my interest is in this country's progress—if the country progresses, we progress, too."

"All the big papers are owned by powerful Filipinos, Father," Luis said. "Dantes is no exception."

"Which simply buttresses my position," Don Vicente said. "But the sugar industry is not good for the country, Luis. I can see that now. We are not even producing enough rice. You often write about exploitation of the poor. Someday you should go to Negros. I have some friends there. Spaniards. And talk about exploitation! They rape the prettiest daughters of their workers. They horsewhip their people when they catch them chewing cane. It's like a thirsty man in a brewery, sipping just a little! And the *sacadas*—this is 1950. They were exploited in 1930 and in 1940. Someday you should write an article on the sugar quota and you will find many interesting things . . . and they say the *hacenderos* of Luzon are the exploiters. All these Visayans, with their easygoing ways, their effeminate intonation—they are the most vicious of landlords."

The drone of traffic drifted to the room—the provincial bus screeching to a stop to disgorge its passengers at the junction, the creak of unoiled bull-cart wheels going through the gate, away from the warehouse at the rear, and toward the open field. His father again, this time with pronounced seriousness: "But more than anything, can't you see? I am no more than an old bundle of bones. I am no longer healthy. I cannot look after the land as well anymore as I should." He coughed slightly, then shook his head and pressed his pudgy hands to his chest. "It hurts, but not as much as when I think of what they are doing to me. These accursed peasants—they lie and cheat and get away with everything because I can no longer ride out there. God knows the hacienda was once the best in this part of the country, better than the one in Santa Maria, Tayug, or San Miguel. Did you know that once upon a time this town was the hub of the rice trade, that we could supply all of the rice needs of the province and even of Tarlac if we wanted to? Hard work—not just mine but also that of your ancestors, my grandfather, your great grandfather . . ."

The same old story again—Luis knew it by heart and was bored by it. His eyes wandered to the spiral iron staircase at the foot of his father's bed, and once more he mused about the tower room he and Trining had never entered. Once, when he was new in the house and had thought he could go anywhere, he had asked permission from his father, who was then propped in bed as he was now, having his tray of coffee, but Don Vicente had told him brusquely that the tower room was private and no one—absolutely no one—ever went up there. Once, when he and Trining were left in the house, since his father had gone to Cabugawan to visit the tenants there, they had, like conspirators, decided to invade his father's eyrie. They had gone gingerly up the spiral staircase, and at the top they rammed themselves against the door. It was securely locked and refused to yield. He wondered, but only for an instant, about the secrets the tower room held; and when he was past his teens he mused that perhaps that was where his old man stored his dirty pictures.

". . . This is a great place to live in, Luis, but one must be strong to live here—and practical; one must know how to deal with the weakness in oneself as with those in others."

Luis bowed, as if in thought, and his gaze wandered to the fine polished planks of narra that made up the floor—long, wide, and shiny, the grain pulsing through. It was almost impossible to get this kind of wood now, for the big trees that once stood in this part of the country had been cut down. Indeed, this house, though a replica of what was burned, was the handiwork of his forebears, the Asperris. It could well be the vaulting monument of their perseverance and their cunning. He knew the story by rote, as his own people in Sipnget had told him—how the Americans came with their transits and their measuring rods, how the Spaniards worked with the Americans, and how with no more than scraps of paper they made binding and permanent the bondage of those who had from the beginning felled the trees, cut the grass, killed the snakes, and dammed the creeks, so that this inhospitable land could be made gracious and fecund.

History is written by the strong? Where had he read that before?

Was it Vic, his half-brother, who had quoted it to him, or one of his radical friends in the university? Again the old anger was brought to life and with it the sense of futility that he could do nothing, nothing, for it was not in him to do battle with the wind, not with his puny body, not with his shallow intellect, least of all with his poetry. He cringed again at having to listen to his father's fears, his expectations, and he listened to the old man as one would hearken to a knell.

"I will go as most men must go, but I want honesty between us. You are my son, my blood is in your veins, my sinews . . ."

I am your son but also my mother's. Luis turned over the silent reply; *the land that you ravaged has claim on me, too, and not just your ancestors from a distant and rocky peninsula.*

"And I want my blood and my life to go on when this mortal frame is no more. I want you, Luis, to marry and have an heir before I go. I want you to look again at your cousin. It is important that this land, this wealth, should not leave the Asperris. It should not go to these tenants who do not understand what it is to carve something out of nothing, who have no pride in their families, in their race. They are treacherous, they are ingrates—they killed my brother, don't ever forget that."

The old man was angry; he was also afraid. Luis could understand it better now—the civilian guards, the patrols, and checkpoints. The Army was never there to protect the poor—it had always been an institution for the preservation of privilege.

"I know, Father," he said, "but if they do want to kill you or me, do you think your civilian guards—"

"Our civilian guards, Luis. Our civilian guards."

"Would the Army be able to defend you? This is not the best defense, Father; it has never been—"

"You have the traditional loathing and distrust of the intellectual for anyone who carries a sword. You have been mesmerized by that old saying, the pen is mightier than the sword. Did it ever occur to you that it was, perhaps, a poet who coined it? People believe it but it is nonsense. The man with the gun is the state, and the state is everything. Can there be progress without order? Without the state and its stability, you have to go back to the jungle . . ."

"This is the jungle, Father," Luis said, surprised that he could now openly contradict his father. "It has always been thus."

"And the predators are people like me?" Don Vicente shook his head ruefully. "And what are you?" he asked. "Will you be the savior of the oppressed and the weak? My son, there are no oppressors, there are no oppressed. There are only people who seize opportunities to make their lives better. The poor are virtuous? The worst enemies of the poor are their own kind—because they are lazy, because they refuse to change."

"It is we who refuse to change, Father," Luis said. "We have grown used to our comforts, to habits of the past."

Don Vicente's voice lifted. "But I have changed, Luis, not just in the flesh. I am no longer the youth who loitered in Europe, who lived lavishly in Manila and loathed every moment I spent in this town. My views—they have changed as well. You don't have to tell me that everything springs from the land and what we have gotten from it must be returned."

Did his father finally believe in justice, then? Or was he again indulging in rhetoric?

Another uneasy silence, then Don Vicente thrust his chin to the door. The interview had come to an end.

The sun-flooded hall was blinding after his stay in the old man's darkened room. In his own room, near the end of the hall, the floor appeared newly waxed and the bed smelled clean, the sheets freshly starched. Beside his bed his suitcases were lined up, and he unpacked them, arranged his clothes in the tall *aparador* in the corner. He walked to the *azotea* and sat on the stone ledge. The faint rustling in the eaves and the sonorous chug-chug of the rice mill behind the house came to him. The brown fields lay beyond the walls of timeless adobe; so, too, did the river dike and the brown dots of buri palms far away.

Trining came out of her room and joined him. He did not notice her until she sat by his side, their arms touching. He turned to her and saw that she had changed from the brown starched uniform she had worn on the trip. It was sloppy and had given her no identity. Now she wore a yellow silk dress that accentuated the soft lines of her young body blossoming into womanhood.

"You seem to know everything—just about all the wrong things to tell him," Luis said petulantly.

Trining looked at him incredulously. "But he knows, Luis—everything—even without my telling him. Do you think Tio is a fool even if he sits in that room all day? He wrote to me about your quitting school. He knows you quarreled with your father rector. Prerogatives—was that what you called it?"

Luis did not answer.

"Besides, it is true. You didn't visit me often enough. I would have seen more of you if only you tried. I am really proud of you, Luis. Just ask my classmates what I always tell them. Why, they say"—she paused and blushed—"I am in love with you. It was very embarrassing for me to appear to like you so much, and you never came as often as I wanted you to—and when you did, you didn't want to take me out."

"You talk too much," he said, dismissing her prattle, walking away from her. He went to the bedroom and flung himself on his bed. The sheets were fresh and cool. Above, from the ceiling, as in all other rooms of the house, dangled a small pink chandelier, and it tinkled as a slight breeze from the open *azotea* door flowed in.

Trining followed him and sat on the edge of his bed. "Well, if you don't like me, at least you could have been sociable with my friends. Ester, for instance—she is your publisher's daughter, and when we came to your office you didn't even notice her. Then at that party at the Cielito Lindo—I had begged you to take me there. Who will take me, Luis? My friends think you are a snob. I had to explain that you are not."

"I am sorry," he said, pressing her hand.

Trining stood up and walked to the door. "Do you want to walk with me around the town?"

"What is there to see?"

"They will see us," she said, smiling. "Four years you've been away. The people would like to see the difference—"

"No," he said brusquely.

"I'll call when supper is ready," she said. The door closed, and he heard her soft humming as she padded down the hall.

SO THIS WAS HOME, this mass of unfeeling masonry, this alien room. But the people that he loved were not here. They were in another time and place, and the fact that he had not written to them for a long time or given them more than the few tidbits that he had thrown their way filled him with remorse. Maybe at this hour his mother would already be cooking supper and his grandfather, as usual, would be by the window that opened to the west, trying to make use of the last faltering light of day, knitting fishnets. Vic would be herding the work animals to the corral if he was with them, if he had not left Sipnget so that he could get some education and improve himself as he had vowed he would. Luis had not written to them for months, and he was sure they did not even know he was home. On his last visit to Sipnget four years ago his mother had cried, saying how tall he had grown. "Jump up you did, like a bamboo shoot!" she said, her eyes laughing and yet filmy with tears. They had tried to make him comfortable as best as they could. His grandfather even vacated his chair by the window and offered it to him.

Trining slipped back into the room quietly. He had closed his eyes but had not really fallen asleep, just drifted into that dulled consciousness between waking and sleep. She was bending over him and shaking his arm. "Supper is ready. Wake up, lazy one," her voice droned pleasantly.

His displeasure with her recent conduct was gone, and looking at her in the gathering darkness, so near and smiling, he raised his hand and caressed her face. She held his hand and brushed his open palm against her lips, her cheek. He rose and pulled her to him, felt the trembling of her lips, tasted their sweet honey-salt, felt her breath warm and soft on his face, smelled the scent of her hair. She did not object. Instead, her arms encircled him slowly, tentatively, almost shyly. Then, with a swiftness that surprised him, she pushed him away and stood up. Her eyes were serious, but they were not angry. "Tio," she whispered. "He is waiting for us."

He stood up reluctantly and changed his shirt while she, too, brushed her dress, although it was not crumpled. That was a beginning, he thought, and before he opened the door Trining tiptoed up to him and kissed him lightly on the cheek. "I think I have been forgiven," she said with a smile.

The dining room that adjoined the hall was lined with glass cabinets varnished rich brown and filled with silver and antique china that his father had brought from Italy and England. On the severe mahogany walls were still-life paintings of ripe guavas, mangoes, and *chicos* in gilt frames. At one end of the glass-topped table in the center of the room Don Vicente sat, and behind him on the wall hung a large silver-framed painting of the Last Supper. A maid stood by with a cut-paper wand, which she occasionally shook over the table.

Don Vicente stopped slurping his soup and bade them sit. Trining paused before her place at Don Vicente's left and with head bowed said grace. Don Vicente looked at his niece, then turned to Luis, who had not observed the ritual but instead had sat down immediately.

"Ah," Don Vicente murmured, "it's wonderful to have someone in the family who will save us heathens."

The girl made the sign of the cross. "I can't eat without praying," she said, sitting down. "It's a habit, more than anything."

"You will go straight to heaven," Luis said. Trining glared at him.

"I do my only son honor," Don Vicente said. "This is the first time I have come out to eat in weeks."

"Thank you, Father," Luis said. *My son, my only son*—the words roiled in his ears. *Father, what is the love you know—you who sent Mother away and took me here? I can go on living, accepting your presents, your protestations of affection—but is this love?*

A beneficent dinner—stuffed chicken, fruit salad, mushroom soup, spaghetti, and roasted eggplants in tomato-and-salted-fish sauce—but Luis had no appetite. Maybe, he thought, picking at his food, at this time Mother, Grandfather, and Victor would be through with supper—perhaps just boiled camote tops and rice—and now Mother would again be before the sewing machine, stitching in the poor light of the kerosene lamp. He turned to the table laden with food, to the servant waving the cut-paper wand to keep the flies away, the cook glancing in through the screened kitchen door, waiting for the signal that meant his masters wanted more. *I see a sullenness in their faces as they serve me. Even in my cousin's eyes and in the face of this man they call my father, I see ridicule and contempt.*

"Anything the matter, Luis?" Don Vicente's voice jarred.

"The trip, Father." Luis had a ready alibi. "All those checkpoints, the delay . . . I've lost all appetite . . ."

His father sighed. "I know, I know, but what can we do? Now, that chicken." Don Vicente pushed toward him the serving tray filled with brown chunks of chicken in gravy. "Try it, just the same."

Luis placed a drumstick on his plate. It was strange how his mother used to do the same, push her plate to him, saying, Here, son, I'm not hungry. His grandfather, too, saying after her in a crude attempt at levity: I am full. Finish this catfish or the house lizards will beat you to it.

Supper was extremely long. After the macapuno ice cream and a few more explanations about his work (a good magazine, one that seeks the truth and, having found it, isn't afraid to print it) he asked his father if he could leave for a walk.

"Where to?" Don Vicente asked, putting his dessert spoon down.

"I was wondering how things in Sipnget are," he said simply.

Don Vicente's face became thoughtful, and his red, baggy eyes narrowed. He shook his head. "I don't want you walking alone—not these days. I'll have Simeon go with you."

"Can I come along?" Trining asked.

"You stay here," Don Vicente told her.

Luis was embarrassed telling his father where he wanted to go. He stood up, avoiding his father's eyes, which he felt clung to him even as he walked out of the dining room. He paused in the foyer. The night was calm, and beyond the long tiled sweep of the porte cochere, the stars were luminous. He went down the stairs, the marble banister cold and smooth in his hand. In the garden the crickets were alive and the scent of azucenas and roses met him like a welcoming wave. Deep inside him he cried: *If I can go to Sipnget and climb another stair, would I belong there, I who have long disowned them?* He remembered with a twinge of regret, of sadness, how he had told all his city friends that his mother had long been dead—she was not, she had done him no wrong except to carry him in her womb when he did not want to be born.

"Luis," Trining said softly.

He turned around. Trining hurried down the landing after him. "Must you really go? Please bring me with you! I would like to meet them."

He shook his head. "Yes, I want to go. That's my family there, can't you see? And you need not meet them. They do not matter to you."

"Oh, Luis," she said, holding his hand.

Does she know, does everyone know the sore that festers in me?
"They matter only to me, and you don't know how much I really miss

the place," he lied. He would have added: That was where I was born, and all that I remember or need to remember is there—but the words just did not take form, for there was this rock in his throat choking him and all he could say hoarsely as they were parting was, "That is where I belong!"

CHAPTER

19

SIMEON HAD an almost paternal feeling for the big car, and in the mornings and late afternoons, when there was no more driving to be done, he would clean and polish it till the black paint was glossy. He would lift the hood and wipe clean the carburetor, the wirings, the steel hump of the engine, and even the backside of the hood. He and his wife—the chubby, cigar-smoking barrio matron who looked after the house in Manila—were childless, and they had transferred their affection to other things, even to Luis, whom they looked after with devotion. It was Marta, too—then a maid in the old Asperri house—who had clasped the frightened Trining, four years old, to her breast, telling the madmen who had already killed the girl's father and mother and were now setting the house on fire that they should spare her who was without sin.

Luis sometimes tried to fathom what went on in his driver's mind, but Simeon was quiet most of the time and there was this meaningless smile plastered on his face when Luis called him down for some small misdemeanor. Luis was almost sorry; the car had already been thoroughly cleaned, and a thick powdery coat would cover it again by the time they returned.

Simeon drove slowly, his headlights picking out the stray pigs along the main street, then they turned right to the narrow *camino provincial.* It had not been maintained; the sides were covered with weeds, and the gravel undulated in piles where it was not swept back by the *camineros* to the center of the road. The night was calm, that vaporous kind, which transfixes the land during the dry season. The dark was pervasive but for a few flickering orange lamps that marked the houses. In the backseat Luis tried to catch a firefly that had been blown in, its pale luminosity popping up and down—but the firefly was soon sucked away and once more Luis was immersed in expectation and apprehension.

"I should be cooling off in a brook now," Simeon said without turning to Luis as the car crawled on.

Luis peered at the left side of the road shrouded with night. They had passed the last kerosene-lamp–lit house, and the road sloped down into the farmlands, anonymous and black around them. All this distance, this vastness, belonged to his father.

"Drive a little bit faster," he said. The car crunched forward. The camachile trees that flanked the road hurtled by. A gray unending stream of night insects caught in the white glare of the headlights pelted the windshield. As the pebbly road rushed toward them Luis searched for the old landmarks, and in a while he recognized the broad end of the bull-cart path from Sipnget that joined the *camino.* Simeon slowed to a stop and Luis got out. A bridge made of coconut trunks laid side by side and covered with matted bamboo spanned the irrigation ditch alongside the road. The land waiting for the plow smelled burnt.

"Wait here," he told the driver. "I'll walk."

Simeon stepped out of the car. "Your father, Apo—he told me not to leave you."

"Simeon," he said firmly, "I am seeing my own village and my family."

A thick layer of dust covered the path and fluffed up at each step, and he often stumbled as he stepped on depressions formed by the steady groove of *carabao* hooves. Tobacco patches on both sides of the path clogged the night with a thick, pungent odor. Insects whirred in the grass that covered the dikes.

I am home. I am home. This is the place honored in the mind and sanctified in the heart. Although he had been away, the sounds and smells were always with him—the aroma of newly harvested grain, the grass fresh with dew, the mooing cattle, the young herder's call for his water buffalos, the cackle of hens, the rustling of bamboo in the wind, and most of all, the tones of his language, for there was in Ilokano the aura and the mystery of things left unsaid. There was the past, too, that did not have to be relived, which must be escaped because it spelled perdition and all the bog and swamp of his muddied beginning. How was it then, how were the hours, the moments at the river, in the water-lilied ditches, the taste of newly harvested rice? *Bring back the strum of guitars, the children's eager voices—all the happiness that ended on a night like this!*

IT WAS HIGH NOON that day, that year, when his father's tractor came. After a hurried lunch he had snatched his buri hat from the deer-horn rack—a relic of his grandfather's hunting days—and gone to the kitchen, where his mother was washing the dishes. Victor followed—Luis was the leader, and Vic was his only follower.

Can we join the others in the road? his younger brother said.

It is hot, his mother said, pausing; see how the land heaves in the heat.

The old man was knitting fishnets by the window. He drew the shiny bamboo shuttle into a loop. Let them go and see how a rich man farms, he said.

His mother turned to them and bade them leave. They rushed down the stairs, into the white powdery road. They did not join the crowd at the bridge or the boys under the acacia trees. They sat on the dying grass by themselves, in the shade of a camachile sapling up the road.

Before long, a rumble came down the road and they saw it—the tractor with a puff of dust behind it, its infernal noise growing louder, its red paint gleaming in the sun. The men stood up from their haunches, and the two brothers joined them. The tractor rumbled closer, and then it was upon them like a snorting bull. Santos saw Luis then, and he beckoned to him. He asked if he was Nena's son, and when he said he was, the caretaker asked him if he wanted to sit beside him. It was something he could not refuse, and much later he remembered that he should have asked Victor to join him, too.

The engine roared again, and its dark fumes almost choked him. The driver flipped a lever forward, and avoiding the bridge, the tractor loped down the shallow ditch, then clambered up the other bank, tearing huge chunks of soil as it made for the open field. It went straight, followed the path, and obliterated the deep ruts wrought by bull-cart wheels and sled runners. The iron treads etched their deep rectangular pattern on the path. More children came from beyond the dike and formed a procession behind the machine. On the seat beside the caretaker, Luis felt his chest bursting.

The dike did not stop the tractor. The machine went up the incline faster than a *carabao* and roared into the village, which had never felt the tread of an engine. As they roared by his home his grandfather appeared at the door. Luis could not look at the old man as they passed. Somehow he knew that his grandfather did not like this intrusion, and he was glad when they finally passed the house and headed for the edge of the farmlands, where the grass grew lush and tough. There the caretaker alighted and dispersed the children who had gathered before the engine. To the tractor's rear the driver attached the plowshares, and then he drove into the tangle of grass and weeds. As it reached the high grass, the machine paused, and into the ground, deeper than an animal-drawn plow could pierce, the steel shares sank, ripped the sturdy soil into clean furrows, and upturned the tough dry earth now moist and rich brown. Behind the newly plowed earth and the prostrate grass they walked and followed the caterpillar as it moved on, unimpeded by rocks and roots of dead trees that had long defeated the wooden plows. Near the river dike the sticky soil where the amorseco grew wild yielded, too, and this patch of land that could never be planted would now be ready for seed. The tractor moved on until it reached the river.

IT WAS LATE AFTERNOON when Luis went home. The excitement had worn off, and the children who had crowded around him asking how it was to be on the tractor had stopped pestering him. He had somehow expected this moment when he would be acknowledged as his father's son. He had seen it in the women from the town who often went to his mother to have the *panuelos* of their *ternos* starched or their Sunday clothes mended. They had appraised him, then talked in whispers. He lingered at the dike until the sun went down, then he went up to the house. He greeted his mother and his grandfather in the ritual that he was brought up in. It was dusk and it was quiet, but Vic broke the silence with questions: Where had he been after the tractor had gone?

Supper. They sat on the bamboo floor around the low dining table that held a plate filled with steaming rice and a shallow coconut bowl that contained roasted green pepper and mudfish.

His grandfather's eyes were on him. It was a busy day for you, Luis, he said; I saw you on the tractor.

It was wonderful, Grandfather, he said; Mr. Santos asked me to join him.

The old man turned to his mother. At least the boy knows what it is to be strong. I think the time has come when everything must change. We must all learn our lesson, and Luis, you had one today. There was a time I knew. There were no trucks then, and even on a fast horse it would take two days to go to the provincial capital. Now just a few hours. The hills were thick with trees and game, and Bagos came to trade with us, bringing venison and woven baskets in exchange for our rice and our dogs.

Father, do not start talking again like you always do, his mother reminded the old man.

But it is true, the old man said sadly. He pinched salt from the platter and sprinkled it on his plate. He continued: The Bagos from the mountains, when this land was not cleared, we talked with one another in a language we understood, and we said, surely there will come a time when men will fly like the hawk, when guns will replace spears and arrows, and wisdom will not be ours to use but will be for the strong . . .

His mother stopped eating. Times have changed, Father, she said, but it has not been very difficult.

The old man did not answer. Time was when a silence like this that now came over them was a bond, time when his grandfather, Victor, and he sat in the shade of the tallest buri palm by the road, after which, with their loads of firewood on the ground, the old man would recall other times, when rains were gentle, when the sun shone and the grasshopper sang, and blessing of blessings, this land was his. The old man turned and gazed upward at the dingy roof.

Smoke from the kitchen stove vanished into the sooty cobwebs and the old fishnets hanging there. Were these all that one could keep?

Vic had stopped eating, too, and his dark face was pensive as he listened to what the old man said: We felled the trees, big trees, which men with their arms outstretched couldn't embrace. The Bagos came with their spears and brought ubi and tugui as big as jars. I had a bow and a spear, too, and we were friends, although I knew that they adorned their dwellings with the skulls of their enemies. We met in the yard and hastened beneath the house where the *basi* was fermenting and where my richest and biggest tobacco was curing. We opened the jars and we rolled cigars, and our laughter reached out to our neighbors, who came and joined us. Ah, those were happy days, and the Bagos were not strangers as people today are strangers, learned men who came from the north with their books and their machines.

That was fifty years ago, Father, his mother said, putting away the dishes; fifty years—you must understand that!

So it was—fifty years! The old man sighed ruefully. But what happened? They stretched the roads across the fields and dammed the creeks, so that the water could flow only to their farms. They built the railroad, too, right across the dikes we built, and finally they brought their lawyers and these learned men said: This land is ours, and this spot, which is just wide enough for your grave, is yours. And we said nothing and did nothing, because they were learned. Of what use is a bolo before a gun? Like the Bagos, we were raised in God's futile ways . . .

His mother stood up and went to the squat earthen stove, held the sooty rim of the pot, and emptied its contents onto the chipped porcelain plate on the table.

Isn't it so, Nena? the old man asked.

But what if it is so, Father? she asked with a hint of displeasure in her voice. She took the empty plate and placed it in the basin of water beyond the dining table. His grandfather sighed. When his mother returned, her face was troubled.

And now the tractor is here, the old man said; every day we are driven farther from our homes. Can you not see what this means? With the tractor we will not be needed anymore, and where will we go? To the farthest hills like the Bagos? They will follow us there, tear away the wilderness that will hide us. They will strangle us with their roads, and we will go on seeking the forest, because there we might find some peace . . .

But, Grandfather, Luis said, you did not see how much easier the tractor can rip a mound apart!

The old man turned to Luis. In the yellow glimmer of the kerosene lamp he could not tell if the old man's eyes were misty or on the verge of tears. The old man turned away and said: Luis, you must speak like this. It is in your blood, and someday, very soon, you will leave this house, because you do not belong here and because it is also in you to be strong.

Outside, the crickets whirred and the blooming dalipawen tree in the yard sent its heavy scent into the house. From the direction of the buri palms a boy herding his work animals hummed an old ballad—Dear, dear raft, come to me, save me before the whirlpool sucks me . . .

His mother rose from the water platform and said in a voice tinged with sadness: Father, how many times have I told you never to bring the child into this?

The old man did not heed her. Someday, he said, turning to Luis again, you will leave us just the same.

You do not know what you are talking about, his mother said; what do you know about the future? So many things about us are unsure. You never went to school, and that is why they made a fool of you. But my boys, they will get educated and they will know how to avoid the mistakes you made. They will have something even if my hands bleed getting them an education.

His grandfather did not speak. He stood up, holding his knees as if he would totter, then walked out of the kitchen, down the stairs, into the dark yard. The cicadas chirped, and a work animal in a corral down the path called its young. His mother went about her chores; she placed the empty dishes on the earthen basin, then scooped the leftover rice from the big plate and returned it to the pot. She spread the rolled buri mat on the floor and brought down the caseless kapok pillows from a shelf on the wall.

Vic sat by the open window. Where do you think Grandfather went? he asked no one in particular. Luis went down the stairs and scoured the yard and the dark approaches to the house. He returned and asked his mother: What was Grandfather trying to tell me, Mother?

She lay on the mat, her eyes on the ceiling, and spoke softly, as if she were afraid that the night, the house, and all of Sipnget were listening to a dreadful secret she was about to break: The ways of people are strange, but bear this in mind—we have done no one wrong.

Why was Grandfather angry, and where did he go?

His mother dispelled his anxiety: Father has nowhere to go. He will come back when he is no longer angry.

Through the open window the April sky was cloudless and the stars burned bright. His mother drew the blanket over her bare feet. The two boys unrolled their mat close to the stairs, and in a while, wordless, they too lay down. She stirred later at the snorting of pigs in the yard. Vic was snoring, but Luis tossed. In the sallow light of the kerosene lamp that dangled from the roof, he saw his grandfather slowly open the kitchen door. Even after the cock crowed on its perch in the madre de cacao tree beside the house, Luis was still wide awake.

THE NEXT AFTERNOON, when he and his brother arrived from a bath in the river, they came upon his mother and Santos, the caretaker, talking in the yard. Her voice was pitched low, and she left the caretaker when she saw the boys. She went up to the house with them, not bothering to ask the caretaker to follow. To Luis she said simply: Now you will see your father.

It was as if he did not hear. He went to the small room, got his books, and leafed through them. She followed him. Well, don't you want to see your father? He gazed out of the small window and saw his grandfather seated with the menfolk, talking at Tio Joven's store.

Don't you want to go? Like your grandfather said, this has to come sometime. The decision is yours. You are old enough now to have a mind of your own.

She would get angry again, so without a word Luis put on his battered rubber shoes and his only shirt, which was stiff with starch. When he was ready she bade him stand before her. This is how it has to be, she said quickly. He knew that she was angry, not with him but with the man in the big brick house, he whose name she always told him to spit at whenever it was mentioned, the man he was going to see, the man whose blood, she said, was in his own veins.

IT WAS LATE when Luis returned to Sipnget. A rooster crowed, the stars were out like jewels in the deep bowl of the sky, the air was sultry and dust was thick on the deserted lane. Were there people peeping through the close windows into the dark maw of night?

It hardly mattered then whether he went back to Sipnget or not. Now he knew what was within the red house, the brightness and the spaciousness, the piano, the table laden with apples and oranges shining with the luster of soft gold. Vic and he tasted apples and oranges only once a year, at Christmas. His mother would unwrap the frayed kerchief she always had tied to her skirt strings, and after she had counted carefully she would hand him and Vic a few coins and say: This is Christmas. And they would buy apples as gifts in exchange for apples they would get during the Christmas party in school.

The lamp in the house still shone, so they would be awake, waiting for him. He went up the stairs slowly and heard the steady whirr of the sewing machine. When he reached the door the whirring stopped. His mother called out to him: Draw the ladder up and don't forget to bolt the door. He did what she told him. It was as if she were afraid a giant hand might slip past the door to snuff out their lives, but there was no such hand and they never had visitors except the women who came to have their clothes mended—and the man from the big red house with whom she argued in the yard.

The small *sala* was littered with pieces of cloth, as usual, and in the center was the old sewing machine with his mother hunched before it. She would be there until it was almost dawn, sewing until she could hardly see.

Her face was expectant when she turned to him: Did you kiss his hand?

I did, Mother.

She seemed relieved. I thought you'd forget, she said; you always forget what I teach you.

The machine whirred again. He took off his shoes and squirmed out of his shirt carefully, so that the slight tear on its back, which had been mended, would not run. Vic was still awake and was looking at him from across the room.

In the big red house, what where they saying now? You will not regret it—that was what Santos, the caretaker, told his father. With his hand upon Luis's shoulder Santos had added: And there is a good head on these shoulders.

The great man—his father—looked at Luis, then the porcine head nodded and smiled—he whose name he must spit at every time it was uttered, he whom his mother had cursed. But Luis could not look at him, nor could he spit at him, so he stared at the polished floor and at his dusty rubber shoes. He could not look at his father, who was all smiles and solicitation.

Yet he went to him, and as his mother had said he should, he held the white hirsute hand and kissed it, knowing as he did that someday, if he grew old and fat and powerful, perhaps he would look just like this man. He would have been glad if he had known this man when he needed him most; he would have been proud to kiss his big fat hand and would have wanted to live in his big red house— but why had his father waited? Why did he not come when he was in the cradle or when he was six or eight and was teased in school— or when they had nothing to eat but rice gruel and leaves of camote and marunggay? There would not have been those bitter moments when his mother would not talk with him, moments when he knew he was not like Victor, nights when she would toss and weep. There would not have been the anguished look on her face when he asked her for the first time: Mother, what has my father done and where is he? My father is not Vic's father—I know that now . . .

He was eight years old then, mud was thick on his feet, his hair unruly, but his skin was fair—fairer than anyone's in the village, although he swam in the river, too, and climbed the camachile trees and like everyone else was exposed to the rage of the sun.

You bear an honorable name! his mother shrieked. She dropped her sewing and towered before him. Her hand fell across his face, its sting sharp on his lips. He stared at her in utter surprise, feeling the pain spread across his face, but he did not cry. He did not move, and he could feel something warm trickling down his mouth, and when she saw this she ran to the kitchen and with a damp towel wiped the blood off his lips. It was not she who had done him wrong: it was his father, and though he could not understand why she had slapped him, he was not angry with her, though always, the memory of her hand across his face and the taste of his own blood would be imperishable in his mind.

December—she had many clothes to sew, but they were neither for Victor nor for him. January—and the harvest would be in, but they would have none of it. Cold mornings—and she would rise before the sun and in the white mists hovering over Sipnget would go to town to get more sewing to be done and through the night, the whirr of the infernal machine in his ears. In March, Luis finished grade school, while Vic, who was younger, had one more year to go. Then April—and the man from the big red house came and said, your father who is visiting from Manila wants to see you. He would have been glad, but he was thirteen and it was enough that there was this frail, sun-browned woman who had slapped him, this old man who loved to talk of days gone by, and his brother—much, much darker than he, who looked up to him, as if he were the only holder of knowledge and virtue.

WHAT DID your father say? his mother asked suddenly. She had stopped pedaling and the machine was quiet.

He asked me if I wanted to live with him, Luis said.

She dropped the colored piece of cloth she was holding and folded her hands at the wooden edge of the machine. What did you tell him?

I said I would ask you first, Mother.

She picked up the piece of cloth and started working on it again. You must go with him, she said; you are going to live with him from now on.

Luis held his breath, not wanting to believe, not wanting to listen to what she had said. You don't mean that, Mother! he cried.

Her voice was firm but disconsolate: You—you have to go to high school and then to college, so that you will not be in want, and someday, when you are older, I hope that you will be kind—much kinder than he—and not wreck the life of one hapless woman.

Mother!

Yes, she said, be kind.

He could not contain his grief anymore. You never wanted me, because I am not like Vic!

She dropped the piece of cloth she was working on and pointed a thimbled finger at him. Do you want to rot here? she asked softly. No, my Luis, you must go, not only because it is your fate but because I want you to. Vic does not have a similar choice, so he will stay.

Luis walked to the open window. In the near distance, the light in Tio Joven's store still burned, and among the men talking was the hunched, unmistakable form of his grandfather. Yes, Luis was different. His classmates called Vic and him "coffee and milk," and although the jesting did hurt at first, he learned to bear it. After all, his mother loved them both in a way that blunted all barbs. He had put the jumbled pieces together and understood—it was he, not Vic, who had sprung from muddied springs.

His earliest memories were confused and inchoate; he did know, however, that before he was born, his mother had married a man from their own village and from this union Vic was born. But that faceless "father" had died before he could remember, and Vic and Luis grew up without knowing what a father was, although they did know the affinity that a host of aunts, uncles, and cousins to the third degree had blessed them with, and most of all, they knew one mother's love.

From the very beginning, too, Luis knew that he was not really from Sipnget and that in time, as Vic had guessed, he would leave. They were in the river then, hurling stones across the broad sweep of water with a sling, diving for pine splinters, which they would dry in the sun and use as kindling wood. They were resting on the broad stones at the riverbank, and after some silence Vic had said: Manong, if you go there, would you still come here and gather this wood with me?

Luis had answered with conviction: No—he would not leave Sipnget. But he did not know then what was to come, the point where their paths would separate, and there would be more water buffalos to bathe, eggplant and tomato plots to work on, mudfish to catch, and sweet corn to roast. There would be more mornings with martins singing in the buri palms.

Now, with a pang of sadness, Luis accepted his being "milk," his being *bangus*—Get out of the sun, *puraw,* or you will become black like Victor; Bangus, go home and help in the kitchen, we will do the plowing! How they had patronized him! He was their kind, their property, the village emblem, and when he reached the age of puberty all the girls would chase him and his mother would watch over him, as if he were a foolish virgin. Now everything would be changed.

I'll go tomorrow then, Mother, he said.

Tomorrow? his mother asked incredulously.

Yes, Father wants to bring me to Manila with him.

Is that all he said?

He looked long at her and remembered how his father had laid his heavy hand on his shoulder. How strange it felt—and stranger his voice when he said: I will take care of you.

He said he would take care of me, Mother.

But she was no longer looking at him. A softness came over her careworn face. Did she love him still, did she want to know more about him, the years he never came to call although he was near, and if they should meet again, how would she—this wasted, dearly loved woman—greet him?

He went to the little room and lay beside Vic, who moved over to give him space. He pressed his cheek against the caseless pillow, and then came this feeling of wanting to shout until the lungs were dry and the parched throat ached with the desire to curse the red house, to curse earth and heaven and everyone capable of perfidy.

The sewing machine whirred, then was silent. He heard his mother walk lightly and approach him, and from the corner of his eye he could see her bend over him, see her wan and wasted face as she tenderly drew the torn Ilokano blanket over his legs.

He turned and whispered: Leave me, Mother.

She cringed, the ancient hurt—as when he asked her where his father was, as when she wiped the blood off his lips—now written on her face. He was not angry with her but with himself. Softly, so as not to wake Vic, he repeated: Mother, leave me.

THE PATH WAS WIDER now. Beyond the river dike, the buri palms were like huge sentinels watching over the land. Luis went up to the dike. Below, Sipnget was not yet asleep. The *amarillo* lights of a dozen kerosene lamps still shone from the windows. He ran down the incline, and the growl of a dog, the crowing of cocks, and the low mooing of *carabaos* came to him. He walked hurriedly and entered the grove of kapok and madre de cacao trees that grew along the path. He passed the barrio school that was roofed with tin, its front gate barricaded for the vacation so that goats and the work animals would not stray in. The Coleman lamp in the village store blazed and bathed with cool bluish light the men seated on the bamboo benches below the grass marquee.

Somebody called his name: "Luis! Luisss!" He recognized Tio Joven's raspy voice, and he waved and went on.

He was back in the familiar haunts of childhood, the dying grass and the old hay. Although it was dark, he could feel that the village had not changed. His mother's house was finally before him. How small it really was—how could it have contained four people? Although he expected it, the sound of the sewing machine surprised him. He pushed the bamboo gate and went up the ladder. The rungs creaked and the whirring of the sewing machine stopped.

"Who's there?" It was his mother's thin voice.

Luis did not answer. Came the drag of bare feet on the bamboo floor, the lamp throwing his mother's shadow on the buri walls, then she stood before him, thinner and shabbier than she was the last time he had seen her. For an instant she just stood by the door, shading her eyes with her palm, regarding him with perplexed eyes. He stepped forward, held the bony hand, and kissed it. She sobbed then, and the lamp quivered in her hand. "Luis, my Luis," she whispered, clinging to him.

He felt ill at ease and he gently broke away. By the window his grandfather, who was weaving fishnets, stood up and hobbled to them. "Must you welcome your son with tears?" he asked. Luis took the old man's gnarled hand and kissed it, too. His mother smiled, and placing an arm around his waist, she drew Luis to the narrow *sala* cluttered with pieces of cloth. She raised the lamp to the blackened iron hook dangling from the rafters, and in the poor light she looked at him again. "You are so tall, much more than I expected— and so handsome!" she sighed. She wiped her eyes with the frayed hem of her skirt and smiled.

The old man asked Luis if he had already eaten. "There is half a roasted catfish in the larder," he said. "I caught it this morning. I knew we would have a visitor."

He could not say no to his mother, who dragged him to the kitchen and set the low dining table. The old man picked up a wooden stool from a corner piled with bamboo fish traps and torn nets and set it before the table. "We don't have anything better," his mother said. She placed before him a tin plate with cold chunks of rice and fish—blackened and stiff—and salt. Luis dipped his hand into the shallow coconut-water bowl, and cupping the rice into small balls, he ate, using his hand. The rice was dry and pasty, the fish tasted bitter and burnt. He did not have an appetite, but he could not refuse.

They returned to the *sala* when he was through, his mother carrying the lamp back to its hook.

Then he remembered. "And where is Vic?" he asked no one in particular.

His mother turned away. "I haven't seen Victor for more than three months now, Luis," she said. "When he left he said he would join a trucking company, carry rice from Cagayan and perhaps go to school, to college, like you. I am sure he is well, although he has not written or visited us."

"He came to me last year," Luis said. "He had a job, but I could see that he needed clothes and money. I gave him some."

"Did he ever come to see you again?" his mother asked.

Luis shook his head. He would have wanted to go about the fields and perhaps, with Vic, swim in the Agno, this time fully provisioned, not with only rice and a cake of buri-sap sugar, as it was when they were young. Or they could drive to the foothills to hunt the elusive wild doves, although that would be dangerous now, for the Huks were supposed to be hiding in the deep folds of those hills. Vic had always known the secrets of the land and was always a better hiker. Luis had envied his brother for the stamina and knowledge he had that could be put to use in the country, where book learning would not catch the mudfish or trap the crab. Luis was certain that wherever he was, Vic was well. He could have helped him if Vic only asked, but Vic did not even acknowledge the books that Luis had sent him, which were nowhere in the house.

How Vic had changed—from a docile younger brother into some-one self-willed and strong.

Luis took off his shoes and sat on the floor. His mother sat on a stool that he had made years back as a project for his "industrial work" in school. The old man returned to his perch by the window, the bamboo shuttle now idle in his hand.

"What are you doing now, son, aside from studying?" his mother asked.

"I am now working, Mother," he said. "It is in a newspaper office, and it is very tiring."

"My poor Luis! I hope that you are never in need—"

"Father gives me more than enough," he assured her. "And with my work, I now have a little all my own." He took his wallet out.

"Don't," she said, pride in her voice. "Your grandfather—we make enough to live on, and you know our needs are few."

"Just the same," he said, thrusting the bills into the pocket of her skirt; she made an attempt to take them out, but he held her hand firmly, brought it to his lips, and kissed it. "Mother," he said with emotion, "please—it is my own money now, and I would like to give it to you."

Her eyes shone, and after a while she asked how it was with him, if he had problems. And he told them in a rambling manner how he was not able to finish college and that not having a college degree was not important anymore. He spoke of how he had quar-reled with his father rector, murmuring, "I defied them all, I defied them all," and when the anger evoked by memory died away, he spoke of the trips he had taken, to Hong Kong and the Visayas, the many friends he had made, many of them writers and poets. They sat there, drinking in every word. And looking at them enthralled by his presence, his talk, it suddenly occurred to Luis how unjust he had been to them, how recreant. It is a sham—the thought rankled him; how can I ever tell them that I have told my friends my mother is dead, that Sipnget does not exist, nor Vic and the past that we shared? God—he closed his eyes briefly and pondered his shame—what has warped me?

"I am so happy, Luis," his mother was saying, "I am so happy . . ."

He sidled close to her and held her hand; her palm was cal-loused, and a wave of guilt swept over him again. In their moments of need, which were many, he had helped them little. His work and his friends were not that much of a distraction; he had simply forgotten them, and realizing this, he now saw the futility of his coming here, the hypocrisy of it all, but he said without conviction, "I need you. I am so far away, and I cannot come here as often as I want. I will just send you money then, and write to you more often . . ."

They were silent.

"What is it that you need? Mother, is there any way you can come and see me in Manila, too? I'd like to give you as much of my own money as I can. The little that you have saved, what are you doing with it?"

The old man stirred and looked at his daughter. "Tell him, Nena," he said.

"What we saved," his mother said, "we gave to our leaders. You don't know who they are, but you must know now. Someday, son, we will get back the land your grandfather lost. Then you won't have to worry about sending us money."

"Who are these leaders?" His interest was aroused.

"Fine men," his mother said, "and it won't be long now before we will succeed. You will see."

"You may be fooled again—if you are not careful," he warned them.

"Who knows?" the old man asked, rising from his seat. He inserted the shuttle into a loose fold of the buri wall, lighted his pipe from the lamp, and sat on the floor. "The drowning man clutches at the water lily, hoping that a leaf will save him. Maybe it is the same with us, but this time we are holding on to something bigger—a sturdy raft, not a leaf."

Luis walked to the window. The night was still, and he could hear the river rushing through the shallows.

"Soon, life here won't be all darkness," the old man mused. "We have the right leaders now, Luis—not the way it was."

"Don't believe everything your grandfather says," his mother said. She was spreading the sleeping mat on the bamboo floor. "But something has to be done. Children are born and there is not enough food for them—and you know why."

This, then, was what they hankered for. How elemental their needs and how little did he heed them. All that he remembered was the greenness of leaves, the taunting face of his father, who by one snap of the finger could dispossess them. Where, then, lay their hope and salvation from years of drudgery? His grandfather's words came again: "Our leaders are different now. They are not after money. We hold meetings and they tell us how we have been slaves, not just here but in other places, other countries. The only strength we have is in our numbers—the poor are much more numerous than the rich. And someday we will triumph."

The old man rambled on, but Luis was no longer listening. The sounds of evening, the howling of a dog, and the stray wisps of laughter in Tio Joven's store came to him.

His mother tugged at his arm. "You will sleep here—in the *sipi*, where Vic and you used to sleep?"

He shook his head. "I have to go back, Mother."

"So it must be," the old man said. "Don't hold Luis back. I think he belongs there now."

"I'd like to stay," Luis said, avoiding the old man's eyes, "but I have to leave early tomorrow."

"So soon?" his mother asked. "I thought you would stay here for the vacation."

"My work, Mother," he said simply.

They accompanied him down the path, beyond the squat cogon houses. The store was being closed when they passed, and his Tio Joven called out to him again, asking when he would come back, and Luis shouted, "Soon! Surely!"

They paused at the foot of the dike, and they would have talked some more but he bade them good night, and after kissing their hands, he went up the path.

The walk back to the *camino*, where Simeon waited, seemed unusually long. It was all wrong—his coming here, his going back to Rosales, to a father as impersonal as his caryatids with archaic smiles.

They drove back in silence. Only when the car purred up the driveway did Luis speak. "We go back to the city tomorrow," he told his driver.

Simeon turned to his master: "So soon, Apo? But we have just gotten here."

He did not have to explain, but he did. "I have work to do," he said lamely. "In my kind of work, Simeon, one does not have vacations." Then his tone became jocular: "Don't you want to go back to your wife? From the looks of it, you would rather be away from her!"

TRINING WAS IN his room, reading the manuscripts in his portfolio. "I didn't misplace any of these," she said, turning away from the writing table. "I was waiting. I'm anxious to find out."

Luis sighed. He removed his shoes and dragged a chair to the door that opened to the *azotea,* where a breeze and the scent of the garden flowed in. Trining followed him and caressed his nape. "You stayed quite a long time," she said. "I was beginning to worry."

"Nothing will happen to me." He held her, pressing her to him. "Do you think the Huks are all over the place? Even if they are, they know who I am. What if I didn't return?"

The girl did not speak.

"We had so many things to talk about. After all—all these years . . ." He rose, looking into her eyes, soft and waiting. "This you won't tell Father," he said.

"What is it?"

"I'm leaving tomorrow. In the afternoon, when he will be napping."

Her reaction was quick. She drew away. "No," she cried. "You can't. You said we would stay here two weeks—or even a month!"

He held her shoulders and said solemnly, "Mr. Dantes's silver anniversary, Trining . . ."

She brushed him away. "You are lying," she flung at him. "At least you can be frank with me. I've known you all my life, Luis. What secret is there between us?"

But how can I tell her, how can I say that I am now a stranger among my own people? "You won't understand," he said softly. "You just won't understand."

"But I do," she flared again. She crossed the room and stepped out into the *azotea.* Above, in the cloudless sky, the stars were luminous. He followed her to the ledge. She turned to him. "I won't tell him, of course, if that is what you want, but when he learns that you have gone without telling him he will be very hurt. And what will I tell him then? Will I lie for you again?"

He nodded.

"Will I tell him that you did not want to hurt him by leaving so soon? The Dantes party is important, and Ester invited me, too. But this is not the reason. What you really feel is nothing but loathing for this house, for where you came from. Luis, we must learn to live with all this—you and I. I am alone, too, and I have no one but Tio and you now. All the way home I was thinking of the wonderful vacation we would have—how we would go to the river and swim, perhaps. You don't know how it is to be shut up here or in that convent school."

"I will write to you," he promised. He took her hand and guided her back to the room. "I will try to write to you every day . . ." But he doubted if she heard his last words, for she had wrenched away and ran, her slippers thumping across the silent hall.

CHAPTER

Don Vicente did not join them for breakfast. Trining and Luis had the long table to themselves. The chocolate was very hot, and the *pan de sal,* since it was baked at home, was much bigger than they got in Manila. Mangoes were in season, and the silver tray was full. How was it in Sipnget then? One fruit had to be divided among the four of them, and the seed was always for him. He would savor it by sucking and licking it till it was dry, then he would slip the seed into the eaves of the kitchen roof and it would stay there, dried and waiting. He never got to planting them.

He had expected Trining to be sullen, but the brief encounter last night seemed to have been forgotten, for her face was aglow. He had known her when she was a gangling girl of eight, and he had seen her in all forms of dress and undress. In the warm morning light she was indeed a woman now, clear-skinned and beautiful.

They were finishing their chocolate when across the hall there reverberated a crash, then his father's startled cry. They rushed to the room. By the time they got there Don Vicente had already risen and was at the door, bellowing to the servants to call the captain of his civilian guards.

"What is it, Papa?" Luis asked, but the old man, blocking the door, merely shook his head. "Nothing, nothing, take your cousin away from here . . ." Through the half-open door Luis could see that the window was broken and shards littered the floor.

Shortly before lunch, after he had apparently thought it all out, Don Vicente asked for Luis to come to his room. By then what had happened was the talk among the servants and the civilian guards on the grounds. Luis wanted to question the commander, but his pride held him back. Why did his father not confide in him? That he did not rankled in him as he proceeded to the old man's room.

Luis found his father immensely composed. He was before the window, gazing pensively outside. He even smiled as he turned. Although the old man had a passion for order and cleanliness, he had obviously left everything as it was for Luis to see. "It was intended that I not be hurt," the old man said without emotion. He eased his corpulent frame into his rattan lounging chair, and with his double chin quivering as he shook his head, he continued: "No, they merely wanted me to get this message."

From the marble-topped side table he reached over and picked up a stone as large as a duck's egg and beside it a crumpled piece of paper—the kind that children use in grade school. He handed the paper to his son. The penmanship was masculine and at the same time very fine. Indeed it seemed familiar, although it was in Ilokano: "The land belongs to the people and the people will get what is rightfully theirs. The next message will be delivered with a bullet. Commander Victor."

Luis turned the paper over to see if there was anything on the other side. His father spoke again: "But I do not see how anyone can throw it clear to the window of my room in the daytime. If he was in the street, he would have been seen. In the neighborhood he could not go anyplace. The guards have checked everything."

Victor—Luis mulled over the name, not only because it was his brother's but because once upon a time, during the war, Vic and he did know a Commander Victor. He, too, came from Sipnget, but unlike most of the young men in the village, he had been able to finish high school. He had ambushed the Japanese almost at will and had distributed food, not only in his village but also to others in need.

Commander Victor was dead. But was he really? There was a new Commander Victor whom he had yet to meet.

Luis walked to the window, which opened to the street and to the town plaza and beyond, to the huddled houses of cogon and bamboo, homes of inconsequential people—clerks, shopkeepers. His father was right—it would require great strength to hit his father's bedroom window. Then quickly it came to him that it could be done with a sling—from across the plaza, beyond the houses, from the line of bamboo at the end of the town, and he remembered how he and his brother used to fling stones, making two or three circular swings with their slings before letting go. How well Victor did it then. While his stone often splashed on the opposite rim of the river, Vic's always went beyond, to wherever he aimed.

"Why do they hate me?" his father's voice prodded him. "I have tried my best to do what I can for them. After all, this land, which my great-grandfather cleared—all of it—bears more than just his pride and our name, and we are duty-bound to preserve it and help those who help us preserve it. Haven't we lived with honor, giving them what is their due, helping them with their problems, no matter how personal? When they are born, when they get married, when they get sick, and when they die—to whom do they come for help? It's I and no one else; I look after them, more than like a father. Can they not see what this means? My brother was the same—he helped them and they killed him and his poor helpless wife, his son. What kind of people are these? Can they not see that we are honorable?"

Luis knew all the words—the rights of the nobility, the responsibilities of serfs—but now they did not evoke anger from him, just indifference, and if he could, he would banish them from his own vocabulary, just as he would relegate all of Rosales to limbo.

"Why do they hate me?" the old man repeated sadly. "Soon it will be a grenade in the yard—or poison in our food. Yet I care for them, more than they will ever know. I have built irrigation ditches for them, sent them to the puericulture center, given rice and money to the priest so that he can go to their villages and minister to their needs. I contribute to their fiesta generously. I have stood as godfather to their children—they are all my children—and they hate me. I can see it in their faces when they come here, whining and begging for help. They cheat me of the harvest, but I continue to keep them because I love them, because they are part of the land, which is part of me. What do they want that I cannot give? They have food, security, and peace. They are happiest as they are, and they do not have a single worry—not a bit of what I have to endure—and only because they are under my wing. They repay me with this—this," he said, pointing to the piece of paper on the table. "Luis, can you explain this to me?"

It would have been the simplest thing to do, to declare that Rosales was no longer the paradise his father had proclaimed, that paternalism was done for, that charity is its own stigma and that the best of intentions are often brutalized and demeaned, but he chose to speak as only a son would: "You must be patient, Father. We are living in difficult times, and this is not your creation. It was created by the war, by expectations that could not be fulfilled. They will learn in time what their place really is, but"—and now he weighed his words carefully, hoping not to displease his father—"we must also understand that if we are to stay here, to be on top as we have always been"—he checked himself and was surprised that he was verbally and emotionally taking his father's side—"then we must also change and learn to understand what is happening below us."

"Just what do you mean?"

"Change, Father, is sometimes imperceptible, because it is slow. You have changed, too, perhaps without knowing it."

Don Vicente smiled. "Yes, yes," he mumbled under his breath. Then, "When you were there last night, how was it?"

"Everything was fine, Father," he said. Don Vicente turned away, waving his son off. "Everything was fine, Father," he repeated as he went out of the room. He was again the boy who played on the banks of the Agno, who shared a roof in Sipnget with another boy and with this boy ate the same soft-boiled rice in the lean months of the planting season. Vic was with him again—the stone, the sling— and he would always be near. If he was darkness, Vic was light, was free, while Luis was encumbered with a past, the remembered experience that brought no certainty, although it was as real as flesh and as haughty as day.

Time that I have lived! It is all here now, compressed in this house, encompassed by this little town. Time that I have lived—there is a creek that passes the village, a creek spanned by an old wooden bridge that was often washed away by monsoon floods. When the rain comes in June the creek slowly fills, then overflows, and the waters could come right to our backyard and we would go to the bridge with long poles and ensnare the pieces of driftwood that have been carried away by the current and we would keep these for firewood. When the rains subside the creek dries up until there are just pools, moss-green and muddy, but we would still bathe in it, for the creek is closest to us and it was here where Vic first told me: Manong, you are white and I am brown. We are brothers, but how can that be? The creek brought us face-to-face. Again, one day, he said: I have been told that you should leave and that if you left, you would not return. I will leave, too, as all of us do leave the place where we were born—but I am sure we will come back.

Vic had returned. That could have been his message that Luis had seen, that could have been his sling. Then it occurred to him that he was ignorant of his brother's movements. If Vic had changed somehow, Luis had helped in the transformation, for it was he, after all, who had sent Vic the books to read and had helped him find the answers. Vic did not have to search far if he had desired to find answers himself, for they were all here in Rosales amidst the implacable poverty and the dullness of the herd.

Luis was free at last from all these, thanks to his benevolent father. He could roam and reap the harvest—but not Vic, although at least Vic now had the freedom to create, to travel an expanse unlimited by geography or vision. Luis prayed to God that in spite of everything Vic would retain this thought at least: that they were brothers and that Luis had not forgotten the jungle's torment. Vic was courage, and what did Luis have to show to redeem his manhood, to attest to his creativity? A few poems? He had the beneficence of a name he was born to bear. If he could only turn back, he could now be by Victor's side as he should be, for his brother was also his fate.

CHAPTER

21

LUIS CHANGED HIS MIND about not saying good-bye. He had expected his father to hold him back, but Don Vicente was more than understanding. He even tried to be blithe about it.

"I see, I see," he said, nodding and grinning, so that the double chin quivered and the bags under his eyes broadened. "Rosales is very dull except for what happened this morning. What is more, you cannot miss the party of the year—yes, I have read about all those European dukes coming. In any case I have already told you what needs to be said. Do not forget—"

"I won't," Luis said, holding the pudgy hand to his brow. His suitcases were packed, Simeon was waiting downstairs, and outside his father's room Trining was pacing the hall, waiting for him. "I won't," he repeated, then he wheeled out.

But what was there to remember? It was a story he had heard so many times, the call to duty and the land, that his future was in politics. It was of course difficult to understand his father's attachment to the land. As a young man, Don Vicente had lived in Spain, visited the old village near Bilbao where his great-grandfather had come from. There was not much now in the Asperri lineage to suggest that it was Basque, nothing but the name, the fair skin, and the demeanor, and those did not matter. His exhortations were sown on barren soil, on the arid reality of Rosales itself. The life of the mind, which beckoned to Luis, was in Manila. It was better to revel in it, to seek the kindred vitality of the young who revolved around the editorial offices, and the nearness of Trining, Ester, and her friends. Although he did not want to indulge in it, he basked in their flattering attention—a result of not only his looks but also because as a poet he exuded some kind of exotic magnetism.

He wanted to spend some time with Trining, but she had waited in the hall only to find out if he would be permitted to leave, and when she found out, she had rushed to her room. He knocked at the door, pleading, but she would not open it. From within came a mumbling sound that could have been her weeping.

He reached the city at dusk. Depressed, he had dozed through most of the checkpoints, and Simeon, still displeased that Luis had cut his vacation short, had been sullenly quiet. The depression lasted for some time, and it was not banished even after Luis had finished the homework he had brought with him.

He developed in his mind a master dummy of the next issue of *Our Time*. There would be a couple of articles on the Bell Act, an exposition on the cultural resurgence in Southeast Asia, a couple of stories, and an essay on the crisis of the Filipino identity. The scenery no longer interested him as it did the previous day. The country was drab, dead brown. The dirty towns through which they passed were all the same, their asphalted main streets lined with wooden shops boarded with impieties of soft-drink signs.

"Do you want to pass by the office, *señorito*?" Simeon's voice startled him. They were now entering the city, and the traffic in Balintawak was tangled again—jeepneys and buses filled with office workers hurrying home. Toward the west the sky was a riot of indigo. Dusk finally brought a sense of peace.

"Home," Luis said. He needed a shower more than anything, to wash away the fatigue. The car could not avoid Rizal Avenue and the snarl of traffic in Plaza Goiti, but in a while they were on the boulevard and Luis felt at home once more in the wide Luneta, now covered with dying grass, and to the right the sea, the stubby trees, all covered with the deep and onrushing dark.

The house was one of those prewar structures spared by the holocaust of Liberation that leveled much of the Ermita and Malate districts, south of the river. It was built by his grandfather in the twenties for Vicente and his Spanish bride.

Sometimes his grandfather drifted into his thoughts, particularly when Luis and his writer friends talked about the revolution of 1896 and how in the end it was usurped by the *ilustrados*. His grandfather was one of them; though he had always considered himself—according to Don Vicente—a Filipino, Luis knew that his loyalties were with that far-off peninsula from which his forebears had come. The old man had been an astute politician, although he did not run for any public office; he knew where the centers of powers were, and when he saw, for instance, the inevitability of revolution, he made the proper noises, which seemed to indicate that he, at least, sympathized with the ill-disciplined, ill-equipped Army. As a Basque, he had always regarded the Spaniard as inferior in the first place. But to avoid total involvement, he had feigned illnesses and was conveniently sick in Manila. The coming of the Americans ended the masquerade for the wily old Vascongado. He saw the inevitability of American suzerainty, and one of the first things he did was join the Federalista party. He would have gotten a very high position in the new government—friendly as he was with those in Manila—but he had decided, like all good Basques, that the future lay in the land, which had, after all, supported him in splendor all through the years.

He was not wrong; it was a time when the haciendas were being forged and sugar plantations in the south were being set up with American and other foreign money. He went back to Pangasinan and the vast lands he had laid claim to and built that region's biggest house, which became a rest stop for any tired and visiting *Americano*. In the process, through the American cadastral surveys that were being made all over the country, he brought out his old Spanish titles, and with Spanish sherry and other forms of concession, he included into the Hacienda Asperri hundreds of small clearings that the Ilokano settlers had made.

The old man liked to consider himself a diviner, a plutocrat ahead of his time. He saw, for instance, the movement of Manila out of the strictures of Intramuros, and he bought lots in Santa Mesa and of course in Ermita, on the boulevard close to the sea. It was in the Ermita house he built where his son Vicente lived, his daughters having married Americans and Spaniards and left for wherever their husbands willed.

The hacienda in Pangasinan prospered, and he died a very happy man knowing that his other son was prepared to take over while Vicente hobnobbed with the rich and the powerful in Manila. He did not know of the ill will that exploitation had spawned, how the house would be burned by the same peasants who he thought were loyal to him. Don Vicente continued living in Manila, depending on the overseers who worked for him, knowing that though he was in the city, he wielded great power. He played poker regularly with Quezon and was on the best of terms with the mestizos who revolved around Malacañang.

Having finished law and studied history as well, he had learned what his father had taught him, and to this wisdom he added his own instincts. He had information on what stocks to buy, where new roads were to be built, and when export crops were to be developed, and his intentional losses at the poker table, which were substantial, were easily recouped.

He contributed, too, to the campaign funds of senators and, of course, to the Independence mission, while in Pangasinan his tenants toiled and filled his *bodegas* with grain. Even when his brother was killed and he had taken his niece under his wing, he did not see the need for returning to Pangasinan; the order of things was secure, the constabulary would see to it that a similar uprising would never happen again.

After the war, his instincts served him once more; he could see the changes coming, and one of the first things he did was rebuild the old house that had been burned, bringing to it many of the artifacts in Manila that were not destroyed; his son was growing, he could leave Manila and go back to the land where he now should be.

Luis had the Ermita house, therefore, all to himself shortly after he finished high school, except on those occasions when Don Vicente visited him, which was quite often at first but soon became infrequent. Don Vicente gambled still, but most of his old poker cronies had died, some of them at the hands of the Japanese, some in exile in America, and the old man did not seem to be at ease with the new occupants of Malacañang. Luis also knew that his father had some special women in Manila. He had never seen the Spanish woman his father married, for she was one of those mysterious creatures who lived in the shadows. The servants talked of her, however, of her madness, of her having been shut up in a hospital in Manila and then in the tower room of the big house, where she would be very quiet except for her whimpering, which sounded more animal than human. There was no medicine, no doctor, however, that could clear her mind, render it lucid again, for what had cracked was not because of some genetic discrepancy or some frustration that had finally surfaced but the heavy accretion of past profligacies, lies, indiscretions, and that hedonist view that regarded woman as a plaything as, indeed, Don Vicente considered his wife when she was younger. But she was a sensitive woman who was not just uprooted from hearth and home; she had also loved her husband deeply and had great hopes about the new land that she thought would be her country as well. When the poor woman finally died, her funeral was just as secret, for she was buried not in Rosales but in a cemetery in Manila. To the best of his knowledge, his father never visited her grave, and not once did he tell Luis of the life they had lived together, even in those moments when Don Vicente was reminiscing about Europe.

The Ermita house was not particularly big by the standards of the district, which was Manila's best housing area, but it was formidably built in Spanish style, with wrought-iron grills for windows and doorways. Red tiles were used unsparingly, and the walls were serrated, although this fact was no longer visible, for the walls had been covered with ivy, which Simeon trimmed. The grounds were wide, the grass was mowed regularly, and the pots of dahlias and ground orchids seemed perennially in bloom. Somehow the Ilokano nature of Luis's housekeepers was evident in the grounds, for at the back, close to the garage where they lived, were plots of tomato, eggplant, and okra, and it was from this garden that Luis often got his fresh vegetables when he felt like having vegetable stew.

The house had four bedrooms, and furnishing and decorating them when he was through with high school had given him some amusement. Together with Trining he had toured the furniture shops and the few drapery stalls in Divisoria. He had had air-conditioning installed in his bedroom and in the room that he had converted into a study/guest room. In the hall his father had placed a grand piano, which no one played except Trining when she dropped by with her college friends. He had a radio/phono, too, in the study, and extra speakers in the living room, and although he leaned toward the classics, Trining insisted on buying and stocking the record bar with her own Latin and boogie-woogie favorites. His library had been growing, but he often lent books to friends, and some of them took advantage of his good nature and forgetfulness.

Marta was watering the gumamela hedges by the gate when the car drove in. She flung the gate open, then ran to open the door of the house.

"I wasn't expecting you so soon, *señorito,*" she said. She switched on all the lights as Simeon carried his suitcases to his room.

He called Eddie at once, and as expected, although it was already almost seven, his associate was still in the office. Luis had left instructions on how the next two issues would be run, and he had hinted, too, that he might lengthen his vacation, so Eddie sounded surprised: "I thought I would be parking on your swivel chair for some time. What's the matter—you broke a blood vessel?"

Luis laughed. "That's a bad guess. It is the place, Eddie." He felt that he was being honest. "Any mail?"

"Contributions," Eddie said, "and some angry letters about the last article on labor you wrote. But they won't sue because they are all crooks. I am glad you have returned, so you can be at the party tonight. You know, only editors were invited—from the entire outfit there are only eight of you going, and you know how the Old Man feels about invitations being rejected."

Luis knew. There was the famous story he had told earlier about how Dantes had eased out one of the executives in his shipping company after the man and his wife were invited to a sit-down dinner and only his wife came because her husband was down with a cold. In spite of such feudal attitudes, however, Dantes regarded his editorial people with more than employer interest. In the mornings when he was in his publishing office he often called his editors in to do nothing but play chess or comment on a new painting or sculpture that he had acquired. All the while the bar at the end of his office would be open and a waiter in white would hover around, jumping to their every whim, dumb-faced to their discussions of politics and culture. It was also at these informal sessions that Dantes gave instructions to his columnists and his editors—he would identify the targets of his derision and his ire, and it mattered not if the sessions lasted until lunchtime, for he would have lunch brought to the room. The editors always knew when the talk was over, for Dantes, almost as a ritual, would open his gold cigarette case and pass around—even to those who did not smoke—Sobranie Black Russians, and then he would light each stick individually with his gold lighter, and after a few puffs he would smile benignly and say, "Well, boys, that is how the cookie crumbles"—an old expression that he never quite forgot from his Harvard undergraduate days. Then the editors would file out, their heads up in the air, for the oracle had spoken and now they knew what to do.

Luis had gone to see Dantes before he left, telegram in hand, saying that he would have to rush home to see his ailing father but that if everything was all right, he would be back. No, he must not miss Mr. Dantes's silver wedding anniversary. The publisher had grudgingly consented to let him go home, "on humanitarian grounds," but he had ended the interview saying, "Luis, you must know that this party is important to me."

There were other parties, and the whole week was to be devoted to them—one for each company, one for close relatives alone, then this major bash, for which the royalty of Europe had been flown in by chartered Stratocruzer and billeted in two whole floors of the Manila Hotel, together with an orchestra from the United States, a couple of opera singers, one from La Scala and the other from the Met, plus the five hundred most important Filipinos, headed by the president and his social-climbing wife.

"Any message?" Luis asked.

"Yes, Miss Vale asked if you had arrived. She seemed very anxious. It was Dantes's daughter who asked for you. Say, you are moving up very fast."

He wondered if Ester had been instructed by her father to inquire or if she had done it on her own, but Miss Vale, Dantes's old-maid secretary, never went into details. She gave out only the barest information, and it seemed that her head was full of secrets but that she stored them for no one but Dantes.

Even when he was in college, Luis did not swallow everything said in the classroom. The family, the teacher, the church—everything was authoritarian, but there was a far more impressive schooling that he had gone through, where one learned freely: the years in Sipnget, which taught him how important relationships were, how people were what they were. It took only a few weeks in the Dantes offices, therefore, for him to know and to latch on to knowledge that was not dispensed in his sociology or political science classes, to amass the information that was never printed in the papers—not even in his own, noted though it was for its liberalism and steadfastness to truth as Dantes—not his staffers—saw it.

As Don Vicente had said, Dantes was no patriot who would sacrifice for freedom and nation; he was a power merchant, selling dreams in his media complex and manipulating men with power at the same time. He could have had his main office in his shipping company and trading firm, which occupied one building in that new community called Pobres Park going up somewhere in Makati, or in his electric and communications building—but no, he chose to have his main offices here in this newspaper building, for it was with his newspapers that he wielded the most influence.

He was an astute politician, although he did not make speeches or run for any public office; in the highest echelons of both the Nacionalista and the Liberal parties, men vied for his favors and trembled at the slightest rumor of his displeasure. It was also believed that he was supporting the Huk movement and that his politics for the future was voiced by his leftist writers like Abelardo Cruz and Etang Papel, fire-breathing "liberals" who knew whichever way the wind blew.

Luis had amazed both of these writers with his insights on rural life, the mute aspirations of those who work the land. Cruz and Papel were city-room revolutionaries who had romanticized their ignorance with facility, and in a sense Luis saw himself in them, for he, too, for all his protestations, was just as comfortable and incapable of sacrifice as they. But there was one major difference, which he prided himself on—he had lived on a farm, knew of the sun's rage, the cold of the waterlogged paddies, and he had exposed Abelardo Cruz's rural knowledge as a book-learned sham. "Do you know how to catch freshwater crabs in the fields?" he had asked the pugnacious editor one evening when they were having coffee after the paper had been put to bed. Cruz claimed he did and even went into the motions of how he did it as a boy, until Luis asked the most important, the most crucial question: "And what if there is no water in the hole?" It was one of the first things any boy in Sipnget learned, for it spelled the difference between life and death. And Luis explained it to them, these champions of agrarian change, these lovers of the poor: "When there is water in the hole, stick your hand in. The crab could be there. But in heaven's name—don't stick it in if there is no water. A snake may be there."

Etang Papel had insisted with her Manileña ignorance and *colegiala* impertinence that the lower classes were the makers of revolution; after all, she read and echoed the *Manchester Guardian* and those books that were difficult to come by but could easily be had if you had friends in New York or in London. But Luis knew that the indolence of the masses was real, that their volcanic angers were the accretion of repressed feelings, for he had seen dogged patience and docile servitude that had numbed their capacity for scrutiny. He had seen them troop to his father's house to borrow money, to reaffirm their bondage—that they were secure in it, that his father could do no wrong. Where, then, was the massive force that could be harnessed? It certainly was not in this city room, it certainly was not in Sipnget; wherever it was, it had to be nurtured, lavished with care, so that it would sprout and grow. And only then . . .

In many ways, he was very glad that he had Eddie to work with; he had met him at one of the college-editors conferences in his junior year. They had gone to the south and stayed for a week as guests of Dantes at one of the publisher's island retreats off the city of Iloilo. And one night the two of them had wandered down the empty beach, and Eduardo Sison, the editor of a small college paper, had talked with him, questioned him, rather, about many of his assumptions, uncaring of the fact that he was a rich man's son. Like Ester, he had asked Luis about his motivations, his insincerity. Eddie, after all, was a self-supporting student who clerked in a Chinese store in the daytime, then went to an accounting class in the evenings. He had a natural talent for writing, but he also had the peasant's natural talent for survival, and because he was a farmer's son, his instincts for what was right were also sharp. When this opening with the Dantes group came and Luis was asked to get a right-hand man, he did not hesitate in naming Eddie. The magazine was about three years old, and there was gossip that the former editor and his associate had been eased out for trying to set up a union. It was a weekly and their deadline was more flexible, but Thursdays were a travail, for the magazine came out on Friday, early enough, according to

Dantes, to beat the Sunday magazines and yet interesting enough for the reader to go back to it for his weekend fare.

It was patterned after the staid English weeklies—Dantes affected a liking for British papers—but its presentation was bright and breezy. The writing was in-depth without being ponderous, and the contributors, whose numbers Luis built up through personal meetings, covered a wide spectrum—conservatives and radicals, campus literati and aloof Ph.D.'s.

He did not know it, but it was Ester who had brought his name to her father's attention. She had heard of him often from Trining, had read his poetry, which Trining would bring surreptitiously to school, and the articles he had written in his college paper and in the other newspapers, for by the time he was in his senior year Luis had already caught the attention of the national-magazine editors for his forceful but elegant prose, and when he met them they were surprised that he was still in college.

Dantes gave his two young editors a free hand, and he was not disappointed. Luis was a good team leader, although there was not much of a team to lead—just Eddie and one staff member, two proof-reader/copyreaders, and a layout artist. Most of the articles were solicited, but in spite of a growing list of distinguished contributors the editors still had a lot of topical writing to do themselves—and fashioning those subheads and those pungent captions was always a dreary chore.

Trining was right—the magazine was his life. Ester took him for a snob when they met for the first time, but he remembered her face, and it was not because she was Dantes's daughter. There was a quality of frailty about her, of tragedy in her eyes. He remembered her, although she wore that anonymous brown, stiff-collared convent-school uniform. She had gone to her father's office that morning and had interrupted a discussion on Hemingway's latest fiction, *The Old Man and the Sea.*

"My daughter," Dantes had introduced her, and Luis had turned to her standing by the table, notebooks in her arm. He merely nodded—an almost mechanical reaction—then went on with the discussion, saying that Hemingway's simplicity was terribly misleading, that this was no simple fisherman out for big game, that the work belonged to the same classic mold as Melville's *Moby Dick,* that it was the story of man searching for meaning, and Ester stood there, listening until it was time for Dantes to hand out his black gold-tipped cigarettes to the two young men, who took them although they never really smoked. He did not speak to her, and he did not even bid her good-bye when he left the publisher's office.

AT EIGHT-THIRTY Luis was ready. He could not make up his mind as to whether or not he should wear a tuxedo. The invitation had left the choice open between black tie and national costume, but it was so warm that he compromised by putting on a *barong tagalog,* with the collar buttoned, over his tuxedo pants.

The Dantes mansion—or compound—occupied a huge lot in San Juan, perhaps a full two hectares of choice land overlooking the city. It had been purchased by the Dantes clan before the war, when such mansions were comparatively cheap and there were still a few nipa houses in the area. The land was rocky, as were most of the environs of Manila, and people were not attracted to it, for nothing would grow on it except sturdy acacia and guava trees.

Five blocks away from the Dantes house, Luis was struck by the immensity of the party. The whole distance was lined with fat, glossy Cadillacs, Jaguars, and Rolls-Royces. Ubiquitous motorcycle policemen from San Juan and Manila directed traffic. It was the party of the year, perhaps of the decade or even the century, but nothing was said about it in any of the papers that belonged to Dantes. It was in the other papers that the event made a splash, for the three big publishers, in spite of their stiff competition for advertising, had formed an informal club where their social doings and good deeds were publicized but not in their own papers—an expression of urbanity that was somehow shallow and hypocritical. It was in the other papers, too, that Luis had read about Sydney oysters and Australian lamb being flown to Manila for this party, along with champagne by the gallon, truffles from France, Roquefort and Stilton cheeses, and other gourmet foods, about how the tables were decorated with tulips from Holland, and then, of course, about the guests—bank presidents from Wall Street, a couple of princesses and some dukes, and a dozen titled personages from Europe.

As he neared the Dantes mansion, a uniformed police colonel stopped his car at the gate and checked his invitation with the guest list, then a police captain gave his driver a card with a number and told him to park farther up the street. They drove into the compound, which smouldered with multicolored bulbs, and the door was opened by a doorman resplendent in the gala uniform of a police colonel. Like most of the big houses in the neighborhood, the Dantes residence was done in the ornate architecture of the twenties and thirties and surrounded by high adobe walls now covered with ivy. The acacia trees were strung with colored bulbs—green and blue and red—and in the carefully manicured gardens were huge candy-striped tents; in the tents were tables. There were four buffet tables at strategic places on the grounds, and beyond, on a stage before the tennis court that was not covered with Masonite, the American orchestra was playing "Autumn Leaves." Luis listened briefly and concluded that the Bayside band was better.

The guests spilled all over, on the terraces, under the high bushy pergolas, and across the grassy lawn. Waiters in white *barong tagalog,* black pants, and white gloves flitted about balancing trays and carrying drinks, and all around was the happy sound of people at play.

The night was unusually cool, and the scent of sampaguitas hovered over everything. In the biggest tent, at the other end of the tennis court, Dantes was seated with his asthmatic wife, and beside them were the president and First Lady. Luis could see them clearly in spite of the distance.

He walked toward the tent, and midway he caught Ester's eyes. She rushed to him, and together they went to her father and mother.

"Congratulations, sir, madame," Luis said, shaking the couple's hands, and Dantes, ever the impeccable host, asked, "I hope your father is well, Luis."

"Yes, sir," he said.

"Well," Dantes said, "Ester, he is all yours."

Luis took another look at the celebrants. Dantes looked older than his fifty-five years, his hair prematurely white and with bags under his eyes, which were perennially misty. His chin always quivered when he talked, and it was quivering now as he chatted with a couple who had just arrived. Luis became aware of Ester's hand gripping his and keeping him from tarrying. "Oh, I'm so glad you came," she said, gushing. "I asked Papa if you were coming, and he said that you had gone home to visit your ailing father. So you left Trining there. She should have come, too. I was allowed four guests, and she is, well, my best friend—but you are here and that is all that matters."

"I wouldn't miss this for all the world," he said, "and not because it is your parents' anniversary but because you are here; I really want to know you better."

She squeezed his hand and said, "Flatterer! But I love it. Would you like to meet my friends, or would you rather join your crowd?" She pointed to a tent close to one of the buffet tables.

They were passing a floodlight that blazed upon a huge statue of ice—a swan in the middle of a big table of hors d'oeuvres—and drawing away from her, he saw how beautiful Ester was. He noted the difference between her uniform and this billowy fuchsia gown she was blooming in tonight. A dash of rouge, a bit of eye shadow—she had the fine features of the Danteses, the fair skin, the imperious chin. Gazing at her in the brightness, he said, "Ester, you are beautiful," meaning every word of it.

She laughed: "If you keep this up the whole evening, I may yet become your girlfriend."

He picked a cracker from the table and scooped caviar from a bowl.

"I'll stay with you and serve you," Ester said, "if you are hungry."

"Starved," Luis said. She guided him to a food-laden table beyond the court where a crowd was busy filling up their plates. She helped him choose his, then took him to a vacant table by the court. She was being the perfect hostess. "I've told my friends I may have a very eligible bachelor—I hope you will not disappoint them," she said.

"I'll stop the presses to see you," he told her. She left him to bring her friends over. He was not really hungry. With a glass of Scotch he went up to the balcony, where he could have an unobstructed view of the garden, the guests rambling around in its great breadth. The orchestra played softly, and couples started moving toward the court. He was not aware that Ester had followed him and was hovering around him, a quizzical look on her face.

"I thought you would be down there," she said solicitously. "I hope you are not angry with anyone."

"Oh, no," he said, laughing. "I was waiting for your gang, but where are they?"

"Dancing," she said gaily, "but I will make up for it. I will be your partner the rest of the evening—if you want."

She took the vacant chair beside him. "I wanted Trining to come—very much—but going to the province was more important. How is your father?"

"Not so well, but he will manage. Old people always do." The orchestra started playing "Stardust." "That's one of my favorites," Luis said. "Learned it during the war. The words are poetic."

"I've read your poetry," Ester said.

"My condolences."

"I like it—but why is it always so sad and bitter? You must be terribly unhappy."

"Are you a psychologist of sorts?"

"No, just trying to understand you."

"I'm an open book. No deep dark secrets."

She stood up. "Let's not waste your favorite song," she said, holding his hand.

They went down the stone steps. At the edge of the court he hesitated, suddenly awkward, knees watery, as if this were his first dance. She was already pressing close to him, however, so he held her narrow waist and her hand went up to rest on his shoulder, her cheek brushing against his chin. He felt the round, smooth, and silky nudging of her thighs, the warm softness of her breast, and all his senses became alive in response to her exalting nearness. He wanted to dance with her still, but the orchestra shifted to an abominable limbo and he said tersely, "There goes our poetry." A young man whose face he did not bother to look at accosted them on their way back to their seats and asked Ester for a dance. Luis let her go.

He slid into the shadows, down the garden slope, where the bougainvillea thinned out toward the rocky promontory. He stood there and watched the city in the distance, aglow like embers, kindling a sky flecked with summer clouds. His back was turned to the music, and soon, so soon, he was hurtling away from this precinct to another time, in a far and forgotten place, and the music was the twang of guitars: I always go back, back to where it all started, to Sipnget, and the village fiesta, lighted by kerosene lamps, the hardened earth for a dance floor, the woven palm leaf for decor, divider, and shade, and the village girls . . .

"At last, I've found you." It was Ester behind him. He turned around, stepped down the rock, and said, "The view from here is lovely. Manila looks like a spread of jewels."

"Not in the daytime," she said. "There's a haze over it, and it looks quite ugly." Then, seriously, "Why did you leave the party?"

"I'm still here, am I not?" he asked.

"I should have asked what you are doing here."

"Not again," he said. He held her arm as they went down the incline. "Don't you know that you make me feel so eccentric?"

"You didn't answer my question."

"Well, I just wandered around and I got to thinking about the town I left, the music I used to listen to. You know, just rambling around in my thoughts—I often do that. It's quite exhilarating."

"How far did you go?"

Luis did not know what to make of her, whether she was making fun of him or was sincerely inquisitive. He decided to be honest. "I was thinking of the very recent past—the war. I had to stop high school, and I commuted between Manila and the province, you know. Looking at Manila from here, with all those lights, and listening to the music, I am aware that time has really gone by."

They went down a terrace and were now on the edge of the dance floor. Luis sat with her near the garden wall.

"We have to live in the present," she said simply, "and thank God we are here, waiting for the morrow."

"You are an optimist, I can see," he said. "But the present is an extension of the past. The connection is not broken at all, and the war—what a big word it is!—it is an extension of peace."

BUT WHAT did he really know about the war? He was too young to have been in the Army and too old to be with the women. He spent the four war years in Ermita, where he grew up to be a young man, pampered, all his wishes granted. He was frightened, but he was never really in danger. It was Vic who knew war, who told him about its starkest details. It was Vic who was in Rosales and Sipnget, who helped to take care of Don Vicente in the earliest days of evacuation. Vic saw the Japanese enter the town, and he saw the pile of Filipino dead—their hands tied behind them with wire—loaded into pushcarts by civilians and taken to the plaza, before the whitewashed Rizal monument, and like so many diseased and butchered cattle, dumped into a common grave. Vic was in Sipnget, too, when the Japanese entered the village, herded the young men together, and picked out the prettiest girls. Now there was another war, and it was being fought in the mountains, in the plains, in Sipnget and Rosales, in dark, unknown warrens of the city, in newspaper offices, and most of all, in the convoluted recesses of minds such as his.

"You are young only once, but you want to grow old before your time," Ester was saying.

"Our tragedy," he said, trying to sound very light, "is that, as a famous writer once said, youth is wasted on the young."

"But I don't think you have really started to live." Ester was prodding him. She had struck at the root of his ennui, and perhaps, he thought later, she was right. He had not begun to live—or love. He had not seen life as Vic had seen it; all that he had seen were the freaks, both of the imagination and of living reality. He had listened once to his grandfather's tales, of *aswangs* making gold out of children's blood, of winged men who could with a wave of a kerchief vault mountain and valley.

"I guess you're right," he said. "Why don't you help me live a little?" He glanced at his watch.

"It is still early," Ester said, "and you asked me to help, didn't you?"

It was a dare he must pick up sometime. Right now he could not stay for another moment. The night was lost, no matter how amusing the conversation and enchanting this girl. In that inner self there was no light; there was this scourge of the searching mind that could not be eluded.

"I have to be up very early," he said. "Aren't you happy that I'm such a thoughtful employee?"

"That's not a nice thing to say," she said. "You are trying to put me in my place, and I am not spoiled."

"I'm sorry."

Ester tried to be light. "And speaking of Father, he sleeps until lunchtime sometimes but still manages to work the whole night. Aren't you really going to meet some of my friends?"

Luis smiled and stood up. "I'd rather be with you," he said solemnly. He had intended to flatter her, but now that he had said it he meant every word. "I really would like very much to be with you again when I can have you all to myself."

Her eyes shone, and he felt that they were looking right through his permeable skull, into the recondite corners of his brain, reading his thoughts as if they were in blazing neon.

"I'm not really a snob—even if you did call me one."

"I did not," she objected vehemently. "Whoever gave you—"

He pressed his forefinger to her lips to stop her from talking further. "I think I am beginning to love you," he said.

Even as he drove away it seemed as if Ester was still beside him. He could still smell her fragrance, her hair, and most of all, he could envision those dark, sad eyes that would—he was now sure—always hound him.

WHEN LUIS DROVE UP the graveled driveway and saw that the lights in his bedroom were on, he decided that Marta must have forgotten to turn them off again. It was her duty to turn off all the lights except those in the foyer whenever he went out in the evening. He would remind her in the morning about her wastefulness. He went up the stairs, fumbled briefly with his keys, then opened the door. Soft music flowed from the radio/phonograph in the study. It was almost midnight, and he did not remember having turned it on when he left. He hurried in and turned the radio off; glancing into his bedroom, he saw Trining, asleep in his bed. He gazed at her with some vexation, which quickly turned into amusement. Trining was in a pink negligée, the hem of which was raised, so that her beautiful white thighs gleamed creamy and soft in the light. He could also see the clean slopes of her breast and its rising and falling as she breathed. He went into the room, bent over her slowly, and kissed her lips. She stirred, stretched her arms, then opened her eyes.

"Oh, Luis," she murmured, purring like a kitten disturbed from a nap. Her displeasure with his having left her was gone, and a smile lit her face. She swung her legs down and stood up.

"What are you doing here?" he asked, wondering how she had come—and so soon. "Had I known you also wanted to return to Manila, I would have waited for you."

"I told Tio that I wanted to be with you—and he put me on the bus. You should take the bus sometime. It is quite an experience. Tio wanted me driven over, but why should it matter how I came?"

Luis started taking off his *barong tagalog*.

"How were the dukes and the princesses?"

"I never met them. Ester said you should have come."

He took his pants off and put on his pajamas. He could undress before her without embarrassment, for they had grown up together, known each other for so long.

"I'll stay here for a month, if you'll let me—or two months. Then I will go back to school."

"You should be in Rosales."

"I can't go back. The house bores me; you yourself hate it. I think I will take up a secretarial course—shorthand and typing. I'll keep house for you, and I can type some of your manuscripts afterward."

"Thank you, but you will only mess up everything."

"You don't even give me a chance."

"And I don't want you to stay longer than you should. People, my friends come here—you know that—and they will talk."

"Tio said I should stay here until school begins," she said stubbornly. "We are cousins, Luis, or have you forgotten?"

He scowled at her. He went to the bathroom and started to brush his teeth. "Have you fixed up the guest room?"

"Marta has done that."

Luis went back to his room, took Trining by the hand, and led her to the sofa, where they sat, her head resting on his shoulder, his arm around her. "How did Father take my leaving so soon?"

"He was very sad," she said evenly, "but I think he understands. Anyway, you have seen him—and he told you things, I presume." Then, somberly: "What's happening, Luis? Are we going to have trouble? Sometimes just thinking about this frightens me and makes me sad. No, not again. Oh, God, not again! You once said that we are far from the—the people. This morning, remembering what you said, I took the bus, and a taxi from the bus station to here. I was not scared. Only once—only once . . ."

"Brave girl." He patted her arm.

"I don't even know now if I should finish college. It seems unnecessary. What do you think, Luis?" She paused and pressed closer to him. "What is going to happen to us?"

He remembered how he had kissed her for the first time the other evening. There were many times in the past when he would embrace her as they danced or horsed around, but there was never any of this closeness and this intimacy that they now shared.

"I wish I could tell you now," he said, "but everything is so uncertain. Let's not talk about the future. Think about something more pleasant."

"Let's talk about Mr. Dantes's anniversary. The grandest thing ever, and I did not go."

"It was fine."

"Were my classmates there? Whom did you meet?"

"None," Luis said, "but I did get to know a bit of Ester, and she set me thinking."

"What about?" Her interest was piqued.

"She rather seems too mature for her age . . ."

"And you think that I am not—that I am a scatterbrain besides?"

He hugged her. "No, but why compare yourself with her? You are prettier, although she isn't bad-looking."

"You can say that again," Trining said boorishly.

"I told her that I'd like to see her again."

Trining turned to him. He could feel her breath warm on his cheek, and her voice was belligerent. "Just what is it that you want to do?" He smiled at her and pressed her close to him again. "Are you in love with her?" He tweaked her nose and laughed. "Well, are you?"

"And if I am?"

"Answer me!"

He gazed at her sullen face, mobile and pretty, and at her eyes, now smouldering. Eyes that could light up and easily beguile him into forgetting that they were cousins. Yes, she had bloomed and was ignorant of the miracle that had transpired. She still had that girlish spontaneity in her moods, in her laughter, in the way she would fling her arms, her nostrils flaring, when she was happy or angry. This was now what fascinated him—the freshness, the vitality of her womanhood. Her cheeks glowed in the light, and her lips, although she was pouting, were full of promise. It was not so long ago that she had been almost tomboyish in the way she moved, in the brusqueness of her speech, and now here she was in his arms, a creature that was ready for the first warm touch of love. "Are you jealous?"

"Tell me, Luis."

"Her father is my boss. I am just developing her acquaintance. No, how can you say that I love her when I have just met her?"

Her face was still close, but the anger was gone. He stroked her hair and then, bending, kissed her softly. Her lips were slightly parted, and her breath was honeyed and sweet. She sighed and embraced him. "It's wonderful. Now I know why they close their eyes. It's more enjoyable that way."

He withdrew briefly and could not help laughing. She laughed at herself, too, then kissed him again. He started to fondle her breasts, and she squirmed. "You don't like it?" he asked.

"It tickles," she murmured, but soon stopped squirming as his fingers touched her nipples. His hand began to wander down the silky line of her thighs. For a moment he could feel her stiffen, although her mouth still clung to his.

"Luis—not here," she said in a husky whisper.

"And why not?"

"It embarrasses me."

"I suppose it always does the first time," he murmured, "but you have to have a first time."

"I know," she said. "I've been reading all those books, and we have had lectures in school."

"Well, this is real now," he said, bending so that they were now prostrate on the sofa. He could feel her gasp for breath. Her embrace had become tighter, possessive. "Luis, what is going to happen to us?" she repeated the question, this time with urgency.

"Love me," he said, pleading.

She nodded and sighed an almost inaudible yes, pressing her eager body still closer to him.

J U N E C A M E in a green that flooded the boulevard. The dead brown of March that had scorched the city was gone. The banaba trees had begun to bloom, and their purple flowers brightened the wide shoulders of the streets and the fronts of restaurants and night-clubs. The school year opened, and a rash of college uniforms—the plaid skirts, the grays and blues—colored the Luneta in the after-noons, together with the olive-gray and khaki of the ROTC cadets having their drills there. The invigorating smell of green things wafted to the house, bringing memories of Sipnget. Trining came, too, every Friday afternoon when her classes were over, and she stayed with him until Sunday afternoon, when he drove her back to the convent school.

It had been a significant year for the magazine, and the signs were clear that it would soon be able to stand alone and would not have to depend on financial assistance from the other Dantes publi-cations, although the magazine had already displeased influential people and business leaders with its satirical and irreverent lam-pooning of their personalities. That they did not make good their threats pleased Dantes very much. Like Luis, he had correctly argued that if it were known that they were bringing pressure on the magazine, it would have confirmed not only their lack of humor but their vulnerability as well.

Luis had really intended to see Ester again, but the opportunity did not come until one afternoon shortly after school had opened. She came to the office with Trining and two other classmates.

"Our first term paper has already been assigned," she said after the niceties were done. She wore no lipstick. Looking at her finely molded face, Luis could see her personality shining through. This afternoon there was something efficient and businesslike about her. "We came to you for advice, really. We do not know anything about the agrarian problem that you have been writing about—and labor, too—and our understanding of our sociology is rather poor. We didn't know that our professor had written for you."

Luis liked the unintended compliment. "Well, for a start," he said, "suppose you tell me if you have been in a picket line—any of you."

All four shook their heads.

"I haven't either," Luis said with a smile. "So this makes all of us students of some sort. The picket line is where you should really go if you want information about labor unions. You will be surprised how crooked the labor leaders are."

"But our teachers—when we talked about this," Ester said, "gave us the impression that you'd be an expert."

Luis snorted. He never liked being called an expert on anything, and his humility was real. "I would suppose that being an editor should qualify me as a jack-of-all-trades, but I really know little about labor problems. A bit about the agrarian problem, particularly sugar—" He paused, suddenly remembering that Dantes was in sugar, too, but Ester would notice this; so he went on. "Politics, the *sacadas,* and sugar colonialism. All these aren't new—you can get more from the files than by talking with me."

"Give us some pointers on how to begin," Trining said. It was a simple suggestion and he was grateful to her, for now he could speak a little from his own point of view. Looking at Ester seated, eagerly waiting, he became ill at ease, and he began to ramble vaguely about the nature of man, the value of labor, and the Marxist interpretation of surplus value; then he shifted to the encyclicals of the popes, the

Rerum Novarum and the *Quadragessimo Anno,* and homing in, he spoke briefly about the class structure of Filipino society, the agrarian origins of the revolution of 1896, the peasant uprisings of the country, and now the rebellion in central Luzon.

He did not know that he had taken so long. Dusk was falling, but the girls did not seem to mind and Ester, particularly, seemed entranced. "It's cleared up a lot," she said when he was through. "I think I know how to go about mine. Why don't you write what you just told us and use it in your magazine? I would like to see it before it goes to print."

He agreed, and as they filed out, most of their questions finally answered, Trining tugged at him and whispered, "You would do anything Ester tells you to do. Now you must write my term paper for me."

A WEEK LATER Ester dropped by alone and made Luis very happy. "I'm sorry," he said, "but the article—it's all finished—is at home. I did it two nights ago, and I just forgot to bring it here. You should have called first, but if you are in a hurry, let us go home and get it." His tone was tentative. He foresaw her indecision, so he added, "I think I will just bring it here tomorrow and give it to your father."

The implicit challenge had been made, and Ester picked it up. "We will go to your place," she said, "any time you are ready."

It was not even five, but Luis stood up, and before she could say another word he was guiding her out of his office. Outside, the heat of the late afternoon claimed them. The Dantes building was in the congested heart of the city, and driving out was a problem. By five, however, they were on the boulevard, which was still sun-drenched. To his right, the sea glinted and the waves collapsed with a murmur against the concrete seawall. The breeze whipped her hair close to his face occasionally, and he could smell her fragrance. Her nearness evoked thoughts and imaginings of the kind of life she and her friends lived, of Trining, too, and all the others who had seemed to him immersed in staleness and boredom, mulling over their sins, keeping all their holy days of obligation, living day to day in the exasperating desire to keep their chastity as the most valuable thing that they would present to those who would become their husbands. It was really quite a shame that Trining had not even put up a token fight. He wondered how it would be with Ester, if she would—after it was all over and done with—go to confession so that she could take communion, or just stop taking communion altogether.

When they were almost home he turned to her and saw her looking at him intently. She turned away, embarrassed. "How is your guinea pig?" he asked. An uneasy laugh escaped her.

"Looking at you," she said, "makes me feel you are sometimes just playacting. You have a driver, a fine home, and yet you sound bitter and discontented—and very proletarian."

He smiled benignly at her. "Don't tell me you don't have a single frustration in the world."

"I do," she said.

"It's all a matter of degree," he said. "Besides, I do not consider myself embittered. Why should I be when I have right now a very pretty girl with me?"

"You are a rogue," she said, smiling. "You will do anything to steer the discussion away and make a compliment on the side. You are a liar, too. You said that you would come and see me, but it is I who makes all sorts of excuses to come and see you."

Her outright confession touched him. "I'm sorry, Ester, but we really had so much to do. Besides, we still have years ahead of us."

"I hope you'll change a little," she said, "acquire a more pleasant disposition—in what you write, at least."

"For you," he said, "I will." Sure of himself, he took her hand. It was cold. "But you must like me as I am."

They were home. He let go of her hand as Simeon swung the car to the left. In the driveway, as soon as he got out, he asked her to come up with him and have a Coke and a piece of cake. He noticed her brief indecision, so he added hastily, "No, don't bother. I can run upstairs and bring the manuscript down."

She stepped out quickly and without another word followed him up to the house.

The blinds were raised and the sun flooded the hall. As he went to his study Ester drifted around the room and out to the trellised *azotea*, where the wind from the sea was coolest. She came back and gazed at his father's Amorsolos on the walls.

"It's lovely here," she said when he came out with the manuscript.

"I'm glad you like it," he said. "As you know, I live alone. I love the privacy and the independence."

She walked to the piano, which seemed to bask in the glow of the afternoon, opened the cover, and drew her hand across the keys.

"Do play," he said, "while I fix up something to drink."

In the kitchen, as he sliced the chocolate cake and prepared the glasses, he heard snatches of Mozart, sentimental and melodious. When he went back to the living room with the tray, however, she stopped and pulled the lid down.

"You play very well," he said.

"Tell that to my mother."

ESTER LEFT at dusk. She had asked him not to bother seeing her home, but he had Simeon drive her to San Juan just the same. They had sat in the *azotea* and watched the sun go down and paint the horizon, the clouds in resplendent ochres, browns, and indigos. They had talked about her paper, classmates, and Trining's new admirer—a basketball player (Trining had told Luis about him). To this last one he had listened with a mixture of contempt and interest. Ester had also talked about her brothers, who seemed to drift, not knowing what to do. Finally she had voiced her disappointment with her own school, the emptiness of it all, the superficiality of the friendships, the senselessness of girl talk, and how most of her friends were looking forward to nothing but sweet domesticity.

As he watched her get into the car and finally drive away, a strange, dull ache filled him. It was not love, he was sure of that. It was something akin to compassion. He worked until past midnight, and although he was tired, sleep seemed far away. He could not quite forget Ester on the *azotea* with him—her smile and the way she spoke earnestly, plaintively. She was not like Trining, who was sensual and all woman, who was direct and who knew what she wanted. It was quite clear—and his knowledge of it made him apprehensive—that he was really interested in Ester, now that the wall of indifference with which he had surrounded himself as far as she and her kind were concerned was crumbling. He was kindred to the emotional beast, he was not immune to the feelings that blighted the poor in spirit, but he was also sure that it was not love.

After Marta had done the dishes and Simeon had checked the locks, Luis was alone again. Marta had thoughtfully, as always, filled the thermos jug near his desk with coffee, and listlessly he poured himself a cup. It took him some time to finish it. Traffic on the boulevard was almost gone except for those leaving the nightclubs farther up the street. When he finally lay down he remembered Ester again, her beautiful body, and he was sure that someday he would have her.

As he closed his eyes, however, in the reddish consciousness that flooded his brain he saw an endless array of wailing babies with his features in each shrieking face. He shuddered.

CHAPTER

24

By CHRISTMAS talk was rife that the Huks were already in the outskirts of the city, that they could now attack Manila at will. Many provincial capitals in central Luzon had been raided and occupied for at least one night before the constabulary could retake them. Luis was certain that the propaganda arm of the movement was working in Manila. He learned from some of his old college friends that a few of their acquaintances in the interuniversity cultural and press groups had joined the Huks. The tension that was reflected in the press and in the government hierarchy was not, however, the kind that tormented him. He had continued his poetry, but it was to him too prosaic, too pallid, and it did not tally with the realities. He could see the greater contradiction within himself as he helped Dantes become richer, at the same time making himself safe from the cares of living, unlike those whom he sincerely felt he championed. There was freedom, yes, but for whom did it work? Certainly it was working for him but not for Sipnget and his people there, for his grandfather and his mother, to whom he threw occasional crumbs.

He did not drink except socially, but now, in the evenings when he could not sleep, he would fix himself a glass of bourbon and toy with it until it was empty. One evening it came as a surprise even to himself that he took not one but three glasses before he could sleep. I must stop this, he told himself, and he got to writing more poetry. He read Mayakovsky and reread Whitman and even tried experimenting in Tagalog and Ilokano with the kind of poetry that he felt the lower classes would understand. It was all a sham, a mistake, that he was writing in English—a language that was for him and the elite—when there should be no barrier between him and the greater masses. Why should the language of science and culture be denied them? Much as he would have wanted to pursue this line of thinking, however, at the same time he felt secure and superior with the fact that he had mastered English and that he would continue writing in it—if only for his ego and for self-justification. It was not the language, after all, that really mattered—it was the heart of it, the art of it. This contradiction was of course an inanity. What really tormented him, as always, was the past, his past, and his recreance to it.

At Christmas he gave his first real party. *Our Time* had already piled up a steady circulation, and advertisements were coming in. More important to him, however, was that the magazine had become credible and prestigious, even to those whose views he disagreed with. It was politically left, but the writers of the right recognized it nevertheless for its liberal outlook, its fairness, and this was not lost on Dantes, who was a businessman before anything else. Dantes had suggested that the party be held in his house, which Luis had recently been frequenting because of Ester. Luis said, however, that it would be better in his own house, which, although smaller, had a wide garden and was more accessible. He knew that many of his friends on the left, particularly the college crowd, would never feel at ease in such surroundings as those of the Dantes residence.

Luis had expected only a few guests, but a riot descended upon him and he was very pleased. It was almost like a reunion with the old college crowd. There were also members of the cosmopolitan set, friends of Dantes, editors from the other Dantes publications, and the inseparable Abelardo Cruz and Etang Papel. Most important of all, Ester was there with some of her friends.

Luis was sorry that Trining was not coming. It would have been an experience for her to know people other than those to whom she was exposed in school, but a week earlier she had gone back to Rosales for the Christmas vacation as well as to look after Don Vicente, whose condition had worsened. She had tried convincing Luis to go with her, even for just a week, not only so that his mind would clear a little but also so that he would be able to see his mother. Luis, however, loathed the idea of staying in Rosales for more than a day, and he had decided that spending New Year's Day at home would be more than enough for him not only to fulfill his filial obligations but also to confront his other self again.

The buffet started at seven, but Luis had started to drink much earlier. By eleven most of his guests had already left in search of nightclubs that were not crowded and churches where they might catch the midnight mass. He was the perfect host, slightly inebriated but gracious, waving heartily, making wry comments once in a while, in keeping with his character, and always saying, "And do come again—if there's going to be another time!"

He had broken into a heated discussion on the *azotea* between Abelardo Cruz, Etang Papel, and a couple of new Ph.D.'s from the university who had just returned from Harvard, brimming with American wisdom and enthusiasm. He had never been apologetic about not having finished his B.A., and particularly after he had read a doctoral dissertation on social change in a Nueva Ecija village. He had been infuriated by the trivia that had come to pass for scholarship.

Papel was huge and homely and had a spongelike mind that soured everything it absorbed; she would have been dismissed as someone's fat old-maid aunt, which, of course, she was not, for in spite of her plain features, she had had a string of men, some of them foreigners who had, perhaps, fantasized about her looks. She was saying that the true nationalist commitment was not freedom from America's apron strings but freedom of the people from their own rich exploiters.

Luis had always agreed with such a statement, but for tonight, he was simply, wearily tired. "Thank God for the poor," he had said, "otherwise, we would have fewer Ph.D.'s and columnists as well."

Papel did not like it and had retorted, "Thank God for the rich, then, for it is they who made the poor!"

His was still the last word: "And thank God again for the poor, for they will make some writers rich writing about poverty!"

Etang Papel left shortly afterward, followed by her coterie. Soon it was only Eddie and Ester in the house with Simeon and Marta, who had come to tidy up the place. Eddie was trying "Silent Night" on the piano with one finger, and beside him Ester sang in a cool pleasant voice, sipping iced tea from a tall glass. Luis joined them, half dragging his feet on the floor, which was now dusty and littered with canapé picks and cigarette stubs.

"Sing louder, Ester," he said. "This is my happiest Christmas."

Eddie stood up. "I have to go, too," he said. "It's been a nice party, Louie."

Luis held him by the shoulder. "And I thought you were my friend," he said. "Stay awhile. You haven't heard Ester play yet." Then to Ester: "Please, boss, do play for us a hymn—any hymn."

"Now, what do you mean, calling me boss?" Ester asked.

Luis laughed. "You are the publisher's daughter, aren't you? You are boss, too."

"That's not funny," Ester said coldly.

"You are drunk," Eddie said.

"I am not, but—Ester, play just the same. I will sing to your tune. Isn't it time we sang something not just to honor Christ but also to those who are in the hills? Let's sing a hymn also for those fighting a private war—those who are now in whorehouses, driven there by decent women."

"You are really drunk." Eddie turned to the girl. "Ester, I think we should go."

"You will do nothing of the kind," Luis said. "In fact, if anyone should go home, it is I. Do you know where home is? It is not in this house or that atrocious feudal castle in Rosales. It is out there, in them thar hills—only there's no yellow gold . . ."

"What's come over you?" Eddie asked. "You just had a most wonderful party, surrounded by the nicest people in the world. What are you beefing about?" He headed for the door. "I'm leaving before I change my mind and call this a lousy party."

"I wish I were dead," Luis said, meaning it. But Eddie had already gone down the stairs. Ester walked over to him and, holding his clammy hand, led him to the *azotea*. From the near distance there came an explosion of firecrackers. It was cooler out in the open, and the sea breeze helped clear his mind a little. He was, however, aware of everything that he had said, and he hoarsely repeated, "I wish I were dead."

"That is not a nice thing to say on Christmas Eve, Luis," Ester said.

"Perhaps I will feel differently tomorrow. I have something for you. It's not wrapped up—it couldn't be wrapped up. It's my heart and I can't take it out. And what is more, it is fouled up, I think. You will not want it that way, would you?"

"I hope this is not the liquor at work," Ester said softly. "We say so many things that we don't mean afterward. And when this happens, it is all wrong. It sours relationships."

Luis listened attentively for the first time during the hectic evening. This was not party talk; they were really alone now. The world had slipped by, and stars swarmed over the sky.

He held her hand and pressed it. "I mean what I say, Ester," he said, looking at her serene face.

"I have friends, many friends," she continued barely above a whisper. "But the relationships are empty. It is not that there is no trust—I trust them as I trust you now, and I hope that they trust me, too. But how can I express it? What I want? What I'm looking for? It is not something that money can buy, else I would have gotten it a long time ago. Do you understand, Louie, what I am trying to say?"

He nodded, for she was now saying something that he had always felt himself; she was giving shape to thoughts that had bedeviled him but that he had not been able to express.

"You want peace," he said simply. "You want happiness, fulfillment—all those wonderful things that come to the yogi, the enlightenment. You want a way out."

She looked at him and nodded.

"There is no way out, Ester," he said. "Not for you. Not for me."

"Yes, there is, for me," she said. "For you, I have doubts. You thrive on conflict. On anger. You are alive when you are angry. I cannot see you in a world where there is peace and harmony."

He shook his head, not because he disagreed with her but because he did not want to believe what she said; it was true, he would be a misfit in a world without anger. Did he really believe in justice, or was he not just rebelling against a past that had injured him? Did he really love the poor, or in professing love for the poor was he doing what was easy, addressing himself to man—amorphous, un-real, without identity—rather than be committed to one individual in need of sympathy, which he could give but would not? And if he loved the poor, would he give them the wealth that was going to be his? Would he be willing to let go of the comforts that he enjoyed so that they—his people in Sipnget—would have something better on their table? He loved Ester, but now he also resented her for push-ing him against the wall, for flailing at him with the truth, for forc-ing him to be honest with himself. But he also knew that to lose her would be to lose his conscience.

"We have to live with ourselves," he said contritely. "That is dif-ficult to do. And the peace that we seek, I suppose, is the peace of the grave."

Her face lighted up, the smile bloomed again. "I have often thought of it that way," she said, rising, a sudden lift in her being. "Then the burden would be lifted, and finally we would be free."

"You agree with me, then, death isn't so tragic after all. And I do wish sometimes that I were dead."

He walked with her to the gate, where her car was waiting, and before he turned to go he pulled her to him and gently, ever so gen-tly, kissed her, murmuring, "Ester, don't hate me for my alcoholic histrionics. *In vino, veritas!*"

She held him and kissed him, then quickly got into the car. Luis walked slowly back to the *azotea*. Along the boulevard the houses were brightly lighted with red, white, and blue star lanterns, with col-ored bulbs strung across their fronts and the trees in the yards. From the direction of Ermita and Malate came more firecracker explosions. At times the voices of children singing carols and the brash music of *cumbancheros* came through, clear and sharp.

The party had actually tired him, and he was most riled by the hypocrites among his own crowd—Abelardo Cruz, Etang Papel—those who prattled about their vaunted love for humanity and un-derstanding of the country's social malaise. There they were, all dolled up, their perfumed hands never having known the brutal hard-ness of a plow handle. His starveling friends were no different. They banded together as if they belonged to a touted though impover-ished aristocracy, and they regarded the masses—the masses, how contemptible, how hopeless they are! Of course, he also used the phrase occasionally—but only when he wanted to make the point that revolution could start not only with the peasantry but also with the middle class, the enlightened bourgeoisie, himself among them. Why isn't there more honesty in this world? Perhaps it is only in art that we can be totally honest. Again, he tried to exculpate himself from the inadequacy of his response. But of what use is art? He was not even sure that the poetry he had written was art. It sounded so effete, maybe because he was looking for the innate music of words or maybe because he was searching deeply for the symbolic meanings of words when there were no symbols at all—just words strung together in order to evoke ideas, images, and the total whole of aesthetic experience. He was becoming an aesthete, incapable of translating his ideas into action. Indeed, he was beginning to wither as he sometimes wished he would.

He went back to the house and wandered about. In the kitchen Simeon and Marta were tucking away the bowls and the wineglasses. The two waiters had gone home, and the rubbish was now in the garbage cans, but the house still looked dirty and the floor was a mess. Marta would have to spend the whole morning cleaning up. "Simeon," he said, "you and Marta go to Rosales for a week. Just be sure you are back by New Year's, for you must drive me to Rosales. Right now I can be alone by myself. And if I forget, do not fail to remind me about your bonus—both of you—tomorrow."

Their faces lit up, and he told them to leave the work—it was late; they could always do it in the morning before taking the bus or train home.

He went back to his room as their footsteps died down on the stone staircase. Slowly removing his red bow tie and his jacket, he sank into his bed. The phone jangled, and half rising, he took it.

It was Ester and her voice was warm: "How are you feeling now? I should have made you a cup of coffee before I left."

"I'm fine," he said, "and I'm sorry."

"You always say you are sorry."

"Blame it on the world—or circumstance."

"You are still sour."

"Even milk sours," he said.

"You are forgiven, then."

"How can I ever thank you?"

"Plenty. We can hear mass tomorrow. I can drop in at your place and pick you up."

"I might not be up early," Luis said, feeling suddenly trapped.

"I'll wake you up."

"I'll be a mess—the house, too. Besides, I've got to work."

"It won't take more than forty-five minutes."

"High mass?"

"Luis, you sound bored."

He could feel the apprehension in her voice. He laughed. "You are going to be a nun."

She laughed softly, too. "Merry Christmas again."

THEN HE WAS REALLY ALONE. The tedium of the day finally possessed him, and he sank in complete surrender to it. He could not remember how much he had drunk, and the urge to have one last nightcap came, but he withstood the temptation. He struck the headboard behind him, cursing, then he reached out to switch off the light. It was then that his door slowly opened and, more surprised than frightened, he watched the man come in.

Recognition came quickly. Luis jumped up and rushed forward to embrace his brother. "Vic," he said, drawing away, studying the sun-browned face, short-cropped hair, buck teeth, and laughing eyes. "Why did you not come earlier?"

"I did," Vic said, "but I didn't want to interfere with your party and I wanted to be sure you were alone. I stayed in the garage."

Luis was incredulous. "Now, that is a foolish thing to do," he said, shaking his head. He was angry. "You know you are welcome in this house. If you didn't want to be with the party, you could have come here and locked yourself in."

"Anyway," Vic said, "I am here and that's what matters, isn't it?"

Luis's mind was keen again. In the soft bedroom light he looked at his brother. It was just two years since Vic's last visit in this house, a visit that had peeved and perplexed him. He knew then that his brother was in need, and he had tried to give him money, but Vic had refused it, saying that he already had a job, that it was enough that he had helped him with his education and with books that he had sent. Luis hoped that his brother would not be as proud again. Tonight, after all, was Christmas.

He could see that although Vic was robust, his clothes were

faded khaki and his shoes were battered leather. He smelled of sun and harsh living.

"Marta let me in," he said simply.

"You could have joined us," Luis said.

Vic shook his head. "Manong," he said, "you know very well that I do not belong to that crowd."

Luis knew what else Vic would say, so he changed the subject at once. "Let's go to the kitchen. There's a lot of food and drink, and I'm getting hungry again."

"Marta gave me something to eat," he said. "I'm really full, and besides, I came here to ask for something important from you—more than food."

Luis sighed. "Vic," he said, "you know I'd give you anything you ask for, but you refuse what I give you."

"I have come here not to ask for help for myself. I know you have it in your heart to help people like me."

"How much do you need?" Luis asked. "I told you before that this house is always open to you. You can stay here if you wish. There's even an extra room. It is so much simpler and easier for you to come and see me than for me to go to Rosales. I've told you this a hundred times. And you haven't written to Mother. I was there last April. She doesn't know where you are. That's not fair."

"I'm sorry, Manong," Vic said. He sat on the edge of the bed, and Luis sat in front of him. "I have not bothered telling Mother where I am, but I told her—really told her—when I left Sipnget that she should never look for me, that I would be all right, and that I would always be thinking of them."

Luis was silent. He was recalling his mother's sadness, her quiet despair, as she spoke of Vic. It was as if she had already accepted the fact that she would never see her younger son again.

"But why?"

Vic smiled and did not answer. Seeing that no reply was forthcoming, Luis asked, "Now, tell me. How much do you really need? If I don't have enough in this house, I can go to the bank first thing after the holiday—and if you don't want to come to my office to pick it up, I'll leave it with Marta."

Again Vic smiled. "It's not money, Manong, although that will help, of course. It is you we need, and others like you—more than

anything now. We need teachers, people with knowledge and understanding such as you have."

"You are talking in riddles. What are you talking about?"

"About us. About Commander Victor."

"He is dead."

"Yes, both of us know that." Then he smiled rather self-
consciously. "I supposed you never knew that his name was not Victor. It was Hipolito, but he was always talking about victory, and
when he was given an opportunity to have a nom de guerre, he chose
Victor."

"But how can I help a dead man?"

"Help me, Manong. I am now Commander Victor."

Luis looked at his brother. Victor was not even twenty, and he
looked more like a village teenager, with his crew cut and his lean,
dark face, but behind the youth was the man who had known travail
as Luis had never known it. Vic was no longer a boy but the man Luis
could never be, and this fact humbled Luis.

"Were you in Rosales in April?"

Again Vic smiled but did not answer.

"Did you know that I was home?"

The same noncommittal smile.

"You know, of course, that I will always help you, that I will do
what you want me to do, because we are brothers."

"I am glad to hear that," Vic said. "I have been thinking a lot
about us. I will be going back to Rosales. It will be my territory now.
I know every village, almost every tree, every turn of the creek, and
every fold of the hill—and a lot of people know me. So I will go
there, but I need you, too, to protect me if necessary, because I can
trust you. Let me make one thing clear, however: the old days are
over. Your father, all his property, must go back to the people whom
he has robbed."

Luis could not believe what he was hearing, and for a minute Vic
droned on about social justice and democracy and the future. What
would all this mean now? He would lose the house in Rosales and
all the land that would be his inheritance. For a while this bleak reality numbed his heart, and for all his protestations, for all that he
had written and said, he had grown to like this ease, this surfeit of
leisure, all that marked him for perdition. He was, after all, his father's son.

Maybe, if he tried to dissuade his brother, there would be other ways, feasible means by which he could remain what he was and yet be totally in agreement with him, support him, and sacrifice for him.

"Vic," he asked, "what do you really believe in?"

Vic paused, gazed at the ceiling, and then looked down at his black battered shoes. "What can one like me believe in? I wish I could say that I believe in God—or any god up there. I wish I could say that I believe in our leaders. One thing I can tell you is that I do not believe in the Americans anymore. We fought the Japanese, didn't we? We were only teenagers then. We were not going to be heroes—whoever thinks of patriotism and heroism when he is there, scared, praying that he can live through the ambush? There were heroes, just the same, and who were they? The thieves who raided the GI quartermaster depots, who robbed the government treasury, the same ones who continue to do it now. These were the people who traded with the Japanese and got rich working for themselves. How can I believe in the Americans when they are responsible for making heroes of these scum?"

"I didn't ask you about the Americans," Luis said.

"Yes, but you cannot avoid them," Vic said. "They are everywhere and, most dangerously, in the dark corners of the mind, especially the minds of the ignorant people we deal with every day."

"You haven't answered my question."

"I am coming to that," Vic said, a smile fleeting across his dark face. "I believe in Mother—our mother." He paused and waited for the word to sink in. "She fed me, she taught me all that I will ever know. Even if she didn't teach me anything, I would still believe in her, because I know she is Mother, who brought me up in this world. There are lots of things in this world that I despise—the lying and the thieving. You don't know how deeply I resent these things, how I rage—but I believe in Mother."

"Do you believe in me?" Luis asked. He had not wanted to ask the question, but he had to know the answer now.

For some time Victor did not speak. When he finally did he looked straight into his brother's eyes. "I wish I could answer you with a simple yes and mean it. We have never lied to each other, but how can I say that I believe in you when I can't even believe in myself now? I am wracked by doubts, by anguish and mistrust. There is nothing anymore that one can be sure of, Manong. Nothing is true anymore except Mother, for she is what she is and we cannot change her. And death."

"I am your brother, Vic," Luis said softly, but within him he was crying out: *Believe me, I am you and you are me!*

"Do you think I will ever forget?" Vic's voice shrilled. "You have done for me what no one has ever done, and I am grateful. Without you and the money you sent Mother I would not have been able to finish high school. All the learning that I got afterward—it came from the books you sent me. The wealth you gave me is here"—Vic pointed to his head—"where no one can take it—not even you. But there is something here, too. Memory. I remember our days together—and our quarrels." Vic laughed suddenly and his laughter was eerie. When he paused, his eyes were misty. "Mother loved you, perhaps more than she loved me, because you were not wanted—and I was. That everyone knew. But where are you now, and where am I? This is the whole point. You will go far, very far, but what of those who are still in Sipnget?"

"And do you not believe me because I am a bastard and because I am only a half-brother?"

"You fool!" Vic lashed at him. "Haven't I just spoken about how we grew up together and lived together? That is something I always look back to with pleasure. That's why I came here."

"And yet you cannot trust me?"

"I trust even Marta and Simeon. Why shouldn't I trust you in another way? But you asked if I believed you."

"There's so little difference," Luis said wearily.

"I said we lived together, but that was long ago and I have never talked with you as I am doing now. In between, many things have happened. You went to the city and I stayed on the farm. I am not saying that you don't deserve better things—you were always smarter than I, and you had a way with words." Vic paused and looked around him. "I had to catch up with my own education my own way, and I know that people change when they live differently, away from the land. Now, tell me. Have you changed? What do you believe in now?"

Luis walked to the window that opened to the bay. The night was calm, a faint glimmering of stars and the silence of a world gone to sleep, and the bay was a black, shimmering stretch—a line of lights where Cavite was. It was long past midnight. Luis turned to Vic and said slowly, "I believe in humanity—not just you or Mother but all mankind. Do I sound like a preacher or a cheap politician making a pretty speech? This is not what I intend to do. Father told me that he wanted me to go into politics. I believe in life, that it is sweet, and that, for all its occasional bitterness, we—man, that is—are headed toward something better—fulfillment. There is much shame, however, and so much hypocrisy around us, and these inhibit our fulfillment as human beings. I am what you may call a humanist. I cannot explain this to you. Life is holy and it is for all of us. God's design I cannot understand myself, and I never will, but I do know that what we are experiencing now will pass and in the end we will all be brothers, not just blood brothers, as we are, but brothers in spirit. Neither you nor I can change the world or human nature, and we can only aim at changing attitudes—and perhaps teach those who have so much to give a portion of their blessings to those who have less."

"Paradise on earth, achieved with human understanding. Not a single egg broken." Vic coughed mirthlessly.

"Do not try to be smart or funny." Luis spoke hotly. "I have been writing poetry, as you very well know—not very good, perhaps, but this is not important. What I am trying to say is that I have hope that there is still truth to be gleaned, even from the garbage dump, if we search hard enough."

"And you think that I have no hope? We fought the Japanese with slingshots because we had hope. We now fight for the same reason. You forget the source of our real strength. It is not people like you, although you can be one of us. We are very rich in numbers. The poor are many—they are the majority. This is all that I understand. As for the good life or reason or the world of the spirit, you can afford to be poetic about it because you are here. You forget one thing: we are there!"

"Is that what they are teaching you in the Stalin universities? I have heard about them."

Victor laughed loudly. "Listen," he said after a while, "we have lots of books, and lecturers, some of whom are Ph.D.'s. Does this surprise you? And we do have schools but not the kind you think. Every day is school day for us. We deal with facts, not with books. We know who is exploited and who are exploiters. If there is a god at all, He is in us—He is not up there. Paradise can be here if we fight well. There is goodwill in men if they are of the same class."

"You sound so familiar," Luis said softly, thinking of his own college days and those sophomoric discussions under the acacia trees. "I am tired of dreams. Why can you not be practical and learn to live with facts, as you say you do? With education—and I am only too glad to help you—you can be more than what you are, whether you are a farmer or a clerk. There is a lot of room. There's freedom, too. Why are you doing this? There must be a reason."

Vic had not stirred from where he sat. "I cannot give an easy answer," he said with great feeling. "I wish I could tell you that I will endure all privation because I love our country, but what is our country? It is a land exploited by its own leaders, where the citizens are slaves of their own elite."

"Be honest," Luis pressed. "Do you think you will be different if you achieve power?"

"I do not know," Vic said humbly. "One cannot foresee the future. I would like to say that I will be Spartan and honest. I am no hero. I would like the good life if I can get it. I would like to have *lechon* every day, to travel and see the world. I would like to be comfortable and not have one worry. But none of these is possible. It is not even possible for me to go to school the usual way, to know myself better . . ."

Luis was silent.

"And you want to know why I am away from all the comforts that I could appreciate, just like other human beings? I will tell you why. I am tired, Manong—very tired. I am tired of everything. I hate the present and I long for the future. It is a future that I hope will at least provide enough food for all of us. I am tired of soft-boiled rice and camote tops and coconut meat and green papayas, such as we have in the mountains most of the time. Once, long ago, I thought that all that mattered was food. There was so little of it—you know what we had in Sipnget."

"You shame me," Luis said.

"But it is true. Remember how it was in the big house? How I used to go there to work and you did not because Mother didn't want you to go to town? How I used to collect the peelings of apples that your father ate and bring them home for us to eat?"

Luis did not speak. He did not want to remember. "All right then," he said after a while, "what do you want me to give you?"

"Give! Give!" Vic flung at him. "I shouldn't be ungrateful, but you always give. People like me—we never get anything that is ours because we worked for it, because we deserve it."

"You are my brother."

"Half-brother."

"We came from the same womb. It is all that matters. We are equals."

"How I wish I could believe that," Vic said, "but it is not so. If we cannot be equal, at least both of us are Filipinos, with the same opportunities. I did not make the laws, nor did I set up the system for mestizos and brown people like me. I would like to think that under the skin it's the same red blood. But blood is cheap, and I will use it to water the land so that people like me will live."

"I will be on the other side," Luis said, "not because I want to be there but because that is where you have pushed me."

"But that is where you are," Vic said, "not because I want you there. You are there of your own free will. You will inherit great wealth. Would you give it up? Why should you?"

"We can share it," Luis said.

"But how far will you go, my brother? If I asked you to get rid of everything and come with me, would you do it? You have much to lose—and if you stay, I will understand. I even understand why you are reluctant to come out in your magazine that you are for us. Yes, we read you every week, and although you seem to sympathize with us, you really are not for us. Could it be that you have forgotten those years in Sipnget?"

"I have not forgotten," Luis said hotly. "I am not turning away from that. You do not know of my turmoil."

"And you think I don't have doubts and moments of anguish, too?" Vic asked. "It has been dirty, dirtier than the war we went through. I thought that after Liberation all the fighting would cease, but it has not been that way. It's uglier now—and so sad—and yet, what must be done must be done."

Vic stood up. He did not even look grown-up. His hands twitched at his sides as he walked to the door.

"You didn't tell me what you came here for—or what I can do," Luis said.

"Some other time, Manong," he said. "It has been refreshing, talking with you."

"One last question," Luis said. "Did you send that message to my father?"

Vic smiled. "You see, my brother, I have not lost my aim."

Luis saw him to the gate and on the way kept saying, "What can I do for you? There must be something . . ." Through it all Vic was smiling, and after he disappeared into the shadows it seemed that a primeval darkness, thicker than the night, dropped like a final curtain between them.

Dear Mother,

It is long past Christmas Eve, and I can think of no better time to write you this letter than now. As you perhaps have already surmised, I am not very religious. There was a time, however, when I was—and I remember how you took me to the church in town during the Holy Week and how piously I followed you as you fingered your rosary and made your Stations of the Cross, how your care-lined face was turned to the prostrate image of a dead Christ at the altar. I still recall that time when I was flushed with fever and Tio Joven applied all those leaves on my chest and rubbed his saliva all over my forehead and I still didn't get well. It was then that you decided that there should be a novena in the house to appease God, whom you believed had been angered. That early evening, after the novena, Grandfather went to the backyard where the dalipawen tree stood, and there, making an offering of the rice cake that you made, the hard-boiled eggs, and the hand-rolled cigar, Grandfather beseeched the spirits: You who have brought fever to my grandson, here is a humble offering. Come now and partake of it, and hurt my grandson no more. That evening I felt the fever ebb, as if it were no more than simple fatigue, although for a week I couldn't stand. I remember how that early morning I went to the tree and saw the cake and the hard-boiled eggs still there and how, because the spirits had not helped themselves to them, I feasted on the offering, against all customary warnings. All this comes to me as lucid as day. It was this that made me realize that food for the spirits could also be food for the stomach.

I am not being facetious. I had not meant to go off-tangent this way. I had meant to start this letter in all seriousness—like an edito-

rial in my magazine, which will never be read by you and by Grand-father and by all the people in Sipnget, although Vic tells me that he reads the magazine every week. I had meant to be poetic, for tonight the Son of Man was born to a mother who, like all mothers, should be revered because it was in her body that she suffered the beginning of life. The birth of Christ is to me the celebration of motherhood, for there are many among us today who would not be loved and who would not be cared for except by their mothers.

I write this letter because just a while ago Vic was here to see me. I asked him what he believed in, and he said he believed in you. I would like to say that I, too, believe in you, but do not think that I will be fair to you or to myself if I didn't explain this belief that is more than belief. I think it is a kind of blindness—or faith.

There are times—and God knows there are many—when I wish I had not been born, but I must tell you that even this suffering that I bear is something that I must experience, both as a poet and as a human being who loves life. It will be difficult for you or for Vic to understand this suffering, for it is a form of ennui that is embedded in the mind, a pain without surcease, even after the wound has healed and the scab has lifted. In fact you will look in vain for scars. It is a malaise that money or circumstance cannot dispel. How utterly simple it would be if it were something a medical specialist could conquer with a new strain of antibiotic. Perhaps a vacation in San Francisco, a new Mercedes, or an eight-carat sparkler—each is a simple-enough solution, but not one of these will suffice.

I am speaking of my birth, dear Mother, my conception, my reason for being here, for being your son and my father's son. It is not enough that I am here, living in comfort, while you are there, suffering. I would like to know how I came to be. I am curious to know if I was born out of love, if I deserve this life that has come to me as a gift from you, and if you regret that I ever came to be.

I will never know the answers, for these are questions I could not dare ask you or Father. At most I can only guess—and that is enough. Even if I do get the answers that I seek, I would still ask why I am here.

Vic knows his reason for being. He has found a cause to which he *can give his life. As for me, I have not found out if this life is worth living. It was, I am certain, given to me in sufferance, and perhaps I am loved not because of myself but because of what I am supposed to be.*

Dear Mother, in spite of all these doubts that rankle in my mind and poison my heart, there is one certitude for you: I love you, perhaps not in the way that you expect me to, sometimes not even the way I would like to, but I love you with a tenacity that I alone can feel. I love you because, as my brother has said, you are all I truly have.

Forgive me then, dear Mother.

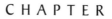

2 5

W HEN LUIS WOKE, the sun was already high. It flooded the room and danced in the cream curtains that stirred in the morning breeze. He could hear Marta puttering in the kitchen and Simeon sweeping the driveway. The first thing he thought of was Vic's visit. He could vividly remember snatches of their long talk, and he had in fact started to think of better replies for the questions Vic had asked and was now better prepared to answer them if they ever came up again. He was now more curious than ever about the reason for the visit, for Vic's having confronted him. He was sure that if he had not spoken so pointedly or tried to dampen his brother's enthusiasm, Vic would have been more open and would have told him what he really wanted to say. It was all too late now; in all probability there would not be another such clash between them and, for all their closeness and for all that was dear and past, never again would Vic confide in him. Knowing this, he felt a great weight press upon him.

Ester called him up while he was having coffee, and her voice smoothed away the numbness of his spirit. "It's nice to hear your voice," he told her. "Would it be too much if you called me every morning to cheer me up?"

"The problem with you," she said with a smile in her voice, "is that you are such a self-centered person, you think only of your convenience. Did it ever occur to you that sometimes it is I who may need the cheering up?"

"Well, sweetheart," he said, "if we are to think of our mutual convenience, the best thing is for us to get married. We can get up together in the morning and cheer each other up."

Ester kept up the banter. "Are you proposing?"

"After we go to church and I still feel the same way, I will."

"Baclaran then," she said. "It won't be crowded today with all those favor seekers."

"I am a favor seeker," Luis said. He stood up, catching a draft of the sea breeze. "But I seek favor only from one virgin."

A gale of laughter. "Suppose I told you I am no virgin?"

"I'm not old-fashioned," he said.

"If you come with me after mass and have Christmas lunch with us, I will believe you."

For a moment Luis wanted to accept the invitation, but he would feel awkward having lunch with the Danteses when he was not sure of how Ester would eventually regard him. "I have an idea," he said brightly. "Let's drive to the beach in Cavite and stay there the whole day. I'll bring lunch."

He could surmise by her silence that she was not so happy about what he had in mind. "You're not going anywhere, are you?"

"No—no," she said, undecided.

"All right, then, I'll be there in thirty minutes."

"I'm already dressed," she said with a laugh. "You get ready in half an hour, and I'll be there."

The sound of a kiss pleased him, and even after she had hung up he was still holding the phone against his ear.

Marta lingered while Luis was having his breakfast. Although she was past fifty like her husband, she had none of that middle-aged look that most women her age had—and the women of Rosales aged fast, oppressed as they were by the drudgery of the farm. Not that she herself was not burdened with work. She had always worked for the Asperri household. After the old house was burned down Don Vicente took her in to look after his orphaned niece in

Ermita. Afterward he sent her and her husband to look after Luis.

"Why did you tell my brother to wait in the garage, Marta?" he asked. "You should have told him to go to my room and wait there or sleep until the party was over."

"But Apo," Marta explained, "I didn't even know he had gone there. I thought you had already seen him, for right after he arrived we didn't notice him anymore."

Luis drank his coffee in silence.

"What is Victor doing now, Apo?" Marta could not resist asking. "We never got the chance to talk with him. He didn't seem to want to talk. Why . . ." the woman hesitated, "why is he so secretive?"

Luis waved her away. "It's his manner," he said, "and you cannot change it."

He was ready when Ester came. Simeon and Marta were not yet prepared to leave, so, just as he had promised, he gave them an envelope with money in it. After giving the couple last-minute instructions, he and Ester went down, carrying Marta's lunch basket. Ester was radiant in a red-printed skirt and blue blouse. "I have heard so much about hangovers," she teased him. "I wanted to see someone with one."

He grinned amiably. "I am made of sterner stuff," he said. "I am sorry to disappoint you." In the car Ester told him that she had brought a bathing suit. Luis reminded Simeon to look after the house very well, then the car was on its way.

"I'm giving them a one-week vacation," he explained to Ester. "I will be alone and liking it."

"With no one looking after your chastity?"

"God is extra kind to bachelors."

The sea breeze flowed into the car, and the fragrance of Ester's nearness was intoxicating. The morning was brilliant, although ribbons of mist hung over the bay, over the hulls of half-sunken ships. "I was wondering," she mused, her hand resting on his knee, "maybe I can come once in a while and clean your house—and cook, too, if you'd let me, just as Trining sometimes does. It shouldn't matter that I'm handy only with a can opener."

"I'm not finicky," he said.

As Ester had expected, the Redemptorist Church in Baclaran was not crowded. Luis was even able to park on the mango-shaded grounds—an impossibility on Wednesdays, when the novena for the Mother of Perpetual Help clogged the church with devotees. The offertory had just started, and Luis was glad that he did not have to sit through the sermon. He had yet to listen to one that would impress him. The priests—Filipinos or foreign missionaries—always had nothing to say except the same clichés about salvation, and they always talked down to their parishioners and sounded as if they were the holiest and the purest of men when God knew that many of them kept mistresses or absconded with church funds. Luis and Ester walked out before the benediction.

The houses along the highway were all festive. Multicolored paper lanterns of various shapes—stars, fish, and octagons—were all over the place, their frills quivering in the December breeze. Roasted suckling pigs, impaled on bamboo poles, were being carried to some of the houses.

They reached the beach resort in about an hour. It was desolate, for people stayed at home on Christmas Day to receive members of the family or godchildren. Only a handful of bathers were swimming in the calm blue water or sunning themselves on the distant curve of sand. The wind was mild and the surf quiet. Luis parked under a clump of short, thorny aroma trees, which would give them shade when the sun got high.

Close by, the laughter of a girl reached them as a boy chased her to the water. They would have privacy in the world—under the trees, in the car—but this was not what he came for. "I am glad you came," he said. She smiled at him. He moved to her and, tilting her face up, kissed her softly. When he drew away, she remained motionless. He opened the door. Simeon had been thoughtful enough to place in the rear of the car a wide piece of canvas, which Luis now spread in the shade.

Ester joined him. "We can sit here the whole day, doing nothing but talk," she said. She removed her slip-ons and dug her toes into the cool, soft sand.

"We have to eat, too," he said, "and other things, besides."

"After lunch, we go home," she said. "I must be home early. Papa does not even know I'm here."

He took off his shoes, too, and stretched his legs. "Is your father afraid that something might happen to you if you are with me?" he asked pointedly.

"Luis," she chided him, "he does not even know I'm with you—and on Christmas Day."

He lay on his side. Beyond the slope of sand, the sea was clear and lustrous. Two boats, their sails tipping and bloated with wind, were riding in the far distance. Beyond them lay the small green hump of Corregidor, and still farther the soft blue line of Bataan and the aquamarine rise of Mount Mariveles.

"You can leave now if you want to. Breathe the word and I'll take you home."

She bent over him and cupped her hand over his mouth. "Don't talk like that," she said. She shook her head. "Please, why do you always want to fight with me? You are so belligerent, and you want me to be your enemy. All right, I'll stay with you all day if that will make you happy."

He sat upright, his manner grown mild, and pressed her hand. "Thank you," he said contritely.

Ester did not mean to drop the subject. "Even to me you are bitter. Do you hate women, or mankind in general? I cannot believe it, but I wish you'd at least be honest with me. Tell me that you overdramatize—like all poets perhaps—that you wouldn't have been expelled from the university had you not fought over such a trifling matter."

"Trifling!" he shouted at her, his humor vanished again. "It is a question of belief, and furthermore, I was not expelled. I quit!"

"Call it what you want," she said coolly. "You would have graduated with honors and not have been a false martyr if you just saw it the other way. The priests are human, too. They had their reasons and they felt cheated. I hear that they considered you one of their best products."

He closed his eyes and strangled the anger that was growing in him. False martyr, human beings—he clenched his fist and struck his palm viciously.

"That would have been me," Ester said sadly.

He turned to her. She was gazing at him with the kind of look no man can fail to recognize, that countenance that can render granite into sand. *What has come over me? What devil anger possesses me so that I lash out at everyone who comes close? I was unhappy because I did not know what to do. I hesitated and wondered. I was afraid that I was not right, that I would end up hurting people, then I looked around me and found that it was not I who was doing wrong to other people—it was they who had hurt and betrayed me, not so much because they had not accepted me but because they had in a sense rejected me. I cannot be close to anyone, not even to those who have reared me—and here is the girl who would give me herself and all the sacrifice this act implies.*

He sat up, stroked her arm, and traced a blue vein with his finger. "I am not angry with you—you must know that. It is with myself that I am continually at war. Maybe that's overdramatizing it again, but like you said, I am egotistical and self-centered." He smiled. "You must forgive me. You are a wonderful creature."

Her humor had returned. "Cut it out," she said. "You know I am no ravishing beauty. It is the blind man who will appreciate me."

"Because he will see something that others will not see—your soul, which is beautiful, too. Do you know what you really have?"

She shook her head. "Flattery will get you somewhere."

He knew it then and he was sure of it. "You have a glowing personality. You are real," he said, and holding her shoulders, he drew her to him and kissed her softly, ever so softly.

AFTERWARD SHE LEFT for the car to change, and when she came back and stood before him Luis realized what a really beautiful creature Ester was. The lavender swimsuit both revealed and concealed. He stared at her and marveled at the shapeliness of her figure, her thighs, the high, pointed mold of her breast, and how elegantly she walked.

"You are undressing me!" she said, blushing. "Come, let us swim."

He did not go with her. "I'll watch," he said. She threw him a kiss and ran down the beach. He watched her swim out, her arms rising and dipping into the water with even grace. One time she dived so long that he thought something disastrous had befallen her, then she bobbed up, nearer the shore, laughing. "It's not so cold," she shouted. She didn't stay in the water long. She was panting when she returned, shaking off her hair the droplets that had seeped into her bathing cap. After taking a shower in one of the bathhouses near the main rest house, she joined Luis and spread their lunch on the plastic sheet that had covered the basket.

Marta had prepared the food well—roast beef left over from the party, Coke, omelet, ox tongue, oranges, and raisin bread. They ate slowly, and when they were through, Ester wrapped the leftovers neatly and placed them back in the basket. She took some magazines from the car, and they leafed through them and argued a bit. It was then that the fatigue of the previous night caught up with him. "You wouldn't mind if I dozed?" he asked. He lay down, and she took his head on her lap. Before he closed his eyes he had one glimpse of her lovely face looking down at him.

It was late afternoon when he woke up. The surf had become a thunderous crash. Ester was beside him. He sat up. The beach was empty, and the slope of sand where the breakers rolled in a while ago had become a chasm, and the waves, massive and white, were collapsing with a roar.

"That was some sleep," Ester said. "I'm glad you are rested."

"You should have wakened me."

"But you needed sleep," she said. "Besides, you were talking in your sleep and it was great fun listening."

"What did I say?"

"Your life story," she told him gaily.

He stood up and stretched his arms. "Thank you for keeping watch," he said. She gathered the magazines, helped fold the canvas sheet, and followed him to the car.

All the way back he drove slowly, although the traffic was not heavy, since there were few commuters from Cavite during the holidays. Dusk had descended upon Manila when they crossed over from Baclaran to Dewey. The bay was shrouded with the purple hues of sunset.

"Do come and cook supper, like you told me," he said. They were on the boulevard, and the façades of restaurants and nightclubs were already ablaze with neon.

"It—it is not proper, Luis," she said tentatively. "Papa—"

He pressed her hand and assuaged her doubts. "I'll take you home after supper. I will say we have been out, that's all. He won't get angry."

"But I also said I don't know how to cook. I am handy with a can opener only—"

He pressed her hand again. As he swung the car to the right, up the driveway, he said, "We will have the house all to ourselves."

She looked at him covertly and asked, "How long will your servants be away?"

"They are certainly not coming back tonight—or tomorrow."

Holding hands, they went up the short flight of stairs. *This is what I want*, Luis thought as blood raced to the roots of his hair. He opened the door and switched on the lights in the hall, Ester close behind him. She switched on the lamp by the piano and went to the kitchen with the lunch basket. Although this was only her third time in the house, she knew it well.

"Shall I start cooking now?" she asked at the kitchen door.

"We have time for that," Luis called from the bedroom, where he was washing up. When he went to the kitchen Ester was still there, studying the refrigerator. He dragged her away despite her feeble protests. His arm deftly around her waist, they glided past the kitchen light, which he turned off, and into the hall. They sat down on the couch near the *azotea* door.

"You are sure Papa won't be looking for me? I think I should call just to let him know." But there was no urgency in her voice.

"He wouldn't care," Luis murmured. Ester lay on her back, her feet resting on the floor. Her eyes were closed, and a dreamy peace suffused her face. "I'm tired." She sighed. "I can go to sleep now and not wake up until tomorrow."

He did not speak. He knelt on the floor, bent over her and kissed her. He felt the warm parting of her lips and tasted the salty sweetness of her mouth. As he fondled the front of her dress she tried to push his hand away and he could feel a tremor course through her. "No," she said with feeling, "I am not ready for it, Luis."

But he did not heed her.

"Louie . . ." her complaint—it if was one—died on her lips.

Long afterward, when he drove Ester home, they were silent most of the way, and although he tried to make small talk, he just could not make himself regard the night as a time of conquest. Even in the depths of his passion, he had not really been unconscious of another reality. She had made the proper motions of pain, of distress, before the final surrender, but a man knows—he can feel this in his bones—and Ester was acting out something that she had already done, although not with him. A man knows, just as Luis knew it with Trining. It was not fair, of course, for him to ask. He had, after all, gotten what he wanted. But why did she have to lie? It would not have mattered much, but what was important was the honesty of the relationship.

Seeing him brooding, she squeezed his hand and asked, "Luis, aren't you happy? Isn't that what you wanted?"

"Yes," he said without feeling. "I am the happiest man in the world."

"I'm the happiest girl in the world," she said, snuggling close.

A ND SO THEY PILED HIGH the hollow dreams and the sense-less talk over many a ruffled moment. The relationship was intense. Although she was barely past twenty, Ester had refined sensibilities and an intelligence that sometimes surprised Luis with its depth and lucidity. She asked him questions that he was afraid to ask himself, needling questions that had to be answered honestly, for they were matters of conscience, and even if his answers often did not reveal his thoughts, to himself at least he was honest. Why did he write poetry—was it out of some deeply felt need to express what he could not express in prose, or was poetry a search for that basic truth without which men could not live with themselves? Why did he sound so private in some of his lines—speaking only to himself? Was his involvement with social justice based on what he perceived to be unjust, or was he obsessed with it because he himself had committed an injustice and was, in a sense, flagellating himself for his final atonement? At times, when he was pushed to a corner, squirming and shorn of defenses as his innermost privacy was gouged, he would be angry at her with a cold and persistent wrath and he would ask her the same question but rephrased—or buttressed, rather—with the sharpness of torture. *Why did you surrender yourself to me? Is it because you think I would be some cheap and easy conquest? When we make love, is your orgasm real or make-believe? Suppose I tell you that I am your lover only because I'm interested in inheriting the Dantes publishing empire someday?* Remembering all these sometimes filled him with remorse, and he would wonder how deeply he had hurt her, but then she always went back to him, like some masochist, and their quarrels, although pitched and bitter, always ended in a passionate reunion, which both of them hoped would not be marred anymore by the kind of disagreements that exposed their nerves raw to the wind. He failed to understand that in many ways Ester, too, was unsure of herself, that she was groping for something to hold on to, apart from the ready pattern that school, social position, and her father's wealth had made for her. If she could not express this in poetry, the way Luis did, she could at least express it in her relationships—and the deepest, the most human, and the most touching of all was her commitment to him.

They were bound to drift apart, however—irrevocably, inexorably. There came a time when to make up was such an effort it drained them of feeling, of expectation. After they had disagreed on his leaving school, on ideas about art and the future of the Huk rebellion (Ester felt that it was justified, but Luis felt that there were other equally effective methods that could be explored and experimented with), the arguments deteriorated and turned to trifles—movies that they saw and novels that they read—and by the time some rash words were exchanged they would be like two beasts, fangs and claws ready to strike.

Their last quarrel concerned the tritest of things—his latest poem, "The Changeless Land." She had read "The Waste Land," and she felt that the similarity was so obvious—but Luis was no Eliot fan and had not even read Eliot's poem. She said that it was unthinkable that someone writing in English in the twentieth century, involved with social change and manners, could avoid Eliot. They were on the *azotea*, and it was past sunset; before them the lights of ships blinked in the wide, blackening bay. Before finally going up they had strolled down the grassy shoulder on the boulevard, following the sweep of the seawall, then when sunset came they danced between sips of Coke and sandwiches Marta had prepared. Now they were estranged again. It was their last quarrel, and Ester declared without rancor, "All is finished—I suppose it is best this way. I am tired of it all, always having to eat humble pie."

"And what about me? Do you think I have no self-respect at all?"

The year had ended—the December picnic, the clinging smell of the sea. "I have tried my best at least to see that we are headed for somewhere, but I will never know. The way we are quarreling over trifles—there's no future for us, Luis, and the best we can do is call it quits while our personalities are intact." She sounded so cool, so detached, and this infuriated him, for he could not feel the same way. It was as if she had robbed him of his manhood and that he had let her do it at will. He watched her every move, her gestures as she sat on the *azotea* ledge and spoke, and he did not know whether he would walk to her and push her, or take her in his arms and end the silly argument with a kiss, or stomp away in superior rage and let her go home alone.

"If I keep up with you, what is going to happen? You will probably drive me to suicide. You are, as I have said before, simply, hopelessly self-centered," she said, trying bravely to still the quaver in her voice.

It was then that he laughed. "You committing suicide? Ester, you have no sense of honor as the Japanese have. It's not in your upbringing. You know very well where you will end, you and your Catholic clichés. You will roast in hell—that is what you believe—if you try as much as pull one pubic hair!"

She was fairly shouting back, taunting him: "You will probably gloat over your victory, for you will then think that I have given my soul and my body away to you."

It was she who stomped out of the house, not even bothering to close the door after her. He heard her car crunch out of the driveway. For a while he was really vexed; he loathed the way she had treated him, but his anger slowly turned to regret that he was not really able to answer her. Finally he came to realize that he had a part in fueling the quarrel and that the decent thing for him to do was to call her up and repeat the same pat apology. If they could never be together again, at least they could part on a note of civility, if not affection. He decided to wait until morning, but when morning came he found no chance to make amends, for as he prepared to go to the office the telephone rang and the message was to alter his plans.

It was a long-distance call from Trining, and her voice was urgent: "Luis, what will I do? You must help me. I don't know what to do."

"Take hold of yourself, and slowly, slowly tell me what the matter is."

"Hurry home, I mean to Rosales—now, as fast as you can."

"Is that all?"

"I don't know, but I think it's serious—and besides, Luis, I want to see you, too. It's been so long now that you have not been here. You can come, can't you? Tio says today—and you need not stay for more than two days."

"What does he want to see me about?"

"He won't say—but if you want a hint, a heart specialist from Manila is staying in the house. He's been here for a week now."

"He isn't dying, is he?"

"I don't know, but a heart attack is often sudden, isn't it?" She sounded frightened. "And suppose he dies, what will I do, Luis?"

"Father is like a bull. He will live to be a hundred."

"It is serious, Luis. Please believe me."

"I'll try my very best to be there this afternoon, then. I have to rush to the office first and fix things up. Tell him that."

IT WAS EARLY AFTERNOON when Luis reached Rosales. The sun was warm, and in its white glaze the town dozed. No change was apparent in the town except for the presence of Army trucks in the plaza. Soldiers in olive uniforms loafed in the shops, on street corners, and in the *barong-barong* refreshment parlors.

Two civilian guards were posted at the gate to the house. They had strung across the gate a barricade of barbed wire, which they swung aside when he arrived. It annoyed him immensely to think that he must live in a fort, but it was, perhaps, for the best. Trining ran down the marble stairs to greet him. She was pale, and because she wore no lipstick, she looked as if she were convalescing from an illness.

"Luis," she said, holding his hand tightly, "I have something important to tell you."

He pinched her chin. "You'd better tell me something really important. It was no pleasure getting here—all those damned checkpoints."

They went up to the house, and when Luis started for his father's sickroom, Trining held him back. "Please," she implored, "it won't be long."

He followed her to her room, its doors always open to him since they were young. Now she locked it after they had gone inside. The drapes had been changed—the heavy purple brocade had become white damask, and on the gray walls were Navarro sketches that the artist had not bothered to frame. On her wide steel bed and on her narra dresser were the coverlets that she had patiently worked on in high school—"to keep from getting bored because you didn't take me out."

"I just don't want any interruption," she explained as she latched the door securely and pulled him to the rattan sofa. As an after-thought, she said, "Do you want a Coke? I baked a cake this morning."

He nodded, sitting back and yielding to the comfort of the sofa. Trining wheeled around and unlatched the door again. Although Simeon was a good driver, the trip had wearied Luis, who had dozed between Angeles and San Fernando. In the hypnotic heat of the straight and glistening road, they had to stop at a shabby roadside restaurant for a cup of coffee and to douse their faces with iced water. Luis felt that he could go to sleep now and forget everything, but Trining returned with Coke and a piece of chocolate cake. Again she latched the door.

"What was it you wanted to tell me?" The cake was very good, just like the ones she baked for him in Manila.

"You eat first." She sat beside him and ran her fingers through his dry mop of hair, then gently massaged his nape and shoulders. When he was through, he asked again.

"Tio is dying," Trining said. "That is what the doctor told me. Tio knows. That is what makes it so sad."

Luis stood up and paced the floor. The news did not jolt him, really. He had somehow expected it, the inevitability of it all. He walked to the window. Tents were all over the school yard, and soldiers were either playing volleyball or lolling about. Trucks, jeeps, and armored cars were parked, too, under the acacia trees, and by the gate was a machine gun behind a protective pile of sandbags.

"If he dies," Trining said softly behind him, "we will be alone. We are all he has. Do you know what that means?"

Luis did not answer. "What are the soldiers doing here, and how long have they been here?"

"The soldiers?" Trining was momentarily baffled. "Oh, they were here when I arrived. There is Huk trouble in the villages and in the mountains."

Luis shook his head and turned to her. "If Tio dies," Trining continued, "will you let me stay in this house, Luis?"

Luis could not help laughing. "Of course," he said. "It's more yours than mine." He walked toward the door, but Trining held him back. "Please, that was not what I wanted to tell you."

"Father is waiting."

"Please." Her eyes were pleading. "There is one thing he wants to see before—before he goes," she said tremulously. "He told me so only a while ago, after I called you. He wants to see you get married, Luis—now, this week."

So this is destiny—he wants an heir, his name imprinted forever upon the land. Luis cupped his cousin's face. "Now, isn't that just like Father?" He smiled. "Always telling me what to do. And who does he want my bride to be? Perhaps he has also made up his mind about that."

"He has," Trining whispered. In spite of her pallor she was blushing. She could not stand his gaze, and she embraced him, saying in a voice that trembled, "Oh, Luis, he wants me to be your wife."

He held her away, gazed at her expectant face, her pleading eyes, her lips quivering and parted, her heaving bosom—all of her which he had already possessed. Then he drew her close again and kissed her. It was a kiss of affection—not passion—and she sighed, holding him tightly as if she were afraid this was the last moment they would be together.

Presently, he drew away. He unlatched the door and, looking back, saw that she had started to cry.

HE DID NOT KNOCK, for the door of his father's room was ajar. Don Vicente was awake. He lay on his high-canopied bed. A massive bulk, he had his head propped up by pillows. The sheets were freshly ironed, and the room smelled of cologne and sunlight, for the shades were up. A silver fruit tray filled with grapes and apples and the cut-glass vases filled with sprays of azucena on the side table brightened the room. His father had grown thinner, but he still looked as solid as ever.

"I heard your car," he said, raising himself with effort.

Don Vicente introduced his son to the doctor, who was swarthy, with a calm professional air. He grinned, rolled up the old man's pajama sleeves, then jabbed a needle into the bulging arm. The old man winced. "That will keep his blood pressure down," the doctor explained to Luis.

"I want to talk with my son." Don Vicente waved the doctor away.

"But don't forget what I told you," the doctor said. "Don't talk too much. Avoid intense discussions." Smiling politely at Luis, he stepped out.

"Did it hurt, Father?"

Don Vicente sank back and said, grumbling, "I get that injection every two days. He keeps changing the place, both arms and"—indicating his buttocks—"down here. No, they don't hurt as much as the thought of what is happening to Rosales, to the land. And I am going to die soon—I can feel it. I don't know when. That doesn't hurt, Luis." He looked at his son. "Please don't make it hurt."

"You will live to be a hundred, Father," Luis said.

"Do you think you can humor me? You young people, you have no idea how real, how permanent death is. Trining thinks that she can joke or tease it away. She should be in Manila, looking after you, but she has to look after me—as if she can do anything. She was so young when it happened. It was I who really brought her up. Such an admirable sense of filial obligation! But I am resigned."

Luis sat back and looked at his father helplessly. In spite of his affliction the old man still wanted to be domineering and sarcastic.

"Now listen to what I have to tell you." The old man's face was turned to the ceiling, as if in thought. "How is your work in the city?"

The question surprised him. "Very well, Father."

"Of course I know that, but that is not what I meant. I have been following your magazine, seeing the advertising increase. Are you happy working for Dantes? Like I told you, he is no angel. With your kind of thinking, you should not be there long—just long enough to get your name established."

"I have a free hand, Father," he said, but suddenly he felt extremely uneasy, now that his relationship with the sugar baron was being probed into. It had occurred to him before, of course, that the Dantes hierarchs were conniving and rapacious, but the publisher had been most judicious with him.

"He is using you," his father was saying pointedly, "your youth, your imagination, your integrity. You will have to leave someday—and make it on your own as soon as you can. In the first place, materially you cannot earn much from the job. You are an Asperri—not a Dantes. Perhaps if you were a Locsung or a Mondovino, you could marry into the family—but you are an Asperri, don't you ever forget that."

"How can I, Father?"

The old man turned to him. "On your own you are not so badly off, you know. The house in Manila—and there are those lots in Mandaluyong and in San Francisco del Monte, in Quezon City. There are five thousand hectares here, the rice mill, some stocks in the brewery, in the mines. My poor brother is dead, but actually his share is very small, for it was I who acquired most of these properties. Maybe just a few hundred hectares will go to Trining. Have you any idea how much all these are worth?"

Luis shook his head without emotion.

"You can put up your own publishing if you wish," Don Vicente said flatly. "Tonight—or tomorrow—I will have the accountant, the lawyer, and Santos come here. You study the Torrens titles—all the papers—and ask me all the questions you want clarified." The old man started to cough violently, his face contorted with pain. Luis rushed to him and tried to hold him up, but the old man brushed off his clumsy hold with a quickness that was surprisingly strong. Luis went back to his seat as the old man's coughing ceased.

"What do you want me to do, Father?" Luis asked.

"It is difficult, *hijo*," the old man said. "I just want to go with my mind at peace. *Requiescat in pace.* I want to know that I leave everything in good hands—your hands—and as I said before, I want the Asperri name on this land."

"I will do anything you wish, Father."

Don Vicente sighed happily. "That's good," he said, folding his stubby hand on the mound that was his belly. "I am glad that is your attitude. Have you ever thought of getting married?"

Luis was prepared for the question. "No, Father," he said truthfully. "I have never given it serious thought."

"You haven't given your word to any girl then?"

For an instant Ester came across Luis's mind, but he and Ester had not talked at all about marriage. He had told her many times that he loved her, and he was certain that in his own fashion he did love her, although there always was in his mind, alive in its recesses, the thought that she had not been completely truthful. It would be so profoundly personal, so demeaning to him, if he were to confront her, so he had never bothered to.

"No, Father," he said firmly, "I have not promised myself to any girl."

Don Vicente wanted to rise a little again, and Luis fluffed the pillows up and added a couple to the pile that supported his father's back.

"I know how young people feel nowadays. How times have changed!" He chuckled. "I want to see you married before I die, Luis. That's a legitimate paternal wish, isn't it? And Trining—I hope that your closeness to each other has not made you blind—she is very pretty. If you have no feeling for her except that of a cousin or even a brother, don't worry. Love will come. She is a very good girl and she cares for you, although you perhaps do not know. I think she adores you. And do not forget, she is also rich—and it will be in the family, intact. No messy legal procedures and all that sort of thing. Your being cousins is no problem. We will get a dispensation from the bishop later. And your heirs—may there be a dozen of them! They will really have something substantial to lean on." A long pause. "You agree with me about Trining, don't you?"

Luis nodded dumbly.

"How long will it take you to decide? Until this evening? The earlier you decide, the sooner you can go back to your work."

Now that it was crudely put to him, Luis did not really need time to think. What would be had been in the back of his mind, inchoate but whole, and Trining had really been a warm and wonderful companion—if only there were more mind in her, not just homemaking and loving. What she had, however, were attributes of the housewife, not the mistress. Whenever she got permission to leave the convent and stay with him she took over the house—the kitchen most of all. She never tried going into meanderings of his mind. She never really reproved him for quitting school and creating havoc with the priests. It would have been easy for Luis to loathe the direct hand that his father was playing in a matter that was intensely personal, but Luis did not resent it. His father was right—there was also the family wealth to consider. How materialistic and crass can you get? The thin, raspy voice of conscience twitted him, but he did not heed it. He loved Trining, too, perhaps in a way that was not as deep as love should be, but he loved her nonetheless and that justified everything.

"The decision is an easy one to make, Father," he said. "Come to think of it, I am very fond of Trining, too, but"—he paused—"do you think she will not object?"

"Hah!" the old man exclaimed, then burst out laughing, shaking with uncontrolled mirth until tears came to his eyes. When he finally stopped, his breathing was slow and relaxed and a warm contentment settled over him. "Trining will grab you with her two hands," he said. "Well, this is wonderful. I knew you would see my point. You will get married tomorrow, then. I'll tell Santos that the papers he has prepared are not going to be wasted." He laughed softly again. "The judge will come here for the ceremony—and the church ceremony will come later. I am sure Trining will insist on that." The old man shook his head, and with a slight wave of his hand he signaled Luis to leave him alone with his thoughts and his happiness.

TRINING WAS WAITING in the hall. "What happened?" she asked, following him to his room. "I am glad there was no shouting, nothing of that sort. You have to be kind to him. What was he laughing about so uproariously?"

In his room Luis started laughing, too, as soon as he had closed the door.

"What is so funny?"

"Us," Luis said. "What a wonderful, compact family we are. All in complete agreement with one another." He realized that she was waiting for the final word. In the fading light of the afternoon he saw that her eyes were beseeching. They had been very close, and he was always aware of her moods, how quickly they changed and how spontaneous they were. "Trining," he said, holding her hands, "will you marry me?"

She gasped, flung herself at him, and burst into tears. "Luis . . . Luis . . ." She was sobbing softly. "I am so happy, so very happy."

Her heart thumped against his chest. She took his hand and pressed it against her belly. "You are here, darling," she whispered. "I wanted to tell you, for some time now, but I couldn't. I simply couldn't—but now I can."

He drew her away. "Why did you not tell me?"

"Maybe you will say that I am proud," she said softly, "but I wanted to be sure of many things. We have always been close. We have done many things together—and naturally. Even making love— it was the most natural thing, and finally"—she paused and did not seem to want to speak further.

"Tell me," he prodded her.

"Well, I could see you paying attention to Ester. I thought that maybe—oh, I suffered. I couldn't go to sleep. You can see I've lost weight, thinking . . ."

He held her close again, and she hugged him, covering his face with kisses. "It must have been that time you didn't ask me about my period. You are so damn fertile." She laughed softly. "Oh, Luis, how many children do you think we should have? I'd like to have a dozen—and they will know more companionship than we did. But I am not complaining. Did Tio threaten you or argue with you about us? I want you—God, how I want you—but of your own free will."

His hand wandered down the silky valley of her thighs, up the mound and unmistakable feel of pubic hair, onto her belly, which he now rubbed ever so gently. He was filled with tenderness and compassion for this girl who had been his companion as well. "I hope we will have a boy," he told her.

THEY WERE MARRIED in the hall the following evening. The town judge, who had once clerked for his father, performed the ceremony. He was a short, paunchy man, and he stuttered badly; his hand was wet when he congratulated Luis and Trining. The town knew about the wedding, and in no time all of Luis's office mates would learn about it, for Luis had sent a telegram to Eddie telling him that he would be absent for a few days, perhaps a week, since he and Trining would be getting married—and would he please look after everything?

There were no guests. For Luis to have invited his mother and his grandfather was unthinkable. Besides, Don Vicente wanted it as quiet as possible, so only Dr. Collantes and Santos's wife stood as witnesses. Don Vicente permitted the servants to watch the ceremony, but they did not file into the hall. Simeon stood at the dining room door, looking in, and Trining wished Marta was present, too, but she was in Ermita, unaware that the girl she had saved was happiest at this moment. Don Vicente did not leave his room, but his door was kept open so he could see everything. When the ceremony, which Trining said later was so brief and unromantic, was over, the newlyweds went to Don Vicente's room and kissed his hand. At seven they had an ordinary supper, and after reciting the rosary in Don Vicente's room they retired to Trining's bedroom, for her bed, as she herself had whispered to him, not only was wider but also did not squeak.

Now there were just the two of them, and with the sounds of evening muted, they sought each other and put the quietus to the waiting and the uncertainty of the past. The window was open. The sky was cloudless, deep black, and sprinkled with stars. The cold of January evenings was in the air. Trining wanted to switch the light off, but Luis stopped her. "Isn't this one time," he said, running his hand across the valley of her breast, "that we shouldn't care if the light is on?"

"I don't want to feel sorry," she said, her face close to his, so that the fine contours of her nose, her cheeks, and her forehead were blurred.

"But I'm not," Luis assured her. For a while they did not speak. In the silence he could feel himself flowing out to her, his whole body lost in the welcome of her being.

"Do you think your mother and your grandfather will approve of me?" she asked afterward. She had asked him to bring them from Sipnget, so that they would be present at his wedding, but Luis knew that they would never set foot in the big red house.

"I'd like to go with you this time—to meet them. She is also my mother now, remember that."

"You will do nothing of the kind. Besides, you cannot walk very far."

She did not bother him again about meeting his mother and his grandfather. He turned on his side and reached for the switch near the bedpost, and as darkness claimed them Luis thought: *This is not wrong, for if it were, then I would feel wretched. Even if it was Father who planned it this way, this is also what I want.* For a while Luis forgot the cancerous hatreds that had embittered him. With Trining beside him, a sense of peace finally came over him, and with it, sleep.

CHAPTER

27

IT WAS A DREARY walk from the *camino*. All around him were the newly harvested fields. There were still a few golden patches waiting to yield to the scythe, and the fields smelled richly of grain and of cut grass. When Luis finally reached the dike his legs were numb. Once, this dike was no more than a rise of earth that followed every bend of the river, but in a few years the path astride it had become a dirt road and the saplings of camachile and acacia on both sides had grown into trees, which helped to hold the earth in place. The narrow road carried no more than bull carts, horse-drawn *calesas,* and an occasional jeepney. On both sides, down to the bank of the river, spread patches of ripening tobacco plots, gold and green, topped with white where the blossoms had not yet fallen. The sun was high, and in the still afternoon the earth seemed to simmer. Astride the dike, he could see the distance he had traversed, and he cursed himself for not having worn sneakers. His aching feet must be blistered by now. His shoes had been newly polished by Simeon, but after he had crossed the muddy harvested fields, they had, like the cuffs of his gray pants, become dusty, the mud having dried on them.

He walked on. Weeds were beginning to obscure the path. There were no quarter-moon marks of *carabao* hooves or the fine polished lines made by sled runners, and the earth was crusty under his feet. The path had not been used for some time, he mused. He stopped and looked back to where he had come from—the wide, flat fields splotched with high mounds of hay, and in the distance the lash of white country road where not a single bull cart or *calesa* moved and the lomboy tree at the edge of the depression from where the earth that formed the dike had been excavated. That tree—he was not wrong—years ago he had climbed it, defying the bees that hived in its trunk to gather its black juicy berries. This was the path, and holding on to a thick stand of grass, he bounded up onto the flat broad back to the dike.

As he stood in the heat of day, he saw before him the barren land. How lonely and empty Sipnget had become—a few buri palms, the bamboo brakes that lined the riverbank, the green puffs of acacia, rows of broken buri-palm trunks left to rot near the riverbank, the water shining in the sun, the broad stony island, and the stubborn reeds, jutting above the water with their catch of moss and water lilies.

Sipnget as it used to be was gone—the store below the dike, the house where he was born, where he had heard the halting screech of his mother's scolding and the soothing remonstrances of an old man. An infernal machine had thundered past Sipnget, leveled the trees and the palms, and furrowed the land into a flat and ugly wound. In a moment of doubt and faltering he retraced his steps—no, he was not wrong, he was in Sipnget, but gone were all the little things that had enmeshed themselves with his life. How could he bring back the village that he knew—blow life upon a desert of brown, so that it might bloom with the old and familiar scents? He ran down the dike, away from the vanishing traces of the path. A sprout of grass caught his foot, and he stumbled on the hard plowed earth. He picked himself up, cursing, shaking the clod that dug into his palms. He hurried to where he knew the first house used to stand. When he reached the place he stooped and examined the ground. Curled up with the dry, upturned soil were cinders and white-bleached roots of acacias and buri palms, like maggots feasting on his past.

All of them in the house in Rosales, including his dear ailing father—surely they must have known what had happened to the village. He had not asked any of them or even told them that he was coming, but they should have told him. On the day he arrived he had asked Santos how it was in Sipnget, and the short, work-ridden caretaker had turned away and—as if he never heard the question—left. Luis was not close to any of his father's workers, not even to Simeon, who had taken him from Sipnget to this big red house, and to the servants, who greeted him politely. He had taken for granted that the countryside—for all its being stirred by the proselytizing of the Huks—would be unchanged, that the village would be where it always had been, the end of dreams. Surely, someone in Rosales must have known that Sipnget was gone. But why did nobody tell him?

He raised his eyes to the sun that singed the heavens, and he was about to turn and go back to the dike when, from the direction of the river, behind the large prostrate trunks of buri palms, he saw a man rise.

"*Hoy!*" He waved his hands.

The figure bobbed up, and he caught a glimpse of an old, anonymous face, but the man bent down again and was hidden behind the trunk. Only his back and the brim of his wide buri hat rose intermittently. He seemed to be busy, rising and stooping behind the trunk.

Luis ran toward the man and in a leap perched himself atop the trunk. Below him the man was tying together burned planks of wood with black, sooty wire. More planks of burned wood were scattered nearby.

"What's happened? Did the whole village burn down?" he asked.

The man went on with his work, his face hidden by the wide brim of his hat, his blackened hands struggling clumsily with the wire.

"Are you deaf?"

"I heard," the man said, still without looking at Luis.

"Tell me, where are the people? How did this happen?"

The man did not speak. Luis descended from atop the trunk and bent down a little. The face was gaunt, the eyes tired, the chin withered, and the forehead wrinkled. Recognition came: "Tio Joven!"

The man raised the bundle of wood and stood it on one end. Picking up a piece from the pile, he rammed it into the middle of the bundle and hammered it, so that the bundle would tighten.

"Luis, the grandson of Ipe." Luis spoke in haste. "You know me, Tio Joven."

The man paused and dropped the piece of wood that he used as a club. He squinted at Luis. Then he picked up his club again and pounded at the plank. "Why did you come here?" he asked without pausing in his work.

Yes, why did I come here—I who had wanted to escape from this land, to blot from my mind the faces of my people? "That's a foolish question," Luis said simply.

Tio Joven peered at him again, but there was no apparent recognition in his eyes. He shook the bundle and tested its tightness. "People change," he said. "Many come here, asking all sorts of questions—and what can I say when I am just here to gather wood for my stove?"

The man stopped and, lifting the bundle to his shoulder, started to walk away. Luis held the man's load and dragged it down. Holding him by the shoulders, Luis shook the man viciously. "My mother and my grandfather and my brother—where are they?" he cried.

The old man shook off his hold and backed away. For a moment Luis expected him to draw the bolo at his waist, but the man did not. In Tio Joven's eyes Luis saw no hatred and no fear—only that resignation of old people who have grown tired of living.

"What do you want me to say?" the old man finally asked, barely raising his voice above a whisper, his eyes throwing glances around him, as if he were afraid that among the dead trunks of palms, in the hot harsh day, someone was listening to the horrendous secret that he was about to tell. "You shouldn't have come here," he said, taking off his wide-brimmed hat and fanning himself. His eyes had grown warm. "It's all too late now."

Luis felt panic pounding his chest. "My mother," he said. "Where are they? Can't you tell me?"

Tio Joven put on his hat and wiped his hands against his faded trousers. "Nena—your mother—she is alive, but your grandfather is dead—and so are many others."

Luis could not believe what he heard. "No!" he cried, and although fear, anger, and sorrow claimed him, no tears welled in his eyes. There was instead this choking weight that pressed upon his chest. "Only a few months ago . . ." He wanted to say that he had been here, but he realized immediately that he had quite forgotten the old folks, that he had not written to his mother at all or attended to her needs, that he had shut her and his grandfather conveniently out of his mind.

"My mother, where can I find her?"

The old man shook his head. "After it happened we did not really know who was alive and who was not. After a week your mother came to where we had evacuated. She was hungry and we fed her. She was dirty and we gave her some clothes. She would go to every man and say, 'Victor—or Luis—you must go home now.' Every young man was Luis or Victor. She had nothing else. Her eyes were red from crying. She carried a small bundle, which she used as a pillow. It contained nothing but old newspapers and letters. She would not part with it. She left at night, so no one noticed her departure. That was the last time we saw her."

"Where could she be now? Where can I find her?"

Tio Joven looked far away. "Ask the wind," he said. "She goes where the wind wills. She was in Rosales, I have heard—in the market, searching. She does not bother anyone. People are kind—they will always give her food, clothing, and a roof over her head."

After a while, Luis asked, "Tio Joven, how did it start, how did it happen?"

"I do not know," the old man said, "but your grandfather, he was among the first to fall. He was feeding the hogs, I think. Two days later—the fires hadn't completely died down and the posts of the houses were still smoking—the dead were still there, where the bullets had found them."

Luis covered his face with his hands and leaned on the buri trunk, his knees watery and shaking. "Only a few months ago—" he said bitterly.

"Time is swift." The old man sighed. "Sometimes we don't notice it anymore."

"Tell me what happened?"

"You never heard about it in the city, not even from your father?"

Luis did not speak.

"Three months ago, or less," Tio Joven said, sitting on the bundle and fanning himself again with his hat. "It is not very clear to me now. Ask those who are in town. They know better."

Luis leaned forward. "Tell me."

"But what use is the truth now?"

Luis turned away. "I have to know," he said quietly.

Tio Joven bent over, rested his elbows on his knees, his chin on his palms. "It's very hazy now," he said, looking at the yellowish blades of grass struggling up from where he had picked up the bundled pieces of wood, "but that afternoon—how can one forget it? The harvest in November was good. Your tia was planning to butcher a pig." He turned to Luis and smiled.

"It was sunset. I was coming up the river, where I had lifted the fish traps. It was a poor catch. I had gone up the gully when the shooting started. I could hear the bullets whistling. I stopped, then I saw the people, the women and the children, running toward the river. I went back and fled to the delta with them, and we hid in the high grass. From there we saw the village go up in fire—all through the night. Then, before dawn, we started looking around for the others in the delta. I called my wife's name, but she was not among those who escaped." The old man's face was inscrutable. His eyes had long been dried of tears, and the story he told had long numbed his senses to grief.

"Why did it happen?" Luis asked.

Tio Joven bit his lower lip and spat. "I do not know—how will I know? They came searching for us in Aguray—in the delta to which we had fled. The constabulary soldiers and Don Vicente's civilian guards—they said that our village was evil, that there were Huks among us, and that they would continue to follow us. We returned here—some of us. We saw for the first time what had happened, and we knew we couldn't stay here anymore. A few days afterward the tractors came."

Luis stood up. Around him the newly plowed earth was waiting for rain and seed. "Grandfather," he asked, "where was he buried?"

The old man pointed to the turn of the river. "There are twenty of them there." The old man rose, heaving his load on his shoulders. Luis walked behind him.

"I am now in Aguray, too. That's farther up the river—if you remember. There's not much to eat there, and we cannot tell when we will have to leave. When the rains come we won't know how the floodwaters will turn. The delta may be flooded, and all the houses of reed and bamboo that we have built will be washed away. They haven't come down to drive us away. Maybe we will go to Manila if we can raise the transport money. We can try our luck there."

Luis took his wallet, pulled out some bills, and handed them to the old man. The old man shook his head, but Luis tucked the bills into the old man's shirt pocket just the same. "Thank you, thank you," the old man said. "You will be going back to Manila? I hear it is very peaceful there."

Luis did not answer.

"We do talk about you sometimes," the old man said finally, "that you will be getting married. You will live in Rosales, of course?"

Luis did not want to talk about himself. "Are all the others in Aguray, too?" he asked.

"About five families," Tio Joven said, shaking his head. "Life there is difficult. There are no fish in the river. We have planted some peanuts and watermelons—seeds that we got from the farmers there, who wanted to help us. We need many things. See, I come this far for firewood." They walked with difficulty, stumbling over dry chunks of earth and deep furrows. The old man stopped before a thicket of shrubs near the riverbank. "Behind this," he said.

Before the mound of earth Tio Joven flung down his load and wiped his face with the sleeve of his shirt. "There are twenty here—we counted them, and we know all of them."

Luis stood before the swell, his arms limp at his sides. Beyond, the river, the sparse growth of weeds motionless on its banks. Above, a smoky blue sky and the sun, which ravaged everything. *I see them all before me now, all who have trusted me because I was one of them. This is my truth, and it would have been simpler if I were ignorant of it and could not trace myself to it. Here I am, the chief mourner, but I cannot cry. I see an ancient and craggy face and eyes that have also seen travail I will never witness. Grandfather—if you are here now, I will hold your hand to my brow and tell you that the world is evil and that not even love such as mine matters anymore. And Mother, you who cared for me simply, where are you? What do I have to offer you? You are here around me—alive as the air is alive and kind as the land that will continue to nurture the seed.*

"Tell me, Tio," he asked without looking at the old man, who now squatted beside him and was starting to pull the strands of grass that had sprouted at the base of the grave. "Who buried them here?"

The old man kept at the grass. "Who else but we? We could have buried them earlier, but we were all afraid to go to the village. When we finally went, they were lying in the ashes, their bodies black and bloated. They all looked the same, and you wouldn't know them if you had not been with them all your life. They left them there—they were not even decent enough to bury them after they had killed them. We had to gather them, each one, carefully, so that they would not fall apart. We didn't want them eaten by dogs—dogs, do you realize that?" His voice had become an ugly screech. "Dogs," he was saying, again and again, in futile anger. "They will pay for this. Dogs. Dogs!"

A warm whiff of wind swept the grass that sprouted from the mound. The grass was yellowish green unlike the grass that covered the dike and the riverbank. Between the blades, shoots were breaking through the soil, straight and firm and sharp. Luis bent down and scooped a handful of earth, which he crushed and let trickle through his fingers.

"I'll come here again," he promised.

"What for?" the old man asked. "We buried them properly. There was no priest—we could not even afford that—but we prayed for all of them."

"I'll come again," Luis said, although the bleak truth was that there was no sense in returning.

Tio Joven bent down and pitched the bundle on his shoulders. Luis watched him do this, and his eyes followed flakes of ash and charcoal as they fell to the ground. "Maybe I will return, too," the old man said. "There is still some firewood I can get." He struggled toward the river and disappeared down the gully.

Luis turned his back to the sun, and his shadow lay like a stub on the ground. A thousand curses stirred violently in his mind, like a pack of starved dogs straining at their leashes. Not many in Manila would believe him if he told them what had happened in Sipnget. His friends would say: Luis, this is the twentieth century, not the Middle Ages. However, he would tell them the truth.

The journey was longer now. The dream is over, vanished like the aimless drift of smoke, like the echo of a gun. It was here on this hallowed land, now violated, where I saw the dream in my grandfather's eyes, in the anger that fed his soul and stirred his withered muscles. We came from the delta one afternoon, on our shoulders old jute sacks half filled with turnips that we had dug. I was tired, and so were he and Victor. We were all gasping as we went up the gully that the carabaos had widened as they trampled their way to the river. I gripped his hand and helped him up. We were to follow the dike home. On the dike's broad back Grandfather paused to catch his breath. We laid our sacks down, and when he had regained his breath Grandfather turned to us and said: If I had my way—and a smile kindled in his face—you both would not be here today, looking for something to fill the supper pot.

I told him that I had no complaints. He stood his full height, his tattered trousers pressed close to his bones by a wind that sprang from across the fields, and Vic and I, we reached no higher than his chest. He pointed to the distance and said hoarsely: See that dalipawen tree there, I planted that like a monument. See how green its leaves—but the tree does not matter, for the markers that are important are those of stone, which the rich man has studded the land with.

With a slow sweep of his hand he traced the curve of the river, which gleamed in the sun, and said: All this—up to the river—was ours, because we cleared it.

My father's men intruded upon Sipnget after that and told this defeated man—my grandfather—long before I was born, even before my mother's time—that everything he had cleared, even the lot where his house stood, belonged not to him but to the man who lived in the big red house in Rosales. Like all the farmers in the village who had clawed their farms out of the wilderness, this man found himself shackled to this land. Times when the stars and the full moon's halo augured a bountiful harvest, times when the river brimmed with fish—these were forgotten. The old people died or left, their homes were swept by typhoons or were torn apart by inheritors, but the big red house withstood all vicissitudes. If they got sick or a child was born, if they married and needed money, to the big red house they went. Debt piled upon debt, and one day Grandfather, no longer able to pay, sent his only daughter to serve in the house, and she, who they said was as beautiful as the morning star, was lost forever to Sipnget.

Father—he was young and handsome then—appreciated beauty and took it where he found it, and a year later the girl from Sipnget returned. The village was asleep. Only the insects in the grass and the

owls in the buri palms were awake. She returned with her shame,
which all the village came to know, and this shame became more than
just the bones and the veins in me; in time it also became this passion
that cannot be vented, these thoughts that cannot be spoken—all that
I cannot be.

Grandfather dreamed. Looking at the hollow creeks and the mouth
drawn like a line, I knew that the maculate dream would endure, but
it had to confront another dream—my father's.

THEY DROVE BACK to Rosales in great haste, and the road, white
and shimmering in the afternoon heat, vanished behind them in billows of dust. The car rattled, but they did not slow down until they
reached the main street and were past the open gate to the *bodega* of
the rice mill behind the house where Santos, the perennial ledger
under his arm and a pencil stuck behind his ear, was looking after
the weighing of the sacks of palay before they were carted to the mill.

Luis bolted out of the car. "Mang Santos!" he shouted.

Santos laid his ledger on the small table beside the wooden platform of the weighing machine and met Don Vicente's son. He
avoided Luis's angry eyes.

"Why did you not tell me? Why didn't you?"

Santos turned furtively to the men heaving the jute sacks from
the platform of the weighing machine into the queue of bull carts.
They had paused and were watching with quiet interest.

"Please, Luis," Santos tried to quiet him, "let's not talk here."

"Why did you not tell me?" Luis repeated.

Santos did not answer. He placed a placating arm around Luis's
waist and led him to the room beside the garage. Santos offered him
a chair, but Luis refused it.

"You are all liars," Luis said. "You came to me, all smiles, wish-
ing me happiness and a long life on my wedding day, although you
knew my mother was lost, my grandfather dead. Have you no heart
at all?"

The torrent subsided and Santos asked, "What good would it
have done if I told you?" The caretaker's hands were shaking. "I am
no one here, Luis—just an ordinary servant, like the rest."

The caretaker's face was frightened, and Luis pitied him. Like the
others, he had grown old serving his father, and now another mas-

ter was taking over. "You lied to me—with your silence. You did not say a thing, but you lied to me, just the same," he said wearily.

"Always remember this," Santos said meekly. "You are your father's son. What happened to Sipnget, to your mother and your grandfather—there was a time I knew them all—was an injustice that cries out to God for vengeance, but who am I to say this? Who can right the wrongs that people do in their anger or in their blindness?"

After some silence, Luis said, "And Victor, do you know where he is? What has become of him? He wasn't in Sipnget when it happened."

Santos rose and went to the grilled window. "We don't know where he is, but the civilian guards and the constabulary think he is the new Commander Victor. They thought he was in the village when they attacked it."

So it was my brother who brought death and destruction to Sipnget, Luis thought grimly. My brother . . .

"A happy day has come, Luis," Santos was saying. "On your wedding day, how could we have told you? Besides, I should not be the one to tell you. Your father knows what happened. Our guards were involved, perhaps less than the constabulary, but they were involved, just the same."

He knows, the whole town knows—and how will I face him now who strapped these clothes on my back? Santos had more to say, but Luis wheeled around and rushed out.

In the shiny, heat-laden hall the calla lilies that had been brought from Baguio for his wedding had wilted in their crystal vases. A garland of bridal bouquet that a thoughtful maid had strung on the statue of the farmer with a plow had dried, and its small petals had fallen, dotting the base of the statue with white. Trining was asleep in their room. He wriggled out of his sweat-soaked clothes and sat on the rattan sofa by the window. The fatigue had reached his limbs, and in a while he rose and bent over his wife, kissed her gently on the cheek, then went out and crossed the hall to his father's room.

Don Vicente was slouched on his bed. As usual, the blinds were down, but the depressing dimness of the room no longer dulled his vision. His father's eyes were closed, mere slits below the black bushy patch of eyebrows. His arms were dumpy at his sides. On his head, as if it had been grafted to the round, fleshy lump, the ice bag was precariously propped, and running down the side of his mouth to his chin was a thin line of saliva. If he had as much as nodded, the ice bag would have fallen, but it did not fall even when he stirred. "Speak, son—what is it that you want?"

Now the baggy eyes were half open and were glued on him.

"I have just returned from Sipnget," Luis said, sitting on the wrought-iron chair beside the bed, watching the rising and falling of his father's broad chest. "I found out that my mother has disappeared and my grandfather is dead—killed by your guards." He thought of sterner words to say, but now this was all he could utter, as if all fight had been drained from him and he had become puerile and timid.

"I knew you would go there," Don Vicente said softly. "I was waiting for you to come and see me, to tell me you finally did go. It is a very tragic thing, Luis—this I must tell you."

Luis bit his lower lip. "There were others killed."

"I know," Don Vicente said, shaking his head. "Tragic thing."

"I have heard of things like this," Luis said, "but in the city, where one is detached from the barrios, I always thought these were exaggerated."

Don Vicente propped himself higher on his bed. "Now perhaps you will tell me what wrongs are to be righted?" The father peered at his son, his thick, pallid lips drawn across the flat expanse of his corpulent face. "Luis—" The old man's voice was almost pleading. He tried to smile, so that the corners of his mouth no longer drooped. "Luis, I have never told you about my past. I did not want to talk about it, but now, now I must. You are my son, you have a right to know it. You know that I am dying and perhaps I deserve to die unloved and—and hated, even by you. However, I was once young, too, and the young have their own weaknesses."

"I have never claimed that I have no weaknesses," Luis said simply.

The old man did not heed him. He went on, his face bathed with the luminosity of remembrance: "I was young when I traveled all over Europe, and I was curious and virile then—not like now. It has been two years since I have had a woman, because I am no longer capable. Oh, what I would give to have one erection! But this diabetes, this drug that works on my heart . . . Yes, it was different then, *hijo.* I traveled all over Europe and had a good share of prim English girls and healthy Nordics, but there's nothing like a Filipina in the way she holds a man, loves him, satisfies him. I should know. God forbid that you become a homosexual—that's becoming so fashionable nowadays—with all that literary life you are living. Oscar Wilde was a homosexual, wasn't he? There must have been others."

"Must I prove my manhood all the time, Father?"

Don Vicente shook his head. "No, *hijo*—I am explaining myself more than anything else. You see, Rosales was not big enough, nor was Pangasinan, perhaps not even Luzon. Your grandfather knew that. He knew I was bright. So off I went to Manila, to high school, like you did, and then I came back to this town and its stupid peasant ways and its ugly peasant women."

"Including my mother."

Don Vicente shook his head sadly. "You misunderstand, *hijo*. Please do not misjudge me. In her youth she was very pretty, and as you would say, I fell for her. It was not like those popular stories you like to repeat in your articles, about landlords having their choice of the prettiest of their tenants' daughters. She was working in the house, and I loved her—you do not know how much. My father knew, he heard about it—and that was why he sent me to Europe for college, and of course I could not but obey. It was difficult tearing myself away from her—you know, we couldn't get married. There was not even a thought about it. For many months she was on my mind, always. You will understand the anguish. I did not write to her, nor did she write to me. I was in Europe. I was going around—"

"And you forgot all about her—and her son."

His father shook his head sadly. "It was not like that, *hijo*." His voice was soft, supplicating. "It was not like that at all. It was human frailty. I came back and wanted to see her, but I had gotten married in Spain, and I did not want to stay in Rosales. Would you want to live here after you have lived in Europe? How many times did I want to see her, to ask her about you, after I found out about you."

"And yet you did nothing to help her when I was a baby—yes, she did tell me this."

"I was away, Luis. I was away, and when I came back and her husband had died and I did see her again, she was no longer the pretty girl I remembered. Work and motherhood had destroyed her."

"And suffering, too," Luis said. "I look at myself in the mirror, and I see you."

"And you do not like what you see," Don Vicente said. "I do not blame you, Luis, but I want you, just the same."

"And that is why I am here—because this is what you want."

Don Vicente turned away, and sobs convulsed his body. "I am dying, and I don't want you to hate me for what happened to Sipnget. I will do anything for you, because—because you are my son."

Luis steeled himself. "Thirteen years, Father," he said clearly. "Thirteen long years—you never had need for us. No, you didn't love her or me at all."

The old man turned to him, his baggy eyes red with tears. "What do you want me to do?"

"There is nothing you can do now," Luis said. "My grandfather is dead. My mother, she is crazy and no one knows how she is. And my brother—only God knows where he is."

"Your brother!" Don Vicente suddenly raised his voice. "He is my enemy. He is your enemy. All of them have become your enemy. Don't you understand? She is a fine woman, but what could I do? I am no god, and I can't dictate to the soldiers where they should go or to the civilian guards who are under their control—tactical, they call it—when they are in the field. They will not say it was a mistaken encounter, but that is what I suspect it was."

"But why did they burn the village? Why did you send your tractors there to erase it?"

"*Our* tractors!"

"Why?" Luis stood up and moved to the window. He raised the blinds a little, and fine powdery dust drifted from the blinds and dissolved as a little sun filtered in. The soldiers who made their camp in the schoolhouse across the plaza were cooking their supper in blackened cans and iron cauldrons.

"The memory must be erased, that is why," Don Vicente said. "Do you think I am not sorry that this happened? But if you must know the truth, blame it on frailty, everything that is natural with men. I don't regret that you were born, that I cared for you and gave you things you needed. You will understand."

Across the plaza a soldier, naked from the waist up, his sweaty chest shiny in the late-afternoon sun, stirred one of the cauldrons with a big wooden ladle. A squad was preparing to leave at the camp gate.

"I didn't ask you to take me," Luis said.

"But am I taking back what I gave you—or boasting about it?" Don Vicente asked. "I couldn't let you suffer, that was all. I was never happier than on the day Santos brought you here, and the other day, when you and Trining were married—what more can a father want than grandchildren?"

"I should have stayed behind, in Sipnget."

"Do not be sentimental," his father said. "What would have been your future there? The things that I give you, they are yours by right."

But these were mine by right, too: the days when we had nothing but salt and rice and camote tops, days when I walked in the sun, looking for crevices in the fields where the frogs hid, so that I could spear them and have something to eat. These were my birthright, too.

The soldiers with their tin plates and spoons were filing out of the schoolhouse and finding themselves benches and writing desks scattered under the acacia trees.

Don Vicente continued, "But I have no regrets except that your mother—"

"Don't talk anymore about her. You can't give her sanity back," Luis said, suddenly turning to his father. The old man was not looking at him. His eyes were raised to the ceiling. Luis strode to the door, but his father held him back. "Sit down," he said sharply, his eyes now wide open. "I am not finished yet."

Luis returned to his seat and met his father's steady gaze. This was the gesture of courage that he had long wanted to make. It is said, his grandfather had told him once, that the field rat that can look at the deadly rice snake in the eye before the snake strikes is saved. *Am I saved now when I have become so pliable in his hands?*

"Do not be rash," Don Vicente continued. "Truth—that which you seek, which I cannot give you—is how we look at things, what we believe. Do not talk about injustice or wrongs. There is always an element of injustice in this world, and many wrongs are committed in the jungle. We all live in a kind of bondage until we die. This, too, is truth, and it is ugly, so we do not call it that."

"How would you call it, Father?"

Don Vicente twiddled his thumbs. "How can I call it anything else? All I know is that we are alive, that you haven't grown up. How about motives, why don't you go into them, too? What is the motive of Dantes, for instance, in building up his image as the champion of liberalism and all that crap? You know that he is not, that he is a vicious plutocrat, but you work for him just the same. You asked me why I had the village plowed. It was not hate—it was remorse. I wanted to start anew, to wipe out the traces of a past that will bother us."

"What about those who lived in the village?"

"*Their* lives—what about mine and yours? Whose is more important? Your mother and your grandfather are no longer there. Don't be sentimental. As for the tenants, they can be accommodated anywhere. The farms they tended—these will still be going to them."

"They are frightened, Father. They will not come back."

"And is that my fault?"

Suddenly Luis felt very tired and his head ached. "We have to have a conscience, Father," he said feebly. "That is what separates us from the animals. It is not the soul or belief in God that distinguishes us—"

"Conscience is for the weak," Don Vicente rasped contemptuously.

So this is what we are up against, Luis cried inside him. The primeval law, the glacial age.

"It is enough," Don Vicente said, "that I didn't approve of it, that I feel remorse about it. It is tragic that they were killed, but there was some firing from the village—don't you understand? They fired back. And there is another thing you must realize—their minds were diseased and their death was inevitable. It's they—or us."

How clear it had become. It was as if his father had been skinned and his insides turned out, so that Luis could look into each internal sore.

"You must understand," Don Vicente continued. "Perhaps I can put it better this way. Look at you, at your friends—the five-centavo guerrillas. Where are they now? Who are those who made money during the war, who survived? The collaborators, the buy-and-sell men who did business with the Japanese." A long pause. "I am not saying that you should be an opportunist, but at the same time you cannot go against the wave. You must ride it and reach some place. To shout against injustice, to oppose it, is sometimes good for the spirit; but be sure it does not destroy you. Just remember this: the laws are made by the strong, not by the weak."

Luis nodded dumbly. There was nothing more that his father could say that he did not already know. He rose, and as he headed for the door again Don Vicente called, "The blinds, Luis. Put them down." But although he clearly heard his father's command, he did not turn back.

Trining had awakened when he got to her room. She was sitting by the *azotea* door, and in the soft light of the late afternoon she was reading Marquand's *Point of No Return,* which he had brought with him from the city. She stood up and kissed him. "Why didn't you wake me up?"

When he did not reply she asked, "How are they? What did your mother say?"

Luis probed into her anxious face, into the soft brown eyes that were always expressive and alert. She did not know what had happened to Sipnget, and somehow he was glad, for if she did and had not told him so, he would have hated her, too. He sat beside her and told her how the whole village had been burned, that there was nothing in the barrio now but ashes and plowed earth. When he had finished she embraced him, her heart thumping against his chest. "The soldiers and Father's guards," Luis said, "it was a mistake and that's that."

"Did you fight with him?"

"I was afraid once," he said softly. "I stayed away from him, because I might say something I need not say. Now I am not afraid anymore. I can even damn him now without caring about what he will say."

Trining shook her head sadly. "You will end up hating everyone, even me."

"How else do you expect me to react?" he asked. He closed his eyes and held her close. *Hate—but isn't this the strongest force man has ever fashioned? The father rector argued forcefully once that love was far stronger, that it was the basis of Christian action and forgiveness its bedrock of virtue. Love, however, does not commit people. It does not draw them together in the same way that hate does. You cannot be Christian and forgive or love the tyrants around you, for in doing so, you will yourself institutionalize their brutality. There is nothing un-Christian about hating those who are unjust. I am a vengeful God—read the Bible again; I come bringing not peace but the sword. So let there be hate, so that we can exorcise the evils that plague us. Only with the cleansing catastrophe of fire can we renew ourselves.*

How readily he agreed now with his brother—but only because the agony was now his.

But what of this girl, this woman who was to bear his child, who had turned to him as her savior and master? He stroked her hair and said, "Don't say that—how can I ever hate you? You are the most wonderful thing that has happened to me."

"If you are filled with anger today," Trining said, "I hope you will have it in your heart to forgive. There is hope, Luis, and time is on our side, because we are young. I have memories, too, or have you forgotten? When they killed my parents and my brother I should have grown up hating those who killed them, but I do not, for you have helped me grow and understand."

Time is not on our side, the thought formed clearly; *time is certitude, time ordains us all to die, as Father will die—but why has he lived so long to warp my life? Time was his friend, not ours.*

THERE HAD ALWAYS LURKED somewhere in the shadows of this house, compounded with its musty odors and clammy surfaces, a pall of inevitable decay so real that Luis could feel it hovering over him. What did his father say? What was it that had curdled all the warmth that once coursed through him? The Asperris were destined to be tormented, to be flailed and torn in spirit. Look at Don Vicente's Spanish wife, whose body was wasted by abortions, whose days were lived in madness. In the end they would all die, and nothing, nothing would remain of them. This was not spoken but implied, understood by the people in Rosales and Sipnget who had watched what transpired in this big red house, who had seen how the Asperris were born, debauched, and how they then passed away—his father's father, the uncles and aunts, until there was no one but Don Vicente.

Luis, however, was not an ordinary Asperri. From the very beginning, a deep, dull ache in his heart told him that he had not really forgotten, that he was still capable of more than kindness. He would be saved from damnation as long as he dispensed with tokens of virtue as he knew virtue when he was young, but as long as he was capable of kindness he would also be an easy victim of deceit. Kindness—as his father had said—was just another form of emotion that man must free himself from so that he would be strong. How much easier it would be if he merely followed what the old man wanted and dismissed the agonies of conscience with the thought that he was committed to something just as necessary—the well-being of no other than himself. This self, however, this bundle of nerves and flesh, this mirror of the inner consciousness that had long been cracked, was the prison from which he would now flee, for it was not just rotten tendon and bone—it was also blood that had been poisoned.

This blood nurtured in a distant corner of Spain was no longer what it was, and its perversion was in him, nagging him, reminding him that in this house was his destiny. He must now take leave of it.

He had already packed and was waiting for one of the boys to fill up the radiator and clean the seats of the car. Trining had made a cup of coffee for him, and he was ready to go. "What will you do now?" she asked.

"I will avenge them, that's all," he said simply.

"Oh, Luis, you will end up fighting your father."

He walked to the *azotea*. The east was paling, and in the orange light the jagged rim of the distant hills stood out. Beyond the sprout of coconuts at the right a dog barked, then the silence of early morning descended upon the town again, punctuated by the crowing of cocks.

Her arms closed around him, and her voice trembled. "I am afraid, Luis, not just for myself but for you. Please take me along."

He kissed her on the forehead. "We have already talked about this. For the moment your place is here. He is sick, and that is a concession I am giving him. It is foolish, you being here and I there, but this is not forever."

She was silent. Then, after a while: "I will call you up as often as I can. Will you try to write down whatever is happening over there, whatever comes to your mind?"

"Every day," he promised. They went down together and she kissed him passionately. "Tell me everything he does," he whispered.

When the car drove down to the gate and into the street it was already morning.

LUIS ARRIVED in the city before noon and proceeded to his office at once. As he had expected, everyone at the desk had heard about his wedding. He had no time for the bantering, and although there was this emptiness in his stomach, he tried to smile. All the way he had carefully planned how he would play up what had befallen Sipnget—the crisis in the rural areas, the immediate need for land reform, and the renovation of the armed forces. It would be one issue devoted to nothing but political reform, and the touchstone would be Sipnget.

Eddie was amazed to see him back. "You deserve a much longer honeymoon," he joked. "Of course I know that what you can do in forty-eight hours would take us ordinary mortals forty-eight days."

Luis grinned. He flung his leather portfolio atop the bookcase behind his desk and inserted a sheet of copy paper into his typewriter.

"Tell me what is so important that you cut short your honeymoon," Eddie said, hovering by him.

Luis looked at his associate. He trusted him completely. Eddie worked harder than Luis himself, but in spite of his ambition he completely subordinated himself to his editor's wishes.

"I've seen something in my part of the country that provides the clue to why the Huks are getting stronger every day," Luis said. "A massacre has been committed. We didn't even get to know about it. Worse, it was condoned and glossed over. Twenty were killed." His voice started to tremble, and he stopped. Eddie sat on the edge of Luis's desk and listened keenly. "In my hometown. The constabulary and my father's civilian guards—they destroyed the village, too."

Eddie rubbed his chin. "Of course you have the proofs, photographs, testimonies—all those things."

Luis glared at his associate. "My eyes—what more proof is needed? I know the village, the people. It is gone. I saw the charred posts, the mass grave where the victims were buried."

Silence.

"You are in for something big, Luis," Eddie said. "Something we might go into with our very lives."

"Yes, and we can't let it pass. I'll have to lay it open—the whole mess. You don't know what this means to me. It is my own father whom I am fighting now. He knew about it, but he kept silent."

Eddie winced. He stood up and went to his desk. "He may have his own reasons, Luis, and they may be good. In any case"—he looked briefly at the calendar—"our deadline is five days from now."

Luis made a listing of the authors he wanted for the special issue. He also checked up on the file of articles that had already been accepted and those that had been set in type, ready to be used. In half an hour he had made half a dozen calls and worked out a dummy. Now the editorial, which he must write—and the article on Sipnget.

HE SHOULD NOT have been surprised to find Ester in his home that evening. Eddie had informed him with a sly, knowing wink that she had called twice, asking when he would return. She had not bothered him in the office, but here she was now, watching him as he moved about, to the kitchen, where Marta was preparing the table. They had greeted each other at the door with a mere handshake, and making a bright effort to sound casual, she had congratulated him. He had in turn asked her to stay for dinner and told her that she did not have to worry about how long she could stay.

"Tell me how it was—the vacation, the wedding," she said, watching him as he helped Marta prepare an extra plate at the table.

"I had not expected you here," he said.

She laughed softly. "Poor Luis—always acting surprised. I was in your office yesterday, and today I called up Eddie about you." Her laughter trailed off into another question: "How does it feel to be married?"

"I thought you wouldn't want to see me again, least of all come here," he said, not bothering to answer her questions. "What is it that's bothering you, Ester?"

"You don't have to ask me that," she said flatly. "But you can ask me why I am not on my knees."

They sat down to dinner, but Luis nibbled at his paella, his favorite, which Marta had prepared. Ester, too, did not seem hungry. "Well, I must want something to be here. Aren't you curious enough to find out?"

"Tell me."

"That's game of you, Luis," she said. "I just want to hear you talk, really, about your town, your big house, your father's hacienda, and of course your wedding night. Know something? I have always known that Trining was very possessive about you, that she really wanted you. Were you nice to her—I mean, gentle to her?"

Her prattle had become quite unbearable. "What are you trying to prove?" he asked.

"Nothing."

He stood up, and because she made a motion to rise, he went to her and eased her out of the room. They went together to the *azotea*, out of Marta's presence.

"You know everything. You don't have to ask questions," he said. She sat close to him, so that he could smell the fragrance of her hair. When she spoke again, it seemed as if she had suddenly aged and her voice was feeble. "Yes, I used to think that I knew most of the answers, that I could even guess what you would do. Tell me how it happened. It was not what I expected of you. Not that I do not think Trining is a good girl for you, but you had some ideas, and marrying your cousin—that was not in the stars."

"Yours," he said, "not mine. Do you find anything immoral about it?" He was defending himself and Trining.

"That's nice of you, thinking that I am still concerned with morality." She had become curt. "Do you love her?"

"Does it really matter?"

She turned away.

"I have no explanations," he said simply.

"I didn't ask you to unravel your dark thoughts," she said. "I can only guess. You know, Father did not approve of you—he thought we were going to be really serious. He wanted me to marry my cousin—you must have seen him. He is old enough to be my father. He is balding, has bad teeth and bad breath—but who cares? He is the only heir on his side—and the family wealth, you know, as the cliché in Negros goes, must not fall into the hands of others."

"It's not a bad idea," Luis said.

"Yes," Ester said. "So you are very rich now, Luis—richer than you thought you'd ever be. Was it your father who told you to marry your cousin, so that your hacienda won't be split?"

"That's not true!" he said, glaring at her.

"All right, then." She drew back. "It may not be true, but it's a fact, isn't it?" She walked to the door and crossed the hall to the foyer. Luis followed her, and for a while, when she turned to him it seemed as if she had regained her spirit, for a smile played at the corners of her mouth. "But we must really see each other again, although the rules are now changed. After all, you are a married man now." She broke into a nervous little laugh. "You must come and see me tomorrow—at six."

He did not answer. She smiled again and did not wait for him to accompany her down the driveway, where her car was parked.

WHEN SHE WAS GONE he went to his room to think things out. He was not going to see her again. He was going to steel himself against the compulsion. To Trining, he was going to be the husband that his father had never been to his mother.

Yet it was only a little past five, and here he was, on his way to Ester's house. The sun was still hot on the pavement, glittering in the shop windows and bouncing off windshields in blinding flashes of silver. It was an easy drive after he had extricated himself from the traffic in downtown Manila.

When he drove in she was reading in one of the wrought-iron chairs that lined the porch of the Dantes residence. Casting her book aside on the low glass-topped table, she raced down the driveway to meet him. She wore a green print dress, and her eyes were alive. Only the nervous flutter of her hands as she clutched at his and the tremor in her voice gave her away. "You are extremely early, Luis"—she smiled at him—"and look at me, I haven't even made myself up."

"You are prettier in the raw," he said.

She pivoted him out of the porch and the shade of the bougainvillea trellis to the lawn, into the cool shadow of the house, and they sat in the garden chairs. "I'll go get some drinks," she said, and went back to the porch, where she vanished behind a ripple of violet-and-green curtains. She had not asked him what he wanted, but Ester was always full of surprises. He felt the old familiarity return. He remembered how he had sat in the same chair, how her mother had always asked him inside, how he had always said that he preferred it here—unless, of course, it was raining—among the palmettos and the well-kept hedges, sipping Coke and nibbling at cookies and exchanging inanities. Those were, of course, the days before they started arguing with each other, before this wall between them was set up by pride, by misunderstanding.

She returned, looking anxious, and placed the cold drinks on the low table. "Pineapple juice," she explained. "I was tempted to fix you a bourbon, but I want to break your old habits."

"You are incorrigible, Ester," he said lightly, "just like me."

"What do we do now?" she asked as she sat before him. "Shall we go see a movie or talk, or shall we go for a ride, like old times?"

"Anything you say."

She started sipping her drink, and sometimes she would look furtively at him. Their talk drifted to Rosales, to his father, to Trining. "Why didn't you bring your wife with you? That's a bit unfair, isn't it?"

His casual reply: "She has to take care of Father for the time being. Besides, she will be with me perhaps on weekends." They rambled on—about the new book she was reading and how difficult it was to get certain titles because of the import controls, until she suddenly apprehended him: "Luis, you are not listening!"

His mind had wandered away to Sipnget, to what he had written and sent down to the press—the utterance of his anguish. He turned to her. The brightness in her eyes had dulled, and in them he saw the shadow of a hurt. She folded her hands serenely on her lap and admitted, "It is difficult to talk as if nothing has happened, when we have really been set apart. Luis, why did we have to quarrel?"

"I don't know," he said dully. "It couldn't be helped, I guess."

"Why did you come to see me?"

"You asked me to."

"You did not have to come."

"I owe you at least an explanation." It was not really that which he owed her; he was drawn to her because she was truth, because she was the mirror in which he could see himself, and he had come to her for sustenance. Indeed he would need her now as man needed light.

"I don't need your sympathy," she told him. "I was wondering—just wondering—I wanted to tell you yesterday, but I couldn't. There are many things you have not been aware of." She turned away, as if she was sorry that she had again taunted him. "I didn't mean to spite you," she added hastily. "Shall we go now for that drive? I promise to keep quiet most of the way."

He smiled at her and held her hand, and her breath was warm and fragrant on his face when she drew near. "I'll get my bag," she said, and went up to the porch again. She came back with a fresh coat of lipstick.

It was dusk when they reached the boulevard. The wind flowed into the car and whipped strands of Ester's hair to his face. They had driven many times along this stretch of asphalt, and it no longer had any surprises for them. The restaurants, the tawdry nightclubs, and the neon lights had long been etched in his mind as props of the nightmare that he now shared with Ester.

"You know," she attempted to say above the steady hum of the car, "we could coast along like this, pretending that we would reach some place—but there's no such place. It's limbo."

"Don't talk like that," he said. "We must stop fighting."

"All right," she said. She sat erect and silent beside him. When they reached the other end of the boulevard, where the stone embankment sloped into an incongruous pile of rocks, beyond which was the sea, she tugged at his arm. "Take me to your house, Luis," she said.

"You must be fooling," he said.

"I'm not."

"No."

"Please, I like it there," she insisted. "We are not going to make love—if that is what you are worried about. It's just that somehow in your room I can tell you things that I cannot say in any other place."

"It won't do any good," he said, trying to dissuade her and swinging the car around the curve, past the Baclaran church. "I am taking you home."

Her voice was pleading. "Please, just this once."

He glanced at her, at the dark eyes pleading. "All right, but it will not do any good."

"I know." She sounded contrite.

THE HOUSE was unlighted save for the twin gate lights. Marta and Simeon had probably stepped out. As he groped for the switch at the top of the stairs she held him back. "Let's keep the house dark," she said. "I want it this way, so I can't see your face and you can't see mine either."

"What are you afraid of?"

She mumbled something about the darkness making people equal. She followed him to his room, and he opened the window to let in the air. In a while his eyes became accustomed to the darkness that was punctuated by the headlights of cars making a turn at the next curve, and he could see her quite distinctly in the soft dark. From the sandy stretch before the seawall the eager laughter of promenaders, mingled with the cries of peanut and balut vendors, floated up to them.

"Luis, will you be honest with me? In my own way I have been honest with you."

"You are asking too much. You don't only want me defenseless, you also want me emasculated."

"Luis, that's not what I want—you have misunderstood. I am committed to you. You must trust me as you would yourself. We are the same, Luis; it's so very clear to me now."

"What do you want to know?"

"Why do you work for my father?"

It was a question he had not expected, and it startled him. Yes, why did he work for Dantes? "Why do you hate your father?" Luis asked instead.

"I could ask you the same question, Luis. Please answer me now."

"Well, it is a compromise with what I believe in and what I can really do," Luis said. "I know that your father is no angel, but I need his paper so that I can air my views. That is one reason."

"And the other?"

"I am human, Ester."

"Thank you for admitting it, but I know my father as you have never known him—and I know, too, why you accepted his offer."

"Tell me."

"No, you tell me."

"He said I could do whatever I wanted—and he meant it."

"You missed the point, Luis. How could you have missed it! He was flattering you, and you fell for it."

For a while he did not speak, and when he finally did he could not bring himself to be angry with her. He asked instead, "Why do you humiliate me? You are so good at it, you will reduce me to nothing."

She held his hand tightly and brought it to her lips, kissed the lean fingers one by one and then pressed his palm to her cheek. "I love you," she said. "I am just trying to help you see how things really are—how my father really is—my family, even me. Can't you see how humble I am before you?"

"I can't," he said but without conviction. The barrier between them was beginning to crumble.

She let go his hand. "You must see it," she said. "It is not easy for me to talk like this, to hurt myself and my family. We are very proud. My father, he would rather lose all his money than surrender, but I— I would have come back to you crawling if I had to do it. Now, let me tell you why Father got you. He said you were one of us, that you would understand and would not make any trouble, like forming a union and that sort of thing."

"I find it extremely uncomplimentary, even insulting, that I was not taken for my own talent," Luis said. "I am not humble and I know I have a little."

She pressed his hand but did not look at him. "I am sorry, darling, I have to tell you this. Papa said the magazine was not making money and could use someone courageous and enterprising, but the first editor did something Father would never condone—form a union—and that was why he had to go."

It all came back to him—his first day in the office, the dirty looks of some of the boys in Editorial at this young whelp of a mestizo, this *hacendero*'s son who was going to run a liberal, leftist magazine. He was a scab, and he knew it now.

"Please do not be angry with me," she begged him. Tentatively he held her by the shoulder—this woman who loved him and understood him—and slowly drew her to him.

"I felt funny at first, reading you. Then I thought maybe you were blind or that you had your own reasons, but I look at myself and I am so unhappy. With you there is a way out, but not for me—I will always be a Dantes. I live the good life, I go to Europe every vacation, wherever my fancy takes me, but I also live in Negros where I grew up, knowing how my family—all my father's friends—make their living. I know some of our workers' children. I played with them." She paused and seemed to choke on her words. "I know poverty, Luis—the most terrible and degrading form. It is right in our hacienda, behind our house, in the *cuartels* of the *sacadas*, in the villages of our plantation workers. And I am eating so well and enjoying it and loving the stage in London and the museums in Paris. I cannot live with myself like this."

"You were born to it," Luis said, "but you *know,* Ester—and wisdom is the beginning of sadness."

"No," she said. "Love is the beginning of sadness." She turned and kissed him on the chin. "Did it ever occur to you," she asked, "that you were not the first?" She looked at him, and in the soft dark he could feel her eyes probe into him deeply, passionately.

"It does not matter really," he said, relieved and also sad that what he had suspected all along was finally confirmed. "But why tell me?"

"I don't really know," she said humbly. "It was very easy to say that I did it to get at my father, to hurt him, but I love you, Luis. When I am not with you something happens to me. I am uneasy. I cannot sleep. I'm tense. Maybe because we are so much alike. Do you want to know—"

"It doesn't matter," he said again and meant it.

She did not mind him. "He was the son of one of our workers," she said, pressing close to him. "I was fourteen, perhaps—and he must have been eighteen. He came to the house every morning to water the rose garden, and I used to wake up to his soft singing—you know, melodious Visayan songs. I would open my window—the garden was below—and watch him work, and although he knew that I was up there, watching, he never turned to me. It was a girlish crush—he was dark, he had good teeth, and his face was warm. I wanted to be near him. One afternoon I went to the group of shacks where he lived. He was there, playing a guitar, when I walked by. There was a duhat tree with fruit—it was not very high—and I asked him to get me some of the fruit. He wanted to climb the tree, but I wanted to feel his arms around me. I told him just to lift me up, so I could reach the fruit. He was strong and gentle, and I will never forget how it felt to have his arms holding me."

She paused, and in the darkness, when he looked at her, her face had become grim. "That was when Father came by on his horse, and he shouted at him to put me down, which he did immediately. There, in my presence, with his riding stick, Father lashed at him, at his head, his back, his chest, and he just stood there, taking everything, not whimpering, not warding off the blows. I screamed at Father, saying that I had asked him to lift me so that I could reach the fruit, and he told me, in Spanish, so he wouldn't understand, 'Go back to the house, you little harlot.' " She paused again, then said, "Perhaps I really am a harlot, Luis—but only to you now, only to you."

"What happened to him?"

"It was a month later that I finally saw him for the last time. By then I had to leave Negros to come to Manila for school—the vacation was over. It was on my conscience—God, how it bothered me! I stole money from my mother, from my father—not much, maybe a thousand pesos, something they would not notice. Then I got my biggest diamond ring. Early one evening, when Father was in Bacolod with his mistress and I knew that he wouldn't be back until dawn, I went to the cane field. He did not want to, he was afraid, but I—I am a little harlot. It hurt, but I didn't mind. I gave him the money and the diamond ring and told him to run away, never to come back, and never to see me again."

"So I must run away, too," Luis said sadly, "and never see you again."

"No!" she said emphatically. "You will do no such thing."

"We are both wiser now," Luis said. "You cannot be my—"

"Little harlot," she finished the sentence with a nervous laugh. "No—not your fault, Louie. And don't get ideas from all the novels you have read—that I am a nympho. I am not and will not be one. And more than this, remember that the Danteses are proud. Very proud."

"What will you prove?"

She rose and brushed the wrinkles from her dress. "Nothing," she said, her eyes shining. "I am not trying to prove anything. I just want to be able to live honestly—with myself."

She did not want him to drive her home, so he walked with her to the boulevard, where she hailed a taxi. And when she had gone, Luis went back to the porch, the darkness above studded with stars. In the tall leafy acacias beyond the high, serrated wall, cicadas were lost in the city.

Words, nothing but words, but they were Ester's, and remembering them, he was filled with gratitude and humility; she had given him a gift of love, which, however she might define it or gloss over it or diminish it, would always be more than what he could give.

CHAPTER

I T W A S O N E of those cool January mornings. The sea breeze and the scent of roses blooming in the patch below his window flooded the room; the sun splashed on the floor and on the cream-colored walls; and the white voile curtains breathed in and out of the wide, bright frame of a window. Marta had switched on the radio in the hall at half volume, and it was playing a schmaltzy tune: "Stardust" again. Mayas twittered in the rubber trees in the yard, and cars hummed on the boulevard.

Luis sat on his bed, then bent low, pressed his forehead to the mattress, and let the blood flow to his brain. After a while in this position, he rose and went to the bathroom. He let the shower run, and soon delicious slivers of cold tingled his nerves. When he came out Marta was already making his bed and fluffing up his pillows. "Are there tomatoes in the refrigerator?" he asked.

"I'll see, Apo," Marta said, walking to the door.

"Slice and sprinkle them with salt. If there are salted eggs, that's more than enough for breakfast."

I am a woman conceiving—he was amused by the thought.

Tomatoes, salted eggs. There's nothing like starting the day with something salty. His body had awakened. Luis went to the dining room, his hair glistening with Vaseline. He ate the tomatoes with relish, and the hard golden yolk of the salted duck eggs was still in his mouth when he glanced at the hall and saw Simeon waiting for him in the foyer, twirling his khaki driver's cap. "I'll go down now," Luis told him. The gold-numeraled clock in the hall indicated that it was past ten. He was late and mildly irritated. If Ester did not talk so much—and thinking of her kept him awake through most of the night—he would have gotten to bed earlier. He dressed quickly, threw his robe on the bed, and hurried down.

Simeon drove fast, but as they neared his office the car got meshed up again in the morning traffic. "Any instructions, Apo?" Simeon asked as he parked.

"Just leave the car and go back home," he said. Ester might visit him again, and he could not tell her to leave. Now he needed her, not as a woman but as sustenance. She should leave him well enough alone, she could not go on fooling herself or him, but the compulsion to be with her was stronger now. "If Ester comes to the house," he told the driver, "tell her to call me up in the office—that is, if I am not home yet."

The Dantes building was near the Escolta, flanked by office buildings and shops. It was one of the newest in the area, for most of the buildings were erected before the war and the Dantes building featured awnings and a marble foyer and was completely air-conditioned. In the back was a big parking area, but it was never really full, for most of the Dantes employees had no cars; Luis, with his big black Chrysler and uniformed driver, was an exception.

He walked briskly through the back door, to the elevator, and pitched up to the fourth floor. As usual Eddie was already at his typewriter. "Isn't it a beautiful morning, Eddie?" he said gaily as he flung his portfolio atop the low shelf of books behind the desk. Eddie paused and looked at him apprehensively. "Better hurry and see the Old Man. He was here quite early asking for you. I think he has been crying—his eyes were swollen and misty—or maybe he had too much drink last night."

"He doesn't drink, you know that," Luis said. He sat on his swivel chair and quickly pored over the mail. Already there was a letter from Trining. He recognized her pastel blue stationery and penmanship—

the full loops, the exaggerated cross of her *t*'s. Contributions—he could discern that by the weight of the envelopes. He separated them from his personal mail and dumped them on Eddie's desk.

"See if you can hash one up to catch up with this issue."

Eddie nodded. Without looking up from his work, he said, "I really think you should go see the Old Man right away, Luis."

Luis pushed the green door, which bore his and Eddie's names in gold script, and went out.

Miss Vale, Dantes's grim and antiseptic-looking secretary, told him to go straight into the publisher's office. Eduardo Dantes was at his desk, his head bowed, his long bony hands folded on the glass top. His temples were graying, and the lines on his wide, sallow forehead were deep. He was fifty-five, but he looked much older and very tired. Having used a great amount of energy building not only his publishing house but also other businesses, he should retire now, but he had said in his characteristic soft-spoken swagger that he was good for another three decades, even if in the last he would have to go to work in a wheelchair, "for that's the way the cookie crumbles." He was always neatly dressed, in linen suits and alligator shoes, and his silk ties were from Paris. He wore no jewelry, unlike many other wealthy Filipinos, who plastered their shirts with diamond buttons and cuff links. He had a simple gold wedding band.

In that particular Dantes manner, he did not look at Luis squarely. "Sit down," he said, unfolding his hands. He started fidgeting with the gold cigarette lighter on the wide glass-topped desk. Luis sat on one of the green leather upholstered chairs that ringed the Old Man's desk. Still without looking at him, Dantes stood up and proceeded to the window. He looked through the clear polished glass as if lost in thought. He brought out a Sobranie but did not offer Luis one. Yes, his eyes were quite swollen.

"How well did you know my daughter, Luis?" he asked distinctly.

Luis was startled. "I wish you'd tell me first why you are asking me this question, sir," he said, wondering what Ester had done. Had she finally gone to her father, just as he had gone to his, and confronted him?

Dantes faced him, his eyes red and filmy. He stuck the cigarette into his thin mouth but did not light it, then he took it and squashed it on the ashtray on his desk. "You are always wary, always trying to walk out of traps," he said. His countenance continued to be sullen.

"That is not a fair observation, sir," Luis said, feeling badgered. "I thought I was impulsive most of the time."

Dantes shook his head and went back to his desk. "This is not a business discussion, Luis, but it is important—perhaps more important than business."

"But I wouldn't be able to know her more than you do," Luis said, shifting uncomfortably in his seat.

"You could have been in love with her," Dantes suggested, looking away.

Luis settled back in his chair and laughed hollowly. "You must be joking, sir. You know, of course, that I have just gotten married."

Dantes turned away, took another cigarette, and lighted it. He inhaled deeply. "That makes it simpler," he said.

"I don't understand."

Dantes sounded remote and his voice was raspy. "Ester is dead, Luis. I hope this means something to you."

Luis clutched the arms of his chair, half rose, then slumped back. "No—this cannot be. No!" he cried, but this was Ester's father telling him that Ester was dead. "I am very sorry, sir," he stammered, "but how—only last night—"

"Suicide."

"No," he cried again. "Why did she do it? It's unthinkable—Ester!"

"This morning," Dantes continued calmly now, "she didn't come down for breakfast. Her room was locked from the inside, so we forced it open. Sleeping tablets—one whole bottle."

Now, with sudden and vicious truculence, bits of Luis's talk with her came back and clawed at him. "She was with me last night," Luis said. "We went out for a drive, and she had dinner in the house. My cook prepared paella, and we talked. We talked. I wanted to drive her back, because I had picked her up. She said she would go home alone. I got her a cab at the boulevard—"

"Was there anything to indicate that she would do this?" The publisher's tone was demanding.

He gripped the edge of the publisher's desk. "I don't know what you are driving at, sir," Luis said grimly. "I liked your daughter very much—although we had arguments, too. I felt great affection for her. I do not deny this, but to imply that I am the cause—"

"No," Dantes cut him short. "I am not saying that, but did she confide anything? I must get to the bottom of it, can you not see?"

Luis sat back and shook his head. "Am I to know everything?"

"Do not misunderstand," Dantes said, opening his drawer. "I have a letter for you from her. It was on her dresser. It surprised me very much that she wrote to you at all."

Luis felt a chill ride to the tips of his fingers. "I'd do anything to have her back," he said with great feeling. "Ester—she is one of the most wonderful people I have ever met."

"She wrote only two notes," Dantes said. His voice seemed about to break, and he paused for a while. "The other was for her mother and me." He placed the sealed letter on his table. Luis took it and hastily opened it. It was, like the address on the envelope, in Ester's hand. "Dear Luis [the greeting was so prosaic!]—Did you know that I once won the school hundred-meter dash? Please forgive me. Ester."

"There is not much here," Luis lied, shoving the letter back.

"Nothing?"

"See for yourself."

Dantes fingered the note silently. "There's nothing? But everything is here. Why should she ask for your forgiveness?"

"She regarded me, I think, as her best friend. She knew that I would not approve of what she did. She was running away all the time—like me. Most of the time. Sir, this you will not understand."

"What was she running away from?"

"I don't know. It could be life itself, and she got tired of running. We talked about it."

Dantes was silent again. "May I keep this note?" he said after a while.

"I've seen it," Luis said simply.

Dantes's lips were drawn. "You don't care—and you say that you are her best friend or sweetheart—"

"Don't think of me that way," Luis said softly. "I admired her very much and loved her in my own way, but not in the way you think. Not that way." He was speaking with candor, and he could hear his heart pounding, the words rushing out in a torrent. "There were many things we had in common. We had a sense of communion although we argued and quarreled, but we were alive, Mr. Dantes. That you must understand. We were not two pieces of furniture. We were alive then, but now she is dead. Do you think this does not pain me at all?"

"Will you tell me why she did it?"

"What do you want me to say?"

"Did you love her enough to want to elope with her—marry her?"

Luis's slight laugh was hollow. "It never crossed our minds. I don't want to make it look as if she was not beautiful, that she had no virtues. Yes, maybe—the friendship could have been more than what it was, but marriage was out of the question. As you can see, I got married—but not to her. No, it was not like that at all. Something I cannot explain—something more."

"What could be more?" Dantes whined, and balling his fists, he struck the glass top of his desk, shaking the big flower vase and the menagerie of blotters, inkstands, and clay figurines that cluttered it. He was now sobbing uncontrollably, and he turned away, his lean frame shaking. "She had everything she wanted. I wanted her to marry properly and be comfortable and not have a single worry in the world! This is how fathers are—wait and see." He turned expectantly back to Luis, his eyes misty and red. "Tell me that you loved her—it would be the best way, and I would understand."

Luis closed his eyes, and in the dark, incongruous depths of his mind there formed slowly, clearly, the image of Ester, just as it was the first time he drove her out to that lonely beach in Cavite and she lay in the shade of the low, thorny trees, listening to the pounding surf. "No," Luis said, gritting his teeth. "It was not that kind of love, or else I should have asked her to marry me way, way back. She knew that, sir. It was something else, just as tender and precious."

Dantes had calmed down. He blew his nose and walked to the window again. "The funeral will be tomorrow afternoon," he announced. "Don't send anything."

Luis looked at the thin, broken man and pitied him. "I am sorry, sir," he said. "Perhaps I can say this: I'll miss her more than you ever will."

As Luis opened the door Dantes called him back. "Don't tell anyone about this—for Ester's sake."

He nodded, then shuffled out.

Dear Ester,

I have never written a love letter and it seems rather late and funny for me to write one, but this is a love letter and my regret is that you will not read it. We are so much alike and so, although you will not read it, I will keep it and go over it every once in a while.

I will not forgive you, for you have caused me unspeakable grief, and more than this, you have planted in my mind the suspicion that I am responsible, not for your life but for your death. Maybe your father is right—I have killed you, and in the process I will also kill myself, not because I love you, which I do, but because we are one.

I will try to write this letter minus the obscurity and ambiguity that you said are my faults. I do agree with you that sometimes obscurity simply is a camouflage for illogical thinking or, worse, bad writing. So, you see, you influenced me, perhaps in a manner that you never realized.

When you were around I had some sense of security in feeling that I could just pick up the telephone and talk with you. I know now that I miss you as one who has lost his sight will always miss the light. So I now feel this overwhelming sense of loss. It is as if I could have been able to save you if I had not procrastinated, but I could not have done anything really except—as did that stupid king—stand before the surf (remember how it was in Cavite?) and bid it stop. I have one royal vice—a self-assurance that is engendered by ignorance.

If I cannot forgive you, it must be you who must forgive me, for I was ignorant and I did not understand the great wrong I had done. There is no way now, however, by which it can be undone, and not even God's mercy can put back in place what I have diminished within myself—and so I must now move about, the incomplete man.

Yet I must atone for myself. I must do this as a cripple and compound my misery by begging. This is not manly. It is degrading, but with you I now have no pride.

I love you, Ester, I love you and it is only in words, for this love is beyond deed. I can only relive the hours we were together, the needless conflict, the intimacy of love's supreme act, and I must now ask why you are gone when you could still be alive, not my little harlot but this earth's most precious gift.

I must now give death—not yours but mine—the contemplation that I have not given it, for your death will also be mine. It is the riddle of the unlived experience, the great emptiness of time that is not yet imprinted in the senses or etched on paper and stone. It is the riddle that we cannot unravel, not because it is a compulsive challenge but because the mind seems somehow incomplete, a vacuum that cannot be filled.

I have always felt that the emptiness of my life stems not from the absence of memories or events but from the lack of courage to go after life itself, the way a hunter would go after the most dangerous game, which is death, the way a seeker would challenge the loftiest peaks. We do not conquer life, no one can conquer what one cannot define, but at least it is there and it is ours to shape and to possess fully, with all the senses working, with all the powers of the heart surging, as we search for the answer to the greatest riddle of them all—death, the ultimate end, the enemy of all men, the final quietus to the noblest of emotions, the tenacity and ethereal creativity of faith. You have found the answer and I have found love.

I have asked my brother, whom you have never met, not to hate but to love. I did not mean it. I had meant to ask you, too, not to hate, but I could not do it. You trusted me and in so doing asked me, too, to have faith. Must this, then, be all? Should we drag our feet, believing that our bones will hold our puny frames against everything—the tyranny of fathers and the perfidy of those who practice treachery? You said that we must love because only by love can mankind be saved and the savages amongst us elevated to the realm of the gods—but how can we love when we are nourished on hate? The old virtues no longer suffice. The world moves farther away from the orbit that was plotted out for us by the great religions. We will not be machines, but we will be something worse—we will be pigs.

It's not five years since the end of the war, and as you know, the theology of self-immolation has fascinated me, more so now that I can see it impinge upon my life. I will not know—never—what really made you do it, for it was not in the name of honor, nor was it failure to serve that compelled you to kill yourself, as it did the samurai. I would flatter myself if I surmised that it was love. I do not think that you were a weakling, either in body or in spirit, to have expressed by this act your rejection and abhorrence of our reality—the sadhu who encases himself with ashes and sends away the spirit from the body also dies. Nor do I think that it was loss of comprehension, for if there was anything that has really impressed me about you, it was your intelligence, which was more than intellect and intuition. It was, I think, an intelligence of the highest order, for it was conditioned by compassion.

I do not know and I cannot know, but this I do know—I will enshrine you here in my mind and in my heart, and I will hate you for tormenting me, but I will cherish you nonetheless, for enkindling, even just for an instant, the faith that had long died in me, so that I can and will escape the fate of pigs.

Thank you, my dear Ester, for humbling me, for making me less the man I thought I was but more the human being I aspire to be.

CHAPTER
30

Now I've done it, Luis reflected bitterly when the first copy of *Our Time,* with the story of the Sipnget massacre, was brought up by the copy boy. The article on agrarian reform was written by a rural sociologist, and the complementary piece on political stability and social change was a contribution from a scholar just returned from Harvard. His own article was extremely calm. He had been worried that it would be truculent and emotional, but it was simple, eloquent reportage, and even Eddie, who did not believe in I-scratch-your-back-you-scratch-mine, had gushed over its polish and forcefulness. Writing it, however, had been more than a drudge. The fury that kindled his vision had made the first draft easy to do. It was the rewriting that had drained him; it had been difficult to speak ill of his father and of the civilian guards, but he had done it with objectivity, and now that the anger had been dissipated a nameless void took its place.

He did not go to the office the day the magazine came out. It was as if he had done the last useful thing for the month and work itself had become some fetter around his neck. Eddie called many times, telling him of his visitors, particularly the team of officers from the constabulary and the imminent trouble that he had raised. Never before had the house where his father once lived seemed so wide and forlorn. In a moment like this it was best that he was alone, so he had hurriedly told Simeon and Marta to go to Rosales on the flimsiest of reasons—that Trining needed them—and told them that he would just call them back. He would miss the couple, but they must have guessed his torment, for they left without complaint.

The nights were most difficult. Between the sombrous dark and moments of fitful sleep he damned himself. Now it was not three jiggers of bourbon but five, sometimes ten. On the fourth night that he had not gone to his office it was half a bottle before he could sleep—and he did not even sleep long.

When he woke up, the bedroom burst in a bright yellow slash and he shaded his eyes with his palms and turned on his side. It had rained—one of those brief, unusual showers in February—and a slow, sinuous breeze filled the room and toyed with the voile curtains. Outside, beyond the rain-polished window, the night was dark.

It was ten o'clock by the timepiece on top of his dresser. He had not slept for more than thirty minutes, but somehow he felt a bit refreshed. He sat up stiff and straight and passed his hand over his thick, uncombed hair. Slowly the hand, which he could not fully control, fingered, too, the stubble on his chin. His toes curled at the edge of the bed, he groped for his slippers and, finding them, stood up. He felt a little dizzy, and he clung for a moment to the bedpost to steady himself. He had brought the typewriter from the library to his bedroom some months ago when Ester had suggested that he work in the bedroom while she was there. Ester loved listening to the hypnotic clacking of the keys. Now his eyes were on the machine and on the crumpled sheets on the floor. He had written the letter, bits of his thoughts, and some stray lines that would go into a new poem, but he had not really worked out anything whole.

He went back to the mirror and peered into it. The face that confronted him looked wan. Around the eyes were bluish rings that he had never seen before, and as he peered at his face, he caught sight of Ester's picture on top of the low *aparador.* He wheeled around, and holding the picture in the light, he examined the swept-up hair, the lips parted in a smile, and the pensive eyes—all her fragile beauty held in a simple aluminum frame. Her dedication was simple: *For*

Luis . . . Sincerely, Ester. He cursed himself again for not having kept her letter, for giving it to her father when it was really his. He must write another letter, another poem, anything that would express this emptiness. He picked a sheet from the ream beside the typewriter and sat down. He was surprised to find that his fingers were unsteady. *On an empty beach,* he typed, *sand and sky and sea—all beyond my reach.* He paused. That was all he could write, for although they burned in his brain, words would not shape into lines and he sat helpless before the machine. He stood up after a while, went to the bathroom, and splashed water on his face. The refreshing coolness was brief. His stomach started to twinge, and he went to the kitchen and opened the cabinets and the refrigerator. There was plenty to eat—tomatoes, oranges, canned stuff, and leftovers in the freezer—but the sight of food now sickened him.

He went back to his room, combed his hair, put on a fresh shirt, then went down. He switched the lights on in the garage. His car was dirty, and although the Chrysler was only last year's model, it looked drab with its thick coat of dust. He had driven through the bad, dusty streets the first night that he did not go to work, and with Simeon and Marta gone there was no one to clean the car. He pressed the starter twice, and the engine obligingly purred—but only for a while. Its hum died into a sputter. He pressed the starter again, then saw that the fuel tank was empty. He cursed and slammed the door.

He hailed the first cab that came along. He had nowhere in mind to go to, so he said to the driver, *"Derecho."* Perhaps there was something to see in the office, although it was already past ten. There would be a few persons still at the desk of Dantes's daily newspaper. When he reached the publishing office he did not bother to get his change. He raced past the parked delivery trucks near the entrance and into the lobby, where the elevator boy was drowsing. There was not much of a crowd in the editorial section, and beyond it, in his office, there was light still. Eddie was working late, reading a batch of galley proofs, when he went in. "Luis, I hope that you are feeling better," Eddie said. "I know how you feel, so I didn't want to bother you, but now that you are here—"

"I came for a few things," Luis interrupted him.

"Take your time," Eddie said. "Would you care to treat me to a cup of coffee? I'm sleepy and I need to go over this." Then Eddie became businesslike. "Can you make it tomorrow? There are a lot of people who want to see you. I have all the names and messages there." He thrust his chin at the pile on Luis's desk. "Tomorrow, particularly, some constabulary officers will be coming. Dantes said you cannot hide from them anymore."

"I have not been hiding," Luis said angrily.

"I know," Eddie said, "but that is the impression one gets, especially after the massacre story came out."

They went down to the ground-floor coffee shop, which catered not only to the Dantes employees but also to the pedestrians and window shoppers. They went to their favorite corner, and Eddie ordered an egg sandwich and coffee.

"Make mine just coffee," Luis said.

"You aren't having anything to eat? You look famished," Eddie said. Luis smiled grimly and shook his head.

The waiter brought Eddie's order. As he started eating he became thoughtful. "This should not go on," he said. "It won't do you any good. Do try to come back to work as soon as you can. There is no therapy as effective as work. About Ester, you should not blame yourself. It was not your fault. The reasons are far more complex than both of us can understand."

"It's not just Ester," Luis said, shaking his head.

"Who else, then?"

Luis sipped his coffee and glanced around at the few customers in the shop and at the waiters looking sleepy and bored—they would have about an hour more to work, for the shop closed at midnight. Luis looked at Eddie and said, "I'm worried about us."

"No, no." Eddie gestured with his hands. "Don't worry about me. I can take care of myself, thank you."

"No, not you personally," Luis said. "Not just you and me, but our generation itself. It is a generation that really is aimless. We say that we have been sobered or matured by war, the generation that could be the trailblazer, for it is the generation that has known the first years of independence. But for a few exceptions, we are headed nowhere. The generation that preceded us was interested in independence. What are we really interested in?"

"Milk and honey. The opium of Hollywood. The chariots of Detroit. Babylon, Rome—the depravity of dying empires."

"We are dying, yes—but where is the empire? We cannot even develop the rural areas, for we really do not care—and those who care want to bring a holocaust first that will sweep away weed and seedling."

"You can lose your equanimity, just thinking about the magnitude of our problems, Luis," Eddie said. "I am sure that Lenin and all those fabled revolutionaries often laughed at themselves. I think they enjoyed a good screw when it was time for screwing—and a good fight, too, when the time for it came."

"I envy them of course—the young people whom we know and who are now in the hills. Of course everything has been simplified for them. Perhaps it is easier that way. We who are left behind are cowards."

"Now, now," Eddie objected, "be careful with that word—*coward*. Don't generalize. Suppose you have a heart condition or you can't shoot. Suppose you are a man of words and you can do more just by opening your mouth. What is total war but total politics, too?"

"Justifications," Luis said. "You are right, of course, but I am tired of justifications. Those who rationalize—and God knows how often I do that myself—are merely draining their blood, and bloodless, they get corrupted."

"Call it justification," Eddie said edgily. He had finished eating and was apparently getting bored. He stared out of the shop door into the street that lighted up with green when the neon sign of the newspaper office flashed. "But doing what we are doing is not exactly a cowardly thing, Luis. Maybe for you it is, for you have everything—but what about people like me? I will be branded the rest of my life, I am sure—and I really cannot afford it."

"You will end up as executive vice-president of the Dantes Shipping Company when the time comes," Luis said, humoring him. "Don't worry. At least you will deserve it, but look around you and who do you see? It's the scum who are getting the largest part of the cake—the thieves, the grafters—and we know it. The traitors, those who collaborated with the Japanese—and it's only five years after the war—it is they who are now in power, and they even call themselves patriots." Luis paused and a chill passed through him. He was merely parroting what his father had told him. The old man was not wrong, he was affirming the truth. He said sadly now, "Yes, it was always the opportunists who destroyed the revolution. It was they who sided with the Spaniards. It was they who shaped our relationship with the

Americans and who sold the Filipinos to the Japanese. I am sure that even now, as the Huks grow in strength, a lot of them are pandering to the Huks."

"But this is nothing exceptional," Eddie said. "I am sure that the Romans found the same kind of panderers when they were building their empire. It is simply survival and preservation of interests."

"The revolution lives, but the dream dies—and we cannot do anything, we who were nourished on that dream, for we are too puny or too involved in the system itself. So my dearly beloved and dying father keeps a company of civilian guards and deems it a necessity, even when his guards kill innocent villagers. We cannot even perish in leisure, for the pain of waiting will be worse than death itself. If we must die—pardon the heroics—death must come, swift and painless, in the manner in which we were reared, afraid of pain."

"I am sure that those whose memories of the Occupation are bitter will disagree with you," Eddie said. "They knew what pain was."

"Not that kind, not that kind," Luis said. "Physical pain is much too simple, although there is nothing quite like it."

"Whatever it is," Eddie said boorishly, "keep it away from me." Then seriously: "Luis, I hope that you will get over it very soon. Just remember, the magazine is your baby now. You gave it life. Of course I can always put it out, but then it will no longer have the personality that you have given it."

Luis stirred his coffee. "I wish you wouldn't talk like some damned preacher, giving me motivation and all that jazz."

"I mean it," Eddie said. "Perhaps I'm also thinking of myself, but I am really trying to tell you that there is no sense in your acting like this. It was not your fault any more than it was Ester's. No one in the office blames you."

Luis leaned forward and glared. "But it was mine, more than Ester will ever know," he said. "I did not give her strength, sympathy when she needed it. I was just too damned concerned with myself." He stood up, went to the counter, and paid the check. Eddie followed him to the door, and in the lobby Luis said, "All right, I will try and make it tomorrow."

When they parted, they shook hands, which they rarely did. The rain started again—a slight drizzle—and Luis ducked in the shade of the marquee. Holding the jacket closer to his chest, he sat on the base of one of the columns. Beyond the ebony pavement came the clop-

clop of horses' hooves on the asphalt. Every once in a while a car sloshed past, its lights flat and bright on his face. When the rain finally stopped he crossed the street and walked toward Plaza Goiti. He looked up; it was midnight and Eddie was still upstairs, working. It had become chilly, and at Plaza Goiti he hailed a cab and gave up the idea of walking until he was tired and could easily go to sleep. He did not stop before his house. He got off a long way from it and walked the deserted seawall. Beside him was the sea, black and formless but heaving and alive. The walk would be long, and it would end in the gumamela-lined driveway. He would go up to the porch, unlock the door, and walk past the silent living room, with its muted piano, which Ester used to play, and its record racks, and beyond, to the bedroom, where he would lie listening to his breathing, to the click of lizards on the wall and the scurrying of mice in the recesses of the ceiling. He would remember what Ester had told him, recall the warmth of her arms around him, the taste of her tears and the thrashing of her heart against his own. *God—we were one, as close as no other two people have been, and she had to run away, not so much from life as from me.*

He sank on the rain-drenched seawall, and bending over, he gave way and finally found release in a grief that wrenched from him a moaning loud and unmanly. He was still sobbing when a policeman emerged from the shadows, tapped him lightly on the shoulders with his truncheon, and asked him if he was drunk. He turned to the anonymous face, and in the first flush of turquoise dawn—for it was almost daybreak—he rose slowly and murmured a flat and level "No." He went up the boulevard and straight and steadily to his house, as if drawn to it by the power that makes a criminal hie back to the scene of his crime.

CHAPTER

31

IN THE FIVE DAYS that Luis did not go to work there had piled up on his desk letters, telegrams, and other messages, most of which he would have enjoyed, for many of them were congratulatory. Seeing them now, he felt no sense of fulfillment, no affirmation of his righteousness. They were merely reminders of a turmoil that had uncoiled. He went over them perfunctorily, then dumped them all in a side drawer.

The phone rang and Eddie answered it. "It's the Old Man," he said. "He wants to see you."

The publisher's voice sounded relieved. "Ah, so you have finally come," he said as soon as Luis was on.

"I wasn't well, sir. I hope I didn't inconvenience you."

"I understand," the publisher said. "If it was a blow to you, Luis, just remember, it was much, much more to us. Have you written to your wife, or called her up and told her? They were such good friends, you know."

"No, sir, I haven't," he said, feeling a pang of guilt. He should have told Trining, but then it was probably just as well that she did not know. Perhaps Marta and Simeon had mentioned the tragedy to her, but the fact that she had not called him up was indication that she still didn't know.

"I hope you are all right now," Dantes said. "Can you come to my office immediately? There are officers who will be here in an hour, and they want to clarify a few things about your special issue."

When he hung up, Eddie was looking at him expectantly. "It's the constabulary," Luis said simply.

"Patience," Eddie told him as he opened the door.

A few of the men at the desks turned to him. Perhaps they knew what was in store for him in the publisher's office, perhaps they envied his courage, which they, in their conformity, in their middle age, no longer had, but he walked on, not wanting to talk even with those who knew him well. This was his problem, and he must handle it alone.

Miss Vale was waiting for him, and she smiled perfunctorily as he paused before her desk. She was efficient, not given to office gossip, and she was one of Dantes's most trusted workers. It was rumored that she was an illegitimate sister of Dantes, but Miss Vale was dark and Ilokano, while Dantes was fair-skinned and Negrense. "Go right in," she said, smiling at Luis. He was pleased to find that with that single smile she could still look like a young girl.

The publisher was opening his morning mail with a gold letter opener, and on his large circular desk were copies of the morning papers, including Luis's magazine. "Sit down, Luis," he said without turning to his editor. "If you want a drink, the bar is over there." Dantes thrust his chin across the expanse of blue carpet, the conference table, to the cabinet at the far end of the big room.

"It's too early, sir," Luis said.

Dantes stood up, elegant in his cream linen suit, alligator shoes, and green silk tie. He cracked his knuckles—a sign that he was nervous—and started pacing the floor, his head bowed, as if in thought. "I have often wondered about you," he finally said, the smoky eyes focused on Luis for a brief moment. "Why should you feel uncomfortable with your money, Luis? It is not a crime to be rich, you know."

"No, sir," Luis said. "I have never considered myself a criminal." He found himself speaking with confidence. "I like my comforts.

They are, after all, mine by inheritance, and I am sure that my father wants me to enjoy them."

Dantes walked over to the narra conference table—a huge, glass-topped, rectangular single piece of wood surrounded by a dozen gilt-edged hand-carved chairs. His voice sounded far away. "Anyone reading you would conclude that you hate the rich and think that all of us are scoundrels who make money exploiting the working class. Even if we do, please do not forget that the poor will always be with us and it is not our fault. They will be there because they are stupid, and they are stupid because they are poor. They are there because they are lazy, they have no capital, no incentives, no imagination, and no will to work. In any society, however, there are those among these wretched poor who will rise. History is full of them. Your own Manila elite—and you know how I despise the new ones—many of them started with nothing but glib tongues and nimble fingers—"

"But do they need to be always with us?" Luis asked diffidently, as if he were addressing the question to himself. "If so, I would then admit that society is always exploitative. We go to the nature of man—his perpetual evil—"

Dantes glanced at Luis, and a small laugh preceded his reply. "Ah, Luis—just like Philosophy Twenty-four again. Ah, my under-graduate years." He sighed. "Soon we will be going into theology, then escapism, then nirvana, and all that sort of thing. I continue to read, Luis, though not much"—he thrust his chin again at the books that lined the huge office. Indeed Dantes was very erudite, and every historian in the country knew of his extensive collection of rare books on the Philippines, including one of the first editions of the *Doctrina,* which was the first printed book in the country.

"I know, sir," Luis said humbly, "and that is why I consider it a privilege that you should even seek my views or talk like this with me."

"Enough of the flattery," Dantes said, but he was obviously pleased. "I love the Buddhists—they seem to have all the answers. I am particularly amused by the Tantric Buddhists. You should see my collection on Tantric art one of these days—mostly from India and Nepal. Ah, but I am straying now. What I want to say is that the poor need not be with us always. That is why we have revolutions—all through history. Don't you believe that the Communists, the Marxists, invented revolution. They had it in ancient Egypt—in Rome, Spartacus. All through history blood has been spilled, and it is not a pretty sight, Luis. I don't really think you want revolution. You are just like me, living with illusions, too comfortable to go after most of them—but, mind you"—he paused and pointed a finger at the young man—"I am not accusing you of insincerity."

"Thank you, sir," Luis said, feeling relieved. The room had begun to get stuffy, and he could feel the blood rising to his temples.

"I think I understand your motivation," Dantes said. "I think you are a bit muddled and unclear, even to yourself. The quest for justice is in every man, even in me. I have vision, too, I like to think. I would like to see this country grow, I would like to see it laced with prosperous towns, with people who have money to enjoy life, to buy the good things in the market, the products we make—"

"Just like America," Luis said evenly, but the sarcasm made its mark.

"Don't talk like that," Dantes said. "You must see progress in economic terms, and its social aspects will follow, since this is a society where awareness of other people's feelings has always been a part of tradition. Can you not see, Luis, what I am trying to do? I want my hands not only on industry but also on communications. Radio and television—we have them now—and power, electricity, and shipping and transport—the whole complex that would make this country surge forward."

With the Danteses in the lead, Luis said to himself.

"I know you have been upset by how you joined my organization, but I cannot stand persons who do not see it my way, which, by God, I know is not wrong. Besides, in the end, you must judge me not according to what I say but by what I have done. And what have I done? Think of the thousands gainfully employed, enjoying some of the best privileges anywhere in the country. Of course this is not just what I want to do, and it is for this reason that I want nationalists on my staff. We must modernize, and this starts in the mind, not in the mouth. We must stop being hewers of wood, drawers of water—to use your awful cliché."

Luis turned the thought in his mind. This was what the Meijis did, this was the siren call being trumpeted in all the new countries— how to stop being slaves not only to tradition but to the mother country.

"For whom are we going to modernize, sir?" he could not resist asking. "For whom shall we break our backs, miss our meals, and even kill our brothers in order to be modern?"

"You are cynical and you mistrust me," Dantes said, a hint of sadness in his voice. "How I wish you did not ask that, for it implies that I am working only for myself. Yes, that is true, I love wealth and the power that goes with it, but I know that I will not live forever—like you, I once had youth, but look at me now. I am not as healthy as I'm supposed to be . . ."

Luis remembered how Dantes was said to have gone to those Swiss rejuvenation clinics, so that he could have more virility—monkey glands, all those things that the rich could afford—and as the rich man droned on, almost like a hypochondriac, about his impending death, Luis not only got a glimpse of Dantes's weakness but also began to think of all those like Dantes who had everything but were aware that everything was ephemeral.

"*Sic transit*," Dantes was saying. "In my case it could be cancer or heart attack—or just the usual complications one expects in old age." He shook his head slowly and his gaze wandered to the city spread before his picture window—splotches of tin and cement, the sickly green trees, and a smoky sky mottled with clouds. His voice sounded remote and suddenly cold. "I have thought a lot about justice, but let me make this clear—it should be my kind. I make the rules, for I am what I am—the patron, the *hacendero,* the feudal lord—all those sociological clichés that you use. I like the role. It gives me a feeling of deep satisfaction, almost orgiastic—to use again one of your fashionable words—of superiority, of achievement, and of doing well. The justice I dispense with is mine, for I am the lord, and this justice will go to the workers, for whom you profess love and affection, not as a flood but as a trickle. If you will pardon my sarcasm, how much do you pay your driver and your maids? What are the terms of tenancy on your father's hacienda?"

Luis bristled and raised his hand in protest, but Dantes waved his protest away imperiously and continued, his voice now raised almost in a rant: "The poor do not know what abundance means. They will not appreciate it, since they are not conditioned to it. We are Western men—our wants, our ambitions are unlimited. They are Asians—primitives with limited wants and equally limited vision. They will always be workers, do not forget that. It is the fate of men to be born unequal. Those with brains will rise in any society, democratic or totalitarian. Ideology is meaningless to those who do not know the difference between caviar and *bagoong*. Margarine, not Danish butter."

Dantes paused and his eyes blazed—but only for an instant. Now they were warm again. "You must forgive my enthusiasm," he said with a quiet laugh. "Sometimes I really sound like a soapboxer or a schoolteacher, and I forget that you are not only an editor but one of the most distinguished young writers in the country today."

Luis carefully brushed aside the compliment. "Thank you, sir," he said, "but I cannot help feeling that you seem to think the lower classes are aspiring to utopia. I can assure you—most of the time all they want is three meals a day, education for their children, medicine when they get sick." He paused, for he suddenly realized that he was merely repeating what his brother had said. "These they do not have. Have you ever been to the Philippine General Hospital, sir?" He knew the question was impertinent, for every year it was to the Mayo Clinic that Dantes went for a checkup. "Have you seen the charity patients there, sleeping in the halls, dying because they have no medicine?"

"That's the government's responsibility, Luis, not mine. There is no employee in our companies who does not enjoy the best medical care and pension benefits—much more than what all those crooked union leaders are demanding. I gave all these benefits to the employees without their asking for them. No one can lecture to me about the rights or needs of the poor."

The intercom buzzed. Miss Vale's voice came clear. "The two officers are here, sir."

Dantes's voice changed quickly. "Serve them something and tell them we will be ready in a few moments."

Dantes turned to Luis and his voice was grim. "You realize that I have been making a speech." The grimness quickly disappeared and he smiled wanly. "I do get incoherent sometimes, but out there are two officers, and before they come in I want you to know that there is only one side—my side. I am not interested in what is right or wrong—or what is true or false. My main interest is that nothing happens to this organization. Let me make this clear—I will back you all the way but only if you subordinate whatever ideas you have to what I have mentioned."

Luis nodded. There was not a single doubt in his mind now that the Old Man had really drawn the line. Yet he could not but appreciate Dantes and his frankness, his simple illustration of what he wanted and what he was. Luis should have had no illusions from the very beginning—as Ester had said, this should have sunk into the depths of his subconscious. If she were here now . . . *Oh, Ester, if you were here now, you would be kind to me, you would comfort me, give me your hand and say that the world will always be like this and we can do nothing about it except be close to each other and share as best as we can the agony of our helplessness.*

"In a way," Dantes was saying softly, "we have been lucky—the Army is not so corrupt or power-hungry as it is in Latin America, and it is easy to work things out because the officers are just after promotions."

"But someday it will be corrupted, sir," Luis said. "It is already starting. As with all our institutions, it will decay, for the Army will no longer have a vision and its highest castes will be only after comforts. This will start at the top, not with the privates and the corporals. But it will spread down, and there will be no stopping it, for the leaders shall have been infected; the colonels will not believe their generals, the lieutenants will not believe their colonels, and the privates will not believe their lieutenants. Patriotism becomes a sham, a means toward getting rewards. A dictator will go masquerading as the man on a white horse. And he will do it easily—for as long as we have an Army that does not side with the poor—"

Dantes had listened, but his was the last word nonetheless: "And what army in the world, ever, has been an instrument of the poor? It has always been, will always be, the instrument of the state—and therefore of the powerful!"

The dialogue was over. Dantes strode to his desk and reached for the intercom.

Two officers, a fat balding colonel and an ascetic-faced major, came in. They did not extend their hands when Dantes introduced them to Luis. "Colonel Cruz, Major Gutierrez." They looked at the Old Man's beady eyes, which did not soften, even when everybody was seated.

"These gentlemen have gone to your town, Luis," the publisher said, "and they want to disabuse your mind about the massacre."

"There is nothing to talk about," Luis said. "Everything was in the magazine, Mr. Dantes. There is no point in discussing it—unless they have something new to add to it. If they have a reply, we will, of course, as a matter of policy, print it."

The colonel took the bluster from Luis. "Yes, there are still many things we can discuss," he said, his voice perceptibly hostile. "Inaccuracies, omissions—all of which have put us in a very bad light. You should have checked all your facts first before you wrote that trash."

Dantes acted swiftly. "Please," he addressed the two officers, "let us go into this dispassionately."

The old hate pulsed in Luis. "There was nothing to check," he said. "I saw the grave where the victims were deposited without decent burial. I've talked with some of the villagers who escaped from your men and my father's guards. I saw the place where the houses stood—a whole barrio, mind you—leveled. I need no further proof."

The colonel was unimpressed. He lighted a cigarette, inhaled casually, and turned to Luis with contemptuous self-confidence. "Since you are so sure, I hope you will consent to hear our side. These you didn't mention—that the villagers were active Huk supporters, that one of the leading Huk commanders in central Luzon is from the village—and I think you know him well. You did not mention that there was an encounter—that the villagers fired first—"

"And twenty villagers were killed and not one casualty among the civilian guards or the troops."

"Only because they were trained well." The major laughed, although his ascetic face remained expressionless. He opened his portfolio and handed Luis a sheaf of papers. "Read it," he said.

Luis took the sheaf and skimmed through it. The report was obviously prepared by a staff member and was an arid bureaucratic piece.

"This is your side," Luis said, "but you are big, and who will take the side of the people—the small people—whose interests, since the government should serve the people, should be your concern?"

The colonel grinned. "You talk as if you were their anointed spokesman. Why don't you be yourself, Mr. Asperri?" Luis could sense the scorn in the appellation. "You know very well you are not small. You are very big, sir." The colonel got a fat envelope from the portfolio. Turning to the publisher, he said, "Perhaps this will prove our point. Read it, sir. This is the handwriting of our editor's father, who is the biggest landlord in the province. It seems hardly possible that he has sired someone like his son. If a father does not believe in his son, who will?"

Dantes read the first page carefully, then the second. He stopped reading. "Your father, Luis," he said bleakly, "feels you were prejudiced when you wrote that article. There was no massacre—just an encounter. So many of them taking place in central Luzon, you know. Even in the Visayas, in Negros, they have started. Furthermore, your father says that these two gentlemen know why you are prejudiced. Would you care to tell me why? Here, read it yourself."

The two officers turned to Luis. "I don't personally want to talk about your past or your personal life," the major said. The ribbon on his chest showed that he was a Bataan veteran. "I can very well understand why you are bitter, but we will have to break our silence . . ."

Everyone knows, everyone! It was a time when he should not have cared, when neither contempt nor praise should have affected him, when nothing should have eroded his belief, but in this moment of truth, he felt clammy and small.

". . . and expose you," the major continued. "Tell the world the reason for your bias, your prejudice. Maybe you do not think that this is fair, but what, then, is the reason for your inability to see it our way? We should ask you, as an editor, to be impersonal, but this you have not been. Well—everything is now in your hands. The future . . ."

The future—did it really mean anything now? His lies—his denials of Sipnget and his mother—had caught up with him.

"What do you say, Luis?" Dantes asked, pointing to the document that Don Vicente had written. "Your own father refutes you."

"We had the whole barrio site examined." The colonel laughed casually. "There was no grave at all. Yes, the village was burned. You know these things happen when houses roofed with thatch are close together. That the whole village was plowed—that is not our doing. It was his father's. We do not deny that two villagers were killed—just two—and I think our editor knows who they are. They were taken away by the villagers themselves when they left. They were buried decently, according to them. I dare someone to go there and dig the land inch by inch and show me the mass grave!"

All is done. Luis gritted his teeth; my own father, he has gouged out my brains and squeezed the air out of my lungs. "Call it what you want," Luis said. "How do we know how you may have exhumed the refugees when I am sure that by now you may have dispersed them? How can I gather testimony from the people who are afraid? The dead will bear me out if the living won't."

The major laughed again in his humorless manner. "I see that you are even superstitious. I do not think that is good for journalism."

The officers stood up, ramrod-straight, and made ready to leave, their Pershing caps in their hands. "You have a very interesting story," the colonel said. "I hope that someday we can have a really long talk."

"In the stockade?" Luis asked contemptuously.

"You misunderstand us," the colonel said, "but perhaps you will be able to explain to me why Filipinos would kill their own brethren. This, in principle, seems to be what you insinuate. We are not wealthy like you, Mr. Asperri. Without the government in which your father has a very strong say, we are really nothing—and who made this government, Mr. Asperri? It's the people of Rosales and Sipnget—and your father and you yourself and Mr. Dantes."

He was beyond the reach of anger, and his voice was clear as he echoed his father: "It is the strong who make the laws, and the laws are not for the weak."

"Your political beliefs," the colonel said, "seem straight out of medieval times. I am sorry, but we did not come here to talk politics. We merely came here to give you a chance to retract before we start any action. It is but proper that you should know where we stand. You are being given the choice, and in your own language, you have a deadline. Mr. Dantes knows . . ."

They tipped their Pershing caps in mock politeness, shook the publisher's hand, then marched to the door. Luis sat back and stared at the papers on Dantes's desk, the affidavit that his father had signed, which the officers had left for him to read. Even the phrasing was unmistakably his father's; so was the uneven signature.

"I hope that you listened carefully to what was said," Dantes said scowling. "We are in a mess. They were here yesterday and told me what they would do. Eddie said you haven't been coming to the office, and I understand. Now this."

"It is part of the job, sir. The risks go with it," Luis said.

Dantes walked to his side and placed an arm on his shoulder. "Luis, let us not make it difficult. I don't want my back against a wall.

I don't want to be forced to select the kind of ax my executioner will use."

"Isn't that what they have already done?"

The publisher's brow knitted, and his thin lips compressed into a line across his tired, aging face. "What is it that really happened, Luis? What is it you hold against your father? After all, one reads in the papers every day about encounters like this, and one must learn to take them in stride. It is not the end of the world if one village is burned down and twenty people—like you said—are dead. You get more killed in traffic accidents in one day in the country."

"We have learned to take murder as an everyday occurrence," Luis said. "When we do this we may just as well stop worrying about whether or not we will ever have law and order. We die when we stop being angry."

"But that's not the point, Luis," Dantes said, moving away and facing the young man. "There is a limit to our capacity. We cannot fight all battles as if they were of the same magnitude. That is the way things run. In some we use high stakes. Others we just ignore—or file away while we wait for a more propitious time. Now, this is what those officers want us to do—print a retraction and declare that there was no massacre, unless we are willing to conduct an investigation ourselves." He walked slowly to the wide glass window through which the sun streamed in. "You have to make the decision," he said softly.

"It is all up to you, sir," Luis said after a while, "but there will be no retraction from me. It is not a question of me and my father involving your publication. That is between my father and me, and we will settle it our way. I will have to resign, and they can sue me as an individual if they want to." He had not really given the idea much thought, but it came as natural as breathing.

"You have made a most difficult choice, Luis," Dantes said, still looking out of the window, a touch of sadness in his voice. "I knew it would be this way, but I hoped that you would see it my way. We really don't have much choice. We can do what they want us to do, or they can come at us in a big way. I will pull strings to save the magazine, but among my priorities—and I am speaking frankly to you—the magazine is not the first. You know very well that I have other interests. I had thought that it would be just some sort of hobby. Perhaps I am speaking much too candidly, making a hobby out of your life, your career—but there it is. Never underestimate the power of the government—nor the bureaucracy as such. I have enemies, too. Perhaps you don't know, but more than fifty percent of your ads have already been withdrawn from your next issue. The advertising department will inform you this afternoon on this when they give you the listing. You know that the government controls newsprint through the release of foreign exchange. That is just the beginning."

"All these simplify matters, then, Mr. Dantes," Luis said calmly.

"But we can back up a bit, Luis." Dantes turned to him. "The world is not really as cold-blooded as you picture it. Look at you— aren't you yourself a paradox? In between is a broad meeting ground, so wide we can both rest on it and give no damn to anyone . . ." Dantes's eyes were expectant.

"I am very sorry I have caused you a lot of trouble, sir, but you know, if Ester were alive"—he choked on the words—"if she were here now and I could discuss this with her, she . . . she would agree with me." He stood up, but Dantes held him back.

"We cannot end this way," he said. "I think we understand each other better now. You spoke of Ester—she was an only daughter, and I was very fond of her. I want you to stay, Luis."

He walked to the door. "It has to be resolved, sir—and I see no other way."

Dantes went to him and they shook hands. The publisher's grip was tight and cold. "You can print the retraction, sir," Luis said. "Eddie is a very good man, and if you decide to close the magazine, I hope you can keep him."

"You want a final statement or something?"

"No, sir," Luis said. The publisher's grip relaxed, and Luis walked out.

EDDIE WAS PACING the office when Luis went in and sat wearily on the sofa beside his desk. "Well," Eddie asked, "what happened?"

"I put in a good word for you," he said simply. "It's the most I could do." He stood up and started clearing his desk, sorting out the articles that he should have attended to. "I don't know if the old man will keep the magazine. If he does, you will most certainly be running it. If he decides to let it go, you will be absorbed in his other ventures."

"How did it come to this? I didn't think it would come to this. Isn't it too much for an exposé?"

Luis went to his desk. "That's the Army for you," he said. "As for Dantes, we are not tops in his system of priorities, that's all."

"Well," Eddie said grimly, "I cannot see what is important and what is not. If he doesn't think twenty dead people important, I cannot work for him. I'm used to the gutter, Luis." He stretched himself on the sofa, flipped off his brown slip-ons, and wiggled his toes.

"I'm sorry, Eddie," Luis said, emptying his drawers of letters, manuscripts. It was like combing into the past—only the past could not be dredged from his drawers and dumped like clips or knick-knacks on his glass top, where he could pick them out one by one and say: This fragment of my life is important.

Eddie watched him wordlessly. "But in a sense Dantes is right, Luis. You are bitter, you know."

Luis threw a fistful of junk into the wastebasket and glared. "I knew the village, I could name everyone in it. They were not just casualty figures—they were people."

Eddie sat up. "I do not deny that," he said. "They must mean very much to you. Look at what you are doing to yourself. Let us not go into that cliché about obligations and righteousness and justice, but you have obligations to yourself, too, and your relatives—your father, most of all. Why should he disagree with you?"

The trash from Luis's drawers was now reduced to a small pile of mementoes. It hardly mattered now. Eddie had given him loyalty, respect, and that kind of relationship that could arise only from mutual trust. "There are things you do not know about me," he said quietly. "It is not that the massacre is not true. God knows it is, but I did not tell you why I have been shaken by it to the very core. My grandfather, he was one of those killed. And my mother, she was betrayed and lost. You may have heard from me that my mother died long ago—that was a convenient lie."

"Luis, it cannot be," Eddie said. "If it is true, then it is not enough that you write about the massacre."

Luis smiled wryly. "How I wish that I could really do something—but what, Eddie? As my father said, it is not the truth that gives us strength. I'm not even half the man that I should be. I am a godforsaken bastard. Go to my hometown and ask anyone you meet in the street. He will tell you how my mother was a maid in my father's house. I had to live that lie in this city, and I tried to belong. Everything is a sham and I wish I'd never been born."

Eddie stood up and embraced him, but Luis pushed him brusquely away. "I don't need your sympathy," Luis said.

"It is not sympathy," Eddie said. "It's gratitude—for trusting me."

"I don't have to be a hypocrite anymore. I can now live the way I like. If I must, I will tell the story all over again. Let us say that I am a mourner and that nothing can comfort me except the truth and the damnation that goes with it."

Dear Father,

Today I thank you not only for this life but also for helping me clear the cobwebs in my mind, so that I may yet know the answer to the riddle that I have for so long tried to unravel. I am, thanks to you, slowly escaping from delusions. Indeed it was most easy to delude myself, to mask a deep and private fear with public avowal of virtue or dedication to some noble folly. Do I really love humanity or truth or that abstraction called freedom? How deceptively simple it was for me to address myself to these ends, and how illusory they are finally becoming.

The reality is not quite like this. In truth I am afraid of losing my comforts, the certainty of the wealth you will give me, all the opulent dreams that are already real, for I know, no matter what I do, that you will not disown me. Your dream, too, is your own mishmash of virtue. You, too, have found it convenient, perhaps, to forget.

When you sent me off from Rosales to a Catholic college you knew it was absurd, for I had never touched a rosary before, and if I had, it was in the manner Grandfather prescribed. (You should have known the old man—you have too many things in common: bullheadedness, love of the good life, and a certain earthy approach to living.) He always looked with skepticism at the many who went to church on Sundays and holy days of obligations, for he felt that most of them desecrated the temple—the cheap, fornicating slobs whose minds, preceding their bodies, committed another mortal sin even as they knelt in the pews to ask that their sins be forgiven. He believed in prayer, of course, but only if it was addressed straight to God. He believed—just to make sure—in the spirits, too, which abounded in the fields, the trees, and the mounds.

Those were four tedious years during which I grew up without family and the pleasures of Sipnget. I was in high school—a junior— when the war came, and you had, at first, thought of going to Rosales but, on second thought, decided that Manila would be safe. You were right; the conquerors did not bother us, and we were adequately sup-plied not just with the amenities that you were used to but with the same dogged loyalty that your encargados *and your tenants had al-ways shown you.*

I will now recall, dear Father, some aspects of those years that I know you did not particularly relish but that, if you understood bet-ter, would have explained to you why things were changing, why I, myself, knew that we must change not only because by doing so we would continue to occupy the positions that we always coveted but be-cause by changing we would also be able to live.

You must remember that day when Santos and other men from Sipnget came and told you that they needed medicines, that the coun-tryside was alive with guerrillas. I had listened and asked if I might go to Sipnget, if only to see my mother, whom I had not seen in years. And you told me to go with them so that I might see for myself and tell you how it was.

I was of course pleased to break away from the monotony of the house. We took the train to Rosales, then hiked for two days until we reached the range. We scaled a steep ridge, and in the glimmer of morning we saw the camp, a cluster of cogon huts at the bottom of a ravine. Trees covered the ridge and the narrow clearing from the air. The men were disappointed that we did not bring more medicines. They led me to the hut in the center, where they said their commander was. They called him, saying that Don Vicente's son had come. The commander came out, a short, well-built man with a peasant's simple, trusting face. His handshake was muscular and gnarled. Come in, Señorito, and make yourself at home in this humble dwelling, he said, grinning. His politeness irritated me. He was a leader of men whose reputation had spread well beyond Rosales. A hardened fighter, he had no reason to appear so meek. It was only afterward that I learned that he was not putting on a front, compared with the constabulary officers whom I had met. At one time (his men told me) he had a priest brought up to the hills because a spy whom he had ordered executed wanted the last sacraments. It was medicine that his men needed most. Malaria, typhoid, and dysentery had thinned their ranks, and they could not bring the sick down from the hills. I said that I didn't see why they could not be brought down. At this his politeness vanished and he laughed aloud. He told a woman passing by with the day's laundry to call someone in the nearby hut, and a one-armed man came. The man used to be a farmer, not a guerrilla, but a Japanese patrol had come upon him—and to the Japanese all those with malaria were guerrillas. They would have killed him had he not escaped. Wounded, he had fled to the hills to become a guerrilla.

I know, Father, that you did not want me to go to the hills again after that first trip, but I did go. I must tell you now that I went with my brother, Victor, and that when you thought I was in Rosales, in truth I was really with them for a few weeks. I saw them kill, but I was not appalled. In their company I was part of a wave. Without your knowing it I had forded rivers and stayed in mountain redoubts, where they made their own laws. It was a time for volcanic angers and it was a time for dreams, and Commander Victor dreamed that someday, when the killing was over, better times would come and he would go back to his farm.

Then peace came and I forgot Commander Victor. I returned to college, to cosmology and protoplasm, the reality and the activity of multiple beings and the place they occupied in the order of causality. I dozed through the devil's rantings, metaphysics, and Father Aguirre's Greek. My professors bored me. They had all shut themselves up in the drabness of their jobs, navigating in narrow circles. Each was placid and self-contained, mouthing dogmas and dieting on imagination. My classmates were of the same mongrel breed—rich, untouched by the war. If they were affected by war at all, they certainly bore no scars. I was the editor of the college paper, a job I relished in spite of the fact that I detested the restrictions imposed upon me by the invisible college censors, priests fastidiously occupied with word and symbol.

You returned to Rosales, too, to build the house that had been burned; you said you wanted to be closer to the land.

The war was over, and the last time I had seen Commander Victor was in Rosales. He was wearing an olive-gray GI fatigue, and he was with a group of nondescript men, drinking in one of the hole-in-the-wall bars that flourished after Liberation. He waved and cried—Señorito, I missed you!

I did not miss him. I had forgotten the men who killed—but not the killing. One morning I received a letter in pencil: "Dear Señorito, this shames me to the very core of my heart, but there is no one I can turn to but you. I need help, Señorito—money—and I hope you will not forsake me, as you never had in the past." The mention of money sickened me, but I realized that he had quailed a lot to write to me. "I am not a recognized guerrilla. I received no back pay, nor have my men, but you recognized me and that is all that matters. My family is hungry. I cannot farm, because I have no carabao. My Garand and tommy gun were confiscated, but my automatic—if the worst comes and I won't be able to pay—I'll give it to you. It is the only valuable thing I have."

I intended to send him a little sum, but somehow, with my schoolwork and other interests, I forgot about the letter. In the following week Santos came to inquire about my needs and to check the house to see if it needed repairs, and to pay some of your Manila taxes. We talked about Commander Victor—and of course Santos knew. Commander Victor is dead, he said. The constabulary had been investigating him for the things his men did during the war, and I would not be surprised if he was even investigated for killing the enemy. He was a poor man, and his wife, said Santos, had come to you to borrow money. You could not refuse, for it was for Commander Victor's funeral. He had blown his brains out.

I can understand, Father, why you have been angered by the change that came upon Sipnget. Aren't these the people you helped in their hour of need? But virtue—as the angels have always said—needs no reward, and if you are virtuous, your reward is not in this mundane world peopled by peasants.

I must now tell you what happened in college. You never asked me to explain, and I am grateful. In the press room that night, where I was closing the college paper, I junked my editorial and decided to tell the story of Commander Victor—his village, how he was delivered to his judges. If he was to survive, he had to use force, the same brute force with which he tilled the land. Wearied by his helplessness, by the weight of a future he could not carry, he surrendered his family to the brutality that he could not bear, and he ended his life with the same gun he had wielded to make secure the men who were his judges.

I justified, as I must now justify, the use of violence to secure justice—and self-destruction as the greatest virtue, for it is from death that we must rebuild.

I did not show the editorial to the college censors—not because I was afraid that they would blot it out but because there was just no time. I had done similar things in the past and received no adverse re-action from them. The following morning, however, the office clerk called me. The whole issue of the paper was being held in the office, and when I got there each news item, each article, poetry, and fiction was marked: Imprimatur, tribunal censorum. My editorial was crossed out in red pencil, and on it was: Donec Corrigatur, tribunal censorum. On my desk, too, were instructions to write another editorial or fill the editorial column with a news story.

It was more than I could bear. I did not go to school the whole day. The following morning, my associate editor came to the house and said that they were printing the paper on orders of the father rector and that I should go with him to the rector's office, for they wanted to clear up the whole mess. I knew most of the priests quite well. I even learned my Spanish from them. I had no foreboding of what was to happen. They were waiting for me, seated before the large molave conference table in the rector's office, looking solemn in their white cassocks. In the center of the table stood a black crucifix, and before the priests was a high-backed chair, which was apparently reserved for me. It was the Inquisition.

"Sit down, Mr. Asperri," the rector said amiably. I took the chair and faced the priests—the rector with his double chin; the father dean, lean, ascetic; and the father moderator, his face burdened with a granite jaw.

"*You understand, of course, why your editorial was censored," the father moderator said. He was from the Basque, like you, although he was not Basque and his Spanish had that Catalan quality of resonance. "It was too strong, and besides, you were really stepping on territory quite alien to you. You know, Mr. Asperri, you have a lot of freedom because we knew you were responsible—but as said, this is now alien territory . . ."*

"*Truth is not alien to me, Father," I said.*

The father dean shook his head. He was a nice man, really, from Seville, and there were times during his lectures in aesthetics when he would close his eyes and be carried away by ideas, the transcendental beauty of faith. Now he was wide-eyed. "Let us not be academic," he said, lisping, his yellowish and filmy eyes probing into me.

It was, of course, useless arguing with them, for they were masters of logic and they led me through a maze, pummeled me, battered me, and humbled me. I said, "I know that you would push me into a corner, as you now have done, but I repeat, I am speaking of one who fought for this country when others who would have fought better did nothing. I felt that I had to do something in this life, which you said would determine the next. I knew in my conscience that it was not wrong."

"*You will continue disobeying rules, then?" The father rector leaned forward, all his superior equanimity gone.*

"*It is not a question of disobeying rules," I said. "It is a question of belief." The father moderator held his thick hand to his lips in mock despair, and the father dean shook the yellow pamphlet, the Rules of Discipline, saying, "You know that there is only one thing left to be done."*

I picked up the threat and said, "You may want to kick me out of the college, but you cannot do this, for when I did not come to school yesterday I had already quit school. I have come here as a matter of formality, to tell you about my decision."

I bolted up, unmindful of their confused and inane protestations, and headed for the door, the sunshine and the free air. I stopped by the office and told my colleagues what I had done, and somehow, the next morning my story was in the papers. Trining came to the house, and in tears she shook her fists at me. One week later Mr. Dantes gave me a job.

I was, of course, worried about how you would react, you being almost wholly Spanish and quite close to the priests in whose hands you had entrusted me. However, you accepted my youthful rebellion, which, as you now know, was also directed against you. I wish it would be easy to attribute this to the phenomenon of growing up, in which we all kill our fathers in order that we may become men, but it is more than this. I will never really be able to accept the fact that as my father you could condemn me and yet expect me to carry on the function of an heir. The line has been broken. It was rent asunder when you denied my mother. I am now free from you, Father. I know this, for I can now damn you to your face.

And yet I do not really hate you or wish you harm. It is what you stand for that rankles—the privilege, the apathy, and the alienation from the people, including me, who have made possible your safe pinnacle. No, Father, you are not ten feet tall. If you can look down on us, it is only because you stand on a pile of carrion.

A part of me shriveled when I left college and still another when I read your letter. Our Time *will go on, but I must leave it in order to appease power. I have finally made use of it, although not in the fashion you wanted, for now I have become free.*

CHAPTER

WHEN TRINING CALLED UP and told him of his father's death he was saddened by it just the same. He expected himself to be indifferent to it, his final release from the encumbrances of the past. Before he received the news he had hoped that he could once more go home and face the old man and tell him what a dastardly act he had committed in condoning the fate of his mother and his grandfather. But now that the old man was dead, now that a heritage of land and power was his, he was touched by melancholy nonetheless.

"He asked for you, Luis," Trining said between sobs. "He said that you should promise not to hate him—that if he had more to give to you, he would give it. He loved you, Luis, in his own way . . ."

Luis remembered how he had gazed at the flabby mass that was his father, his half-closed eyes that had lost their luster, the hands that no longer gestured or groped for the folds of the sheets. He remembered him prostrate on the high carved bed, his head never steady, as if he were in the midst of a nightmare. He had expected a note from him to return to Rosales, so that his father could explain everything, but no such letter arrived. He did receive letters from Trining, aside from the occasional phone calls, telling him that Don Vicente had bided his time, hoping, perhaps, waiting, perhaps, for his only son to yield to the compulsive call of blood, but not for the world could Luis have said: Father, in this moment when truth and forgiveness—and even love perhaps—are within easy power for us to release from the prisons of our dark, tormented minds, I come to you.

Luis did not go. The old man had lost.

Luis did not bother Eddie with the news. It was shock enough for Eddie that Dantes had announced Luis's resignation. Shortly after the phone call from Rosales, Eddie visited him. It was early evening, and although he had nowhere else to go, Eddie did not want to linger. "I just dropped by to tell you that you need not worry about me anymore," he said. "I have been given a new job by Dantes—just like you said. I said some things I should not have said." He sounded very wretched. "I owe you many things, Luis. Do not think that I am disloyal—but I am poor, unlike you, and I need a job to eat—"

"You don't have to apologize," Luis said. He asked Eddie inside, for they had been talking on the porch, but Eddie drew back and, fidgeting, said, "I didn't mean to stay long."

"You can't risk being seen with me anymore?"

"That's not fair," Eddie blurted out.

"It could be true, you know," Luis said, "but don't look so guilty and crestfallen because you are still working for Dantes."

"I really must go—"

"Don't," Luis begged him. "I just got a phone call from my wife. I should regard it as good news." He held Eddie and drew him up, and soon Eddie was his old self again. He immediately went to the bar and poured himself a Scotch.

"What is the good news?" he asked without interest.

"Father is dead," Luis said simply.

"You should grieve." Eddie was aghast.

"In a manner of speaking," Luis said thoughtfully, "I am sad. I suppose I will miss him eventually."

"Don't speak lightly about death," Eddie said. "They say that when a blight strikes it doesn't come once. Remember what happened to Job? I am sorry, Luis—really very sorry."

Luis said, "But this is what I wanted to tell you. Can't you see? I'm now really on my own."

Eddie shook his head. He had downed his drink, and he walked to the foyer. Luis wanted him to stay longer, but there was nothing more that they could talk about. "So, you see," Luis told his friend as they went down the stairs, "I am an orphan now—and free."

"No one is ever free from one's self," Eddie said dully. They had reached the landing, and the light shone on Eddie's face.

"This is good-bye, then," Luis said.

Eddie gripped his hand. "There is no good-bye between friends."

Luis watched him walk down the driveway and disappear on the boulevard, where night had fallen. It was warm outside, but he did not yield to the temptation to walk over to the seawall. He bolted the gate and went up to the house.

In the morning he went to the gas station down the boulevard and bought a liter of gas for his empty tank. Then he washed the car; he had not worked with his hands in a long time, and he rediscovered the pleasure in it. He changed his wet clothes and tidied up the house, first sweeping the kitchen and ending up in the garden, where he piled up the dry acacia leaves and burned them. It was almost noon when he finished, and although his bones ached, he marveled at the satisfaction, the release from tension, that the work had given him.

From the library he picked out some books, Mayakovsky and Walt Whitman, Sartre and an anthology of Asian poetry. He arranged them in a trunk in the rear compartment of the car. He then disconnected the house main switch and locked all the windows and doors until it was stuffy and warm.

It was dusk when he reached Rosales. As he drove into the town the Angelus pealed, dirgelike, and some of the townspeople paused to pray. The massive gate opened, and he drove straight to the landing, where Simeon was waiting. He handed the keys to the driver and instructed him to leave in the morning for Manila. He hurried up to the hall filled with people, none of whom he recognized, and went straight to the bier at the other end, before the statue of the farmer with a plow. He felt he had to see for himself. He stood between the tall brass candelabras before the elevated coffin, and his eyes wandered up the lacquered wood to the glass-encased viewplate. It seemed as if the man inside, obese and darkened by embalming fluid, was a stranger. Staring at the face of the corpse, Luis felt no sharp incision of grief. His father would have a mausoleum in the town cemetery—perhaps the biggest, the grandest. Santos must already have made arrangements. As for his grandfather, Luis was certain that the old man's remains had been exhumed along with those of the rest and he would not even know where his grandfather was, in what unmarked and unremembered spot of land the old man had finally found the resting place he never had in life.

And his mother—where could she be now, that poor, deranged woman roaming the streets, sleeping on sidewalks, and seeking food in garbage cans? He imagined her on street corners in Manila, in rags, talking to herself, seeking Luis or Victor, carrying a bundle of old letters and clippings. How now would he look for her? If he did find her, would reason return, would she recognize him and say, My son, my son—or would she run away from him as one would from the reincarnation of evil, the spirits that abound in Sipnget and bring fevers to the young until they were appeased with offerings? This, too, was his father's doing.

Forgive me, I cannot wail like the women. Everything that I have felt for you has become a festering wound whose pus, finding no escape, has gushed into my bloodstream and fouled my heart and transformed it into unfeeling rock. How can I cry, how can I rile the fact of death, the end of all tissues, diseased and sterile, when it is death alone that can erode the rock? I have not known the kind of love a father gives to his son. You have not held my hand, carried me on your shoulders, tousled my hair, or held me in your embrace, so I must not mourn you, Father, but the past, which I did not shape, since the present is decayed beyond redemption. If I mourn, it will not be for you but for a baby yet unborn, the days of darkness upon which it must crawl, the future that would wrinkle its face, so that long before the happy time, it would be ready for the grave. I mourn the dear ones who died at twilight, my kin in the wilderness firing at their kindred. I mourn for those who, like you, are great and indolent, seated in the safety and comfort of important offices. They are dead, Father, without knowing it—and for them there is no salvation. For these I grieve—but not for you. Forgive me, then, my father, forgive me.

A hand rested on his shoulder, and he turned to his wife, her eyes swollen and red from crying. "I am back," he said simply, stepping away from the bier and the heavy, nose-clogging scent of funeral wreaths. Arm in arm, they went to their room, where the murmur in the hall diminished into an almost imperceptible hum, and they looked at each other.

"I was afraid you would not come," she said. "I was not thinking of myself but of you. Everyone knows you are all that remains, and if you weren't here, what would people think?"

"Let them think whatever they want," he said. "I was not present when they buried my grandfather, was I?"

She did not answer, and he told her what had happened in Manila—the confrontation in Dantes's office and how he had been eased out. He told her, too, about Ester—not the anguish he felt over her death but the simple fact of it and how it was just right that in the end he had severed all connections with her family. "It's all over," he said, sitting on the stool before her wide narra dresser.

She took everything calmly, as if no tragedy could ever faze her, and she went to him and held his head in her arms, her large belly nudging his shoulder. "Luis, what is happening to the world? I only hope that, no matter what, you will be with me. Do you think you can endure living with me all your life?" She moved away from him and lay on her bed, her face contorted with pain. "Come." She beckoned to him, trying to smile.

He sat by her side. She took his hand and held it to her belly. "Feel it," she said. He could feel the smooth swelling, the slight movements of the life imprisoned there, and a swift, physical sensation akin to joy lifted him.

"Feel it?" she asked.

He nodded. "Does it hurt?"

"Only when it moves so much," she told him. He laid his hand again on her belly until the movements ceased. Then, bending over, he kissed her and buried his face in her breast, murmuring, "My wife, my wife."

This is me inside, this is me living, complete, a proof that I am here—now. I can say that I have lived and planted well, although the soil was barren and the air was polluted. I can explain this nameless life, but how can I explain myself?

"I need you, my husband," Trining was saying softly. "I hope you will give him a happy childhood."

33

THEY BURIED Don Vicente Asperri the following morning. It was a warm May day, and a fierce sun bathed Rosales with a searing brightness. All the town officials were gathered in the house, five congressmen from the province and three senators, all in dark suits or *barong tagalogs,* and the whole front of the house was lined with big black cars. Luis received their condolences with indifference and fretted at the toilsome length of the funeral service in the hall. When the coffin was brought down the marble stairs the senators and congressmen vied with one another to hold the carved silver handles as if the chore was a privilege for a chosen few. If only his father could see it all now, he would be pleased at such fawning gratitude from the big men whom he had helped. Now it was to ingratiate themselves with Luis, the next Asperri, the only Asperri, and around him they hovered—powerful men—knowing that the mantle had been transferred to him.

With Trining, Luis was the last to descend, and at the landing the solicitous crowd milled around them, recreant favor seekers all. In the driveway, which was cleared so that the couple could pass, the town police, in starched khaki uniforms and black armbands, formed a two-file honor guard, and beyond the gate, in the street—where the coffin was pushed into a shiny funeral coach drawn by four black horses—were the inconsequential people of Rosales, the tenants, the mob that had come to pay the great man their last respects. The shuffling of stolid feet and the low, hushed voices merged into one depressing hum. It was warm in the yard, too, and the sweaty smell of people was heavy in the air. The brass band started the Funeral March, and the policemen in the driveway moved to the gate and into the street, where they led the procession, their flag drooping in the immobile air.

Behind the funeral coach, Luis and Trining, in their Chrysler, led the mourners, followed by the politicians, the provincial and town officials. Behind them, inching their way along the main street, were three trucks from the rice mill, all bursting with funeral wreaths, with streaming black ribbons, purple lotus flowers, and greens. Behind the trucks the multitude, on foot, kept pace.

The Catholic priest, who lived on Don Vicente's grace, timed his arrival perfectly. Accompanied by two acolytes, the young priest walked down the street with burning incense. He went to the rear of the funeral coach and intoned a prayer, then the funeral procession moved on.

Trining turned to Luis. Above the dragging cadence of funeral music and the shuffle of feet on the asphalt, she whispered, so that Simeon would not hear, "You must forgive him. He is dead and cannot hurt you anymore."

But it is the dead who hurt us most, for we cannot ask them questions, bring them to heel, or confirm with them what it was that made them what they were. Even in death, something of the man lives on— the visitation of his sins. What he did is not confined to himself. The wars he sanctioned go on long after every bone in his virulent body has become one with the soil. Upon this soil we feed and we imbibe the same virus. Death is the ultimate truth, not for him who is gone but for us who still live. "Yes," Luis said softly, "he can still hurt us, perhaps not so much by what we remember but by what others will expect of us—Asperris. We carry his name, you know, and that is a burden."

The procession left the asphalted street and proceeded to the dirt road leading to the cemetery. The street was now lined with sorry-looking houses roofed with thatch and walled with buri-palm leaves. People came out of their houses to line the street and gaze at this most impressive display of big cars. Never again would Rosales have a funeral of such magnitude. Never had it had so many politicians and officials gathered together, all in the name of Vicente Asperri.

Had it not rained a few days back, dust would have risen to suffocate all of them. As it was, only a thin, powdery cloud rose, and it covered the coach ahead, the carved cherubs on its hardwood door, while the black wooden wheels creaked in their slow turning. In about half an hour the procession reached the cemetery at the southern end of the town, and the crowd made way for Luis and his wife and all the personages gathered around them as they headed for the small *visita* in the center of the cemetery—a dilapidated structure with a rusting tin roof and four posts gone awry. Near this the Asperri mausoleum stood on a lot wide enough for a house. It was walled with white Romblon marble. Here lay Don Vicente's father, his brother, and his sister-in-law, their black marble tombs shaded by lowland pine. There was a tenant whose sole duty was to look after it, to trim the gumamela hedges and water the plots of African daisies and amarillo shrubs, so that, although the whole cemetery had not yet responded to the touch of May, this particular plot was green and abloom.

The politicians vied with one another in hoisting the coffin out of the coach. They carried it to the chapel and set it on a low platform. Santos walked over to Luis and asked if he wanted the cover removed. Luis shook his head. Out of the tightening circle that surrounded them the priest came forward and stuttered the last ritual. When it was over he went to Luis, his breath stinking of tobacco, and said that he hoped everything would be well, that Luis would continue to be the Catholic that his father was. Then the politicians and their wives crowded around Luis, asking him and his wife to visit them in Manila. We have known your father's greatness, they all said; and we hope that you will not forget us . . . The band played "Nearer My God to Thee," and the tomb was sealed. It was time to leave; he took Trining's hand, turned listlessly to the assemblage, and attempted a smile, after which they walked to the car.

They were silent all the way, and when they went up to the house Trining said, "I know what you're thinking of." They washed their feet with warm water, which a servant had placed at the top of the stairs, and they shed their outer clothes of black. Marta had insisted that this be done, so that no abomination would visit them.

Luis remained silent, and in their room Trining repeated, "Luis, how much better it would be if you just talked."

The warm water had banished the tiredness from his feet, and he sank into bed. The heat in the room descended on him like a solid mass, pressing down and seeking every minute pore of his skin. Trining went to him and sat on the edge of the bed. She was wearing a comfortable maternity dress, which she had ordered from her dressmaker in Manila. Although the dress was chic, it could not hide the contour of her belly.

"My grandfather . . . Father is there in that handsome mausoleum—and my mother, I don't even know where she is. Can't you see how terrible it is? So now I am the lord and master of this castle—hah!" He laughed without mirth. "Did you see how they came to me, the politicians? Have you ever seen such a funeral? Can you not imagine the power I now hold—to do with as I wish? Stop the waves, do not dirty the hem of my royal robes—"

"Luis, what are you talking about?" Trining was distraught.

He sat up beside her, pressed her hand, and said softly, "Even a king does not have all the power in the world, sweetheart. There are things I must do myself, with no help from anyone."

"I'm your wife. Do let me help."

He held her face and kissed her softly. "How do we go about living with this blot in our minds?"

"We can try," she said hopefully. "There must be a way we can get to those who knew what really happened. Santos—he should be able to help." Her eyes shone.

"They are all cowed," he said. "Do you think you can find even one who would stand up to the constabulary? They have never been on the side of the people—all those officers are always on the side of the rich."

"Which we are," Trining said flatly. "So there must be a way that we can find out. We start here, in this house, and if we cannot get anything here, we can go to Sipnget, or that refugee village."

"Aguray."

"We can even go to the mountains, if the answers can be found there." She was looking at him intently, searching his face, and he marveled at her tenacity—this frail creature, reared in comfort, who now, in his moment of need, was by his side.

AFTER LUNCH they hastened to Don Vicente's bedroom, which would be dismantled, and the maids hurried out, emptying it of its memories of sickness and death. When the room was finally bare and Don Vicente's clothes were packed in mothballed lockers, Luis called Trining and pointed to the spiral staircase that went to the tower. Like him, she had never been up there. It had been locked all these years. He had once asked the servants about the tower, and they had told him that it was there where Don Vicente Asperri's wife had lived and wasted her years in lunacy, cursing her husband who lived in the room below and slept away from her, on their wide matrimonial bed, cursing him for having failed to give her a child.

Luis slowly led Trining by the hand up the iron spiral stairs that were wiped clean, as were the wooden steps. They reached the top of the flight, and slowly Luis opened the door, which he thought would be locked. It was not. They stepped into the room in awe, expecting to see things they had never seen, perhaps old and rusting lockers brimming with unspeakable secrets. The room was airy, not cobwebbed and musty, and it looked lived-in. There was a writing desk and a sofa, and there was a shelf of folders, which, he soon found out, contained all the issues of *Our Time* published from the time he took over its editorship. There also were carefully bound issues of the college paper that he had edited. There were scrapbooks containing Luis's letters when he was in high school, old pictures of himself on a picnic by the river and with his school debating team—and wonder of wonders, there were the poems he wrote in his teens, poems that seemed so effete and unreadable but that sent a pang of nostalgia coursing through his being. He had often wondered where he had placed all these, and now here they were, all neatly arranged and bound together, as if they were meant for posterity. So it was here where his father had cared for him in his own fashion. It must have been an effort, going up the stairs in his condition, but here he had peace—and communion with his son, which had not been possible in person.

"Oh, Luis," Trining said, "he loved you. He wanted so much to know you. Can you see it now? Can you forgive him now?"

Luis strode to the window, a hundred thoughts crowding in his mind. Beyond the acacias and the coconut palms the whole town was spread around him. Through the clear glass panels he could see it all, even where Sipnget was and the river like a silver ribbon in the sun. And every day that his father spent here he could see the village, too. Luis shook his head. "I was something special, perhaps," he said softly; "I can understand that, but I am not just an Asperri. I come from that place over there." He pointed to the distance.

They went down to the library, which adjoined Don Vicente's room. It was here where all the important papers were filed—the Torrens titles, the stocks in the mines and in the brewery.

Santos came up to explain things. "You know, *señorito,*" he said, "I owe everything I have to your father. I will serve you as well as I served him, and whatever little knowledge this ignorant brain holds is yours to use."

Luis said, "I want the truth. I want to find out what really happened to Sipnget. More than this, I want to find my mother and to see where my grandfather was buried."

"But what good would it do, Apo?" Santos asked. "The dead are dead—they cannot be brought back to life, and it really matters little where they have been buried or even how they died."

"It does matter," Luis said, "if they are your relatives!"

"I am very sorry, Apo, but sometimes, for someone like me, silence is the only answer. You understand, Apo, I will serve you in the best way I can, but there are things I cannot do, for I am not strong."

"All right, then, where are the civilian guards? Who pulled the triggers?"

"They have been disbanded, Apo. The constabulary disbanded them after you left."

"We cannot find even one?"

"Even if we did find one, would he speak? You are asking him to swing from the loftiest tree."

"Would you be a Judas to me?"

"Even the weak have a right to life, Apo."

EVEN WITH SANTOS'S REBUFF, Trining was doggedly serious about going to Sipnget and beyond—to Aguray. She was hardly in any condition for the walk—and not even a jeep could go to Aguray, for it would mean not only fording the river where it was shallow but also walking the dunes on to where they became alluvial.

As she prepared in the evening for the trip—lunch basket, walking shoes, umbrella, and thermos bottle—Luis hoped that she would at least know how it was with his grandfather, although he had now become thoroughly skeptical that he would find even a trace of the exhumation and reburial.

Trining had her own defense against disappointment—the walk would do her good, and she needed it for the baby. They started out early in the morning with Santos at the wheel of the jeep. The sun was not yet up, and the town still slept in that brief coolness that always preceded the humid onslaught of May. Santos drove slowly over the road, which had begun to rut. Trining had dug out from the closet a green parasol and sneakers that she had used in her physical education class in college. The walk would be nice and cool if they got to Sipnget before daybreak.

Luis did not have a single worry about his physical safety, and he refused the pistol that Santos said he should carry. When they reached Sipnget, however, a little apprehension came to him. He was, after all, no longer Luis from the village. He was now one of the region's wealthiest men. The sun broke through the thin morning haze. The air was rich, compounded of morning dew and the earth that had begun to stir. A new bridge made of unsplit coconut trunks lay across the irrigation ditch, which had been dredged. Santos assured him that the bridge was sturdy, and they drove over it. Then Santos carefully eased the vehicle down the uneven path, over deep ruts made by *carabao* hooves, which were beginning to disappear. They drove slowly, knowing that Trining in her condition would be uncomfortable at every little bump.

The dry season was over. The huge blotches of burned fields were now mottled with touches of green. The mud holes and even the irrigation ditch alongside the path had dried up, and water lilies, matted and dead, clung to the uneven floor of the ditch. Soon everything in the waterways would stir and the brown would disappear under a blanket of green.

"I came here once, long ago," Trining said when they were near the dike. They had not spoken much on the *camino provincial*. "It was November, and harvest time."

Luis knew well that season when the whole land seemed ablaze with golden fire and the air was brilliant and scented. It did not last more than a month, for the scythe subdued the fields in no time and the fire of torches blackened the fields, singeing the hay to the very skin of the earth.

The trail made a curve, and there, beyond the thin veil of grass, stood the dike. The old duhat tree and the buri palms were gone. Luis was not surprised. With the people of Sipnget no longer there, it was natural that the landmarks would also be erased. They stopped in the shade of a stunted camachile tree, and Luis helped Trining out of the jeep. She smoothed the creases from her skirt, and for a moment, as if in pain, she held her belly and did not move. "Don't you think you should stay here with Santos and wait for me?" Luis said. "I can go alone, I know the place. It is quite a walk, but I should be back in three hours."

Trining was resolute; she left several sandwiches for Santos and followed Luis toward the dike. The path that led to Sipnget was completely obliterated. The dying grass hid every trace of the old path. Even the clean straight lines that sled runners and bull-cart wheels had etched upon the dike had been wiped out. He held her hand as they went up. The sun was still soft and mild, and although they had both walked a considerable distance, they were still fresh, free from the ravages of heat and humidity. Once she stumbled as she stepped on a loose clod, but she quickly braced herself and, clinging to Luis, went up the dike. How thorough the destruction of Sipnget was! Not a single tree, acacia or palm, stood where the village used to be. The tractors of his father had done a tidy job—the furrows were immaculate and straight. They went down to the stubble field, and for Trining, the walk on the plowed earth was extremely difficult. There was no path to the river except through that brown serrated land. They reached the riverbank after great difficulty and looked down on the delta, silver and brown in gashes of sun. He turned around and saw how all the trunks of buri had been removed. There was no curtain of grass, no mound.

"I don't know now where the grave was," Luis said, admitting defeat. "God, it could have been anywhere here, even on this very spot where we are standing."

She pressed his hand and did not speak. "Can we go back to Santos and ask him?" she asked after a while.

Luis smiled. "It was not he who wanted this land plowed," he said. "No one but Father and his friends. Whoever worked here will not speak with us now." He turned again to the river. "It is a fine day for a woman with child to go walking," he said lightly. "Aguray lies beyond."

They went down a gully choked with weeds and rotting banana trunks. In the soft sand of the riverbed they walked again hand in hand. The water was only ankle-deep in many places, but in a few weeks the rains would come in earnest and the water would rise, muddy-brown and swift, and it would no longer be possible to cross the river except by raft.

"Why should they stay there?" Trining asked. "Why don't they come back to Sipnget or to any part of the hacienda, where you will let them farm?"

The sun was now warm, and Luis opened her umbrella and shielded her from it. "We stayed there once during the war," Luis said. "It is quite inaccessible during the rainy season, when the river is flooded and portions of the delta become a swamp. Now that the delta is dry, so is Aguray. It is a kind of stopover, a temporary haven. I am sure that they are merely biding time, that when it becomes more propitious, they will come back."

She paused, her brow glistening with sweat as the baby inside her stirred again and she grimaced with pain.

"Are you sure you want to go on?" he asked.

She smiled at him. "Yes," she said. "We are here now. We must proceed."

He led her to the shade of the tall grass and let her rest on a huge, smooth boulder. He took off her sneakers and rubbed her feet. She watched him, his devotion, and when he was through he took off his shoes, too, for now they would cross the river. He folded the cuffs of his pants and placed their shoes in the lunch basket.

The water was cool, a murmur over the pebbles. It rose no higher than their knees at the deepest, and they walked slowly, holding hands. He was afraid lest she stumble where the stones were mossy.

Her thoughts were far, far away. After a while she said, "Luis, I don't know, but there's just the two of us. We don't need much, do we?"

"What are you thinking of?"

"If it is the land they want, don't you think we can sell it to them cheap—or even give it to them in time? I know Tio would not do it if he were alive, but he is gone, Luis. We can leave Rosales, go to the city—anywhere you want to go, maybe America or Europe. You can write there, and I will look after you. Just us—I will love it that way."

What he heard pleased him and he would readily have accepted her idea, but it suddenly occurred to him that he wanted to keep everything intact, that he wanted to play landlord, too, in a fashion different from his father's. "It is not that easy," he found himself saying. "Even charity is not that simple. It has to be administered with great responsibility. That means slow, hard work. It means surveys, seeing to it that the land is equitably divided and that it goes to the right people. It means the building of institutions that will replace us—perhaps some sort of bank for crop loans, or a lending agency to which the farmers can run when someone in the family gets sick or gets married. Also, someone has to teach them the basics of farm management—you know, all these things must be done professionally . . ."

She was looking at him intently, and when he paused she said, "It would be simple, Luis, if you really put your mind to it."

"Yes," he said. "It can be made simpler, but it means that we couldn't get away. It means we will have to stay here—and work."

"There are always problems coming up—like those clouds. It has been very warm. Do you think it will rain?"

He followed her gaze. The clouds were dark, and they stretched up the hollow curve of the sky. "If it does, it will do us good," he said. He guided her to the shallows, and the water sloshed around their ankles and sang among the pebbles and the moss-covered boulders. As they went farther across, the water evened out and Trining did not bother lifting her skirt. Then they reached the other bank and walked barefoot on the sand, which had begun to warm. This was the first time he had come to Aguray since the war—and although the yearly monsoon blotted out the trails, new ones were always etched on the sandy loam at the beginning of the dry season and one whose sense of direction was as keen as the wind's could not miss Aguray.

Now they came across the small clearings, watermelon and cucumber patches that seemed abandoned, for there were no signs that the thatched sheds at the fringes of the clearings were inhabited. Before noon they rested again in the shade of a lone acacia tree on the sandy plain. Trining opened the lunch basket. She had not forgotten her husband's preference for salted eggs and tomatoes. They ate slowly. Trining held her belly once, pain beclouding her face, but only for a moment. She drank cold water from the thermos bottle, and soon she was fresh and ready for the walk that lay ahead.

At high noon Luis stopped and pointed to the far end of the wide delta, to the trees and the bamboo clumps that marked Aguray. "There, that's where they should be," Luis said.

They hurried on, past the thicker growths of grass that sprouted from the dunes, past many clearings planted to root crops and sweet potatoes, all of which were overgrown with weeds. It had become very warm, and Luis took off his shirt. Trining continually mopped her brow with her scarf, and although she tried courageously to keep in step with her husband, she started to lag behind and Luis had to walk slowly. "You cannot go farther," he said, drawing her into the shade of another camachile tree before the riverbank. She was panting and pale, but she smiled wordlessly. He smothered the grass in the shade, and spreading his damp shirt on it, he bade her sit. She did not want to but he was firm, so she sat down slowly, holding her belly. All around them the grass was tall, ready to burst into white plumed flowers. A cloud of dragonflies hovered over them, the gauzy wings glinting like specks of silver against the sky. He let her rest until her breathing was easy again, then he helped her up and they walked down the sandy bar, up the gully that led to Aguray.

During the war Victor and he used to go to the village and feel secure—but only during the rainy season, when the river was full and Aguray itself was isolated. There were so many small islands of sandy loam there, each with its own moat, and one could not easily cross the waters and navigate unless one came from the place and knew each of the waterways, for every year these changed, depending on the way the current moved.

He ran up the riverbank, which was a low incline, and looked down at the Aguray that he knew. This was the haven that he and Vic and Commander Victor had known—but if Sipnget was now gone, so too, was Aguray. There was not a single house in the sandy wasteland. He raced down the path, which was still unclaimed by grass, and he came across yards where thatched houses once stood, where people used to gather in the early evenings. Nothing was there now. He turned to his wife, who had followed him, and tears scalded his eyes as he said, "You can see for yourself—they were hounded even here."

"It is not true!" she cried. "There must be a way we can find where they are! They cannot vanish like smoke. Santos—he would really know. He keeps that ledger. The soldiers, the policemen in town . . . You are the *hacendero* now. They must respect you and give you what you want." The words poured out of her in a torrent.

"Trining," he told her softly, holding her by the shoulder, "no one can help us. This was their last refuge, and they had no cause for leaving it. I do not think even Santos knows where they have gone."

He turned to the hills at his left, the rugged bluffs that loomed so near although they were kilometers away. "There's only one place they could have gone to, and we cannot follow them there."

"We can!" she cried. "If you want to—and I want to—we can follow them wherever they have gone to." She freed herself and walked away, her steps rigid and straight, as if in a trance, then she broke into a run for the river and Sipnget. He called to her to stop, and when she did not he sprinted after her. Catching her, he held her quivering body close to his, sought her warm, pained face, and kissed her—her lips, her damp nose, her eyes, her hot, salty tears—and when she tried to break away again, he pinioned her arms until her struggling ceased and she started to moan and the sound that came from her was the anguished cry of a wounded animal. "She is my mother, too. Isn't it so, Luis? And I have not even seen her and presented myself to her. I want to thank her, my dear husband, for bringing to this world the person I love . . ."

He slipped an arm around her formless waist and let her cry. When she quieted down he led her back to the river. He picked up the empty lunch basket, the scarf, and the umbrella that she had left at the bottom of the gully, and shielded her from the hot westering sun.

They were on the riverbed again. The sun was hidden now behind an ominous mass of clouds that spread out across the sky. "It's going to rain—if the wind does not blow those clouds away," he said. She looked up at a sky that had darkened. Soon it would be June, and if the rains came on time, there would be grasshoppers on the wing, mushrooms in the bamboo groves, and spiders in the bushes at dusk. If it rained on time, the seed would also sprout on time, and somewhere in this vast and blighted land, unmarked by a cross or hedge or man's lament, lay his kin—and somewhere, too, his mother would be walking, searching . . .

"I don't care anymore whether or not it will rain," Trining said in a strained voice. "I just don't care anymore."

Rᴀɪɴ ꜰᴇʟʟ the following afternoon, preceded by incessant thunder. The four o'clock whistle at the rice mill had not yet blown, but the shower hid the sun completely and it seemed as if dusk had come. Luis had not closed the windows in their room, and the gusts had made a wide wet gash on the floor. He dragged the high-backed narra chair across the floor and set it by the window. With a towel he mopped up the water on the sill. He flung the towel to a corner, where the maids would pick it up, together with his soiled clothes. He took a bedsheet, and wrapping it around his shoulders, he sat by the window and gazed at the town raked by mist and wind. He hoped that he could write, and he had a bookcase carried in from the library. In it were most of the books he had brought home from his city shelves. He found out, however, much to his discomfiture, that running the farm, along with the host of other responsibilities that he had inherited from his father, was turning him into a drudge involved not just in looking at figures but also in dealing in a very personal way with tenants, overseers, and even some of the townspeople and officials themselves. The first few days after his father's burial were spent in meeting people, in trying to remember faces and first names, the way his father did. Even the smallest decisions were left to him; making them was what his father did, and this was not entrusted to the lawyer, the accountant, or Santos. This fact impressed upon him how authoritarian his father had been and how, therefore, his father must have been responsible for what had befallen Sipnget.

No new desires moved Luis in his new position, and the mind that had prowled the past terrain of anger and of remorse and dwelt briefly on those few moments of happiness with Ester could not find a moment of inspiration. He was a fugitive in the silence of his house. The time he now had on his hands was not time at all, for the essence of life eluded him and what he wrote was no more than a jumble of phrases, a few typewritten pages, verbose, clumsy, clipped together, or crumpled into little balls in the mesh wastebasket near his desk.

The dry season was not really over. Beyond the wet sweep of the *azotea,* the wide garden with its azucena pots was starting to sink in a flood. Beyond the pall of rain the adobe walls and the wide asphalt ribbon had acquired a polish and the neighborhood children had rushed out, naked, and were running up and down, shouting, holding their faces to the sky taut with storm. Some of them climbed the short banaba trees that lined the street, all the way down to where the gray-green hulk of the *municipio* stood; they plucked twigs off the trees, which they shook at one another. It was wonderful to be young and splashing in the rain. In Luis's mind he raced with the children, and he felt the slosh of the rain on his bare feet and the tingling drops on his skin. But this season of fresh green would not last—the rain would pock the plaza, and there would be muddy craters where the pigs would wallow. The weeds would grow everywhere, and the green would acquire a dirty hue.

He did not see his wife come in. He became aware of her only when she sat on the broad arm of his chair and rested a shaky elbow on his shoulder, her breath warm on his cheek. "You will never make a good housekeeper," she chided him. "Look at the floor—it is all wet. And your things piled up there. And all that waste paper. You forgot to close the window again."

"I was asleep," he said, his eyes still on the children on the asphalt, who had started playing leapfrog. "Besides, I want it open."

"Aren't you cold?"

"You see I have a blanket about me."

She brought her swollen body closer to him. "I thought you might want to be more comfortable." She was soft and warm, her breast against his arm, a strand of hair across his cheek. "I am having some coffee brought in. You should go out. Do not confine yourself so much in this room. You will end up being a monk if you don't watch out."

He leaned on the sill. "Must you recite the things you do for me? Must you always be giving me advice?"

Her hand was cool on his nape. "Please do not be vexed with me," she said. "I just cannot bear seeing you like this—an hour or two in the office below and the rest of the day here. Do you want to go to the sea? To the beach in Dagupan? Or to Baguio for the weekend? Or do you want to see the latest movie in Manila? Whatever you say, but please do not shut yourself up here. This was just what Tio did."

"You don't have to tell me that. I know."

"You used to wake up early—in Manila—and stroll down the boulevard, and at dusk you would walk to the Luneta. This is not a time for walking, but tomorrow, if the sun comes out, we will go for a walk. I need it. We can follow the dike, and as you used to do, we may be able to get some saluyot for lunch."

"No, Trining," he said, "what I want is peace." Rain lashed the ditches; the huge leaves of the lilies in the garden trembled, and gusts of wind swept the *media agua*.

"You will get wet here," she said, tugging at his pajama sleeve.

"The worst that can happen is for me to catch pneumonia," he said.

"You do not appreciate the fact that I care," she said bitterly.

"But I do," he assured her, trying to hide his irritation, "but I need time for myself."

"It is not time for yourself that you really want," Trining said, bending so low that her cheek brushed his. "You are looking for something you will not find. After that trip to Aguray, Luis, I have come to accept it—that we cannot find them. There are things that we must accept because we have no choice."

"You are beginning to sound like Father," he said.

"I am only trying to help. Aren't you glad?"

"God, I'm glad," he said. "I am glad for the food you stuff me with, but do not pamper me. I can leave today if it will make things easier for you. I can return to Manila or go back to Sipnget and start building again. Perhaps that is the best way. You know, I married you so that our house and our landholdings wouldn't fall into other hands. With me out of the way, you can have it all."

She stepped away, staring at him, her lips quivering. "Luis, how horrible can you get! Is that the reason—the only reason?" She was frightened. "Please let us not quarrel. If you want me to stay away, I will—but don't say these things. Do you really mean them? Then why didn't you tell me before?"

The outburst had left him shaky but elated somehow. Now he was calm. "I'm sorry, Trining," he said quietly. "I am not myself anymore. I cannot think straight anymore. Please leave me alone."

She stood before him, speechless, then turned and walked out of the room. As the door closed after her, the cold, hostile silence came back, stronger than the rain. He went to the bed and lay down. If anybody could give him comfort, it was his wife, and yet he was shutting her off, hurting her. *There must be something bestial and satanic in me to make me hurt like a sadist those closest to me. Ester, and now Trining.* He rose quickly and called out, "Trining! Trining!" When she did not answer he went to his old room, to the kitchen, then to his father's room. She was not in any of the rooms. One last place—the library. He flung the door open, and there she was, on the couch, her eyes wet with tears, her faced contorted with pain.

"I'm sorry, my darling," he said, bending low. "Have I hurt you?" She nodded but smiled, then kissed him. "I am in pain, Luis. I think I'm going to have the baby soon. This is a different kind of pain I'm feeling now."

He rushed out of the room, called for Santos, and told him to get Trining's doctor. When he got back she had wiped her face. Although her eyes were red, she was smiling. "It doesn't happen that fast," she said. "The pain comes in several intervals. Maybe I should go to the provincial hospital or leave for Manila, whichever you think is best."

When a woman gives birth, he remembered the saying clearly, one foot is in the grave. Why did he not even have the decency to be more attentive to her in this time of need? "You are all I have now," he said, "and I have not been a good husband to you during the last few days. Forgive me."

"There is nothing to forgive," she said.

He held her hand. "I have committed many crimes—I mustn't commit one more. I cannot go around sending to perdition those whom I love."

"Don't talk like that," she said, trying to rise from the couch, but he restrained her.

"It is true," he said sadly. "Ester, I have a feeling I was the cause of it all. Before she did it—the last night she was alive—she was with me. I feel responsible, for I could have stopped her. I don't know why she did it—I can only suspect. She did not expect us to get married, Trining, and she loved me. Please do not be angry now, but I think she killed herself because there was no future for us, or because she—she was pregnant, because she was carrying my baby. I cannot be sure. I can never be sure . . ."

Trining closed her eyes and shook her head vehemently. "Stop telling me. I don't want to hear it. I don't want to hear it!"

"I am sorry," he said, "but it's better this way. You will get to understand me better, know what I am. I feel that I hurried Father, too, to his grave, that I did not help Mother and Grandfather. Now I am also hurting you. God, I don't want to hurt you!"

"Then stop talking. Stop talking about Ester!"

"It was not love, Trining," he said. "I didn't promise her anything. I could have promised her something from the beginning. You were the first girl whom I asked to marry me. With Ester it wasn't love, it was something else."

She half sat and covered his mouth with her hand. "Don't talk anymore," she begged him.

"All right," he said, shaking his head. "I am like rust. I destroy everything I cling to. The dog in the street that bites its master's hand might be forgiven, but not me."

She swung down from the couch and stood before him. "You won't leave me?" she asked. "No matter what, you will not leave me?"

"Why do you ask?"

"I just want to know how long you will be needing me. It will not be forever. If you say so, you are lying. You don't have to put up appearances, not with me. I will just assume that someday you will leave me. Luis—that I won't be able to stand!"

The light from the open window grew dimmer; the steady thrum of rain presaged high waters. He rose and embraced her awkwardly, for her belly stood in the way.

"Don't promise me anything," she said.

"I love you. You will be the mother of my child."

"You don't have to kill me if you don't want me anymore. I will leave you in my own way—and it will be forever, too."

He bit his lower lip, kissed her, and drew away. *All my life I have made no sacrifice. I have never given up even one fingernail. All my life people have shown me the truest measure of their devotion. Love— if to love is to be willing to be used, then I do not know love. Nothing throbs here within, not a heart, only a cold and mechanical pump.*

"No, I will never leave you," he said, but he knew he was not telling the truth.

DR. REYES, who owned the small hospital in the town, was shivering when he arrived. He was the town's best doctor, and although he was short and lean, there was energy and skill in his meager frame. "It is not yet your time, Trining," he said as he entered their room and brought out his instruments. He was very casual about it all. "The blood pressure is normal, respiration is normal—but the pain, how long are the intervals? More than thirty minutes? But this is so soon—you are not due until about six weeks from now or thereabouts. Did you exert yourself? Did anything excite you? This could be a premature birth, you know, but thank God, we now have good hospitals."

"No," she lied, not looking at her husband. "Nothing exciting has happened, but I did go for a long walk last week."

It was not necessary, said Dr. Reyes, that they go to the hospital immediately, but Luis was insistent.

"Well," the doctor said, "I wish I could say that my clinic is good, which it is, but really, if we are going to any hospital at all, we might just as well go to Dagupan. It has one of the best in the north. There is a very good obstetrical staff there, and it has the latest instruments. I don't want to take any risks."

Santos drove them in the Chrysler. The rain was coming faster; it covered the land completely, and at times Santos had to switch his headlights on. There were ruts in many portions of the provincial road, and each bump was mirrored in Trining's twitching face.

By the time they got to Dagupan, it was already night, the street-lights were on, and the rain had diminished to a drizzle. One foot in the grave—and he had settled for the provincial hospital when it should have been that specialists' hospital in Manila, with its array of the country's best doctors, anesthesiologists, and pathologists. It was a consolation that Dr. Reyes had assured him that although it would be a premature birth, he expected the delivery to be quite normal. Trining was as healthy as a cow, he had whispered to him.

He got a suite and a couple of private nurses to take care of Trining as her pain progressed. She did not deliver on that day or the next but on the third day, after Dr. Reyes and his team had finally decided that she needed a cesarian section. Luis followed her to the operating room. He would have watched it all had he not felt sickened. He had to go back to the suite, a wad of cotton drenched with ammonia clasped to his nose as he felt nausea coming.

He did not faint. He sat through the two hours, and when it was over and Trining was wheeled unconscious to the recovery room he rushed to Dr. Reyes.

"I am no surgeon"—the doctor's face was grim—"so I merely assisted, but the surgeon we had, as you very well know, is one of the best. We did all that could be done. Trining is safe—she will be recovering in a few days, and then she can go home."

"Why did she have to go through surgery?" Luis asked. It was a foolish question. It had been explained to him earlier when he signed the paper stating that he was permitting a surgery. If it had not been done, her pains would not have ceased, the baby would not have been born, and the mother would have died.

"She is all right," Dr. Reyes repeated, "but we had to remove her uterus. You know, this means she cannot have another baby. Her ovaries are intact, so there will not be much hormonal change, but babies—that's out of the question now."

"And the baby—is it a boy or a girl?"

Dr. Reyes could not speak. The grimness of his face deepened. He beckoned to the new father to sit with him on one of the long sofas near the lobby. There, quietly, the doctor told him what had to be said.

When the doctor had finished, what stuck in Luis's mind were his words: "It will require courage to look at the baby—and more courage to accept him." Courage! If only his father were here now, he would perhaps curse heaven. It was not possible that he who had everything, who had worked so hard to leave his name upon the land, must now himself be blighted. Perhaps it all started with him, his genes diluted with sin. *It is not I, it is not my fault or Trining's,* Luis assured himself; *it is not I, it is not I.*

But it was he who had planted the seed that had brought forth this thing that Trining would have to see, too, and have the courage to accept.

WHEN SHE regained consciousness her first words were, "How is my baby?" Her breath still smelled faintly of anesthesia. She had lost blood, and although she had been given a transfusion, she had the pallor of the sickroom.

"It's a boy," he whispered, kissing her, "and he is well, but you cannot see him—he is in the incubator. He is such a tiny creature. The doctors say he may have to be brought to Manila within the week for special care. They don't have the facilities here for him." He was carefully preparing the ground for the fact that he did not want her to see the child. She smiled at him and pressed his hand. "You will be all right," he continued. "They had to cut you up. They had to remove your uterus, and you won't be able to have any more babies, but that was the only way you could be saved."

"Oh, Luis," she broke into a sob, "and I wanted to give you a dozen children!"

He stroked her brow until she quieted down. He had carefully instructed the people who were taking care of her never to mention the baby to her or let her see it.

After two weeks, when she was finally able to move, he brought her back to Rosales together with two nurses. They placed a bed for Luis in the library so that Trining could occupy their room alone until she was well. It was only Santos and the two nurses who knew about the baby, and Luis had instructed them to keep their mouths shut, not only before Trining but also before everyone else.

Returning to his chores fatigued him. There were decisions to make—the introduction of fertilizers in certain areas around the hacienda, the purchase of four new tractors, and the setting up of the first cooperative, which he had planned. Above all, the anxiety of watching over Trining, of seeing to it that she would not know. After supper, which he took alone in the dining room, he went to her. She was propped up on a stack of pillows and was reading the Manila papers that had piled up. Her complexion had improved. Color was returning to her cheeks, and her eyes were warm again. He kissed her passionately and whispered, "I can hardly wait—but it will have to take a month, I think."

She pinched him and called him a dirty old man. He kissed her again on the brow, this time tenderly, and said that he was sleepy and must rest. He closed the door of their room and crossed the hall to the library, where his bed was made. The moment he lay down, without even putting on his pajamas, he fell asleep.

He woke up at about midnight—that was what the clock on the wall above the writing desk said—and the first thing he was conscious of was that he was not alone in the room. The lamps were on and the light etched everything clearly—the writing table, with his typewriter on it, the bowl of chicos and bananas, and the thermos jug with coffee. Seated before him, at his right, was Vic—lean and dark and serious of mien, looking intently at him.

Startled, he spoke hoarsely: "Vic, how did you get here?"

His brother simply smiled. "I have been waiting for over an hour, and I have finished reading most of your magazines," he said, "but I did not wake you up, although I switched on the light so that I could read."

"But how did you get here?" Luis was incredulous. He sat up and groped for his slipper. "You must not stay here another moment—and you know why. You are a wanted man, and just across the street are soldiers."

Vic shrugged. He stood up and peeled a banana. "I am safe here," he said. "Isn't this your house, Manong?"

Luis went to the door and bolted it.

"I assure you I am safe," Vic said. Then, thoughtfully: "But I must ask you and your wife to leave as soon as you can, tomorrow morning if it can be done. Go back to Manila and stay there. I don't know how you will do it, but give the land back to the people. Of what use is it really to you?"

"So this is what you came for—to make a pauper of me," Luis said.

Vic shook his head. He had grown thinner and older since Luis last saw him. His clothes were the same decrepit gray trousers and colorless shirt. "Make a pauper out of you? Do you know how I live? Many times we have nothing to eat but green papayas, guavas, sometimes no salt, and our stomachs are full of sourness. We are bitten by leeches and mosquitoes, and some have malaria. But we are not bitter. How can you be a pauper? You will never be one."

"Why do you want us to leave?"

"Because you are my brother," Vic said, "and I don't want you to be like Grandfather—or Mother."

"Do you know where she is?" he asked shrilly. "I went to Aguray—my wife and I, searching."

"I searched for her, too," Vic said, "in the villages and in the hills. She had been there and people saw her, but I was always too late. She must have gone to Manila. How can we find her there? You can move more freely than I. I can easily find her in the places I know—if she is there—but in the city . . ."

Luis sat silent and helpless. "I did what I could, Vic. I am a writer—and I wrote. I was eased out of my job, you probably know that, but do you know how it happened? Who did it?"

Vic said simply, "Don't worry. Justice will be done, I swear. God," he muttered, "if You are here, then You are my witness. I have sworn it!"

"Why do you come like a ghost?" Luis said after a while. "Why should you still care whether I am alive or not?"

"There is one thing we have in common," Vic said. "We have the same mother."

"Yet," Luis said evenly, "you really do not care; you would rather see me dead, so that it would be easier for you. If you only had one hour to spend in my place, you will realize that what you want is not that simple. I agree with you that the land must go to the people who farm it—but how will they progress without someone like me to give them money when they need it? Why must they spend so much on fiestas when it is unnecessary? Who will sell their products? Who will teach them about farm management, fertilizers, and crop rotation? These problems cannot be solved with guns."

"Excuses," Vic said coldly. "I could kill you now if I had the hatred to do it, but what would that do for us? My enemy is larger than you and all your grandiose plans, which made it possible for your father and you to be what you are and for us—our mother and myself and all the people of Sipnget—to be what we are."

"It is history you want to destroy, then," Luis said. "You cannot destroy what you have not created—and the past is bigger than any of us."

"We make our fate," Vic said with a laugh. "Did you not make yours? And all the time you ran away. In the war you were safe in the city and no one could touch you."

"I had difficult times, too," Luis said, "and I was with you, too, though briefly."

"Excursions," Vic said contemptuously. "That was what they were—you were having fun. It was life or death for us. We were hounded like dogs then. It is the same now, only the hunters are no longer Japanese but our own brothers. I am alive, maybe because I ran, but we will not run anymore. Now we have to kill."

"How easily you say it," Luis said. "Is it all that necessary? The world is changing, and what really is a few decades in history? The wealthy that you rail against—they will disappear in time. Look at me, Vic. I work—I am not really all that interested in the land Father has passed on to me. You are welcome to as much of it as you want. The wealthy who do not work will be replaced by young ones who have brains, whether they come from the lower class or from the middle class. It is really a cycle—that's a very good Buddhist symbol."

"I only know that this is my time," Vic said with conviction, "and I know that it is wretched."

"There will always be the poor among us," Luis said, and remembered what Dantes had said: "The Communists have not abolished poverty. In fact you can say that the Scandinavians and the

Americans have done a better job of that. And the poor sometimes get to love their chains."

"That is what we are here for," Vic said. "To break the chains for them."

"The chains will be broken when the time comes—not by you," Luis said. "Look around you. The changes are coming. You cannot tell hundreds of talented young people that they cannot use their talents. They will."

"Talent is not enough," Vic said. "They are not men of the future. It is the new men who will bring change, and their future is not in America but here. Did you ever think about the foul legends that our generation has fed on—that when God created the world and was fatigued by His labors He sat down to shit, and this shit is this group of islands? This is just one of the myths that we will destroy. I will forget the past; no, more than this, we will destroy this past, whatever the Spaniards and the Americans left, whatever they planted in your minds. We will do this—start anew, from a clean and empty sheet. We will write what the future should be. This is necessary, and urgent, for we cannot build until we have destroyed this past. Can you not see? It taunts us with its false promises, it corrupts us with its evils—"

"And I will quote to you an old Ilokano saying," Luis said. "He who does not know where he came from cannot know where he is going."

"But I know! I know!" Vic said, his voice rising with emotion. "If I did not know, how would I know what to destroy? How would I know my enemies?"

"Enemies?" Luis asked. "Who are your enemies really, Vic? Across the street, in the schoolhouse, are soldiers. They are farm boys. Their parents could be like those in Sipnget, and they are just as poor. Do you want to kill your own kin?"

"Do you think I like it?" Vic asked. " 'Any man's death is also mine'—you have quoted that idea to me before. How can I forget that the soldiers we fight could have come from Sipnget? But they are not people—they are instruments of the rich."

"How facile you have become with words," Luis said.

"No, Manong," Vic said. "It is you who are good with words. You are the poet, but sometimes I wonder if you really have a purpose, if your poetry is worth anything at all. You have a wonderful home and friends who appreciate your talent, but you grow fat, you grow old, and soon you will discover that you are nothing but skin and bones. What is the reason for your poetry?"

Luis said sincerely, "I do not know. As a matter of fact, I don't even know why God created us. We are very poor likenesses of Him, you know."

"I did not know that words—and you are a master of them—had sharpness and poison. With words you have also killed perhaps, although more slowly and more painfully. With us it is the body that dies, it is the body that will kill—faster and therefore more kindly," Vic said.

Words, words! Luis felt a cold rage rising in him. "You cannot take words and isolate them any more than you can say that you have killed a man and destroyed an instrument. This is reducing man to an object—and you are more than that."

"Yes," Vic said. "I know I am more than an object, but in this process I am just an instrument, too. Therefore I must be useful—and I will be useful not only to myself but also to thousands like me, who may never get the opportunities you have."

"You are also my brother," Luis said sadly, the anger ebbing out of him. "You are the boy I grew up with, who swam the Agno with me, the friend who gathered camachile along dusty streets, caught frogs in the cracks of the rice fields. You are not mindless, you are not heartless, you are not a machine."

"Manong, my brother, how beautifully you express yourself. But when you left Sipnget, when you left Mother, you left her forever. You were the son who was loved, because you needed love, and we loved you, but this love has not been returned. You know it and only you can explain to yourself why this has been so. I realized this when I saw you last time. I had come to ask that this love that you said you had be expressed in sacrifice. But you were incapable of sacrifice. If hate is strong, all the more should love be. My coming here shows this. It is in memory of our boyhood that I come here, wanting you and your wife to live. You cannot ask from me anything more. I have nothing else to give." Vic was silent and transfixed before Luis—and tears were streaming down his dark, sunburned face.

Luis embraced him. "My brother, my executioner," he whispered.

Vic pushed him away and without another word walked to the door. Luis did not follow him. He did not see where his brother disappeared. He did not know who guided him out of his fortress. When he sank into his bed a thought coursed through him like ice: all these years he had always felt himself superior to his brother, maybe because he had more education and had seen more of that broader landscape extending beyond Sipnget, and what he had seen and experienced had imbued him with more knowledge, more sensibility. He was, after all, a poet, and he could be really capable of love that was not love of self but love of life—and therefore of death—so that he should be able to give himself to death's embrace and mock that which is also the end. He knew now, however, that this was not so, that this was self-deception instead, and that, as his brother had said, he was incapable of sacrifice. And the poetry that he had written—which could hardly be understood even by those with facility in English—of what use was it? Of what use was life? He had believed that he had simplicity, but now he knew that he was obscure instead, not because he did not know what he was saying but because his own feelings were inchoate and therefore devoid of real passion. What, then, was in his arteries?

He breathed heavily. The house was quiet, but the silence was that of a sepulchre. The whole world was quiet. There was no one awake but him, and for the first time in many days his thinking was clear.

CHAPTER

36

My Brother,

    When I saw you tonight, when in a moment of truth you came to me with a profession of love, my deepest regret was that I had none to give. You said that you had none, either, but you did give me something—you affirmed what I had always known to be the greatest manifestation of love or hate—and that is the willingness to lose the physical self. More than this loss, however, is the total commitment of the mind to an end that gives no glory, no reward, no immortality.

    My brother, you will be reborn, even before you meet Him who is our last arbiter. I know this, for you—not I—are the new whom we have all been seeking. I have often wondered about the shape and color of this new man, this archangel, this man whom we have sought to be the ultimate modernizer. Now I know what he looks like. He may think of himself as a machine or as a weapon, but I know that he is much, much more than this—he is a spigot of true blood and a coil of complex nerves, and although he may regard his life with some con-

tempt, the truth is that he gives values, far more than I can adorn mine with the hypnosis of words. He is the poet, not I.

Words—these are the jewels that I must polish. I must now try to answer as truthfully as I can, at least to myself, without having to justify myself, the question of what I have done with words—of what use is poetry, of what use is art.

I will not now try to be as obscure as Ester—whom you will probably agree with—once said I was. In fact I would like to think that poetry or art is the most luminous, the most lucid, of all forms of communication, for it goes straight not to the mind but to the heart. I would be at a loss, however, to describe how the process comes about—and because the process sometimes defines the nature and uses of art, you must forgive me if I find no real explanation for the uses of art.

What I can tell you is what it is against. It is opposed to the debasement of the human spirit. It is against anything that brutalizes, primarily because it is an affirmation of life—and anything that brutalizes denies life. How simple it would be for me to say now that art is life—not death—and that art, with all its inanities, its obscurity and its lack of purpose is, perhaps, like you, the ultimate conqueror of death.

This, I think, is what I have tried to do—to create, for myself at least, something that could make me more than what I am, coward and weakling, a man who has forsaken his past and his loved ones, a man who has lived on hate as I know my kind of hate and yet must learn how to live, if only to assure himself that he is an artist.

I think that I am, as usual, flattering myself again, thinking of myself as a creator, equipped with the finest sensibilities, and therefore special. How I would like to call myself a new man—but I know that I am not and that by your light I will never be really committed to life in such a way that I can vanquish death in the manner in which you have flung yourself completely toward its defeat. It is you then, my fearsome executioner, who is the artist, the rebel and creator, for it is you who will make beauty out of the ugliness that pervades our lives, out of the dung heap that surrounds us.

As for me, there is no single shred of doubt in my mind as to the future that I face, a future that I will have no hand in shaping in the way that you have. My mundane task is to survive—and to survive I must stay away from the turmoil of conflict and the putrefaction of despair. My sight is limited. I look around me and see the vastness of a landscape that has been charred into ruins. I see nothing but the rubble of dreams, and I am puny and weak, and I cannot do anything but quiet this helpless rage and remember that I no longer belong.

In spite of this I will try to live with my concept of honor, to accept the limits of what I can endure. If I am driven forward, inch by inch toward the grave, it is by compulsion and it is only with death that the tyrant within can be vanquished.

God, I am afraid. I would like to think that I can be brave as in the harsh physical sense I was once brave. I have seen death and laughed at its ugly face, but I have not really conquered him, for in the end he will triumph and he knows it.

But my death has happened and it has been swift and even sweet, for it has been administered with grace, with love—not hate. Goodbye, my brother.

CHAPTER

37

THE LOUD METALLIC CLATTER of vehicles and the shouts that rocketed up to the house from the school yard where the soldiers were camped woke Luis up from a dreamless sleep and made him aware that something important was happening. Somehow, Vic's nocturnal visit seemed unreal, but the letter, which he had written in longhand, staring at him from his writing table, brought him back to the reality of Rosales, to Vic's admonition that they must now leave. The air was ominous, and although the morning was bright and the day was alive, a sense of foreboding knotted his chest. He went to the room where his wife was. She was already awake, and the nurse was giving her breakfast—tomato juice, eggs, rice, and a thick slice of ham. Every night she was given sleeping pills, so that she never woke up until morning and had not had one listless night since her return from the hospital.

"You slept well?" she asked, her eyes shining. He nodded absentmindedly and took a sip from her coffee. He sat beside her at the small table, and his hand went up slowly from her flanks to her breast. She nudged at him, implying discretion, for the nurse was in the room, although her back was turned to them.

"You can sleep with me tonight, Luis, if you wish. It gets cold, and I need you to keep me warm. I am better now and won't need any more injections."

"Except one," he whispered in her ear; she quickly pinched him as she whispered back, "Not for another two weeks. Do you want me to go back to the hospital?"

The nurse left them discreetly, and as soon as she was gone Luis said, "The soldiers are leaving. They are taking everything with them, even the tin tubs where they store the mush. I don't think they're coming back."

They walked to the window. In the rain-washed morning the soldiers were loading their bedding and tents into the six-by-sixes lined up in front of the schoolhouse. The trucks were already bursting with equipment, but the loading seemed but half finished. Two officers in sweat-drenched khaki were shouting orders at the men in battle greens, weighed down with bandoliers and ammunition cases, which they balanced on their heads. People were gathered around the trucks. Food vendors were cornering some of the soldiers poring over lists and arguing about debts.

The first two trucks were filled with nondescript crates, and the families of the soldiers—mothers suckling babies, kids too young to understand what was going on—moved to the rear, and a jeep and an armored car with its mounted fifty-caliber machine gun advanced to take their place. Some of the shacks beyond the schoolhouse, which the soldiers' families had occupied, were torn down and all salvageable materials—tin sheets and wooden sidings—had been loaded into the vehicles.

They are leaving us, Luis mused darkly, *and I will never know who among them destroyed Sipnget.*

He turned away from the window. "Why do you think they're leaving?" Trining asked, tugging at his hand.

"They're in a hurry, so they must have been called to a place where they are needed more."

She was looking intently at him. "And with them no longer here, who will protect us?"

He wanted to tell her of Vic's visit, but he had never told her much about his brother except that he was intelligent and continually asking questions and that he wished Vic could have gone to college. It was now clear that Vic had really come to warn him, not just to continue the old harangue. Somehow, in the recesses of his mind, no matter what happened, he would be secure; for all the truculence of Vic's rhetoric and the oppressive tension that pervaded the plain, he was convinced that he was no enemy.

"Surely you don't believe all those stories about the Huks. I would be more worried about the constabulary and the civilian guards. Look what they did to Sipnget."

"Don't the papers tell the truth?" Trining asked. "Look at the stories about Santa Cruz, San Nicolas—the Huk massacres in the Army camps they attacked. And San Nicolas is only twenty kilometers away."

"Twenty-three," he corrected her.

She stood up and went to the window again. "We should get out of this place, Luis," she said heavily. "I see no future here, nothing but days we cannot call our own. If we go back to the city, we can lose ourselves, and my baby will have better care, not like in the provincial hospital where we left him." She turned to Luis. "Why can I not see him? Is he so shriveled and ugly—that is what premature babies are supposed to be—that I may lose all composure upon seeing him?"

For a moment Luis was taken aback and did not know what to say. Then he surmised that the nurses must have been telling her things, hinting. "What did the nurses tell you?"

"Nothing," she said, "except that premature babies look ugly sometimes and they never really put on flesh and their skin never really stretches until they are nine or ten months—and that's a pretty long wait, isn't it? And look at the milk in my breasts that should go to him, poor thing."

"He is being taken care of properly—"

"We should really get out of Rosales." She was determined. "I'm afraid for you and what could happen here. We can rent a small house and sell the house on Dewey—even this house, if it has to be that way. Both are too big for us, anyway. We can live like ordinary people, with just one maid. I'll do most of the housework and the cooking. But let us go while there is time. This afternoon."

He could not face her, for now it seemed that he must stay in Rosales, not because he wanted to defy his brother's warning, not because he did not want to give Trining the peace of mind that she sought, but simply because he knew in his bones that he could not live elsewhere—not in the city, which would remind him of Ester and of the lies he had told. Living here would be living with the truth, no matter how damning it was. Living here required courage, too, which he must now possess. Most of all, being in Rosales would confirm, for him at least, that illusory contract he must have with his own people.

"No, Trining," he said evenly. "This is where we must stay. I'll have the baby taken to Manila this week, so that he will have the proper care, but we—we must live here, for this is where we belong. I see now why Father was so concerned, why he returned here."

Her reply was a long time in coming. "I'll stay with you. I'll follow you . . ."

"To the ends of the earth." He laughed lightly and kissed her on the cheek.

The nurse knocked on the door. The commanding officer of the detachment was downstairs—and would Don Luis please give him five minutes? He was sorry that he could not call earlier, but their order to leave was sudden. He told the nurse to ask the captain into the hall and to please wait.

When Luis came into the hall the captain was staring at the mellowed frames of European Postimpressionist paintings that his father had brought home from his trips. The captain was a short, wiry man, probably in his early thirties, with prominent cheekbones and a narrow forehead. He appeared spare from a distance but on closer look was actually firmly built and muscular. He saluted Luis, then came forward and extended his hand. Luis saw him almost every morning getting into a jeep or armored car, then disappearing up the dirt road that led to the foothills and returning again in the late afternoon, his gait as brisk as ever. He had come for a visit one evening, but only Santos and Trining received him. He is a lonely man, Trining had told him later, and Luis had said brusquely, the guilty are always lonely.

Luis shook his hand. The officer's grip was clammy and tight. "I am very sorry, sir," he said, "that I have to say good-bye the first time I see you."

Luis motioned him to sit down on one of the overstuffed leather sofas in the hall, then asked a maid to bring some coffee.

"We are going up north," the officer continued. "We did not re-

ceive our orders until early this morning on the radio. There seems
to be more trouble there."

"Once it was confined to central Luzon," Luis said, a wisp of sadness in his voice. "Now, it's all over the country—in the Visayas, in
Mindanao . . ."

"Yes," the captain said, "and fighting them is like ramming a steel
fist in the air. They are everywhere and nowhere."

"They are wherever there is hunger and exploitation," Luis said.
"They feed on greed and injustice."

The officer looked down and seemed thoughtful, then he turned
to Luis, his eyes burning. "I wish I could form opinions as easily as
you," he said, a hint of impatience in his voice. "It is of course very
sad that my orders will always be to seek and destroy them. They are
worthy opponents—some of them could really teach us tricks in
guerrilla warfare and intelligence work. I am particularly impressed
by Commander Victor—his daring, his brilliant tactics. The batallion
has lost more than twenty men to him, and we haven't captured a
single man from his unit. Yes, I know he is your half-brother, and I
am sure that you still hate us for what happened in Sipnget. I just
want you to know that none of my men were involved, that it was
after the incident that we—all of us—replaced the detachment here."

"I don't want to hear about it," Luis said.

"I did not mean to digress," the officer said. "I just brought it up
so that you would know that I know."

"Don't you feel a little bit uneasy, Captain, fighting your own
kin? I imagine you must be a veteran of Bataan."

"Yes, yes," the captain readily answered. "I was interned in
Capas—the Death March, all of that. Yes, it was different fighting the
Japanese. But it is our lives or theirs—it is really that simple when
you are in the field." He cracked his knuckles. Perspiration had moist-
ened his face, and his shirtfront was wet. "But what can one do? We
are not landowners like you. We are professional soldiers—at least
the officers, like me. Of course those boys down there, with their families—they are not professionals. They joined the Army because it
was just another job. God knows how difficult it is to get a job. Not
one among them wants to go to the hills to fight—and yes, some of
them have relatives, too, on the other side. No, sir, it has not been
easy and it will never be. There is really no sense in going after your
own kin, but we must keep our house in order. I am no student of

politics the way you are, but if this country disintegrates, there are powers ready to grab us. One can say that under the Americans this may not be possible—but the Huks are anti-American, although I do not think the Russians are helping them. Why can't they be just nationalists? It would be better that way. Even then, this I want to assure you—they are doomed."

"Why are you so certain?" Luis asked, his interest aroused.

The coffee had been brought in, and the captain took a cup. "I am sure," he replied, "because there is freedom in this country. Oh, you will disagree with me—this freedom works only for the rich, for people like you, and it does not work for the poor. But there is more to it than that—there is freedom to express opposition in words, even in action occasionally. There is a kind of mobility, too—is that the word? People are able to rise from their low origins. Look at me, sir. Maybe we will not go beyond a certain position, but we can move. And the government, for all its shortcomings, is an elected government. There is communication between the politicians and the people—open communication, sir."

"There is one thing you miss," Luis said. "Revolutions are not made by the masses. They are made by new men, by people like you—if you were on the other side."

"And if I were there—thank God, I am not," the captain said, his voice excited and high-pitched, "you know what would happen? I would get killed—or I would surrender in the end. Your brother, sir, will get killed, no matter how fast he runs—that is, if he does not surrender. It is not a question of the Army being a superior force. It's a question of forcing a revolution upon a society that is malleable, that will change with the needs of the hour. This is what the Huks misunderstand, Mr. Asperri. They are blind to it. As the problem intensifies, the government will become frantic—it will institute reforms, try to win the Huks and their friends back to the fold, with promises, with concrete programs, and who can then fight the government and the powerful men who run it? These men—for all their corruption—are malleable too, Mr. Asperri. They will change, and when this happens the Huks will be destroyed. It is really as simple as that."

"And in the meantime, while we wait for this change, there will be more people killed, more poor people sacrificed in the name of reform?"

"I suppose it has to be that way, Mr. Asperri," the captain said.

"I thought," Luis said, "that the war just over taught us at least one thing—the meaninglessness of violence. It did cheapen a lot of our values and this that is happening now. Do you really think it will strengthen our society?"

The captain sighed and slapped his thigh in a gesture of futility. "We have our favorite hopes," he said. "You have yours—and I understand your views, your affection for your brother. You may even be giving the Huks aid, but if you do, please think it over. They are doomed, and you are simply lengthening their agony. You really cannot fight the government, which, in a way, is of our own making. This is what we often forget—whatever its shortcomings, this government is ours."

The officer glanced at his wristwatch. "It's time I went back," he said. "I wish I could return and have a long talk with you and tell you about our side, too. Those boys out there, barely out of their teens, are farm boys—like I said—and they are not concerned with politics or philosophy. They are concerned about the money they will send home if they survive their patrols—fringe benefits. These are the things that interest them. The right formula for patriotism—love, duty, honor—it's for the birds, isn't it, Mr. Asperri? Or for people like you and me."

Luis smiled wanly. The officer stood up, and Luis accompanied him to the stairs, where they shook hands again, this time warmly.

"You need not worry," he said as he turned to leave. "A new detachment may arrive tomorrow or within the week. Our patrols are out every night, and if an attack should come, your town police is quite ready—and radio contact is very good. Assistance will be immediately available."

IT DID NOT RAIN the whole day, and the heat had become oppressive—it rose from the earth, too, like some diaphanous spirit in possession of everything, and even the massive house seemed to have been conquered by it. Trining, who normally complained about the heat, now did so with vehemence. The generators had just been brought from the city. The air-conditioning and refrigerating units in the house had malfunctioned, perhaps from the excessive heat itself, and now there was no light as well. At dusk, however, it finally rained with a suddenness that was both welcome and soothing. The evening that came soon after was fragrant with the scent of green things.

For the first time since she got back from the hospital, Luis slept with his wife in their room. Luis went to sleep swimming in the pleasantness that had come with the July twilight. He had tried reading some of his new poems to her, but she had lost interest after the first two, had turned on her side and gone to sleep, so he had lain them down; soon he was dreaming that he was strolling in a field of water lilies and that as he stepped on the soft purple blossoms they were not crushed at all but yielded instead to his feet and sprang up, larger and prettier, as he moved on. He saw the field spread about him, a throbbing purple sea that melted into a bowl of glazed blue sky.

It was a shot that woke him up, sending consciousness coursing through him like fire. He opened his eyes and strained his ears. In the dark, somehow, all sounds seemed more defined. Now the shots burst again in quick fury. He turned quickly on his side, and in the dimness he saw that his wife had sat up. She reached out for his hand. It was cold and trembling.

"Something is the matter, Luis," she whispered. "I called for the nurse, but there was no reply. She is gone. I called for one of the servants—there was no answer either. We are alone in the house. Something is the matter."

Another burst of gunfire rang out, and Luis thought it did not come from afar but from the vicinity of the *municipio*.

"It's the Huks," Trining whispered hoarsely, her breath gusty on his face, her heart pounding against his chest. He held her, and although he had started to tremble, he assured her. "If they are Huks, they will not harm us. There is something I should have told you long ago—my brother, Victor, is one of them. The Huks know that we are brothers."

The shots came nearer now, the inaudible cries and the howling of dogs. They were coming from the east, from the foothills, and the sounds were now at the entrance to the town. Whoever they were, the shouting was coming in a flood that could not be dammed. Their cries exploded sonorously in the quiet, as if the mob was now downstairs, taunting the silent ghosts, crying: Our moment has come.

"What shall we do?" Trining asked.

He tried to calm her, saying, "Do you know what they are really after? They will raid the *municipio* first, get the guns of the police and loot the municipal treasury and the stores, then they will leave. This is the way they always work." He wanted to believe his words. "We will be safe—my brother . . ." But he did not finish what he wanted to say—that they would be safe because he had done harm to no one.

To no one? He turned the words briefly in his mind and tried to convince himself that they were true, but he could not now lie to himself, not in this hour of need. He had not harmed Ester and his mother and his grandfather and Victor—they who were closest to him; he had only denied them, and denying them, he had killed them. He had done harm to no one, and now rocks crashed through the panes, smashed into the room. Bullets ricocheted from the stonework and the aging wood and sang deep into the caverns of his redoubt.

"No!" he cried. "They cannot do this to me. I am their friend! Not to me!" He rushed to the window and flung it open, so that he was framed there, his arms flailing as he shouted to the huge and formless blackness before him. "Vic, it is I, Luis, your brother. You don't know what you are doing!"

He could not see the shapes that moved below. Trining pulled him away from the window just as the giant veil of darkness before him suddenly exploded in sharp orange flashes of thunder. He found himself being dragged to the floor, among bits of glass. Again the horrendous shouts, like a curse, burst in unison in the street below in all its frightening clarity: Commander Victor! Commander Victor!

The firing and the stoning ceased, and the shuffle of feet below moved on. He stirred, the dust of the floor gritty on his lips. His wife, beside him, groped in the dark for his hand. "Luis," she said softly, "I've been hit." She pressed his hand to her breast. It was wet and warm.

"My God!" he cried, and gathering her gently, he carried her across the room and laid her gently on the bed. He moved quickly, groped for the light switch twice, thrice, but it did not work. The generators were out; the complementary power from the town powerhouse had been cut off, too. It was elementary strategy—they must have cut off the communication lines as well. Rosales was now sealed off, and there would be no help forthcoming unless the news was relayed to the constabulary by wireless.

He bent over her and asked, "Does it hurt?" In the dimness he saw her shake her head. He ran to the hall and called the servants—Santos slept in the room near the landing—but there was no movement in the house except the patter of rat feet in the ceiling and the túmult of his own breathing. He rushed to the servants' quarters beyond the kitchen. Lighting a match, he saw that all the cots were empty, the drawers, too, and on the floor were scattered pieces of clothing that had been left by the servants as they fled. Trining was right—they were alone in the house. Everyone was gone—Santos, all of them whom he trusted, who would do his bidding without question. The servants had known about the attack, and none of them had warned him. Was it because they hated him and wanted him to die—or was it because, no matter what he did, he would always be his father's son? He felt miserable at their perfidy, they who had lived with him, who had partaken of his food and played with him in his childhood.

He strangled a sob and fled back to their room, where his wife lay bleeding. I must stop it, he said to himself, and in the darkness he groped for anything to stop the bleeding. He lighted a match and in the feeble light Trining's face was dreamy and unafraid. "Does it hurt?" he repeated, wanting desperately to hear her assure him that it did not. She shook her head.

"Luis, my Luis," she said softly, "it is the same thing all over again, but I am no longer scared the way I was—and I was not even hurt then. No, I am not afraid at all—but for you, my husband, I am afraid."

He found a candle at the bottom of her dresser and lighted it. Quickly the things in the room jumped up. He saw the medicine chest that the nurse had brought. He pushed down her nightgown. The wound was above the right nipple, a neat little hole, and from it a stream oozed, not in spurts but in a slow, sure trickle. She had bled much, and the whole front of her nightgown was drenched.

"We must get out of this house," he said, and proceeded to help her up so that he could carry her, but she held him back and, smiling bravely, said, "They will kill you the moment they see you. Just try to stop the bleeding."

He opened the medicine cabinet, took out wads of cotton and

bandages, a bottle of Merthiolate and sulfa powder, then went back to her. He worked swiftly, although his hands shook. He sprinkled the wound with the powder, swabbed it, then padded it with cotton. He was not sure if the bleeding would stop after he had plastered the dressing, but this was better than nothing. "How do you feel?" he asked when the job was done.

"Weak," she said, looking at him with misty eyes. "Luis, I am going to die and my poor baby, my poor baby—I have not even seen him."

Tears welled from her eyes and wet her cheeks. Luis eased her back onto the bed and wiped the tears and the beads of sweat that glistened on her brow. She mustn't die, he prayed, looking at her face, which was now quiet as a child's and as lovely. She mustn't die, he prayed, hoping for daylight and the end of this nightmare. He blew the candle out and took her hand. Her pulse was weak but steady.

Bending over her, he whispered, "You will be all right." He felt her lips touch his cheek. Now was the time to tell her—she must know about the misshapen thing in the hospital, about that Asperri who would inherit all they had if it lived. If it were to live! He would forsake it; this was not his, nor was it Trining's—this thing with handless arms and footless legs, this grotesque thing he had sired. What infernal seed had he planted? What evil was it that thwarted his father's dream to perpetuate his name upon the land he had coveted? Was this the coagulation of all his sins, all the frustrations he had passed around as his blessings? But it is alive—this baby, this son—and it cries and its eyes are human, although as yet they are unseeing. It would require courage to look at it, the doctor had intoned, and resignation to accept it, but it was pity now—and charity and the purest kind of love—for Trining to be shielded from the truth. Bending over her again, Luis said softly, "Don't worry about your baby. At least it is safe. You will see him. Just wait."

"If I die," Trining said, "will you marry again? If you do, Luis, please take care of him, see to it that he is loved, that he will have a happy—a very happy childhood—" He did not want her to finish, so he bent down and smothered her face with kisses.

He went to the window and peered carefully into the street that was now empty and silent. From the direction of the *municipio* fresh volleys broke out and the plaintive cry "Commander Victor!" in unison, as if a cheerleader for a basketball tournament had trained the shouting throng—only the cry was harsher, louder, and seemed to ignite the air. That was what happened when they raided a town or a capital—they always shouted the name of their leader for all to hear, as if doing so would give their unit prestige and strike into the hearts of their victims the fear and the respect that their leader evoked. There was the first Commander Victor whom he and his brother knew, who blasted his brains out with his own gun, and there was a new one now—and there would be a third and a fourth. There would always be a new commander each time one died. These leaders never died, for how can a ghost, a dream, be nailed up in a coffin and shut up in the hollow of the earth?

ALTHOUGH THE SHOUTING had ceased, the gunfire persisted, not in volleys but in isolated bursts. They must be looting the Chinese stores now, and he wondered how Go Chua and his waddling, unctuous assistant, the ascetic Joaquin Lee—all of them who occupied his father's *accesorias*—would appear. Perhaps they were helping the raiders themselves fill up their jeeps with cases of canned food, shoes, clothes, and sacks of rice.

There was a chance that he could steal into the car with Trining and make a dash across the town and head for the city, but he quickly gave up the thought. His brother was not dumb. He must have placed roadblocks at all entrances and exits of Rosales. But why didn't they rush the house when they passed? It was a simple thing to do, smash the iron gate, proceed to the *bodega,* which was still stacked high with seed palay and newly milled rice, and they could have gone up the marble stairs and blasted open the steel safe in the study and made off with the thousands of pesos in it. The answer to his own query came viciously—they did not bother because they knew that he and his wife were now alone, because they were like ripe guavas about to fall at the slightest breeze, because to enter the brick house was like entering an unguarded treasure trove.

Luis crouched low, hiding himself from the street, and slipped through the *azotea* door. Through the low stone balustrade he peered into the street and beyond—into the town. No shape emerged from the darkness—just the fine uneven line of the horizon against the sky dotted with stars, for the rain had gone and with it its portent of clouds. They were taking their time, and if they did tarry, there would be time for him and Trining to escape. He rushed back to their room, and in the dark, to which he was now accustomed, he saw that their bed was empty.

HE RUSHED OUT, shouting her name, and at the other end of the hall he caught up with her wobbling to the door. He swept her up in his arms and in spite of her protests carried her back. She was light and helpless as a child. Perhaps she did not hear him call her name, and when she snuggled in his arms, her face pressed warm and cool against his cheek, she asked, "Why were you so afraid? I just wanted to make sure the door was bolted tight. They must not harm you, Luis. Even if I die you must live."

"They will not harm us," he assured her, but he knew he was lying. There was no place for them that was safe, not in this house, not in Rosales, not in Manila even, for it was not so much violence that they could not escape; it was life itself—crude, cunning, and vengeful. But they would leave behind this abomination that would inherit all of Rosales—the land—and the thought of it sickened him. At the same time it confirmed for him, at least, the irony of his being here.

"If they break into this house, will they burn it?"

He shook his head. "It will be a waste," Luis said. "My brother knows much, much more than that."

"Your brother?"

"He is Commander Victor," he said simply.

Trining did not speak. It was better that way. She must now know and understand that this fate was not just theirs; it was also shared by someone who had, after all, come to warn him in a final gesture of remembrance and love.

"Forgive me," he said brokenly. "Vic came here last night; he told me to take you away, to leave immediately. I did not heed him—I was so sure—and I was thinking only of myself."

"Do not blame yourself," she said softly. "Please do not blame yourself." He was holding her hand and he felt her stiffen. "Oh, Luis," she whispered, "it is beginning to hurt."

"Please, God," he cried softly, "please do not let her die." Then he mumbled senselessly into her ear. "When morning comes the servants—and the doctor—will be back. I will not leave you. I won't leave you."

Trining stretched her hand out. Her voice was composed and clear. "You are cold," she said. Indeed a breeze had sprung in through the smashed windows. "Lie beside me," she said. He looked at her face again in the soft dark and listened to the rattle of gunfire in town, then he pulled the sheet over her, leaving her pallid face and her arms, limp at her sides, uncovered. He lay beside her, and as he did so she closed her eyes and only her breathing, quiet and measured, assured him that she was still alive. His hand went under the sheet and passed over her breast, over the wound. Her skin was warm, and there was no trace of wetness around the bandage.

So this was how it would end, in the cold night, with his brow moist with sweat, his wife dying beside him.

Violence was bearing down upon him and on this house, which his grandfather had helped to build. There was no town then, no main street—just a rise of ground covered with shrubs and trees strangled by vines. The shrubs and the trees were all burned by his grandfather and his grandfather's people. They had chanced upon this land—away from the harried coastal strip in the Ilokos, from where they had migrated—and they helped build this house, this room, where he now waited.

It was quiet again. Cicadas complained in the drenched acacias in the yard, and a dog barked in the street. He turned on his side and gazed at his wife's quiet face. Her eyes were still closed, and remembering her pain, he stifled the urge to touch her, to wake her up if she was asleep, to disturb her. Quietly he stood up and went to the window. Beyond the moss-covered wall and the asphalted *camino provincial* lay the black fields of Rosales. Below, in the garden, were tumbled pots of dahlias and roses that Trining had tended. The shattered glass crunched at his feet as he moved away from the window. He turned the bronze latch of the door to the *azotea* and peered out. Nothing stirred there. He stepped out and leaned on the iron pergola, to which a screen of bridal bouquet clung, its small white blossoms, like his light blue pajamas, distinct in the black. The town could clearly be seen from this vantage, and in some sections of it flames licked at the sky, red throbbing hues that melted into the darkness. Portions of the town were burning, maybe the *municipio* or his father's *accesorias*. From this distance the destruction seemed beautiful. It was as if he was in Sipnget again. He remembered one early twilight when he and his grandfather were setting the yellowed grass afire. He had thrilled then to the crackling of the flames as they enveloped the field so quickly. He had to run, shaking off wisps of warm ash that had swirled up with the flames, then drifted down and covered him—and everything.

The rain at dusk had washed the *azotea,* and portions of the tile-work were glazed with water. In the reflection the flames, bright as sunset, painted the bowl of darkness above. Now the crackle of burning wood and the hiss of flames reached him and he closed the *azotea* door and went back to the room.

He bent over Trining and listened again to her breathing. It was even and slow, and happiness lifted him, away from this room and its portents. *We are alone now, the two of us. You should not be destroyed, you should live—it is I who should go. You have a great love for life, your youth is fresh, and it will be wasted. Forgive me for giving you not the future but this.*

This was the other violence—the mind that was warped, the peace that was shattered and could not be mended. He had seen and known the other kind, seen the mutilated bodies, the clean bullet holes through which life had escaped, the sightless eyes that could no longer guide one along the path of vengeance. He had stood before that unmarked grave in Sipnget—and what had that violence done to him? It had not made him weep. It had not made him strong. He had continued to speak, but to himself alone, and they understood him not, not his father or his tenants—they never knew what it was that he really wanted to say, whether in his poetry or in his prose, what it was that made him procrastinate. Was it really love that moved him? What is the truth that one must believe in now? Passion could well be evil. Logic, then, is what lasts. It cannot be destroyed—like facts, like numbers, like history. Perhaps the answer was in religion and God—how he sought it and how he followed it, through a long and perilous journey, along crooked paths, and in the process, God, how he had lived and yet not loved! If he did love, Ester would not be dead, or Grandfather—and now Trining.

He thought of writing a letter again, but to whom would he address it? *Dear Trining, dear world, dear son, who will inherit this rubble: what will happen to us is an indictment against our time. We have everything and nothing. We die in peace, yet in anger. We were born* to a world rotten with evil, although we all pledged ourselves to what was good. We spoke softly, but our hands were rough and we lived long and life shortchanged us.

If I live through this, dear wife, dear son, please remember it was not my intention to hurt or to destroy, but I have done these nonetheless. The spring was clear, but time had muddied it. I hate ugliness, but it is part of me, perhaps because it is also part of birth—that miraculous happening is preceded by agony, as is the dawn by the dark, impalpable night.

Words, words—nothing but words. What am I doing? Playing with words when life is about to ebb from her. I must at least prove to myself that I am not a lamb being led to the slaughter, that I made my choice long ago and I must now protect this choice. He went to his father's room, beyond the long, silent hall. He knew every piece of furniture in it, and he ransacked the glass-paneled case by the window. The gun was there, all right, where he had returned it when Santos had urged him to carry it—and a cartridge box, too. He weighed it in his hand and deftly flipped its chamber open. It was fully loaded.

He was ready now, and he went back to Trining, the gun at his hip, the cartridge box in his hand. She was sitting on the bed. He went to her and told her to lie down and not move. "When it is light, the soldiers will come. Then it will be safe and we can return to the city."

"You have told me that—"

"But it is true, it is true!"

"No." Her voice was soft but firm. "I am going to die, and you will, too, if you don't escape now. I have thought about it, my husband. It is better that you live. You cannot escape if you carry me—you will be slow, you will be spotted, and they will kill you. Please go now while you still can. You can leave by the back."

He shook his head. Her hands reached out to him, and he embraced her. She had become cold. She sank back into the bed, and although he could not see her eyes as she turned away from him, he knew she was crying.

"Do not cry," he said, holding her close. "I cannot leave you. I will die first."

"My husband, my Luis, we cannot fight," she told him. It was the first time she admitted the truth about themselves. Tenderly he kissed her again. "What is going to happen to you?" she asked.

As if it still mattered, when long ago the primeval sore had claimed him—and yet here she was, like the others who called him friend, worrying about him. He went to the window. The fires had now become wilder, as if the whole center of the town, the market, were now engulfed in flames.

"You can escape. It is so simple," she insisted behind him.

He went back to her. "One thing is sure," he said. "I will not leave you. Why should I? This is the least that I can do for you, and this I did not do for the others."

"Do not talk like that."

"It was so easy to hate—"

"It was not hate," she said, reproaching him softly. "Its other side is love."

Luis laughed drily. "The difference is now very hard to draw, although everything started out so pure. Look at it this way—the muddy lowland river gushes out of clear springs in the mountains. The world began with two sinless people."

"Don't talk like that," she said, pressing his hand to her breast.

"I am sorry," he said, bending over and caressing her hair. It smelled of freshness and life. "There is an old saying: *In vino, veritas*—in wine, truth. I think it should be changed to: In violence, truth. The truth now, my dear wife, is that I have sinned, not just against all those whom I loved, including you, but most important, against Mother and all that she was. I forsook her, but I will not forsake you now. She was everything—Mother—the grace and the patience of the earth. How she sacrificed for me, but what did I do for her? No, I will not leave you."

It was as if he had intoned an ancient prayer, the *oracíon* that warded off evil, for the great weight on his chest seemed lifted at last. He had decided that this was his fort, that they must not touch her, the contemptible mob. He heard her sigh, and bending over her, he touched the bandage on her breast. It was wet and warm, and fear rushed back, massive and all-engulfing, but he tried to ward it off, speaking softly: "What do you feel? God, do not leave me. You cannot leave me," he cried, holding her tightly, and he glanced at her face, but her eyes were closed. "My wife, do not leave me. There are just the two of us now—just the two of us."

"Luis." It was a soft, gurgling sound that escaped from her lips, then she was limp, and although her face was still warm, he knew that she was dead. He held her more tightly now, sobbing loudly as he had never cried before, for this was the girl he had grown up with, who knew him as no woman had ever known him, and she was dead. He kissed her lingeringly on the lips, which were still warm, then slowly he laid her down, folded her hands neatly on her breast, smoothed out her hair, and gazed at her face, lighted now by the glow of the fire and quiet in repose.

He went out into the hall. Near the window the bronze statue of the farmer with a plow gleamed in the light of the burning town. There was a shuffle of feet in the street below, raucous peasant voices and the snort of jeeps. He turned to the *azotea,* and through the broken glass windows, the town—all of it—seemed ablaze. The sky was clear but scabbed with clouds. The air was cool. He closed his eyes and inhaled deeply.

Would death hurt? The knowledge would be meaningless, but even then he wanted to know how it would be in that last moment when that wakeless sleep would come at a time when all his faculties were working—and it was just as well, for there would be no real life in old age when the bones would have become brittle, the mind senile, and the flesh shorn of its nerves.

Down the street the howling of dogs increased. The shuffle of feet on the asphalt had heightened. Like him, they were young— these peasants, riffraff, the aimless generation, which had finally found something to latch on to. These were the young who would always be marched off to a tree and hanged, the pawns who must answer always for their father's dementia. And the young could do nothing really but accept or forget, as he, too, must now accept.

The shuffling of feet had ceased. The voices below the house were a murmur. They were there, waiting, waiting. It would be simpler if he went to the window and shouted his defiance at them, but that would be foolhardy. It pained him to use the gun, for he had never used one before, never aimed at any man, although as a boy he had gone hunting in the delta with his father, and during the war he had fingered captured Japanese rifles—but to grip a gun and point it at another human being was to play God, to pass irrevocable judgment. He crouched below the statue of the farmer with a plow, the cartridge box on the floor before him. The base of the statue was wood, but it was thick molave and it would give him some measure of protection at least. Protection? What high wall, what bastion could protect him now from this primeval anger that had been released? Yet it was an anger that he had shared and fed on, because he believed in it, because it represented that bleak and trackless waste from which he had come. But this anger was not a mover or a compulsion. It was some effete luxury that titillated the mind and adorned his prose, his poetry, as frills adorn a curtain.

Now this anger had come to claim him, and strangely aware of this, he felt no impulse to reject it. He no longer felt rancor for his father nor for Dantes, nothing but an overwhelming indifference. Now he was simply tired.

What a waste—the thought crossed his mind: *If I should live longer and if there still be plenty of potent chemistry in this flesh, I would be like that son I leave behind. I would only bring rot to those whose lives I will touch. Better, then, to be exorcised from this land, better to succumb finally to the avenging fires that I have fanned. What have I known that would convince me that life has meaning? My wife, the dearly beloved life and youth that she gave up for me; the beautiful world of Sipnget, the mornings washed with dew; Mother's touch . . . If I die tonight, it will be just a physical death, for I have long since died and only memory has framed me, here where I have trod, and searched and searched but found nothing.*

Dominiko-Kai
Shibuya, June 29, 1972

AFTERWORD

SELF AND NATION
IN LITERATURE

M ANY YEARS BACK, a group of Ilokano writers from central and northern Luzon invited me to talk at a workshop they had set up in my hometown, Rosales, Pangasinan. They wanted me, with my background as literary editor and novelist, to clarify some of the problems of craft that had been bedeviling them. I did not think it was a difficult assignment; I had done some writing in my own language several years back but had stopped and devoted myself to English, as demanded by my job.

A few words about Ilokano: it is spoken today by some fifteen million Filipinos in northern Luzon and in Mindanao. In Hawaii, the majority of the citizens of Philippine ancestry are Ilokanos, which is perhaps why Marcos elected Honolulu as his place of exile. We are an adventurous people, hardy and given to thrift and perseverance. We are supposedly endowed with *carabao* patience and cast-iron stomachs, but more than these ethnic idiosyncracies, our language is very precise and sensual, and in the back of my mind I had hoped that I could enrich my writing in English by extracting from my native Ilokano the same nuances and musicality that

Richard Llewelyn drew from his native Welsh or, on a much more magnificent scale, James Joyce, from Irish. In fact, one Filipino writer with an Ilokano background had done this successfully: the late Manuel Arguilla. He flavored his stories with the earthiness, the vivid color, and the vitality of Ilokano. Had the Japanese not killed him, his work would have fully flowered and would have brought about—at least for our writers—a deeper appreciation of their native languages—all ninety of them—and the richness they could have imparted to English.

But this is digression; I had meant to say that I was going back to my hometown after many years of living in Manila and elsewhere in Asia. I relished going home; all the remembered words came alive again. I could understand everything that was said in Ilokano, including the archaic expressions and the poetry bubbling all over the place. Slowly I came to realize that I had missed a lot.

Then it was my turn to speak. I started in my own language, but after the first phrases of elaborate greeting, I found myself fumbling, groping for words. The ideas were crystal-clear, but I could not express them and I strained with an expression that had become alien to me. In the end, I had to give up Ilokano and speak in English. I had never felt as I felt then, the terrible sense of inadequacy and helplessness.

They all understood me, of course, for English is one of our three official languages, but the experience humbled me and impinged upon me the fact that, perhaps, I cannot go home again.

I am sure that this experience can be duplicated easily in any part of the world by those individuals like myself who have become urbanized. I am sure that many of us in Asia have raised questions that probe deep into the very core of our personalities and even into the very purpose of our inconsequential lives.

This is not just the result of our history but the complexity of the Philippines itself. Although Tagalog, the national language, can be understood in almost every part of the country now, the language of science and culture, of government and the elite, continues to be English. With a population of seventy million, a third of our people is capable of communication of sorts in English, a fact that has been embroidered into the dubious statistic that we are the third-largest English-speaking country in the world.

Theoretically, the Philippines is ripe for the media revolution, and as a publisher, I should now be printing thousands of books for this mass market. But we do not read, and most of our people are more comfortable with comic books and TV. Moreover, our low per capita income seems to indicate that a Filipino will take care of his stomach first before he attends to food for the mind. And who can blame him?

What, then, is the future for English? As the lingua franca of the region, it will continue well into the future. But to modernize, we have to develop our own language even, perhaps, at the cost of ignoring altogether our other languages. In promoting this national language, we will also give a genuine cultural base for nationalism. This is no longer an option; it has become a compulsion.

It is perhaps too premature to say that our literature in English may probably decline. This is what happened to the prose and poetry in Spanish written in the 1880s and up to the early 1920s. Even the novels of José Rizal, our national hero, are now seldom read in their original Spanish, although they are required reading in English translation in our schools. Our Spanish poets Fernando Ma. Guerrero and José Corazon de Jesus are unappreciated except by scholars in search of footnotes. Indeed, the literary hiatus between our Spanish past and the American era is wide and final, and Spanish as a literary language in the Philippines is dead. This may well be the price we have to pay so that a national literature will evolve, one that will be read by all our people.

The shift to Tagalog, however, is slow. It could be hastened, but there is continuing opposition by Tagalog chauvinists who refuse to accept the first verity of language, that of communication. Some of these oppositionists wield influence in government and have vested interests as teachers or as bureaucrats; some still insist on the use of archaic Tagalog, on a complicated grammar that favors coinage of words when there are equivalents in popular use. They use *aklat* ("book") when everybody uses the Spanish *libro*.

PERHAPS IT IS TIME that the Institute of National Language be led and staffed by non-Tagalogs so that the grafting to the national lexicon of non-Tagalog words that are widely used could be hastened. By provoking non-Tagalogs to opt for their own languages in opposition to Tagalog, by making language a vehicle for Tagalog chauvinism, the issue of language, which is central to Philippine development, has been derailed, and what is worse, instead of unifying Filipinos, it has sorely divided us. The worst enemies of Filipino nationalism, therefore, may be found in the Institute of National Language, among them the late Lope K. Santos, who forced upon the school system his *balarilà* ("grammar," in Tagalog).

The past has created attitudes embedded deep in our cultural matrix that are just as pernicious. No less than a cultural revolution can exorcise us of such attitudes and their stigma. We may have survived three hundred years of Spanish tyranny, forty years of grudging American benevolence, and three brutal years of Japanese occupation, but we continue to languish in the prison created by this past. How many times have we been awed by our neighbors, by their granite monuments and fabulous ruins, by their classical arts and dances? Go find us a temple, we often tell our archaeologists—half in fun but in our heart of hearts with wishful longing—but we know these monuments are not there, that we may have to build them ourselves. We do console ourselves with the thought that these monuments of past grandeur could be—and are—anchors to poverty that cannot be lifted. What, then, is the Filipino artist? Is he a helmsman beholden to no celestial guide, to no route to his past as Asia knows this past? We have no moorings to break away from and we hope to God that we are not drifting, that we can, perhaps, be light-bringers, although it is a feeble light that we are holding up to our own benighted people.

WE CANNOT BUT ACCEPT the history that has shaped us. When Spain came to us with Catholicism, she destroyed the beginnings of an indigenous culture. Spain also imposed a social structure that afflicts us to this day. It is a structure of power and privilege wherein the social elite is also the political and economic elite whose power and privilege were not earned but mandated, as evidenced in the land grants or *encomiendas,* in the bulk space of the galleons that sailed to Acapulco. It was a system of exploitation and forced labor that enabled the chosen few, mostly Spanish mestizos, to amass fortunes without lifting a finger at honest toil, and it was from such beginnings that the obnoxious attitudes and values of colonialism were ingrained later into the very culture of our people.

Toward the last decades of Spanish rule, the desire of the *Indios* to be educated could no longer be restrained. Some were already in the priesthood, and families who could afford it sent their children to Europe for their education. They imbibed the ideas of the European Enlightenment. They were not so much interested in an independent Filipinas as they were in proving themselves equal to their Spanish overlords. They set up in Barcelona *La Solidaridad*, a fortnightly edited by Marcelo H. del Pilar, wherein they espoused ideas of equality, cultural nationalism, and democracy. They satirized the friars and showed an erudition that proved to themselves, at least, that they deserved seats in the Spanish Cortes.

This period is known as the Propaganda Movement, and the brightest lights of our Spanish literature shone in the pages of *La Solidaridad*. The newspaper was banned in the Philippines; like most exiles, the Filipino patriots and writers were condemned to penury. Penniless and often at odds with his own countrymen, Marcelo H. del Pilar is one of our tragic figures; soon after the paper was forced to close for lack of funds, he died in Spain of starvation.

Rizal foresaw the coming of America not only to Asia but to the Philippines, and America did come. Our literature in Spanish was fired by anti-American feelings after 1898.

The soldiers from Idaho and Montana became overnight teachers, and there were more to come: the first Peace Corps, the Thomasites, those dedicated young Americans who arrived on the S.S. *Thomas* and set up the beginnings of the public school system.

Our first literary models were asinine. In high school, we read and delighted in O. Henry's trick endings. We did have some classics, the Gettysburg Address, the hortatory writings of Tom Paine, but in a sense our colonial educational system fostered a culture that did not emphasize our Filipino-ness. In fact, in the late sixties, I was forced to write to the principal of the academy where my boys went to school; their elocution text included only one Filipino author. Looking back, I am convinced that this educational system created for many of us a warped view of our own society; it made us hanker for the luxuries that we could not produce. Worst of all, we came to accept cultural symbols that were alien to us.

The Americans, with their sincere naïveté and mixed intentions, as evidenced in the Washington archives, could not help themselves, either. Our elite, from the very beginning, chose to collaborate almost uncritically with them just as they collaborated with the Spaniards and the Japanese. In literary terms, it would take time before we would appreciate the "flowering of New England" and those writers who gave American literature its sinew and its marrow.

By the thirties, Filipino authors with new sensibilities, like Paz Marquez Benitez, Narciso G. Reyes, Paz Latorena, Federico Mangahas, and Salvador P. Lopez, began to surface. Shortly before World War II, our literature in English had completely changed from the suffocatingly simple stuff of the twenties.

The war came and its brutality was deeply imprinted in our psyche; we continue to this day to ask questions about Japanese culture—how a people with highly polished aesthetics, with austere and contemplative philosophies, could surrender themselves to the obscenities of barbarism. During those three years of Occupation we were taught a new language, but at the same time the Japanese promoted Tagalog as the national language in a manner unequaled during the American regime. Tagalog literary magazines, associations, and literary experimentation flourished during this period. Another astute quality of Japanese propaganda was to point out our Asian-ness; it mattered not that we were under the heel of an Asian people—did they not prove themselves superior to the white race?

The Occupation brought to the surface fatal flaws of our society: the collaboration of the elite with the Japanese and how readily they gave up the ideals of freedom.

THE HISTORY of our literary development is one of dilution, infusion, and impermanence. It is not strange, then, that some of us who today write in English feel that we are holding on to ropes of sand, that we may become irrelevant and extinct, unread by our people just as our literature in Spanish is entombed in Filipiniana indices.

This is not to denigrate the achievements of our writers in English who have joined the mainstream of English letters and honored the language with their excellence. But in writing in English, we also accepted the encumbrances of the language. We had to accept as part of our tradition Shakespeare and Dickens and Faulkner, just as those who wrote in Spanish had Cervantes and Lorca as hallmarks of their tradition.

This is not what I personally want, this fact forced upon me by my history, by my profession. Language is not just grammar and syntax, or poetry and prose; language is also a way of thinking, a culture. I do not deny my debt to English literature, my appreciation of its beauty, but English is also associated with my colonial past and its excesses, and because I have succumbed to it, it continually reminds me of and crucifies me for my weakness.

And much as I appreciate Faulkner and his commitment not only to the agrarian South but to man, much as I identify with Dickens's righteous indignation at man's inhumanity to man, both are alien to me; they come from another planet, and in our tortured geography they have little to say to me.

My tradition is the village, its filth and its poverty, the agony and the confusion of my striving to be free from it yet be part of it.

Tradition—what a beautiful blind, what an ambiguous, all-purpose façade; like patriotism, it can very well be the last resort of scoundrels or writers grown obese with comfort and adulation. It is, of course, never enough. One can find in it his hope or his perdition and for most of us, it is usually the latter. The businessman who hires his relatives no matter how inefficient they are is paying a heavy price for his tradition. The Filipino critic who lavishes praise on his incompetent writer friends because he does not want to ruffle their feelings is no different. Literature suffers because writers give their books to colleagues who will then write glowing reviews or saccharine introductions.

These acts are done regularly in the Philippines and they can be easily rationalized. Aside from the desire to maintain "smooth interpersonal relations," jobs are difficult to find, and coteries are not just for social and intellectual amenities; they are also for assistance, which comes in the form of awards, fellowships, and grants. All down the line, from the editors of literary magazines to the teachers in the universities, this social system operates. The public does not really care, consensus becomes the final accolade, and sometimes, only in private conversations or in our innermost thoughts is the true worth of many of our writers ever acknowledged.

And because criticism is permissive, literary reputations—as with other reputations—are easy to garner; mediocrity often masquerades as genius. Some writers who have not produced any body of work acquire a tremendous literary following, even the National Artist Award!

This is one reason, I feel, why little is known of our literature in English outside of Manila or, for that matter, of our Spanish literature. Many of our writers are contented and smug with their reputation at home, but more than this, if we try to get published abroad and are rejected, we feel that foreign editors and publishers do not understand us. It will be difficult for us to realize that our shortcomings could be on craft, that our skills can be honed not only by dogged perseverance but also by an honest tradition in criticism.

But all these do not really add up to the greater malaise that permeates the Filipino literary life: the seeming irresponsibility of many toward our own society and, therefore, to the great themes in art itself. These themes are, in a sense, unchanged since Rizal's time—the disparity between the countryside and the city, the poverty of the masses and the sickening affluence of a few.

Our critics abroad and at home who hear this complaint often conclude that we are utopians. Indeed, the utopia as we understand it is far removed from Plato's *Republic* or from Thomas Moore's definition; most of the time, all that we desire are clothes for our people, three meals, potable water, garbage collection, education for the children. There is nothing utopian about needs as basic as these.

Some of our writers have recognized this, but others have shied away not only from this truth but from the other truths of society. If they had not done so, there should be a great novel on rural life, on the peasant revolts that have shaken up the countryside intermittently all through the Spanish regime and up to the present. By extension, there should be other novels on the Japanese occupation, not just Stevan Javellana's *Without Seeing the Dawn* and Edilberto Tiempo's *Watch in the Night*. To this day, one of the best literary documents to come out of the Huk experience is *The Forest* by William Pomeroy. There is reason enough for many of us to disagree with Pomeroy's ideology, but there can be no quarrel about the literary validity of his book, which recounts his life as a hunted man.

COMMITMENT—again, one of those megaton words loosely used in the Philippines today. To what or to whom must the artist be committed? Certainly to his art, first and foremost, because he will survive only to the degree that he is devoted to his calling. Beyond his craft, this art, is that transcendental rationale that constitutes all art. Different societies have described it according to their lights, but I would borrow the famous fifth-century Chinese critic Hsieh Ho's first principle, that it is the concept of "spiritual energy which animates all things." Though fundamentally metaphysical, it may well be—for those of us who are not Buddhists or Taoists—the belief that in contemporary terms must have sustained Solzhenitsyn through the bleakness of Soviet disapproval. It could well be ideology, too, though nothing as pedestrian as rightist or leftist or even nationalist. It is, after all, the inner strength which finally enables the cripple to rise, the spirit which renders the impossible easy to contemplate, the vision which arms the artist in his demolition of the reality that suffocates him and replaces it with his own truth as only truth can liberate.

Many of us have searched for this truth, this vision, but because we have missed it, we are creating a culture that is not just derivative, but one that makes a mockery of decency and makes our collective death wish loom real and near. This theme is epitomized in E. P. Patañe's classic story, "The Bomb." The fisherman in the story could be any Filipino, and like most fishermen in our country, he has dived to the depths where the American navy dumped many bombs after World War II. He brings up one such bomb, and with primitive implements proceeds to open it to extract the gunpowder that he will then use to dynamite the water and kill the fish.

Many fishermen have been blown up with just one mistake. Whole neighborhoods—as attested to by our newspapers—have been wiped out. The fisherman knows this, his wife knows this, and this most memorable story ends with the fisherman trying to open the bomb—but around him are his wife and children.

Life is absurd—if it should end, let it end for us all. We can extend this fatalism to almost every Filipino aspect of life. We have denuded our forests for the Japanese plywood industry. In so doing, we have also removed much of our watershed; the mountains are bald, and our reservoirs will soon dry up or will be rendered useless with silt. Floods ravage the fields, and money that should go for dams goes into the pockets of the elite. We went through notions of free elections but ushered into office evil men. We exhort the young but our youth are as corrupt as the leaders they criticize.

Our revolutionary elite was bought by the Spaniards at the Pact of Biak-na-bato; the Japanese did the same and so did the Americans, who gave them high positions, annual proffers of sugar quotas. Our writers can be enthralled by the blandishments of power, social position, adulation. Under Marcos, some became speechwriters, propagandists. It is easy to rationalize this sellout by saying that they have to live. But one can live as a baker, the way the poet G. Burce Bunao elected to become before he left for America as an exile, or as a merchant of folk art and handbags like the short-story writer Gilda Cordero Fernando.

Today, as in the recent past, I tell my writer friends to leave if they have the opportunity to do so, to work elsewhere where their imagination can be given free rein, where the obdurate demands of living do not obstruct the free will, knowing as I do that the spirit of inquiry, without which the literary imagination would shrivel and die, was stilled by Marcos.

In December 1958 a hundred writers met in the mountain city of Baguio and argued about the writer's responsibility to the country, never about the government's or the state's responsibility to its citizens. The theme of the PEN-sponsored conference was "Nationalism and the Filipino Writer." A tenacious group of "committed" writers felt that literature must be nationalist or be damned as useless. They argued that the writer, if need be, write propaganda for social change.

This is, of course, extremely understandable. One of the greatest dilemmas that confront our writers is how to be useful to a society undergoing traumatic change.

Some of the vociferous propagandists of that meeting became powerful members of the Marcos government. Did conditions change merely because a few writers opted to work for the dictator?

"No artist," said Nietzsche, "can tolerate the real."

Indeed, Nietzsche confirms only too well the artistic sensibility, the fact that the artist is the perpetual rebel seeking that elusive truth, or beauty, or perfection, although these may never be, for as a Chinese sage once said, "I searched and searched for the truth and in the end found there was no truth."

GLOSSARY

accesorias	Apartments; literally "outbuildings." Word used widely until the 1950s.
amarillo	Orange-colored flower, or orange; literally "yellow."
anisado	Aniseed wine.
aparador	Wooden cabinet for clothing.
Apo	Respectful form of address.
areglados	Agreements, "done deals."
arroz caldo con gallina	Chicken and rice soup.
asado	Pork cooked in a reddish, savory sauce.
aswang	Malevolent night creature, half woman, half bird.
azotea	Roofless area attached to the rear of large homes.
bagoong	Salted fish sauce.
Bagos	Non-Christian mountain people.
banca	Wooden boat usually hewn from one tree trunk.
bangus	Milkfish.
barong tagalog	Loose-fitting, long-sleeved shirt—the national dress of the Philippines for men—made from gauzy pineapple-fiber fabric, often embroidered on the collar and facing.
basi	Sugarcane wine.
bodega	Storeroom, usually separate from the house; granary.
buntal	Fine soft grass woven into hats.

cadena de amor	Weed that grows luxuriantly, with a pretty pink flower.
caldereta	Goat meat stew.
calesa	Horse-drawn buggy.
camineros	Road workers.
camino provincial	Provincial road.
capre	Big dark ghost who inhabits large trees.
carabao	Water buffalo.
caretela	Horse-drawn two-wheeled cart.
caromata	Larger type of horse-drawn vehicle.
castaño	Chestnut-colored horse.
cavan	Sack of grain, sugar, or seeds.
cédula	Residence certificate.
cerveza	Beer.
chico	Brown, golf-ball-size tropical fruit.
colegiala	Female college student.
colorum	From the Latin mass, but meaning something phony or illegal.
comedia	Folk dramatization of the Christian and Moslem wars.
comprador	Merchant.
cuartels	Barracks.
cumbacheros	Folk band composed of not more than six musicians with harmonica, guitar, bass and bongos.
derecho	Right (direction).
dinardaraan	Pig innards stewed in vinegar and pig blood.
drill de hilo	White cotton material used for suits.
encargado	Person in charge; administrator of a plantation.
feria	Fair with sideshows, etc., during fiestas.

galletas	Cookie-like biscuits.
gobernardorcillo	Town mayor.
hacendero	Landlord; owner of hacienda or big tract of land.
halo-halo	To mix, usually sweets in crushed ice.
herbolario	Folk medicine man.
hijo	Son.
hospicio	Retirement home for old priests.
Huks	Communist-led revolutionary group that fought for agrarian reform in the Philippines after World War II; it grew out of an anti-Japanese resistance movement during the war.
Iglesia Ni Kristo	Church of Christ.
ilustrados	The first Filipinos, usually of means, who studied in Europe (beginning in the 1880s) in order to become "enlightened"; literally, "learned" or "well-informed."
kundiman	Sad folk song, usually Tagalog.
lechon	Roast suckling pig.
lengua	Tongue, usually ox tongue, prepared as a special dish.
macopa	Tropical fruit, shaped like a pear but smaller.
Manong	Affectionate, respectful form of address for older brother or man. Ilokanos do not call older relatives by their given names alone.
media agua	Awning over a window, to stop rain.
media cuerpo	Half the body, as in a photograph or painting.
Meiji	Historical period in Japan from 1867 to 1912, the Meiji Restoration.
merienda	Afternoon snack.
morcon	Large sausage, usually homemade.
municipio	Town hall.

nanca	Jackfruit.
pancit	Noodles.
pan de sal	Salted bun.
pañuelo	Stiff kerchief that is part of the traditional Philippine costume for women.
puraw	White.
sacadas	Migratory sugarcane workers.
sala	Living room in large houses.
salapi	Literally a fifty-centavo coin; also denotes money, lucre.
sin vergüenzas	Without shame.
sipi	A small room attached to a peasant's house where pillows and the rice bin are stored.
tama	Correct.
terno	National dress for women.
tinto dulce	Sweet wine.

ABOUT
THE AUTHOR

WITH THE publication of *Three Filipino Women* by Random House in 1992, the work of F. Sionil José began appearing in the United States. He is one of the major literary voices of Asia and the Pacific, but (after encouragement by Malcom Cowley and others) his novels and stories are only gradually being published in the country that figures in much of his work as both a shadow and yet a very real presence.

José runs a leading bookshop in Manila, was the founding president of the Philippines PEN Center, publishes the journal *Solidarity*, and is best known for the five novels comprising the highly regarded Rosales Saga *(Dusk* [Po-on]; *Tree; My Brother, My Executioner; The Pretenders;* and *Mass)*, the second and third novel of which make up this book. He is widely published around the world and travels steadily.